ASURA

TALE OF THE VANQUISHED

The Story of Ravana and His People

ANAND NEELAKANTAN

PLATINUM PRESS

ISBN 978-93-81576-05-2

Illustrations Amplecreation Studio
Cover Design Mishta Roy
Layouts Ajay Shah
Printing Manipal Technologies Ltd.

First published in India 2012 by
PLATINUM PRESS
An imprint of
LEADSTART PUBLISHING PVT LTD
Trade Centre, Level 1, Bandra Kurla Complex
Bandra (E), Mumbai 400 051, INDIA
T + 91 22 40700804 **F** +91 22 40700800
E info@leadstartcorp.com **W** www.leadstartcorp.com

US Office
Axis Corp, 7845 E Oakbrook Circle, Madison, WI 53717, USA

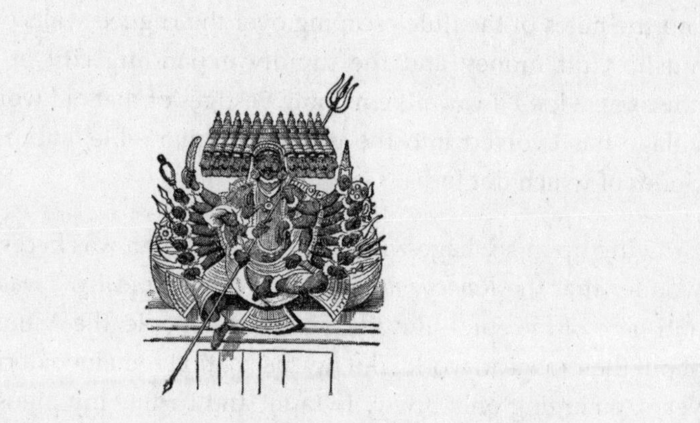

TO MY PARENTS,
THE LATE SHRI L. NEELAKANTAN AND
CHELLAMMAL NEELAKANTAN,
WHO OPENED THE MAGICAL WORLD
OF INDIAN MYTHOLOGY TO ME.

About the Author

I was born in a quaint little village called Thripoonithura, on the outskirts of Cochin, Kerala. Located east of mainland Ernakulam, across Vembanad Lake, this village had the distinction of being the seat of the Cochin royal family. However, it was more famous for its hundred-odd temples; the various classical artists it produced and its music school. I remember many evenings spent listening to the faint rhythm of *Chenda*s from the temples and the notes of the flute escaping over the rugged walls of the school of music. Gulf money and the rapidly expanding city of Cochin have, however, wiped away all remaining vestiges of that old world charm. The village has evolved into the usual, unremarkable, suburban hell hole, clones of which dot India.

Growing up in a village with more temples than was necessary, it was no wonder that the *Ramayana* fascinated me. Ironically, I was drawn to the anti-hero of the epic – Ravana, and to his people, the Asuras. I wondered about their magical world. But my fascination remained dormant for many years, emerging only briefly to taunt and irritate my pious aunts during family gatherings. Life went on. . . I became an engineer; joined the Indian Oil Corporation; moved to Bangalore; married Aparna and welcomed my daughter Ananya, and my son, Abhinav.

But the Asura Emperor would not leave me alone. For six years he haunted my dreams, walked with me, and urged me to write his version of the story. He was not the only one who wanted his version of the story to be told. One by one, irrelevant and minor characters of the *Ramayana* kept coming up with their own versions. Bhadra, who was one of the many common Asuras who were inspired, led and betrayed by Ravana, also had a remarkable story to tell, different from that of his king. And both their stories are different from the Ramayana that has been told in a thousand different ways across Asia over the last three millennia. This is then *Asurayana,* the story of the Asuras, the story of the vanquished.

Anand Neelakantan can be reached at: mail@asura.co.in

Dasamukha

Why is Ravana portrayed as ten-faced?

While the ten-headed, twenty-armed figure of Ravana as the supreme anti-hero, is familiar to every Indian and scholars of Indian mythology, few really know why he is portrayed in this manner. Traditional Indian wisdom places importance on the control of one's emotions and projects the intellect alone, as the being supreme. The great King Mahabali, advises Ravana to shun the other nine base emotions of **anger; pride; jealousy; happiness; sadness; fear; selfishness; passion** *and* **ambition. Intellect** *alone is to be revered. Indian spiritual gurus have always stressed the need to overcome the Self' and have considered these emotions detrimental to the elevation of the soul.*

But, in his response to Mahabali, Ravana justifies and exults in the possession of all these ten facets, as they make him a complete man. Mythology thus portrays Ravana as Dasamukha, *or the ten-faced one, while his twenty hands denote prowess and power. Ravana sees himself as the epitome of a complete human being; without any pretense to holiness or restricted by social and religious norms. He is as good or as bad as any human being, and as nature intended man to be. Society is unable to curb his other nine faces, as it does in the figure of Rama. So Rama may be seen as God, but Ravana is the more complete man. Our epics have used the ten heads of Ravana to symbolize a man without control over his passions – eager to embrace and taste life – all of it.*

Ancient India at the peak of Ravana's Asura Empire

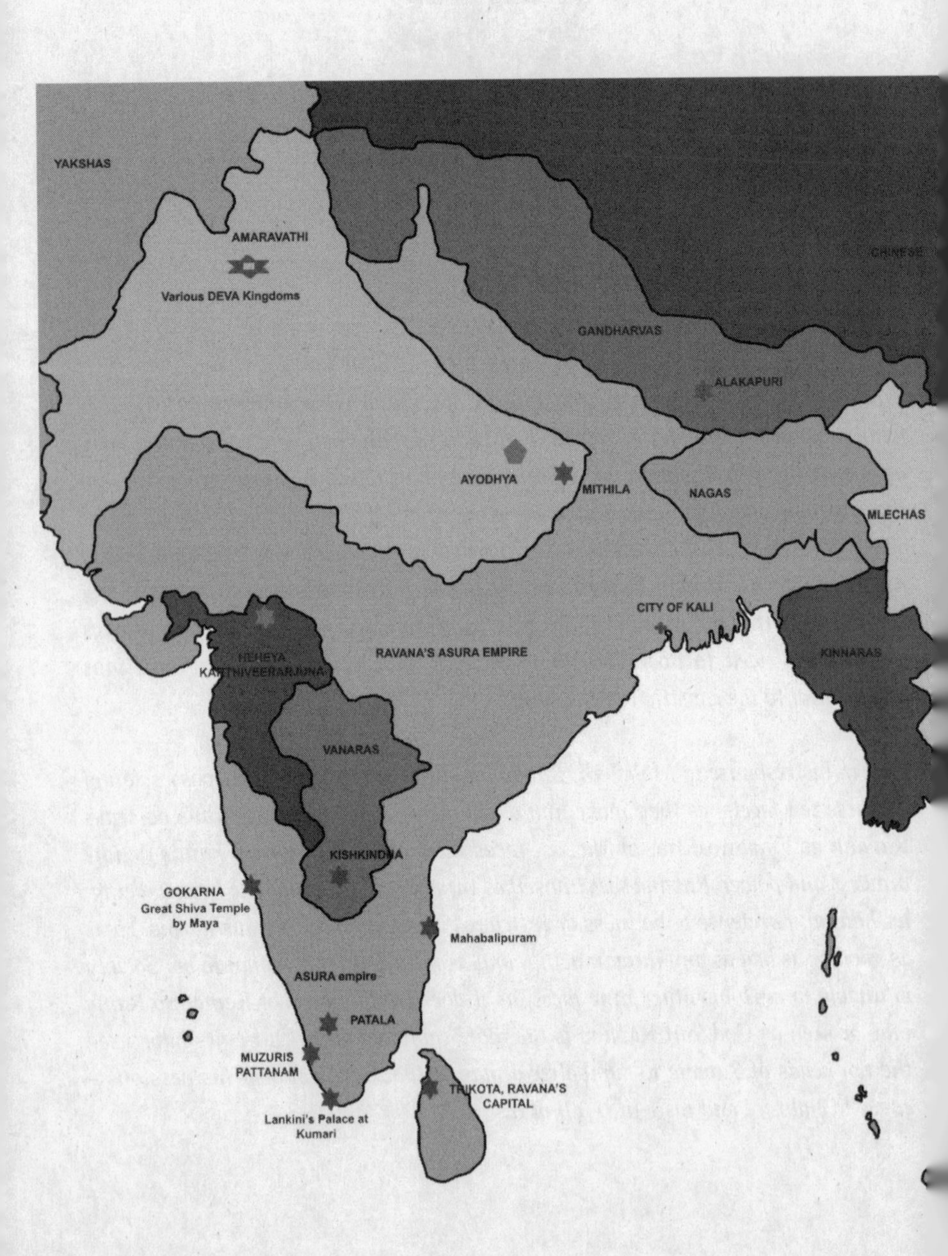

Contents

1 The End

Ravana

Tomorrow is my funeral. I do not know if they will bury me like a mangy dog or whether I will get a funeral fit for an Emperor – an erstwhile Emperor. But it does not really matter. I can hear the scuffing sounds made by the jackals. They are busy eating my friends and family. Something scurried over my feet. *What was that?* I haven't got the strength to raise my head. Bandicoots. Big, dark, hairy rats. They conquer the battlefields after foolish men have finished their business of killing each other. It is a feast day for them today, just as it has been for the past eleven days. The stench is overpowering with the stink of putrefying flesh, pus, blood, urine and death. The enemy's and ours. But it does not matter. Nothing matters now. I will pass out soon. The pain is excruciating. His fatal arrow struck my lower abdomen.

I am not afraid of death. I have been thinking of it for some time now. Thousands have been slain over the last few days. Somewhere in the depths of the sea, my brother Kumbha lies dead, half-eaten by sharks. I lit my son Meghanada's funeral pyre yesterday. *Or was it the day before?* I've lost all sense of time. I have lost the sense of many things.

A lonely star is simmering in the depths of the universe. Like the eye of God. Very much like the third eye of Shiva, an all-consuming, all-destroying third eye. My beloved Lanka is being destroyed. I can still see the dying embers in what was once a fine city. My capital, Trikota, was the greatest city in the world. That was before the monkey-man came and set it on fire. Trikota burned for days. Shops, homes, palaces, men, women, and babies, everything burned. But we restored it. Almost every able man joined in rebuilding Trikota. Then the monkey-men came with their masters and destroyed everything. Hanuman did that to us. The monkey-man brought us death, destruction and defeat.

I don't want to dwell on that. I should have killed him when my son captured him. Instead, I listened to my younger brother, who plotted against me. But treason and betrayal is nothing new to the Asuras. I was naïve. I foolishly believed that I would always be loved by my brothers and my people. I never imagined that I would be betrayed. I feel like laughing. But it's not easy to laugh when one's guts lie spread around like a wreath.

Sounds of joy float down to me from my city. The enemy is celebrating his victory. The monkey-men will be busy plundering Trikota. My temples will be looted; the granaries torched and schools and hospitals burnt. That's how victory parties are. We have done that and worse to many Deva villages, when the Goddess of victory was my consort. Some ugly monkeys must have entered my harem. I hope my queen has the sense to jump from a cliff before anything happens. I can't control anything now. I can feel the hot breath of death on my face. The jackals have come. *Which part of my body will they eat first?* Perhaps my guts, as they are still bleeding. *What if a part of my breastplate chokes a jackal?* I chuckle at the thought. A jackal sinks his teeth into my cheek and rips off a chunk of flesh. That's it. *I've lost this bet too.* They have started from my face. Rats are nibbling my toes.

I, Ravana, have come a long way. Now I do not have anything left to fight for; except this battle with the jackals. Tomorrow, there will be a procession through the streets. They'll raise my head on a pole and parade it through the same roads that saw me racing by in my royal chariot. My people will throng to watch this spectacle with horror and perverted pleasure. I know my people well. It will be a big show.

One thing I cannot understand is why Rama came and stood over me after

THE END

I had fallen. He stood there as if he was bestowing his blessings on me. He said to his brother that I was the most learned man in the world and a great king and one could learn the art of governance from me. I almost laughed out loud. I had governed so well that my empire lay shattered all around me. I could smell the burning corpses of my soldiers. I could feel my Meghanada's cold and lifeless body in my arms even now. The acrid air of a smouldering Trikota smothered my senses. I could not save my people from these two warriors and their monkey-men. And he was saying I was a great ruler? I could appreciate the irony of it. I wanted to laugh at my enemy; laugh at the foolish men who trusted me and who were now lying all around, headless, limbless and lifeless. I wanted to laugh at the utopian dreams of equality for all men on which I had built an empire. It was laughable indeed. But that was no way for an Emperor to die. I have worked hard and fought with the gods and their chosen men. I doubt if heaven has a place for people who die of laughter.

Then just as suddenly as it had started, the rats and jackals scurried away. A shadow, darker than the dark night, fell upon me. A dark head with curly hair blocked the lonely star from my view. *Is it Kala, the God of death, who has come to take me away?* I struggled to open my eyes wider. But dried blood held my eyelids together. *Is it one of Rama's lowly servants who has come to severe my head and take it back as a trophy?* I want to look him in the face. I want to look into his eyes, unwavering and unflinching in my last moments. Something about that head and curly hair reminds me of my past. *Do I know him?* He leans down and looks at my face. *Ah! It is Bhadra.* My friend, perhaps the only friend left, but I do not know if I can call him my friend. He was my servant, a foot soldier to start with. Then he got lost somewhere along the way. He strolled in and out of my life, was sometimes missing for years together. Bhadra had access to my private camp when I was the head of a troop that resembled a wayside gang of robbers rather than a revolutionary army. Then, he had had access to my private chambers when I was the king of a small island. Finally, he had access to my bedroom when I was ruling India. More than that, Bhadra had access to the dark corners of my mind, a part that I hid from my brothers, my wife, my lover, my people, and even from myself.

What is Bhadra doing here? But why am I surprised? This is just the place for people like him who move around in the shadow. I can hear him sobbing. *Bhadra getting emotional?* He was never angry, sad or happy. He acted as if he was very emotional now. But I knew he had no emotions. And Bhadra was aware that I knew.

"Bhadra, carry me away from here. Take me away to..." My strength failed me. Actually, I don't know whether the words actually left me or died a silent death somewhere in my throat. Bhadra shook his head. I was cold, extremely cold. My life was ebbing out of me. Then Bhadra hugged my head to his bosom. I could smell his sweat. Pain shot through me from every angle and spread its poisonous tentacles into my veins. I moaned. Bhadra laid me back on the wet earth, wet from my blood, the blood of my people, the blood of my dreams, and the blood of my life. It was over. A sense of sadness and emptiness descended on me.

"I will complete your work, your Highness. Do not worry. Go in peace. I will do it for our race. My methods may be different, even ignoble, compared to yours. I too, was once a warrior, but I have grown old. Arms frighten me now. I'm terrified of war. I can't even hurt a child. Nevertheless, my methods are deadly. I will get revenge for you, me and our blighted race. Rama won't go free for what he has done to us. Believe me and go in peace."

I did not hear most of the things Bhadra said. Strangely, however, I was soothed and slipped away from this foul-smelling Asura and drifted back to my childhood. A thousand images rushed to me. My early struggles, the pangs of love and abandonment, separation, battles and wars, music and art, they flashed through my mind in no particular order, making no sense. Meaningless, like life itself.

I sensed Bhadra bowing down to touch my feet, then walking away. "Bhadra. . ." I wanted him to come back and take me to some doctor who would put my intestines back, fit my dangling left eye back into its socket and somehow blow life into my body. I wanted to withdraw to the Sahyas forests in the mainland and start a guerilla war, as Mahabali had done years ago. I wanted to start again. I wanted to make the same mistakes, love the same people, fight the same enemies, befriend the same friends, marry the same wives and sire the same sons. I wanted to live the same life again. I didn't want the seat Rama has reserved for me in his heaven. I only wanted my beautiful earth.

I knew such things were not going to happen. I was sixty, not sixteen. If I lived, I would be a one-eyed, dirty, old beggar in some wayside temple, with stinking, tattered clothes. A long way from what I once was. I wanted to die now. I wanted this to end. I wanted to go away. Let the burning cities take care of themselves. Let the Asuras fight their own wars and be damned along with the Devas. I only wanted to return to my childhood and start over again, every single damn thing, again and again, and again. . .

2 The seed

Ravana

The monsoon wind swirled around the small hut hanging precariously on a mountain cliff. Another push by the roaring wind and the hut would plunge into the black torrents waiting hungrily below. Then we would be just specks of death washed ashore. It would have been better had it ended like that. *But this was just the beginning of the end. Could I be obliterated from the leaves of history – just like that? Hadn't I a mission to fail?* I didn't know it then, but I had been born to fulfil someone else's destiny. To allow someone else to become God.

Huddled together with three siblings and a morose mother, I looked down at the brightly lit palace of my half-brother. It was quite near, yet a world apart. I had been there once, hidden behind the shawl of my poor, black mother, my younger brothers tugging at my fingers. My sister was lying limp like a dirty old rag, tired and hungry, on my mother's shoulder. We were poor, dirt poor. The only thing we had in abundance was poverty. And hunger. Also shame.

As a last desperate effort, mother dragged us to beg before her stepson, Kubera, the lord of all wealth, the richest man on earth. In the glitter of the palace and the sickening fragrance of abundance, we stood there with a begging bowl. We got our alms, a few pieces of gold and also many derisive glances from my stepbrother's wives. Our needs were few and his time was too precious to waste on us. A flick of his hand, some small change, and he thought no more of us. Until the day I reminded him of our existence quite rudely and loudly. But that happened much later. By then we had ceased being beggars.

I gained my biggest asset from that arrogantly opulent palace of avarice and greed – my burning ambition. The fire of hunger would never quench the flames of ambition the palace ignited in me. I knew then that the world he owned and much beyond, would be mine and mine alone. Today might very well be the last day I will be with my mother. Tomorrow, if our small hut survives this torrential rain, we will start our journey. I believe there is a world out there to conquer. A better world awaiting us.

My brothers and I never had an education to speak of. No Brahmin was ready to take us for free even if we worked for them. We were wild, black and naughty. We had learned that we were half-castes. Our father was a famous Maharishi, but had little use for us. He was immersed in his own world of learning to care about his progeny. He was a Brahmin. My mother was of an unknown Asura caste. He kept the relationship an open secret. He knew enough of the Sanskrit Vedas, which the Brahmins claimed contained all the learning of the world.

Father wasn't a bad man, really. He was like any other member of his caste; gloriously self-centered. He considered that we were suitably rewarded with his mere presence in our home. And conveniently forgot that humans need food to live, too. Oh sure, he named us after demons as we never showed any interest in his teachings. Many a time, we mocked him and ever so often, I boldly questioned his faith when he and his friends chanted the Vedas. In our mud veranda, Kumbakarna, Soorpanakha and I mimicked them. Only my youngest sibling, Vibhishana, watched with awe. His eyes used to be fixed on the Brahmins as he listened to their jabbering with rapt attention.

This was after my father gave away all his money to my stepbrother, Kubera. We were left with nothing. Growing up was difficult, a continuous numbing ache, the kind which throbs and slowly spreads its black fingers over one's soul. Yet, we never strayed from the path of righteousness. Our sense of justice differed from what the learned and privileged considered right. We decided our righteousness and we defined our rights in our own way. We learned that the truth could be bent to suit one's needs. Our dharma was based on simple things: a man should be true to his word; he should speak from his heart and shouldn't do anything he considered wrong. One should not cheat even if one was sure to fail. One should honour women and not insult anyone. If there was injustice, we had to fight it at all costs. We never knew any of the great teachings of the ancient Asura or Deva saints. We followed no tradition. We were almost bastards.

The next day, we would be leaving this island. I had heard that there are great nations to the north. I would travel across the length and breadth of India. I wanted to climb the snow clad mountains of the Himalayas, swim against the dangerous currents of the Ganga raging in her full monsoon fury. I dreamed of passing through the thick forests of the Vindhya and Sahyas and seeing the monkey men and the kingdom of the Yakshas and Kinnaras. I dreamed of being in the music-filled world of the Gandharvas. Oh, what a world to conquer! What a life to enjoy! One day Ravana would rule the world. From the mighty Himalayas to Lanka, nay, from Lanka to the Himalayas; I would rule the world; with justice, peace and prosperity for all.

Looming in the shadows of my myriad dreams, there lingered a small doubt. Were these wonderful dreams just hunger-induced hallucinations? I might die today, caressed by the black waves and dragged by the roaring currents. My life might just flicker for a while and end in dark silence. Then who would ever now the passions and ambitions I held close to my heart? Who would know what glories I had planned for my people? My life would be just like the foam on the frothing black waters down below, soaring, ever-expanding, there now but then gone into the unknown.

My mother's tears burned a hole in my soul. She wanted us to go out and conquer the world, yet she wanted us nearby as well. Perhaps, she saw the fire raging in my eyes and decided not to stop us. When I looked back, I saw my mother, a hunched-back figure in tattered clothes, hugging my ugly sister. She was the most beautiful baby for us, but when I saw her with the sense of fairness my mother had instilled in us, I had to reluctantly agree with my father's belief that my sister was the ugliest creature he had ever seen. I hated him for that statement. I hated him even more for the fact that it was true.

The gatekeeper of my half brother's palace was sitting on the beach with his friends. They roared with laughter at the sight of us three teenagers struggling with the catamaran and raised a toast to our death. They even insulted my mother with indecent songs. I wanted to wring their necks! But I had promised my mother that I would not use violence until I got wise to the ways of the world and the sense to use my power with fairness and justice. I fixed my teary eyes on the distant shoreline – there lay my hope of success in this cruel world, my world and my guru.

My brothers and I travelled through the thick, evergreen Sahya forest. We saw glorious palaces and ports; ivory and sandalwood and peacocks and monkeys. We saw ships with kaleidoscopic-coloured sails sailing to distant lands, laden with gold and diamonds, pepper and spices. We saw temples where the Gods resided and demanded a portion of the earnings which men strived hard to earn. And we also saw the representatives of those gods who plundered in God's name. The cities were bright with lights as brilliant as the sun and the women, beautiful like those in paradise. I saw with mixed emotions of pride, jealousy and anger, the ships on which my half-brother's flags fluttered.

Whichever city we went to, Kubera's enterprises had an office. He ran a tightly controlled business empire from his palace in the island. Equestrian messengers carried important letters to his business partners and trade guilds. He owned more than a 130 ships, which sailed to Greece, Egypt and China. I was sure any junior manager of his numerous units would have welcomed us to their gold-brocaded offices, had we identified ourselves as Kubera's siblings. But that was the last thing I wanted to do.

I could have easily led a comfortable life as a clerk in any one of my half-brothers offices. It would have ensured that my family got at least one meal a day. But how could I forget the bored look in my step-brother's eyes when he dismissed us from his palace with a few gold coins? I would rather die of hunger than demean myself for a lowly job in his business empire. It might have been false pride. Many worldly-wise people have said so, to get along in the world you had to be practical and satisfied with what your measly life offers. But I was a dreamer. And I did not want to just get along in this world. I wanted to own it. Why were our people so meek and humble? That was something I always wondered about. Why were only a few able to control the power and wealth while the rest obliged them, and even laid down their lives to help this small selfish gang oppress them and their children? Was it fear? I don't know. But wherever I looked, I only saw oppression. Money, caste, rituals, traditions, beliefs and superstitions all conspired together to crush the humble majority. Why couldn't there be a more just way of living?

The moment I started asking *why*, I was branded a hothead. The Brahmin friends of my father once tried to banish me from the village saying I was possessed by evil spirits and that I was a *Rakshasa,* a demon. Perhaps I was too young and brash and my view of the world was yet to get tempered with experience. Except for my youngest brother Vibhishana, who was always quiet, I could see the same restlessness in the rest of us. I believed Vibhishana was a bit of a nitwit. But he was the darling of our village while we were growing up. He followed whatever was laid down in the books and never asked any questions. There were many times when I felt that Vibhishana was most suited for this society and that he was going to make it big in life. And I liked him. He was so small and vulnerable and I always felt he needed to be protected from this cruel world.

I desperately needed some confidence. I wasn't intelligent in the conventional sense either. I could not recite the Vedas backwards the way Vibhishana enjoyed doing. In any case, I thought the Vedas were a load of humbug and it didn't matter which way you recited them. Some jobless Brahmin like my father, created them thousands of years ago. Instead of making themselves useful, the Brahmins prayed to the Gods they themselves invented for the rain, the sun, horses, cows and money and many other things. It must have been very cold, from whichever cursed places they came. Otherwise, why would they croak like frogs and appeal to the Gods after putting hundreds of assorted twigs into the fire?

Perhaps I was prejudiced. I shouldn't think that the work they were doing, as Yajnas, was useless. In fact, it served as a perfect tool to mint money and gain material favours. They were no fools-these Brahmins. They knew how to project even the mundane tasks of burning twigs as earth-shaking, scientific discoveries and claimed to tame the forces that controlled the world. And it was funny that the majority of people like the carpenters, masons and farmers who were doing something meaningful, had become supplicant to these jokers croaking under the warm sun, sweat pouring from their faces in front of a raging fire and chanting God knows what.

They had a Yajna or a *Puja* for everything under the sun. If you had leprosy or a common cold, there was a God to whom you had to offer a special puja to appease him. You wanted your pestering wife to elope with your bothersome neighbour, there was a puja for that too. You wanted your cow to have a calf or your wife to have son, the Brahmin would help you. He would just conduct a *Puja* and a divine calf or son would be born. You curried favour with the Brahmins and your son would become the biggest pundit in the world by the age of sixteen. If not, he would perhaps become rowdy like me, who did not respect Brahmins or rituals. He would become a *Rakshasa*. I think there are many more *Rakshasas* among us now. Perhaps, it was because the '*why?*' virus spread. Couldn't the Brahmins conduct a puja so that our heads were cleared of sinful thoughts? This is something I have to ponder over when I have time.

Wherever I travel I find imposters claiming to have direct access to god and fleecing people. It is strange how kings of antiquity suddenly became Gods. How they metamorphosed into specialty Gods is even more amusing. I am no atheist. I strongly believe in God and am always willing to pray for my material and spiritual progress. But for me, God is a very personal thing and prayer needs to be spoken silently in my heart.

3 Captives

Ravana

The Asuras were a casteless society and had a highly democratic set up where an elected council, instead of a king, held actual power. They were also a roaming tribe, hunting and raiding for their existence, but somewhere, perhaps 2000 years ago, they settled down in cities and towns along the river banks. It has been said that the Asura kingdoms had roads paved in gold. But what an empire they built! It sprawled from the Indus in the west to the Brahmaputra in the east, and from the Himalayas in the north to the Narmada in the south. It could easily have been the biggest empire on earth at that time. When the kings of Egypt were busy building great tombs to bury themselves, the democratic council of the Asura kingdom was busy laying roads, building hospitals, drainage systems and everything they thought was useful for the people.

My mother claimed that she belonged to a prominent Asura tribe, the Hethis. Few believed her. However, it made me proud to think that I did indeed, belong to an elite Asura tribe. Though Asuras were never overtly religious, we had our own gods. Prominent among them was Shiva or Parameswara. We learned that Shiva was a great Asura king of antiquity, when the Asuras were a wandering tribe. I love to think that he is *The God*. He was my personal favourite.

It might have been about a 1000 years ago, when the horse-mounted, savage tribes of central Jambu Dweepa plundered the Asura cities in the great plains. A council of ten kings led the mighty Asura, and they met the horse riding savages. The mighty Asura army met the horse-riding savage tribes near the river Jhelum. The leader of the plunderers was named Indra, who through his atrocities had earned the title, *Purendara* or 'Slayer of Cities'. Thousands were slain; women irrespective of age, were gang-raped, children burnt alive and granaries plundered. Magnificent cities crumbled. A civilization was destroyed and the clock of progress was set back by centuries. The Asuras lost everything and they fled to the south. The Nagas withdrew to the eastern hills and the Kinnara and Yaksha kingdoms were wiped out. The Gandharvas became a wandering tribe and soon got long lost in the bylanes of history and mythology.

The Asura civilization was at its peak during the invasion, but they had lost their fighting power. Culture, music, art, architecture had conspired to blunt the fighting prowess of the asura armies, which in fact, was nothing but a charade. There was no efficient leadership, no professional command and no strategy or plan for national defence. It was no wonder that the mighty Asura army was routed by a handful of aggressors under Indra's dynamic leadership. Of course, the supremacy of the Asura race could have been highly exaggerated. A defeated race often uses its cultural supremacy to cover the shame of defeat. The victorious party was always portrayed as barbarians who defeated and destroyed a highly-cultured and well-developed civilization through deceit and sorcery.

But the Asuras fought back. They staged a battle from the south to reclaim their lost land. They won occasional victories and even held sway over all of India at times. However, it was the intellectual war that they were losing. Tribes which came from the north-west, had begun losing their moorings and a synthesis with the Asuras had begun. They stole the great Asura God, Shiva. Brahma, the teacher, also became their god. However, the most prominent God who suddenly appeared was Vishnu. The Brahmins, who were the official priests of the Devas, began formulating complicated rituals. They found that the main strength of the Asura cities was its cosmopolitan culture. The Asuras were a free people. Their fertile imagination made Shiva into a lovable God who demanded nothing, and no ritual was required to pray to him. He was the Asura's friend, cousin, son, father, or anything one could imagine. In many cities, Shiva was portrayed as a phallus, to celebrate virility and fertility.

Once the cities were conquered and the temples destroyed, the Brahmins demanded the conquered people worship a formless single God called Prajapita Brahma. This was an alien concept to the Asuras and led to riots. It was decided to leave the religion of the natives alone. But the spin-doctors of the conquerors started working overtime. They began ascribing divinity to their own leaders. And soon, the ruling class started calling themselves Gods. These Gods multiplied to thousands and then to lakhs. The Brahmins occupied a position below their rulers, who called themselves Devas. However, as the complexity of society and meaningless rituals increased, the Brahmins began to gain control of society. This happened over centuries, but the amazing thing is that the Brahmin spin machine never got tired and was largely successful in holding sway over the conquered population. The conquered were called Dasas and made to do all the work necessary to ensure that the Brahmins and the ruling class lived in perpetual mirth and enjoyment. They were bad rulers and pitiful administrators. Their self-centered rule drove huge populace into the hands of rebel army and only the meek and invalid stayed in the slums of their cities.

The Deva capital city of Amaravathi, paled before Patala – the temporary capital of the Asuras in exile. Amaravathi, once a huge city at the mouth of the Saraswati river, was now a miserable old shanty town. It was built by the Asura school of Mayans, who were great city builders. Almost all the available books on art and architecture, city–planning, parks and amusement centres, temples and theatres, had been produced by them. Once the Devas settled in the great northern plains, they started building a few scattered cities and founded their own school of art and architecture. But the Vishwakarma school paled in comparison to the Mayan, even though ideas were liberally lifted from the Mayan books. What they achieved, as far as I heard, was some shanty towns on the river banks of the north. Mithila and Ayodhya could perhaps have been their best towns. Going by the accounts of travelling mendicants like Narada, who was an inveterate liar, these towns were neat and not overgrown like the others that abounded on the northern plains.

I had never ventured this far north but wherever I travelled, I saw unrest. The Deva empire was slowly crumbling under the relentless pressure of guerilla warfare. I could feel the distant rumblings of a massive uprising. For years the defeated Asura tribes had been fighting a bitter war but were only partially successful in reclaiming the asura territory. For a few years, some life was injected into the dead dreams of the Asuras by men like Mahabali of the Keralaputra tribe, who held sway over all of India for about 18 years or the supposedly invincible twins, Hiranyakasupu and Hiranyaksha, in south-central India. But they all collapsed soon enough.

Initially, the Asuras had superior warfare strategies, better engineers to create machines of war and great generals and kings to lead the battle with valour. But the cunning of the Devas and the treachery of their own people ensured that the Asuras snatched defeat from the jaws of victory. It was obvious that the Asuras lacked unity. One–upmanship, false pride, over-confidence in their powers and of course, the belief that the Devas would fight the war fairly; something that the Devas always believed but seldom practised, ensured that the Asura tribe would wander in the wilderness of India for a 1000 years.

And then began an intermingling of the tribes. No one can really claim to have pure Deva or Asura blood. The deep black Asuras mixed with the pale Devas, who in turn mixed with various shades of skin colour ranging from the yellow of the Gandharvas, to the pure white of the Kinnaras, and the pitch black of the Yakshas. It was not unusual to find a pitch black Deva maiden with blue eyes or an Asura man with yellow skin and brown hair. Nor was it considered extraordinary to have a coal black brother with grey eyes and straight hair, a very fair sister with dark eyes and wavy hair and another sibling with yellow skin and curly black hair in the same family. I myself am fair complexioned with thick wavy hair and deep black eyes. My sister is as dark as midnight with straight hair and brown eyes. Kumbakarna is stocky with black skin and black curly hair and black eyes, whereas Vibhishna is light brown with light blue eyes and brown wavy hair.

Mixed races were held in contempt earlier. The Devas shunned them like lepers and they were laughed at by the Asuras. Stung by social antipathy and disdain, a group of this mixed race withdrew to the forests of central India. They were weak and uncultured, even by Deva standards and chattered incessantly without doing any productive work. They led a crude and miserable existence collecting berries and honey from the forests, living in tree houses and caves and occasionally raiding nearby villages in search of gold and women. They came to be called the monkey tribe – the Vanaras. They were mostly ignored and often considered boors. In the Deva or Asura languages, the word *Vanara* was a curse word and to call someone a Vanara was the ultimate insult which resulted in duels and death.

The Vanaras led a miserable life until Bali appeared. He burst upon the scene like a clap of thunder in summer. Bali was a great tactician and a superb military general. After suppressing the opposition in his Vanara tribe, he became their supreme leader and a brutal dictator. Along with his younger brother Sugreeva, Bali raided both the Asura and Deva tribes several times from his capital, Kishkindha, on the banks of the river Tungabhadra. Soon the Vanaras extended their sway from the Western Mountains to the Eastern Hills and were threatening the borders of Lanka. In the north, all the petty Deva kingdoms up to the Ganges River lived under constant fear. But Bali maintained a peaceful relationship with Karthi Veerarjuna, a powerful tribal monarch and descendent of an aborigine tribe, who were the original settlers of India. He ruled the narrow coastal strip on the west coast between the sea and some table–land on either side of the Vindhya mountains, on the banks of Narmada.

The situation was dangerous. Power balanced precariously between Karthi Veerarjuna in the west, Bali in Central India, the decimated Indra empire (split up as numerous petty Deva kingdoms between the Himalayas and the mighty rivers of the north), and the warring Asura tribes of the South. The condition of the Asuras was the most miserable. Poverty, disease, famine and misery ravaged the once-famed cities. Apart from the architectural splendour and thriving commerce of a few port towns like Muzuris and Kaveripattinam, the majority of Asuras lived in squalor, without any hope or self-esteem. Money was concentrated amongst a few like my step-brother, Kubera. The military leadership wasted themselves fighting foolish wars with the Devas, the aborigines, the Vanaras, but more frequently, among themselves, without any plan or strategy.

We crossed the river Poorna. The forest lay trapped and immobile, tangled in a haze of creepers and vines. I was rather apprehensive. These forests had become hiding places for guerillas belonging to various Asura tribes. We decided to continue but were suddenly surrounded by a group of armed men. I was impressed at the skill with which they surrounded us. Twenty taut bows were ready to sing. I stopped Kumbhakarana with a glance. The oaf was struggling to get his rusted sword out of its tattered sheath. I was not a coward, but the three of us were no match for the twenty archers surrounding us. This wasn't the time to play hero and I didn't know whether they were Karthiveerarjuna's policemen or Asura guerilla fighters. They were too dark to be Devas.

A well-built man with greying hair approached us and pointed his sword at my neck. Another, much younger, started searching us. I was wondering if I could kick the man in the groin and get hold of his throat, when another man pressed the tip of his sword to the hollow of Vibhishana's throat. My brave young brother started whimpering. I got the message and kept calm. This is no time for heroics, I told myself. Then, tied and blindfolded, we were half-led, half-dragged through the bushes and heavy undergrowth of the jungle.

4 Guru

Ravana

We stood shivering inside a cave, waiting for someone to appear. There were noises emanating from its depths. Suddenly all the noises ceased and a frightening hush descended. My heart was beating violently and I was embarrassed to find Vibhishana crying. My heart went out to my younger brother. He was so innocent about the ways of the world.

And then a deep, resonating voice ordered that our blindfolds be removed. As they were lifted and our eyes adjusted to the darkness inside the cave, we saw a very old man seated on a large stone chair. He stared intently at us. I held my head high and glared back at him. Slowly, imperceptibly at first, but then engulfing his whole face, a smile crossed his face. As if touched by a magic wand, the tough and mean-looking old man was transformed into a man of vigour and vitality. His face emanated a serenity beyond words. His smile conveyed the wisdom of ages. Slowly recognition dawned on me, it was *Mahabali*!

Here was the greatest and mightiest of all Asura kings. The wise, the strong, the learned, the kind, the perpetrator of social justice, the icon of dharma – paeans run out when one thinks of Mahabali. But was a hint of contempt hovering at the back of my mind? Mahabali had conducted brilliant military campaigns, vanquished his foes and ruled over a continent justly, but he lost his empire because he did not want to back out of a promise he had given to a poor Deva Brahmin, Vamana Vishnu, seeking alms from the mighty Emperor. When Mahabali's reign was at its summit, the Emperor conducted a *Rajasooya,* to proclaim his suzerainty over all of India. Kings, chieftains, rajas and maharajas, belonging to all the tribes and kingdoms of India assembled at the Asura capital of Muzuris to pay homage to the king of kings, Mahabali. As a part of the ritual, the Emperor promised a boon to anyone who asked for it. It was at that time that the Vamana Vishnu, disguised as a poor Brahmin boy, asked for three feet of land to set up a Brahminical learning centre in the Asura capital. Not wanting to go back on his promise, Mahabali gave permission to Deva Brahmins to preach their religion in the Asura capital. Soon, this small centre grew into a massive missionary institution. It became the hot-bed of conspiracy and court intrigue. Finally, before the Asura elite could work out what had hit them, Deva Brahmins had overcome the last Asura empire.

Mahabali was banished to the underworld and the empire he had built for over two decades, soon exploded into hundreds of warring petty kingdoms. But Mahabali continued to live on in legend. I was amazed to see my childhood hero in the flesh. But I was disappointed as well. Mahabali did not match the chiselled image of my hero which a hundred childhood fairytales and legends had sculpted in my mind.

"We have been trailing you for the last few weeks. What brings you to these parts where no one dares to tread? These are dangerous times and this is no place for fools like you to loiter about." The deep voice boomed through the caves and snapped me back from my reminiscences.

I bowed to the great soul before me and said, "Great King, we are seekers of fortune. We are from the Pearl island of Lanka in the southern seas." I tasted mud in my mouth when I said this, but I couldn't escape from my roots. Even our address was borrowed. "We are the sons of Kaikesi and half–brothers of Kubera. I am Ravana, and these are my siblings, Kumbakarna and Vibhishana."

A small frown appeared on his old haggard face. There were deep thought lines on his broad forehead. And there was a clear chill in his voice. "Your notoriety precedes you, Ravana. I suspected as much. My informers have brought news about your misdeeds of the past few years. It is indeed unfortunate that the Asura tribe produces such useless hotheads as you. You call yourself a warrior? But my boys were tailing you for the past eight days. They could have slit your throat many times over in the last week. And you call yourself a warrior! I think your mixed blood has got to do with this total incompetence. Stop playing a buffoon and be worthy of the ambition that burns in your heart."

Anger rose in me. What right did this old loser have to tell me off? Yet, I knew he was right. I was angry because it was true. I was an indifferent student. My mother wanted me to become a world-conquering warrior, but my non-caring father wanted to fill my head with Brahmin 'learning'. Could we afford a good teacher? Did we have the opportunity to learn to be good warriors? I had many reasons for not succeeding in life. I clenched my fist to keep my temper from exploding. I left that mundane existence because I had the fiery ambition to become something. I saw Kumbha trying to untie the chords. His eyes had become red with rage.

Then I understood. The Emperor was merely testing my patience. Perhaps this was the Guru I had been looking for. But anger still simmered within me. I didn't want to submit so easily. I could not be so easily tamed. I looked scornfully at this man and his delusion of grandeur. But my tongue appeared to have dived deep into my stomach. I could not retort. Mahabali exuded raw power. I was suddenly afraid. And then it dawned on me; this was a turning point in my life. An array of emotions flashed through my mind and I stood paralyzed before the Emperor, exposed and naked. I could feel his glance taunting me, challenging me, soothing me, frightening me.

"You may be of some use to this world after all. Initially, I thought of you as one of the dregs who populate the forgotten and forsaken Asura outposts like pests; who dream of glory and do nothing; who revel in a past, real or imagined and wish for a miracle to save themselves and their race. But Ravana, I can see a spark, a small one perhaps, but a spark indeed, which with the right breeze can be blown into a raging fire. I do not know, whether you are the promise of our miserable people or their curse. You could be both and many things beyond.

Something tells this old man that you have a grand ambition and you will not stop anywhere until you achieve your dreams. You do not know what power you have suppressed in your restless and aimless mind. A small speck of hope is rising in me, that you, with proper training and guidance can become the salvation of a million people – the people who have been trampled upon, who have been banished to the nether world of nothingness. The same people who are being crushed under the foot of an unscrupulous enemy. Ravana, welcome to the humble abode of Mahabali. Stay as long as you want, but more importantly, learn. Come with an open mind and remember that this place has a lot to teach you."

The old man had style. Then with a wave of his hands and a kind smile, the corners of his mouth twitching with a slight hint of a taunt, the Emperor dismissed us.

I kept thinking about Mahabali as we followed a slightly built man with a flowing white beard, through the enormous cave. Mahabali's fall was ridiculous. It did not have the glory and heroism associated with the fall of the other great Asura empires before him. The great Asura empire of the famous twin brothers Hiranya and Hiranyaksha, had almost achieved supremacy over all India, when Hiranya was gored to death by a wild boar. Hiranyaksha was betrayed by his son Prahalada, who had conspired with Indra, the king of the Devas.

Prahalada was a weak king and the empire soon went to pieces. He ruined the country with heavy taxes. Farming and pasturing were ruined, trade guilds migrated and art died. Meanwhile, a new menace had entered the scene – a mad Brahmin called Parasurama – Rama with an axe to grind, who formed a group of thugs to start a series of terror raids in the south. Anarchy and arson spread and his thugs were dreaded across the country. They sneaked into palaces, looted them, butchered the occupants and set fire to the city. Whenever Parasurama conquered a land, he ensured that the Brahmins occupied the highest posts. Erstwhile priests like the Malayans or Vannans, were banished from the cities to the villages. Ineffectual King Prahalada obtained peace from Parsurama at a great and humiliating price and ensured the ascendancy of the Brahmins in the Asura social order.

A change took place when Mahabali ascended the throne after Prahalada died. Indra could never have anticipated that Prahalada would have such a grandson. Within a decade, Mahabali had overthrown the yoke of Indra's empire and in a few years he had conquered the entire subcontinent. This was before Karthiveerarjuna had reestablished the aborigine or Adi Dravida empire on the west coast, and Bali, the mighty Vanara king, was even born. For the next 20 years, Mahabali ruled with flourish and Asura art and music reached its peak. Great cities were built and trade exploded. The world came to his doorstep. Oh the glories I have heard about those times! The old men of our villages never stopped talking about those days – days that I believe have been glorified beyond recognition.

Vibhishana was trying to make conversation with the old man. But he only replied in grunts and snorts. When we reached a corner, the old man abruptly stopped and turned to us. "These are your sleeping quarters. Tomorrow we will start the lessons."

Before we could thank him, he had left. We lay there thinking of our future. I kept thinking of my mother and sister. I hoped a hurricane had not blown our small hut over the cliff. I thought of my miserable childhood when even the old and stale food our neighbours gave us tasted good in our hungry mouths. I thought of the day when all four of us became sick with stomach aches after we ate like pigs in my half-brother's palace; our poor stomachs unaccustomed to ghee or fruits rebelled, and we were miserable for almost a week.

I thought of the opportunities lost by each poor, black, Asura child; the poverty, the filth, the flies, the shattered childhoods, and a familiar numbing pain started gnawing my soul. My father's leering face jeered at me, screaming repeatedly that I was a black and good-for-nothing evil-spirited loser who was a burden to the world. I think of the nights when we spoke only about the various foods and delicacies which we had only heard about but never seen.

My mother's sobs touched a soft spot somewhere inside me and I wept for our misery, the struggles that lay in the future, our shattered hopes of the past, our people and our tribe. I wept for our helplessness, frustrations and

broken lives. I even wept for the blackness of our skin. I sobbed for our ignorance and the cherished nostalgia about the imagined glory of our people. Tears could neither wash the colours of our heroism in poverty nor the foolhardy resolve of our people to die for a cause. Neither could it wash away the callousness of people like my half-brother, who was insulated from this world of emptiness. Then I wept for myself. Then, through the darkness that covered us like a blanket, two pair of hands embraced me from either side – the tired hands of my brothers, who I vowed I would protect with my life, who I believed would die for me. We hugged each other and wept together for all the miseries we had faced.

Slowly it began to sink in. A small seed of hope so casually thrown by the old Emperor began to sprout. I hugged my brothers hard as I began to think that my talk about conquering the world was not the empty daydreams of a destitute child. Maybe the future had promise. Tomorrow was another day and a new beginning.

5 Dasamukha, the ten-faced

Ravana

The old man with the flowing beard woke us at dawn and marched us to a nearby mountain stream to do our morning chores. He was quite loquacious at the moment as if he had suddenly discovered that he had a story to tell and found in us a most willing audience. "People call me Brahma. That is my family surname. Teaching runs in our blood, and we have been Gurus since ancient times. There were four Gurus in the Council of Knowledge, and each year, they decided the syllabus for hundreds of schools spread over various parts of the Asura empire. We created the Asura world as we know it today. My family created the law and were worshipped as Gods. Along with Shiva's family; who right from the time of the great empire on the banks of the Indus, protected farms, property and animals, and were called the Pasupathis owing to their function in the society. We developed a civilization."

He rambled on, "Then the Deva invasion began. The first act of Indra was to burn down our cities, schools, temples – everything that encouraged progress. We had at that time, in collaboration with the architect and engineering guild of the Mayans, achieved great progress in technology. We had even developed a flying machine – the *Pushpaka*. However, only a prototype had been built. The invasion changed all that. The head of the family and the fourth member in charge of science and technology, was among the first victims of the marauding barbarians and Asura science died with him. The head of the Mayan school escaped in his flying machine in the nick of the time and his successors are now protected by your half-brother, who has appropriated the *Pushpaka* flying machine prototype. I do not know how many centuries will pass before man masters the sky again.

My ancestors specialized in arms and manufacture of military equipment. The Brahma family who specialized in arts, crafts and music are under the protection of the Gandharva empire. Bali, the great Vanara king, protected the Brahma teachers of architecture and is building great cities in middle India. The tribe of the fourth Brahma, who joined the Devas, specialized in philosophical discourses. They are now the intellectual gurus to the Devas. So, even though I will be imparting knowledge in all possible branches, I shall specifically concentrate on arms and military strategy. As warriors, I believe that is the most crucial knowledge you should possess."

He had our attention. We had a vague idea about the evolution of the Brahma clan but it was surprising that the old man who sat cross-legged before us, was actually the bearer of such ancient wisdom. He hardly looked like a great guru. He was rather plain, short and bald, with a pot belly. But the flowing white beard and the twinkle in his eyes betrayed the genius hidden beneath that old and worn shell.

From that day, as the sun rose over the Sahyas and the majestic Poorna river that wound its way through the green mountains turned purple, a new epoch began in our lives. Brahma was our long-lost father, the mother we left behind, our Guru, our God, our saviour. Knowledge in its purest form, refined by scores of generations of knowledge-seekers of the Brahma family, poured from the old man. It engulfed and enthralled me. He taught us long-lost arts, long-forgotten texts and more than anything else, planted in my fertile but restless soul, the quest for knowledge. It was he who taught me to listen to the music of nature. He showed me how to listen to the chirping of birds, he made my mind dance to the tune of the flowing wild brooks, he made my inner self soar with the eagle flying high in the sky. I felt cleansed. If I owe anything to anyone in my life, it is to my Guru. He gave shape to my ambition, wings to my dreams, clarity to my vision, and power to my arms.

In my irresponsible teenage, I would dismiss the Vedas and Upanishads as humbug. But Mahabali and Brahma opened to me the magical world of the sacred texts of the ancient Asuras and Devas. I stood astonished at the grand philosophical speculations these books espoused. They were the works of supreme intellectuals and men of genius. It was a far cry from the trivia that people like my father were propagating in the name of Vedas. The rituals, the animal sacrifices, the curse of caste - none of these had the sanction of the Vedas nor were they divine proclamations or edicts. By the time Brahma and Mahabali had reached the commentary on the Atharva Veda, I was confident that I could challenge any pseudo scholars on the Vedas. The real meaning of the sacred texts gave me greater determination to attack evils like caste, animal sacrifices and other rituals being propagated by the priestly class. I was determined to curb meaningless rituals and sacrifices and put an end to the curse of caste.

We had nearly reached the end of our education. The last few classes were with the great Emperor himself. He spoke in length about mind control and mastering the senses. The path he proposed was rigid and straight. It was tough, challenging and totally impractical.

"Anger is the lowest emotion. It clouds the intellect and can make you do foolish things. You become blind to reason and react only with your body, without thinking. This leads to failure in every sphere. Uproot this evil from your system.

The next base emotion is Pride. Arrogance stems from pride and kills clear thinking and vision. Pride makes you underestimate your foes and overestimate yourself. Jealousy is a vile emotion, and mastering it is one of the most challenging tasks a human being has. Jealousy makes you pine for other man's kingdom, wealth, wife and fame. This emotion has lead to many wars, bloodshed and tears since time immemorial.

Happiness and sadness are just two eternal truths like day and night. A man of superior intellect is never affected by these emotions. They are not base emotions at all but a reflection of our thoughts, a reaction to our perspective on things we see, hear and do. Equanimity is not only desirable in a warrior, but a must. Without it, you are as good as dead in the battlefield.

Fear is not an emotion, it is a disease. It spreads from the leader to his followers and vice–versa. Nothing has killed more men in war than fear. What should a warrior fear? Death? But death is what everyone achieves ultimately. Is it wounds that you fear? What is more important? A pint of your blood or the nectar of victory? *Think*. Thinking will clear such doubts.

Nothing is more condemnable than selfishness. A man who thinks of himself alone is the most unlucky person of all. Why is one born? Is it to get fed and grow fat? Is to procreate and multiply like pigs? Is to defile this good earth with bodily wastes and then die without creating any ripples in the world? What is his life worth if it does not light at least a small light in the darkness that is crushing our people. Ravana, abhor this vile emotion of selfishness.

Love is a chain that ties you to the millstone of make-belief. A warrior should focus on victory and victory alone. That should be your only Dharma. Do your duty to your people, parents, wives, sisters, brothers and Gods, but never ever love them. Love makes you weak. Love has unseen bondages that take you into the abyss of failure at that crucial moment when victory and failure get balanced. Beware of love.

Finally, control your ambition. Ravana, I can see the fiery ambition burning in your eyes. But do not be reckless. Take only what life offers you as your own. Let your life follow its own tide. Aim for things and strive to achieve them, but always keep your feet solidly on the ground. Think, think and think, before you act.

The only thing worth preserving is your mind. Your mind absorbs the knowledge you gain from your Gurus, your books and your life, and refines it to great wisdom. It is what you have to develop. Every living minute you have to strive to feed your mind with fresh and positive inputs. This will give clarity to your vision and immense power to your action. You will make fewer mistakes and also learn faster from them.

Ravana, you have a great destiny before you. I have never seen anyone who can mend my broken dreams. Never before have the poor Asuras had someone so suitable to lead them to victory and eternal glory. Ravana, lead them with wisdom and empathy. You can give them back their lost empire and redeem their forgotten civilization, you can colour their aspirations and fire their imagination. I can visualize you flying atop a fiery horse, your sword outstretched, your thick black mane flying in the gusty wind, leading the bravest Asura warriors to charge upon Deva forces. I can see the Deva cities crumbling. Yes, I can hear the distant tremors of a coming storm. They are faint now, but the power they are going to unleash on this holy land of India will be tremendous. They will uproot the current system, demolish a million myths and rewrite history. Ravana, I believe, the world will be yours, unless you forget the ten lessons I have just mentioned. I believe Brahma has done enough for you to shed the nine thinking heads from you. Only the most important one, the mind, remains. The education you received is the ultimate sacrifice, your tapsya. You are now refined intelligence in its purest form. And with clear logic and action, you will lead the Asuras to regain their past glory. Go Ravana, and own the world!"

Was it the foolishness of youth or an inner urge to speak my heart which prompted me to contradict the great Emperor? I have yet to figure it out. But even now, as I am being eaten alive by rats and jackals, I believe the things I told him then. I can still see the look of astonishment, then anger, then infinite and indescribable sadness, which played upon the old face. It hurts me to even think of it, but my youth gave me the impudence to press on.

"Your highness, these are noble thoughts, but what you are demanding is impossible. I am sorry to say this, but is the shedding of the nine emotions or nine thinking heads as you call them, which I need to shed for the sake of success, practical? I am a good student and I have learnt my lessons well but I shall always have my own opinion about things. Do not think that I am arrogant. Please hear me out.

You were talking about anger, your Highness. I agree, that misdirected anger can cause harm. But is it not a basic emotion of life? If I do not get angry at the plight of the Asura tribe, that once-mighty race which built the greatest civilization the earth has known till now, how can I claim to be one of its worthy sons? Can't I be furious when thousands live in inhuman conditions under the yoke of Deva kings and their vassal Asura fiends? If I cannot feel frustration about the forgotten Asura arts, demolished Asura religion, pulverized Asura temples, destroyed Asura kingdoms, and cowering cowards who drag themselves on all fours in front of Deva kings and petty nobles claiming to represent Asura interests, tell me sir, what emotion should I feel? Is it not anger that will electrify my thoughts and push me into positive action? I am sorry sir, but I will never lose this emotional head – the head of anger.

Why should pride and vanity be held in contempt? I feel proud about my people, our race, our culture, language art and music. I feel proud about myself for having immense energy and the will to succeed. I do not believe that a person should always be meek, beg for food or live in eternal poverty and all the stuff which Brahmins preach but not a single one ever practises.

If I struggle hard in my life to achieve success, I have every right to be proud of it, I have every right to bask in vanity and luxury. Why did the kings of the past build great temples and cities? Why did the nobles donate towards charity and religion? Is it not to exhibit their vanity and pride? Most humble men are either hypocrites or have much to be humble about. Success breeds pride and vanity. And pride is the only reward of success.

Jealousy is the biggest force that motivates humankind. Why do empires compete with each other? Why do kings try to outsmart each other in what they do, if not motivated by the jealousy they feel? Jealousy is the driving force of progress, envy is the motivating force of life. The need for importance is the most important of urges after the basic physical urges of food, shelter and sex. Even these basic urges have their root in jealousy. To deny jealousy is to deny the basic instincts of man. Sorry sir, but what you are asking is impractical.

You talk about equanimity in sadness and happiness. Is this possible ever? When my beloved ones depart from this world, should I remain calm? Should I deny myself the consolation of crying? If I become incapable of feeling happiness, what shall become of me? If I do not find happiness in the beauty of the rising sun, if I cannot feel ecstasy in the smile of a little baby, if I cannot lose myself in the happiness of music, is life worth living?

Fear is the greatest instinct of man and beast, and you ask me to ignore it. Sir, I am not afraid to say that I am scared. I am frightened of many things. I am no coward but fear sleeps somewhere in my heart. I am afraid of death and the people who claim they are not afraid of death. They are either foolish and will drag others down with them also, or they are evil men who hate everybody.

I am afraid of losing many things, worthless though they may be, but I would have gained them through my sweat and blood. I am afraid that my loved ones may fall prey to disease. I am afraid that some battles might claim my faithful brothers. Strong rain can wash away my sister and mother into the waiting ocean. I am aware with every breath I take that I take steps towards my death. But I do not fear fear so much as to deny its very existence. It is this fear that helps me remain prepared for dangers that I must face. It is fear that makes me understand that there are things that I cannot control and helps me to understand God and myself.

You call selfishness a base emotion. But it is this trait which has built great cities around the world and the very foundation of ambition. Without a highly centered ego and the desire to achieve the treasures of this world, would one succeed in life? When I see a lovely girl, a fascinating place, a charming village, a sparkling diamond, a prosperous country, ambition flutters in my soul. I want the charms of this world to be mine and mine alone. You may try to kill my base thoughts, but my King, pardon my impudence and tell me in all honesty, was it not from the same selfishness that you built an empire? You did not become a mendicant, but strived to become the Emperor of the whole world. If it was not for this base instinct of selfishness, why did you slay thousands in war? Why did you lead your mighty armies against the Devas? You had one aim only, you wanted glory for yourself, your clan, your tribe – whichever way one looks at it, the word *you* is prominent. I want to achieve whatever you achieved and much more. I am willing to risk being known as the most selfish man in the world, rather than dying unknown as a selfless non-entity."

The old man sat there with fire in his eyes. I felt myself cowering. But, as I had started, I did not want to leave things unsaid. I collected my thoughts and pressed on, "It's pity that you and Brahma look down on love as a base emotion. Without love, without the king of emotions, nothing exists. There's nothing more pure than the love of a mother for her baby. If one has not felt the painful need to be with one's lover, if you do not feel the love for your own brothers, sisters, your father who made you, your mother who carried you in her womb and raised you with her blood and milk, for friends and those little cherished moments of togetherness, your wife for sharing your life with you and for your children for carrying your life forward, then is this life worth living? Is it not love for your country, tribe, language, religion, Gods, and so many other things, which may seem trivial but which are so preciously held in the bosom of men, that has led to so much bloodshed and war? People have died for love in the past and will continue to do so as long as the world exists. I shall always love the things I have told you about. But yes, I shall love myself above them all. Without me, nothing which is lovable has any meaning to me. I love because I exist and I exist because I love – I love myself.

Ambition is the key to progress. Without ambition, the kings of Egypt would not be so busy building those pyramids right now. Without ambition, men would have remained hunters. There would not have been wheels, horsecarts or chariots, magnificent cities, temples and palaces, nor majestic sailing ships. Without ambition, we would not have had a Mahabali or Indra. Ambition is the horse that pulls our lives forward.

The amazing speed of progress man has achieved in the past few years would have not been achieved without that small flame of ambition in the minds of a few men, which was fanned to become a huge fire by the other emotions you have urged me to shun. Pride in one's capability gave men the confidence and ambition to grow; jealousy that someone else would achieve more prodded him to work hard and more efficiently; the quest for happiness resulted in ever-expanding ambition; the fear of sadness kept him awake at night and pushed him further; the fear of failure made him more careful and God-fearing; selfishness glued his family, city, clan, tribe and country together and made him strive even harder. Love for life and the things which made life precious, made him protect his achievements. and I am sure an undying ambition for more will lead mankind to progress. Progress, which we cannot even imagine, can never understand in our short lifetime.

My beloved Emperor, please do not feel sorrow if I speak my heart. You were talking about intelligence being the only head worth having. I agree it is important. But history teaches us that without any of the other emotions, it is just an empty skeleton. There is no life in it. Sir, it was not the maharishis or sages who built civilizations but extraordinary men, who never controlled their emotions, but let them flow in the direction which nature intended. No mendicant living in a forest ever conceived a great city, no sage was determined to built the great temples, no Brahmin desired to built great ships for commerce and trade. These were built by men who had pride in their veins, anger in their minds, who cried when they felt sad and laughed when they were happy, who were frightened when confronted by forces or events bigger than themselves, but strove forward with determination and a selfish love for all that they cherished. They constantly kept raising their levels of ambition. Intelligence is just a tool to serve our emotions and I want to live as God intended man to live.

My aim is neither become God nor achieve moksha. At best I think, those are old wives tales. I do not believe in a heaven where you will be given all that you purposefully denied yourself in this world. I do not believe in rebirth, when I will be born as a Brahmin if I do good deeds in this life – good in the way the Brahmins describe. If being born a Brahmin is the ultimate reward, then I may even refuse to die for fear of being reborn.

I am sad to disappoint you, but I shall live like a man and die as one. I will never try to be a God. I will live exactly as my emotions tell me to. I do not want to be a model man for future generations to follow. My life begins with me and ends with me. But I will live my life to its full and die as a man should. So borrowing from your words, I shall be a man with ten faces – I am *Dasamukha*."

A thick silence followed. Brahma stood staring at his bare toes and the shrunken Emperor's fiery eyes bored through me. I found a sudden energy flowing in my veins. Until I delivered my long speech, I was not myself sure of my life's philosophy. Until then I had wondered if I was betraying the trust the great old man had placed upon me. But suddenly I found I was looking at him with a new pair of eyes. He was shrinking fast in my estimate. He was just a shrunken, beaten, half-dead old man who had a pretentious air about him, as if he was still ruling the country. He was just a mountain rat, hiding from Deva forces and fighting his own puppy war in his backyard.

The voice I heard then was a weak murmur. He tried to rise himself but crumbled before me. I watched in horror. The pale figure slowly rose to his knees. With glassy eyes, he stared past me and then quite melodramatically raised his head and stared. I had no time for an old man's ramblings. I turned my back and with a deliberate toss of my head, walked out with my brothers following me. Vibhishana, with faltering steps, turned back many times towards the old man who had now raised both his hands towards the sky and was rambling. But Kumbakarna followed me with steps more determined than my own and a smile on his lips. A motley crowd of Mahabali's warriors followed me, their swords and shields clattering as they walked.

I stepped out into the blazing sun with my band of followers. The earth was fresh from a recent shower, as if the Creator had just finished his work and gone to bathe. I inhaled the smell of the forest blooms and wet, red earth. The chirping of birds was music to my ears. The world lay with wide open arms, inviting me to join in this exhilarating journey of life. As I took my first step, I heard a sharp-pitched wail from the cave I had left behind. My spine chilled but I walked on, trying hard to close my ears to the old man's soul-piercing wail that rose from the depths of that stinking cave. "What have I unleashed?!" the crazy old man kept wailing. I soon shut out the miserable sounds and the world the old man represented, from my mind. I forgot about it for a long time until it came back to haunt me in my sleep. But that was later, much later. I am now running ahead of myself.

6 Devil's raid

Bhadra

I had been fighting this fool's war for the last few years. I fought under Mahabali for six years, then tried to form my own group and failed. Then I fought under Sumali. I was neither a great fighter, nor a great organizer. Short, plump, with soft hands, I am just an ordinary man. Just like a vegetable vendor, the bullock cart man, peddler in the market, or even the washerman. I am a nobody. I do not have a steely glare and arching brows. My nose is not hooked and my lips do not draw a determined, straight line. I do not have high cheek bones or a cleft chin. I had another name earlier in my life, but now I am known only as Bhadra.

I never had large ambitions. I looked after my farm on the banks of the river Poorna. It had some pepper vines, a few coconut palms and two cows. I was happy with my wife and a lively three-year-old daughter. My village was small but it had everything – the sacred grove, a small shrine for Shiva, a toddy shop and a small school, where basic crafts like masonry, farming, mathematics and other necessary subjects were taught. There was also a house of pleasure, a quack who called himself a doctor, a priest to fleece us, and a public bath where we bathed along with our buffaloes. I lived like my father, who had lived like his father. My children would also live like me, growing up in the same street, bathing in the same pond, falling in love with the dusky beauties of the village, marrying, procreating and dying quietly, mourned by a few and not in the least missed by the world.

My life would have gone on like that, without any punctuations, to end simply with a full stop. But the arrival of the Devas changed everything. We did not know who these creatures were until they came and knocked us down. I remember those days with horror. We heard the rumblings of distant war through the occasional traders who came to collect pepper from our farms. They spoke about how the Deva forces were grouping under Vishnu, the chief Deva, and how Mahabali was bracing for war. We ignored these rumours. These were unimportant things and happened to someone else in far-off places. Kings fought wars and won or lost their kingdoms and their lives. We were the lesser mortals and cared nothing about the dirty world of politics. I believed that Mahabali was invincible. He was thought to be just and tried to rule with his subjects in mind. Atleast that is what the village elders told us and we had no reason to disbelieve them. We continued to live the same way no matter who ruled in the distant capital. So long as they did not bother us, we would always say they were good rulers.

On a dusty evening, when we were returning from work on our farms, a messenger appeared on horseback. He was a tall fellow with smallpox marks covering his face and a strange expression in his eyes. He asked us to demolish our Shiva shrine and surrender to Vishnu. He was treated well by the villagers, but sent back with a warning that he should not invite the wrath of Shiva. In fact, the messenger went into the Shiva shrine and offered prayers before leaving. The whole day, we spoke about the Devas. Some said the Emperor had already fallen and fled underground, and that Vishnu had become our new Emperor. They claimed that the messenger was proof of their theory. Others said that Mahabali had moved over to the Deva clan and was rapidly converting all the Shiva temples to Vishnu temples. There was a row in the toddy shop and my friend got punched on his nose by an angry Shiva fanatic. I was happy that there was finally some activity in my quiet village. Usually nothing exciting ever happened here and one new day was as dull as the next.

That is, until the night I was woken by my wife. I was angry to be rudely shaken from my sleep and wanted to thrash her for her impudence. Then I saw that there were strangers inside our bedroom. My first thought was, which I vividly remember even now; 'Oh god! What will I give these people to eat? They have come after dinner time.' Then anger came. How dare they break into my bedroom? Slowly, fear crept on me. Who were these people? Why were they here? My neighbour, that idiot who spat red betel juice into my courtyard every day and enjoyed the fights that followed, was being burnt alive and brightly lighting up his front yard. In that ghastly light I also saw an orgy taking place in my neighbour's yard. The cuckold whose wife flirted with every male in the village, was getting it from more than six persons at the same time. But she was screaming. The Deva warriors had taken our village. The whole village was burning. People were running about like scared chickens. I saw people being hacked. Houses were ablaze. Warriors on horseback with their fair, devilish faces, were jeering, howling and killing people.

The strangers were leering at my wife now and I could feel her trembling. I scrambled up and threw my arms protectively around my family. The devils howled with laughter. Then I heard the crackling sound of fire as it ate through my hay roof. Someone hit me with the hilt of his sword. The bridge of my nose cracked and searing pain shot through my body. A boy, barely fifteen perhaps, lifted my daughter by her legs, swung her like a rag and smashed her hard against a mud wall. I heard my beloved daughter's skull crack open. Her blood and brains splattered across our faces. The devils laughed again. I went numb and collapsed onto the floor. My wife fainted. I desperately tried to grab my wife as they dragged her away into the darkness. My fingernails scratched lines of blood on her arm, but she slipped away. I tried to stand up. There was blood everywhere. I slipped in the blood and my hands touched my daughter's shattered head. I shuddered. I did not want to look. I had to find a weapon. Anything that I could use to smash the skulls of these bastards. Somehow, I had to save my wife.

My wife's shrill screams got lost among many similar cries rising all over the village. I walked, even as my strength oozed out of me and tried to grab a pillar of the verandah. It was solid bamboo but with dismay I found I could not lift it, let alone use it as a club. I jumped on the swine who were raping my wife. Bare handed, I fought tooth and nail, but I was no match for the mighty Deva warriors. I was down in a second and they started punching me. Solid wooden shoes kicked my face and I was dragged in the mud. Blows rained upon me. Mercifully, one bastard plunged his sword deep into my abdomen and all I knew then was darkness.

When I awoke, it was still dark. There were flames everywhere but they were slowly dying out. I could hear the distant howls of jackals. Another day has dawned, I thought hazily, and I have to go and milk the cows. But I just lay there. The earth was so cozy, cool and comforting. Then slowly, very slowly, reality crept in and I sat up with a jerk. Needles of pain pierced parts of my body which I didn't know existed. My eyes were welded together, caked with blood. I struggled to open them. Then I saw some Deva bastards sitting under a tree, getting drunk.

All around, my village and my entire life, lay shattered. I tried to stand and might have broken a twig in the effort. The noise sounded like a bolt of thunder to my ears. The ghostly figures looked back. I sat without moving. 'They know I am alive and they are going to kill me,' I thought. For a moment I was relieved the Devas decided not to investigate. Then I saw him. A dark, tall figure was walking towards me, his sword drawn. I panicked. As he came near, I saw that it was the same boy who had splattered my girl all over the wall. He was drunk and wobbled on unsure legs. I waited, my hands searching for anything I could use as weapon. The boy stood near my head, swaying a little. Someone called out to him. He hesitated. By then my hands had found an old knife abandoned by somebody, and in one fluid movement I struck it into the boy's groin. I was surprised when he fell on the top of me without a sound. I pulled out the knife and struck him again in the nape of his neck.

"Hey!" there was surprise and shock in the voice of the man who was running towards our tangled forms. I saw others following him. I struggled to get away from the boy but he was heavy. I was drenched in sweat and blood by the time I wriggled out from under him. Instinctively I ran into the forest bordering my village. I ran with whatever strength was left in my body, away from these demons, away from my past, away from the life I had known. I kept running for the sake of my dear, useless, meaningless, hollow, shallow life. I panted and puffed my way towards safety, slipping on the decaying carcasses of my brothers and friends. But it did not matter then. They were just carcasses, waiting for the vultures to finish what the

Devas had started. Death was following me and I was chasing my life which was running away swiftly.

A sharp pain pierced my shoulders and I saw fresh sprouts of blood dripping, marking my trail. The bastards were shooting me. Arrows whined past my ears and landed with sickening thuds in the tree trunks all around. One of them could split open my throat and then this nightmare would mercifully end. Then everything faded away. I had a weightless feeling, as if I was floating. A sea of dark green swallowed me. Branches hit my face. I was falling, falling rapidly down a dark abyss. So this is what death was like. So sudden and kind. The caresses on my face, the sensation of weightlessness, the pleasure of floating, and whack!. For a moment I was dead.

When I came back to the light, I was lying on a crude rope cot inside a stinking cave. There were moans coming from all around me. I tried to sit up, but was forced to sink back as pain grabbed me in its claws. I turned my head slowly and saw that there were many people lying around the cave in various stages of decay. I shivered. Was I a prisoner-of-war and at the mercy of the Devas? But when had the Devas ever taken prisoners? More over, I was a civilian and not a soldier. I lay there with useless thoughts buzzing in my head which I tried to make sense of. The sound of people talking floated down to me, "Half of them will definitely not make it. The others might take at least a month to even start walking." The tongue was definitely classy Tamil, the kind used by educated and pretentious city folk. I realized I was not among foes. But the voices sounded matter-of-fact and their dark prophecy filled me with indescribable terror. Slowly, like waves lapping the banks of the Poorna, bubbles of memories rose from my drugged mind and broke into my consciousness. It hurt so much that I started wailing. Many cries echoed through the cave from the throats of men waiting for death. I heard the voice of a defeated people moaning the loss of simplicity and a meaning in their lives which they never had. Perhaps, it was in one of those moments, when I lost myself amidst the cries of my people, that I vowed revenge against the Devas.

7 Lore of the losers

Ravana

We had been walking like this for four months and were now tired and hungry. I sensed most of the warriors were bored when I started my usual morning discourse, "Today we will learn about the war of the ten kings, that led to the Asura empire's final collapse and the advent of the Devas. Initially, the Devas were just a nuisance to the mighty Asura kings. They went on rampages in the border towns once in a while. However, with the advent of Indra, things started to change rapidly. Indra had nothing to lose. Tales of his savagery preceded him. He had ransacked many small kingdoms north-west of the Himalayas and burned beautiful cities. He butchered all living beings in a captured city and lit huge funeral pyres, around which the Devas danced and chanted.

When the ten kings of the Asura Council decided that it was time to teach these barbarians a lesson, Indra had already established himself with his sharp shooters in the barren and snowy ridges of the rugged mountains of Gandhara. The mighty Asura army, even without great military or tactical superiority, would have simply crushed the small contingent of Deva marauders by its sheer numbers and superior arm power. But in the narrow valleys of the Gandhara, the elephants of the ten kings were quite useless. The Asura kings were used to fighting in the wide open spaces between the Ganges and the Indus. The elephant battalion, the infantry with heavy clubs and swords, the chariots, which were more like goods carriers and carried reserve weapons and men, were more suited to wide open spaces.

But Indra showed his brilliance when he chose the narrow Gandhara valleys to encounter the Asura kings. He waited in the heights of the mountains for the Asura kings to come and fight the battle on his terms. The Asuras were quite confident of the outcome. They had faced countless attacks from other tribes from the north and north-west before. This was just another of those picnics, when they would crush the enemy, capture their leader, forgive him magnanimously, and offer the vanquished party a banquet in their palaces.

Poor devils, they did not know who they were dealing with. This was a different kind of enemy – vicious, ruthless and with an indomitable will to win. I have never been to Gandhara, but what we learned from Brahma gave us a pretty good idea of what it could have been at the time of the war of the ten kings."

I had drawn a rough map of north-western India on the sand and was surrounded by my brothers and Prahastha, a capable middle-aged man, who was the captain of our soldiers. The other warriors listened carefully. Prahastha claimed he was my mother's distant relative and hence my maternal uncle, though I doubted it. On the other hand, my mother had many Asura relatives, so it could have been true. If he thought I was going to bestow special favours on him after I became king, he was going to be disappointed. But Prahastha was a capable and intelligent man and I respected him.

I paused when I saw some of the soldiers getting edgy. I felt sorry for them. Most of the soldiers were illiterate and poor. They would have been farmers or artisans or traders in normal times, but driven from their homeland, they had followed their once-great Emperor, who had promised them their old, secure world. They were betrayed and had now put their hopes on a homeless young daredevil like me, to deliver back to them their long lost world. Perhaps I was becoming a megalomaniac, but certainly I would try to deliver them their dreams.

"Indra, had initially made a tactical blunder. He had attacked the walled city of Pragya, on the banks of the Sarswathi, which was a major port of King Pramyudha. He was not a man of half measures. He unleashed his entire army. 500 elephants, 10,000 infantry with heavy swords and clubs, and 500 archers in bull chariots, burst out of the city walls. Indra had a small army of 600 mounted archers. He put 200 of them to attack the city's front gate and tried to enter the city from the rear. Pramyudha opened all four gates and his mighty army divided itself and converged at the front.

Indra was shocked by this daring move. Like a cornered rat, the Deva army fought back viciously. But there were far too many Asura forces. Moreover, the wide open plains gave the Asura army room to manoeuvre. The Devas, on their horses, were easy targets. From atop elephants, warriors showered heavy javelins and spears and the heavy arrows made the Deva armours look like onion peels. Indra ordered a retreat, but it was impossible to get out of the mess he had led his army into. More than 80 percent of his army was butchered. But Indra fought valiantly with his sword and even managed to wound Pramyudha.

It was foolish of Pramyudha to get down from his elephant and challenge Indra. And while Pramyudha fought Indra, the idiotic Asura soldiers stood in a circle and clapped and cheered with each thrust and plunge of the combatants swords. It was as if the Asura warriors were being entertained. They even cheered Indra for his superior swordplay!

Pramyudha played by the book. His footwork was perfect, so were his jabs and thrusts. But Indra was fighting for his life and he referred to a very different book. Quite unexpectedly, he threw sand into his opponent's eyes with his shield. At the same time, he deftly cut with his sword. Pramyudha, the accomplished swordsman that he was, ducked, but was a bit too late. He received a deep wound on his shoulder and fainted in the battlefield. In the confusion that followed, Indra forced his way out of the shocked crowd, thrusting his sword into three soldiers who stood in his way. He quickly mounted his horse and vanished in a trice, followed by a handful of survivors."

"Tell me any story about a fallen king, and I will show you someone whose foolishness is only exceeded by his vanity," Prahastha added.

"True," I continued, "Had the fallen king let bygones be bygones and gone back to ruling his kingdom, Indra's attack would have been but a small footnote in history. Instead, his huge ego was hurt. Pramyudha did not take solace from the fact that his subjects had been spared the fate of citizens of other cities which had fallen to Indra. He was not satisfied that, except for his personal defeat at the hands of the enemy king, his army had succeeded in crushing the Deva army. His image had taken a beating. Asura kings of yore did not have divine right to the kingdom. A king was an elected leader, the most accomplished person in the city, a great warrior. And that was all."

"Pramyudha learnt from his court spies that his popularity had fallen among his subjects and that he would not get re-elected. He needed to take drastic action to restore his prestige. Such thoughts are devastating for a king. There ought to be no personal failures or victories. If your army has won, it does not matter whether your opponent is a better swordsman than you. But the Asuras always wore their egos on their breastplates. Their thinking thus became clouded and the chain of strategic mistakes began to unwind," Prahastha added, while I drank water from the pitcher.

I could see that the audience was listening with rapt attention now. Pleased, I continued, "The king sent spies in all directions. He had to somehow trace Indra and take revenge. Paramyudha also called on the General Council of the Asura kings. This was a body of equals from all parts of India. Ten kings met once a year to decide about water sharing, fixing customs, excise, and toll rates, port levies, and to exchange musicians and artisans. An emergency meeting was rarely called, unless there was a grave threat to the security of any of the kingdoms. Generally, the kingdoms maintained standing armies, but because of rapid cultural growth, their fighting prowess had greatly declined.

There was something mysterious about this land. When great conquering armies succeeded in their mission and settled down between the great Indus-Ganges plain, they seemed to lose their tough edge and got rounded and feminine. The land changed them from great barbarians to gentle creatures with a taste for the fine things of life. This happened to all the great conquering armies before the Asuras, and you can see it now happening to the present Deva kingdoms of the north.

And it happened to the Asura people as well. But, the kings wanted to think of themselves as the descendants of great warriors who swept through the country. They were supremely confident about their military might. The army was nothing more than a bloated organization with musicians, dancing girls, magicians and petty tricksters, acrobats, cooks, flower vendors, traders and priests. The numbers we heard of in stories were untrue. In an army of 10,000, only a few were actual warriors. The others accompanied the army to the battlefields and made a nuisance of themselves.

Six of the ten kings disagreed at the General Council meeting that Indra's attack was not alarming. They believed that any prosperous city could be attacked. But Pramyudha carried the day with his convincing arguments. He said that the tribes which raided the frontier towns of the Indus plains never dared to attack the capital city of a prominent kingdom. This group, Pramyudha thought, did not seem to be the usual raiders who attacked the granaries and carried away whatever they could. In fact, these people had shown unusual daring and cunning and they were using a strange animal to carry out their raids. The Asura army was surprised by the deftness of the animals, which unlike bulls, were swift and agile. Unless this enemy was crushed, Pramyudha argued, our people would live under the constant threat of these barbarian hordes. However, that night the Council adjourned without a decision.

The morning session broke when a messenger entered the camp of the Asura king of the north-western territory, and announced that horseback tribesmen had set Multamukha on fire. This was a major city on one of the most prominent trade routes that stretched from the mouth of the Ganga to Gandhara and beyond. The attack tipped the scales. All ten kings decided to join hands and form a huge army and decimate not only the horse-mounted tribes, but also all the small-time pirates and robber gangs who attacked the major trade routes to the great cities of Egypt and Mesopotamia.

The Council met for the third day and war plans were drawn up. Pramyudha won the generalship, not because of his seniority or prowess, but because he was the only one who did not have any second thoughts about following the enemy into unknown territory. Most of the kingdoms were comfortable and no one wanted a war. Trade was booming and life was generally good. The old crowd of daring soldiers who had followed Shiva on their bulls, slept on dirt, and ate once a week, had vanished. These were men who had tasted the sweetness of life and did not want to fight extended wars with tribes that had nothing to lose.

Pramyudha started from the bank of the Indus, with over a lakh of archers and warriors armed with clubs, spears and curved swords. About 10,000 elephants and 3,000 bullock chariots were accompanied by 10,000 drummers, flutists, dancing girls, camp builders, bards to record the heroics and render songs of Asura bravery, and the other dregs of society who usually accompanied an Asura army. This mighty crowd – there is no more suitable word, crossed the Indus and Sarswathi rivers and started hunting down small-time robbers and marauding tribes. The army marched on with great success. Pramyudha maintained excellent communication lines with runners carrying messages between the villages on the way. Spies informed the Asura king about enemy hideouts and the army descended with surprising speed and ruthlessness on the villages suspected to harbour enemy spies.

Pramyudha became drunk with success. His spies informed him that Indra was fleeing with a small army towards the north-western mountains of Gandhara. Pramyudha's bards sang praises about him and this ruffled the fragile egos of the other nine kings, who were reluctantly accompanying the army. They found themselves demoted to minor leaders in Pramyudha's service. Pramyudha himself was becoming haughtier by the day. Initially he ignored the advice of the other kings. Later, he openly criticized them and made fun of their military strategies."

I pointed out the course of Pramyudha's army, marching happily towards disaster about 1000 years ago. The soldiers leaned over to get a better view of the rough map I had drawn on the ground.

Prahastha took over, as I was feeling parched and needed a break. He started in his throaty voice, "The army was no longer a compact fighting unit by the time it reached the rugged plains at the base of the Hindukush mountains. Three kings had rebelled and threatened to leave with their armies if the campaign was not called off. By this time, Pramyudha had started talking about conquering the West, including Egypt, and proclaiming himself the Emperor of the world. When the three kings rebelled, he promptly arrested them for treason and after a brief trial, executed them openly. That sent a shiver through the army. Their morale was already at its nadir.

The campaign was not turning out to be the picnic they had imagined. The great march was taking its toll. Soon, a large part of the armies belonging to the executed kings, rebelled, and many others deserted. Pramyudha hit back with brutal force. The bards sang that he slayed 9,000 of his own armymen. He also sent a huge contingent to chase deserters and bring them back to be executed after a mock trial. Some of the warriors remained neutral during this time. It seemed that the Asura army would inflict a defeat upon itself through this rabid infighting. Finally, Pramyudha was able to persuade six kings to remain with him and the rebellion was put down with great difficulty. But he had lost precious time. It was already winter by the time he decided to penetrate deep into the mountain country in search of Indra and his army

Viboga, the king of Varanasi, asked Pramyudha to wait until summer, but Pramyudha declined. He wanted to capture Indra and drag him back to his capital at the earliest. He, who would be the Emperor of the world, would not be cowed by steep mountains and snows. Against better counsel, Pramyudha ordered his army to move north-west. The narrow mountain roads were slippery. The elephants slipped and fell into gorges or on the road, blocking progress for hours. Bullock-drawn chariots and even elephants, had to be abandoned on the narrow road. The infantry column broke up and soldiers walked as they pleased. The heavy axes, clubs and bows were difficult to carry and most of the soldiers, coming from the sweltering plains, were not used to the freezing mountain cold. To add to their woes, Pramyudha kept all his supplies in the bullock carts and these had to be carried uphill by the warriors. The motley crowd of dancing girls, bards and musicians; magicians and priests; became a nuisance and slowed down the progress drastically."

I took over the story from Prahastha, "The mob walked for more than a month in search of the elusive Indra and his followers. Many deserted the army and others died due to the elements and exhaustion. The men had exhausted most of the supplies and except for an occasional mountains goat and small birds, nothing else was edible. More than half the elephants were dead and bullocks were killed to feed the hungry and tired army.

The army had lost most of its heavy weaponry. The dregs had already fallen behind and the column of soldiers stretched more than seven miles. The group of dirty, ragged men, with heavy unwieldy weapons, slowly and painfully dragged themselves through the labyrinths of the treacherous mountains. In the past year, they had not seen a single Deva soldier. The only time the Asura warriors had taken to arms were against themselves and highway robbers, on this great march.

By this time, Pramyudha also had discovered his folly and wanted to turn back towards the cozy comfort of his beautiful capital city. But the army was hopelessly lost. Many of the mountain passes were now closed due to avalanches and landslides. Pramyudha sent messengers upon messengers, in all possible directions, asking for help and supplies from petty Asura chieftains. But not a single messenger returned. It is believed that these messages were intercepted by Indra's army. Then, when the Asura army's morale was at its lowest ebb, on a cold, foggy morning, Indra's horse-mounted archers started raining flaming arrows on them. Pramyudha's army was stuck in a narrow, mountain gorge and stretched over ten miles in single file formation."

I made a circle around a point in the map to emphasis my point. "Indra trapped the mighty, numerically stronger, Asura forces in a narrow mountain gorge with deep canyons on one side and high rugged rocks on the other. Perched on agile horses, the Deva archers rained lightweight arrows on the helpless Asura crowd. Indra had hardly 500 warriors to take on a 50,000-strong Asura army. But what followed was plain slaughter. The heavy arrows of the Asuras could not defy gravity and reach the mountain tops where the Deva archers had stationed themselves. Axes, clubs and spears were quite useless. There was nothing the Asura army could do to stop the huge stones which came rolling down, crushing scores of men in their way, but to wait for their turn to die. After a brief attempt to fight, the majority of the army fell into a disorderly retreat.

Pramyudha, despite all his faults, was brave, and he attempted to raise the morale of his fleeing army by trying to climb the rocks where the biggest group of Deva archers was placed. With adroitness, he started to shoot arrows with surprising accuracy and succeeded in hitting quite a few Deva archers. Seeing their King's valour, hundreds of Asura archers started following him. But the majority of his army fled, and except for the brave king of Varanasi, who tried to dissuade Pramyudha from this doomed campaign, the five other kings of the Council also fled with their armies. In the stampede which ensued, thousands were trampled to death and many found their graves at the bottom of the ravines.

Pramyudha and Viboga fought their way uphill with their small crew of a few thousand. Even this small determined troop outnumbered the Deva army. Indra understood the danger and quickly led the fight himself. Once more Pramyudha and Indra were face to face in the battlefield. Viboga was fighting his way up and shouted at Pramyudha to retreat and let him lead. But this was the chance for Pramyudha to avenge himself for the shameful defeat he had suffered in the last combat with Indra. He cornered Indra, who soon got tired, defending the powerful jabs, cuts and thrusts of his opponent's sword. But unlike the Asuras, the Devas do not stand in a circle and applaud good swordsmanship when their leader's life is in peril. A cleverly aimed arrow hit Pramyudha's neck and emerged from his right eye. The shock paralyzed Viboga and in those split seconds, seven Deva swords hacked Viboga to pieces.

Pramyudha continued fighting for a few more seconds, but Indra, with a clean sweep of his sword, gracefully severed his opponent's head. His cry of triumph sent shock waves through the remaining Asura warriors. Indra raised the severed head of Pramyudha on his sword tip for all his opponents to see. The Asura army was in full flight. Indra allowed a few thousand to escape and then closed in to butcher the unfortunate multitude left behind. Thousands were slain on that fateful day.

The disorganized Asura army was forced out of mountains by the Deva warriors, who knew the territory well. Once they reached the plains, the Asura army in full flight, pursed by mounted soldiers, numbered only about 200. The five kings who had taken flight, could have turned back and conducted an organized counter attack. The horse riders were in the open where the heavy equipment of the Asura army could have wiped them out. That was the reason why Indra had tactically kept his army at a safe distance, beyond the range of the heavy Asura arrows, but within the range of his lighter arrows. Soon, the Deva ranks swelled with fortune hunters and deserters from the Asura army, the kind of people who always want to be on the winning side. The news spread that the Asuras were in full flight after a rout and the Devas were following them. Robbers and other wild tribes, who had gone into hiding when the mighty army was sweeping northwards, came out and joined the Deva ranks.

The first to know the taste of the Deva's might, was the motley crowd of drummers and dancing girls and other useless crew members who were returning home, unaware of the fate of their army. They were first overtaken by the fleeing Asura army and then the swelling Deva hordes descended upon them like a plague. The mob was out of control and except for the original hundred warriors, no one listened to Indra's command. The majority were aboriginal tribesmen and plunderers who stopped at each village to loot. They ransacked houses, plundered cities on their way, hacked thousands of ordinary folk to death, and gang raped women. Soon, citizens of the big cities began to flee even before the defeated Asura army reached them. It became a human avalanche and riots broke out. Utter chaos reigned with an entire country fleeing from a handful of barbarians. Then the Asura army also started burning down cities during their flight, lest they fall into Deva hands. The public took to arms and the standing armies of small towns joined the public to stop the fleeing Asura army from looting their own cities. Civil war broke out.

Rumours spread that the five kings had joined the ranks of the Devas and had murdered the other five, including the charismatic Pramyudha. Soon the Asura kingdoms were fighting each other while the Devas grew in strength. Indra's prestige had risen tremendously after the Asura rout. Soon, other wandering Deva hordes joined him, while the mighty Asura empire disintegrated before their eyes.

It took seven months for the great empire to crumble, an empire which had taken a thousand years to reach maturity. Once Indra felt confident that the Asura empire was weak enough, he blasted through the cocoon of the Asura's protected existence. It is a great lesson for all students of warfare and statecraft on how to treat a conquered land.

A civilization draws its pride from the cities it has built, the books it has produced, the artists and artisans it has bred, the temples it has built and so on. A conqueror's first duty is to aim the mightiest blow possible on these edifices of civilized existence. Indra did it beautifully. He demolished all that was possible. He burned libraries, butchered poets and architects and pummelled the temples and hacked women and children. Soon, everything the Asuras held precious was destroyed. And from there, the original Indra got the name *Purendra* or 'slayer of cities'. Soon, the Asuras had to go underground and there was occasional resistance, but mostly ineffective. Indra built an empire with the skeletons of the Asura civilization as its foundation. For nearly 300 years, the country was under the total control of the Indra dynasty.

During this period, the plains soothed the Deva temperament. Art and culture once again regained their sway and the Devas began to lose their fierceness. They also became creatures of comfort. Great cities, though much inferior to those of the Asuras, were built. The process of synthesis started at the end of the second Indra's reign. Shiva, who was the supreme God of the Asuras, came to be accepted by the Devas also. The great teacher of the Asura tribe, Brahma, was also accepted as God. The later Indra kings were weak and soon became mere puppets in the hands of Vishnu, who was the commander-in-chief of Indra III's army. By the end of Indra XI's reign, the Vishnu clan was virtually ruling the country and the Indra kings were just token monarchs: like the Shiva kings of the Asura tribe, who had become just a small power in the upper Himalayas, near Kailash, long before the rule of the ten kings.

The Vishnus ruled for nearly 700 years in the name of Indra. They were successful in preserving the Indra name and the Deva culture and were hailed by Brahmins as preservers of a social order. Soon, a curious set of thoughts got mixed up. I do not know whether it was Brahmin slyness or mere coincidence, but Brahma, the original possessor of knowledge, was hailed as the Creator; Vishnu as the Preserver of the system; and ironically Shiva, who built an empire, and not Indra, who destroyed, was hailed as the Destroyer. They were the three Gods of India – the *Trimurti*.

The first members of these families were hailed as Gods and are still revered by the Devas. We accept Shiva as God and also the first Brahma as God. But the Brahmin insistence that Vishnu, a Deva commander-in-chief and a mere servant of a Deva king, be considered the supreme God, was hard to accept. There were great rebellions by the subjugated Asuras against Vishnu. Some great men like the Hiranya twins and Mahabali, succeeded in establishing an extensive Asura empire rivalling the empires of old, for a short period of time. But in later years, just as the Asura empire was divided into ten kingdoms, so was the Deva empire split into many petty fiefdoms.

When an empire crumbles and many small states spring up, we know the time has come to build a new empire. When half-castes like Bali in Central India, and aborigines like Karthi Veerarjuna in the Sahya mountains, are able to carve huge kingdoms out of the Deva empire, we know that history has come full circle. Indra had but a small army to take on the mighty but divided Asura empire. I hope you have learnt the lessons of that eventful war which resulted in the fall of our people. The time has come for us to return the favour.

Remember that the mighty Vishnu family also has weakened itself through in-fighting and only a small group, ruling the tiny princely state of Ayodhya near the River Sarayu, is worth mentioning. Our beloved Emperor Mahabali believed that its young prince, Dasaratha, a relative of the present king Anarnya, was the only one among the Devas capable of building an empire. So let us continue our struggle until we get ourselves horses and arms. Then we'll show the Devas that they have forgotten the lessons of history."

The lecture was rather heavy for the crowd assembled before us. It was better to give them short, simple orders which they could follow, instead of indigestible doses of history. I was disappointed that no one had contradicted me or raised any questions during my long address. They just sat there staring stupidly. If I was to quench even a little of my fiery ambition, I would have to devote a great deal of time to developing leaders. One day, the passive submission of this group could be advantageous to me. What my predecessors had tried to do was to run a republic. They wanted democracy, where each man, like this bunch of idiots in front of me, decided the future of the nation.

What such a race needed was a strong dictator. Mahabali tried to become one and failed. He was too soft to be a dictator. Earlier kings like Hiranya and his brother, were cruel and ruthless, and were so harsh that they lost popular support. What they needed was someone who was intelligent, ambitious, strong and ruthless, and of course, benevolent – perhaps someone like me.

I gave the order for the congregation of would-be warriors to break for lunch. I sat with my brothers and cousins under a banyan tree, not too far from the meadow where the warriors were making merry and cracking raunchy jokes. We started with the leftover debate of the past few days. Where should we start our campaign? Vibhishana wanted to capture the small Deva village near the river Kaveri. It had a small fort, granaries, a tiny school, but nothing else. The people were dirt poor and a small band of malnourished men guarded the dilapidated fort. It would be just a token victory. Kumbakarna was dead against it, saying that it would be a waste of effort and alert the other Deva kings about our army. I thought it a bit preposterous to call this motley crowd an army, but allowed Kumbakarna to get away with his illusions. He wanted an all-out campaign against Karthi Veerarjuna in the northern Sahyas. My uncles, Malyavan and Sumali, wanted none of this. They wished to continue the guerilla warfare against the Central Indian Deva kingdoms and finally take on Amaravathi.

It was a long and drawn-out dream without any strategy or plan. I was part-amused, half-irritated, with this elaborate joke of the past few days. I was trying hard to make this a democratic forum, where we would take a decision with mutual consent after due discussions. But, I was convinced that democracy would not do with these people. If they, who were my close kin, could not agree upon the direction the campaign should take, without stopping to think whether we had the arms, means and men to conduct the same, how could I expect the common Asuras to think with any clarity?

"Enough!" I was getting flustered and wanted to end this farce. "I want to attack Lanka and that settles it. I will not allow any further discussions."

"But…" I stopped Vibhishana with a steely glare and saw with dismay that he cowered before me. Either I was getting better at intimidating people or my younger brother was a bigger coward than I had previously imagined. Before my uncles could start rolling out their grandiose, hare-brained schemes, I said with determination, "First someone has to get our mother and sister from the island. It might get too dangerous there. Then we will plan the campaign to attack the island. I want the throne where that oaf of a half- brother is resting his fat arse and I want it fast."

I can still see the shocked expressions in my uncles' eyes. They were shocked by the language, the tone and my expression. In their code, leaders had to be polite, use civilized language, and hear discussions out before humbly requesting everyone's cooperation. I have, at the most conservative count, violated at least five codes of Asura honour. But I did not care. No more flowery language in chaste Tamil, no more elaborate rituals for me. I would set my own codes and those who wanted to could come with me.

8 Maharaja

Ravana

I have noticed this man since the day he accompanied Sumali, though, there was nothing in him to be noticed. He was one of those low cadre soldiers who are so essential in any army, but who are usually thanklessly forgotten. He was always trying to get near me. He wanted to get something across badly. I called him and asked what he wanted. I should have done so weeks ago but had decided to impose distance between the officers of the army and the lower ranks. Earlier, we three brothers would get drunk together with all our comrades. But I had begun to feel uncomfortable with such a show of camaraderie.

It all changed when my uncles came with their band of two score soldiers to swell the ranks of my mighty Asura army. My uncle Sumali, made sure that we at least resembled an army and not a street gang. He had given us a long talk. This might be the biggest Asura weakness – the propensity for long talks. He tried to drive it into my head that if I wanted discipline in the army, I had to respect hierarchy. To respect hierarchy, I first had to create it. I learnt fast and was soon treating everyone else with contempt and people were meekly taking it.

The dark young man came up to me, bowed reverently, and placed the refreshments close by. I did not want to look at his face. I was afraid that if I looked hard enough, I would see the contempt and hatred this class of people hid behind their meaningless servility and excessive deference. He stood close to me for some time and when I did not acknowledge his presence, he left silently. Why was I so concerned about whether they respected me or not? Banishing that foul-looking man from my mind, I tried to concentrate on the organizational structure for the army.

We had agreed on a council of ten officers, including my uncles Prahastha, Sumali, Maricha, Jambumali, the erstwhile governor of East Lanka's Pearl Islands, and us three brothers. There was also Rudraka, an able commando from Mahabali's elite protection wing and the only one to escape alive, by masquerading as an alms seeker, when the army of Vamana Vishnu attacked the Emperor; Dhumraksha, the man who was the supply and distribution chief of Mahabali's army and Vajradhamstra, the commander-in-chief of Mahabali's forces. There were other minor officers who commanded smaller units. My silence ensured that I was chosen as commander-in-chief. It was only when I felt the exhilaration and relief of being chosen as commander, that I realized how much I had wanted the post. I sensed some restlessness in Prahastha and Vajradhamsra, but they and the others, knew they were not up to the task. Six years of battles with no result does not inspire confidence in the troops. So they lost out and accepted it like gentlemen.

The unspoken agreement was that every decision would be by vote and I would only be a token chief. We Asuras, unlike the Devas, were yet to evolve an advanced level of political administration. This was an area in which I wanted to emulate the Devas, who had a clear administrative system where the king or Raja was the supreme ruler. He is divinity in action, the living God on earth, and he decides what is good for his subjects. The advantage is that decisions are fast and implementations swift. The disadvantage is that with a bad ruler, bad decisions are also implemented quickly and the country could suffer. While we Asuras waited for our councils to reach a decision even during war, the Devas took our country from us.

Anyhow, my assumed divinity, which I had started believing in since I was lying to myself quite often these days, stood as a barrier between me and the dark, stocky young man. I was rather confused and decided to discuss the matter with Sumali. After all, the dark man could be a spy. He was watching things with hawk's eyes and I had seen him find chores which ensured that he was near us during our council meetings.

I was sitting deeply immersed in my thoughts, unable to formulate any concrete plans for our forthcoming attack on Lanka. I could feel the stress and wanted to smash something, or shout at someone, to clear my mind. I had impulsively said that we should take Lanka from my step-brother. Now I realized that the move did not make much sense.

Kubera's palace was inside a well-guarded fort, atop Trikota, a huge rocky mountain. Whatever sparse vegetation existed earlier, had been destroyed by Kubera's security forces seven years ago: when Varuna, a pirate who ruled the seas around the mainland, in a daring attack under cloud and forest cover, nearly captured Lanka. He torched the city and took hordes of gold and imported horses; silks and women from the palace. The fort was made impregnable after that, with all the vegetation cut from the hill and watch posts every hundred yards. Mounted guards patrolled the streets and the beach. They were ruthless and efficient and numbered over a thousand. They had successfully repelled Varuna's attack thrice in the last seven years and even succeeded in sinking three of his ships. It was rumoured that Varuna had moved to the eastern seas. Kubera even acquired a fleet and built a powerful navy. These heavily armed ships patrolled the seas and piloted the trade ships in and out of the island's port.

But more than the strength of Kubera's army, it was another factor which sent shivers down my spine. My mother and sister were still living in that dilapidated shelter at the edge of the cliff, overlooking the sea, assuming they have not died of starvation or from the elements. If Kubera sensed that I planned such mischief, he would kill my kin in a second or worse, take them hostage. I did not have a standby plan for that. But the Council had decided that Lanka should be taken at any cost. The wealth of the island was fabulous and would help us raise a huge army and navy to take on the mainland. No other conquest would help us raise enough forces to take on the might of India.

"Sir, may I speak?" I gazed at the stocky, young man and was rather irritated. It was the same man who had been following me with his gaze for the past few days.

"What do you want? Don't you have anything better to do?" I was surprised at my own harshness.

He stood there, his eyes even with mine. I was a head taller than him but he looked at me squarely. There was no threat, neither any fear. I waited for his eyes to fall, for him to cower and stare at his own toes. But the man before me showed no nervousness. The classical sign of an Asura faced with authority was to fall on his knees and grovel. My race, in its march towards progress, had forgotten that people can be equal and there was something called the middle path. In this man, I met someone who could handle equality. I was surprised and irritated to find the man showed no fear of my authority and did not act humble. It was absurd; the very notion that he was my equal was absurd. Or was it? I had behaved just like him a few months ago, before Mahabali discovered me.

Then I understood. I saw that he was a man who had lost everything and was living only for a purpose. There was something inside him which was taut and ready to burst. Here was a man who could control his emotions and merge with his surroundings. He could lie still like a cobra in the grass and strike with deadly venom, attack with passion, soundlessly and ruthlessly. His eyes were glassy as he stared at me. Suddenly I was afraid. My hands clenched the butt of my sword, ready to strike if this cobra made any move. Without any warning, he shocked me by falling at my feet.

I was angry and relieved. Angry that he had shown the same Asura behaviour of submitting to authority. Relieved because I did not want to fight such a primitive force. There was something crude, raw and fresh about the man. He was the original force of nature, the very salt of the earth. The fact that he was an ordinary man made him extraordinary.

"Trust me, your Highness, my King; I shall serve you better than anyone ever born. I shall lay down my life for you. Make me your servant. I know you are our saviour. You are our God-sent king, who has come to rescue the Asura tribe from the clutches of the Devas." He suddenly broke into sobs and his whole body shook. I stood there embarrassed by the sudden display of emotion. He clutched my legs. I did not know what to say or how to react. This was not what I had expected. Then I saw Prahastha running towards us with his sword drawn. I stopped him with a flick of my fingers, amazed by how even the proud Prahastha stopped abruptly because of my small gesture.

How amazing! If more people fell at my feet like this, I might not only start enjoying it but even start demanding it. The initial pity had vanished and was replaced by a love mixed with contempt for the hapless human being lying at my feet. I could feel that he was completely under my power. I could kick him, drag him, and even behead him, and no one would raise a finger. I was also terrified. What would happen to me? This kind of power came with the burden of responsibility as King, to hear the woes of one's subjects and find solutions to their problems. I would do that. I would be the kindest king in the world.

I raised him up with my hands and stared into his face. His eyes were red and I thought his emotions were genuine. But I could not fathom the depths of his eyes. The sleepy, glassy eyes were like those of a snake. Something sinister was lying dormant there and I was afraid to touch it lest the snake wake up. "What is it that I can do for you?" I assumed my kindest voice and wondered if the pitch was rather too shrill for a king.

"Your Highness, we have been discussing about you becoming the King of the Asuras. We want you to be crowned as soon as possible. All the soldiers in the camp believe that you are the true successor of Mahabali and we want you to lead us. I come as a representative of the soldiers who are willing to live and die for your success."

"You are aware that I am your commander-in-chief and you live and die for our cause, just as I do." My tone was severe, yet I couldn't hide my excitement. The rank and file of the Asura army wanted me as their king. The Council could think I was too young and brash for such a responsibility but my soldiers wanted me as their leader and that was more important. I was uneasy that I had thrust myself on the Council as its chief. Now this beautiful young man was addressing me as king and not plain 'Sir', as the soldiers address their superiors in the Asura army. I was pleased but saw Prahastha wince and made a note of it in my mind.

"Your Highness, we want you to be our King. We have fought enough for the Council. We lost every time because someone in the Council was not beyond treason. We want a King like that of the Devas, a king fit to rule us and all of India from Lanka to Gandhara. We want an Emperor to rival the rule of Mahabali. Nothing short of this great dream will inspire us, your Highness. We shall be happy to die for the sake of the great Asura empire you are going to build."

"We will have to discuss the matter in the Council. What is your name?"

"Bhadra, your Highness. Bhadra from a village on the banks of the Poorna. We shall await your decision, your Highness. Please forgive my impropriety, but we had no other choice." He walked backwards with all the deference due to a king, without turning his back on me. A great cheer erupted from his friends waiting a little way away.

Prahastha came and put his hands on my shoulder. "Let's call the Council." His voice was steely-toned but I could not have cared less. My ears were receptive to the slogans rising from the soldiers' camps, *'Long live Maharaja Ravana!'*

"The Council is dismissed." I smiled at the shocked face of Prahastha and added, "You are my Prime Minister."

I walked away, leaving Prahastha to ponder. Somewhere in my mind I felt I was being manipulated. I glanced over to the camps and saw Bhadra standing alone, leaving the merriment to his comrades. There was a small trace of triumph at the corners of his mouth. Our gaze met and the smile vanished. He bowed low. I walked past the camp with what I believed to be a royal gait, amidst the cheering of soldiers, to my camp. I had to get my mother and sister back before I started the campaign. That was my last thought before I slipped into a dreamless sleep.

9 Maricha, the beloved

Ravana

I saw them accompanying my uncle Maricha. My sister had grown up; not exactly pretty, but one could not miss the bubbling energy in her. I was in a meeting with my council of ministers. It was no longer a democratic forum but I made sure that their voice counted. It was a charade and everyone knew my wishes would be carried out to the last. But the Asura need for a good debate and argument, was satisfied.

The meeting stopped and everyone stood up. My old uncle Maricha was smiling and waving his hands at us. His twins were tottering behind, followed by his still-pretty wife. My mother and sister were behind them, and they were waiting for us to stop the all-important meeting to come near. Vibhishana rushed to them like a lost puppy who has just found its mother, yelping and shouting with joy. I also wanted to run and embrace my mother and sister, but was not sure that kings behaved that way. Kumbha was running behind Vibhishana and the twins ran towards him, screaming and laughing loud enough to frighten the birds perched above us in the forest canopy. I walked, in a manner I considered to be a majestic gait, with the tall and dignified figure of my uncles Prahastha, and the ever-frowning Sumali, following behind.

"Did you have any problems on the way?" Uncle Prahastha had no time for sentimental niceties.

"Only Varuna's dhows, but we managed with a small gift."

"He gave away Sulakshana's pearl necklace to the pirates. She worked hard for seven years in that Guild to earn it." There was affection in my mother's voice. Maricha shrugged his shoulders as if to say that giving the pearl necklace to pirates was an act of no significance. I touched his feet and embraced him.

"So you have become the King eh?" My uncle back-slapped me hard. I stood there grinning like a child who has just scored well in an oral exam. "Now we have to find you a kingdom."

The soldiers laughed and I fought hard to keep my smile in my face. His humour could be biting, but how I loved the old rascal. We vividly remembered when as teenagers, my uncle and aunt coming to our battered shack with two babies who were not more than a few weeks old. It was one of those harsh monsoons and we fervently prayed to Shiva that the hut would withstand the storm. They looked tired and worn, my uncle in rags, with a bandaged head and his arm in a sling, and my aunt smiling despite looking like someone who was about to fall down and die. They clutched the babies, one each, and my mother, who has the knack of understanding without words, stood up and took both babies from their tired arms. We shared our sparse *kanji* with them and they slept the whole night through.

The babies were too weak to cry, but I remember my mother worrying about their feed. My aunt was past the age of having babies and we were sure the children had been adopted. My uncle and aunt had always been poor after he lost his kingdom, yet these kind acts came naturally to them. We did not know anyone in the village who would be kind enough to lend us some milk. Our neighbours were too poor to own a cow and milk was a luxury.

As usual it was Kumbha who came up with the idea. We decided to steal the milk from the only man who owned a cow, rather, hundreds of cows. It was difficult but possible. The danger element added a thrill to our adventure. Vibhishana was reluctant, but did not protest for fear of being branded a coward, which he definitely was. He agreed to stand guard and warn us as we jumped the fence and entered Kubera's stable. It was pitch dark and we groped around the stable to find a cow to milk. None of us had any experience of milking cows. The stable was stinking of cow dung and urine and those big, buzzing mosquitoes that resemble miniature flying tigers, were happy to taste blood in the early morning hours. It was beginning to look like a bad idea and we wanted to get out. Someone coughed outside and our hearts jumped into our mouths. We heard a soft whistle and panicked. It was Vibhishana warning us that someone was coming. We ran, but lost our bearings. The cows woke up and started bellowing. Torches were lit. They were heading straight towards the stable. Somehow we got out, only to find ourselves trapped between the palace guards. We fought and knocked down a couple of them, but were soon overpowered. They tied us up and then the beating started. They beat us with clubs; they shattered Kumbha's tooth; and burnt us with torches. We howled and cried after a few minutes of attempting a dignified silence on being tortured. The beating continued till daybreak.

When I woke, blood had caked on my face and every pore of my skin hurt. Kumbha had woken earlier and was staring at me through his swollen, black eyes. His face was a mess, with his nose and teeth knocked out and his lips cut. He winked at me and smiled and at that moment I loved him more than anyone in the world. I knew that one day either he or I would lay down our life for the other. I smiled back. We were tied to the stable pillars and left alone. Then I wondered what had happened to Vibhishana and in that silent communication between people who deeply love each other, I saw the same question on Kumbha's face. We were terrified! We looked as far as our necks could stretch to see if Vibhishana had been beaten and tied to a pillar like us. But there was no trace of him and we were sure the guards had beaten him to death and buried him quietly. Or he had informed my mother or the village elder perhaps, to come and plead with Kubera to release us.

We had not attained maturity of age and according to the Asura code of law, we could not be jailed nor could our arms be chopped off. We would be forced to work in Kubera's oil mill or farm, as slaves for a few months. Kubera the millionaire, found that this type of punishment made economic sense and saved him a few coppers. He was half-Gandharva, half-Brahmin and not Asura, but he made sure he followed all Asura laws – non-interference in the natives' religion and beliefs, he called it. It allowed him to concentrate on trade and commerce. I saw Kumbha staring vacantly, silently praying for Vibhishana to be alive. Tears were rolling down his cheeks and he made no attempt to turn his face when he saw that I had noticed. My own eyes were brimming with tears.

An old guard came and untied us and Kumbha collapsed onto the floor. The guard lifted him roughly and called for help. I could barely walk. Two guards carried Kumbha on a thick bamboo poll, like a wild beast which had been just hunted down. It was almost noon and the air was hot and humid at the peak of the monsoon season when the sun peeps out to bake the red muddy earth for a few hours.

Kubera, the *Money-God* and the giver of justice, was seated on his throne, busy signing palm documents with his royal stamp and barking instructions about various vagaries of commerce, shipping rates, pepper prices, gold equivalent for cardamom weight, etc, which would be carried to the respective officers in the various ports of the island and then back to the merchant king by messengers on swift Arabian horses. There were other criminals waiting for the God of money to dispense wisdom and justice but in this world of high profile trade and commerce, everything else was insignificant.

I saw Kumbha had passed out and was afraid I would follow him. I wanted to hear what our punishments would be for trespassing on the *Money-God's* property. It seemed like an endless wait and for the first time in my life, I pondered my mortality. I was too young to think about death, but with every inch of my body hurting, thoughts of death came easily. It was then that I saw my uncle among the crowd, restlessly waiting for judgment. We made eye contact and he smiled that beautiful, heart-warming smile that made me forget the pain. A few of his front teeth were missing but I could feel the sincerity of the man. He looked concerned and at the same time, I felt that with him around, nothing bad could happen to us.

Two criminals who had stolen jewels from the temple were the first to go on trial and before they could plead their innocence or the city police could arrange proof for examination, Kubera pronounced them guilty and ordered their arms chopped off. There was a loud wail from a woman, probably the wife of one of the men. The man was probably a craftsman before poverty had driven him to steal from the Gods. Now the State would take away his arms and the Gods would have their jewels back. Justice was exact and swift and the crime rate low.

Kubera was an efficient ruler, especially for the trading class, who were assured of a safe city. His popularity among the middle classes was always great. The rich did not care who ruled, as long as they were allowed to be rich. The poor could not afford to care and nobody asked their opinion in any case. Only the middle class mattered and any half-witted ruler knows how to pamper them. One of the men offered himself as slave. He claimed he was an expert weaver and said that he would weave for free. Kubera immediately reversed the sentence and the weaver's new punishment was to be a slave for the next ten years and keep weaving and making money for the establishment.

The next man was too proud and offered no apology or deal. He was taken away for his arms to be chopped off. In any other country he would have begged, but as this was a prosperous country, begging was not allowed. Beggars were banished to the interiors or more often taken to the sea and drowned with stones tied to their necks.

"Next," a soldier stationed near the throne barked. Kubera was looking at some business papers in the meantime. He was an efficient time manager. We were shoved forward by the guards. "Accused of trespassing into the royal cowpens and attempted theft of cows," barked the police commissioner.

"Not guilty," I wanted to roar, but only a shrill, boyish sound came out. A sudden hush fell in court. Nobody has ever dared to speak in court when the King was present. Kubera was immersed in his palm leaves and it took him a few seconds to register the silence. He deliberately read through the entire document and put it aside. Then he raised his head. A smile spread across his face. He was a handsome man and the smile made him more so. But there was something creepy and spider-like in his movements.

"My, my, who have we here? My beloved step-brothers. I am honoured. If you had asked, I would have gifted you a few cows. Instead, you wanted to steal. How natural. I see you have taken after your mother. So, what do you prefer, your arms chopped off; your noses cut off; or a plain simple branding on your cheeks that you are thieves? I cannot be blamed for nepotism."

"Sir, I have a request." Maricha walked into the centre of the court and a hundred pairs of eyes bored into him. I believe he had broken the elaborate Deva court decorum. These uncouth Asuras! They behave like children. It is perhaps the Deva's burden to civilize us. I watched with horror at what my uncle was doing. I wanted to scream at the top of my voice and stop him, but I did not for fear of punishment. The old fool was blundering on, the old lovable rascal. I felt some small hope that we might be let off easily. "Sir, these are children and they scarcely know what they were doing."

I felt my cheeks growing hot as all eyes turned towards me to see the foolish boy. I was sixteen and still being referred to as a child. Even if I got out of this, I would be taunted for the rest of my life by my friends. I had missed a few sentences, immersed in my teenage wrath, and it took a while for the enormity of what my uncle was saying to sink in.

"So you offer yourself in return for the freedom of these ugly brats? I hope you are not in an extended state of inebriation from last night's revelry and that you are saying it of your own free will. You say you are a soldier, but you have a few missing teeth and an arm in a sling to prove that." The laughter in the court echoed around us and my cheeks burned when I saw my uncle standing there with his right arm in a sling, dignified, his eyes staring at a distant point a few inches above the fool who was playing the buffoon king.

"Six years in the oil mill." The order passed like a lightning bolt and I shivered. Kumbha showed signs of waking up. I could see that even

Maricha was shocked. This was too harsh for a small trespass. I could see tears sprouting from the old man's eyes. I could see the face of his wife and the twins. I had brought this upon the old man. How old was he? Thirty, thirty-five perhaps? At sixteen, everyone over twenty looked old. Six years meant that he would be fourty-one by the time he got out. That is, if he made it at all. The oil mill was the most dreaded of all punishments. Instead of bulls, men were tied to the mill and walked round and round, grinding sesame seeds or *copra* into oil. It sapped the life out of them. Twenty hours of back-breaking labour, 365 days multiplied by six, for the old man. Just because his hot-headed nephews could not help playing heroes and trespassed on the premises of their step-brother, the merchant-king.

"And add one year more so that this old bastard learns how to address a king. Sir, indeed! Next."

I heard this with horror. This was justice. Fast and swift. For contempt of court, my old uncle got one more year of slave labour. My uncle stared at his toes. The guards came and handcuffed him. He was then bound in chains and shoved hard by the guards. People laughed. My people, the Asuras, laughed when one of their kin was treated like an animal for no fault of his. Someone whistled. We were dragged out of court and dumped outside. The State had no use for us anymore. Our bones were broken and our internal organs damaged. So we were discarded like gnawed chicken bones. Chewed out by the State. Then, the first stone hit me. Soon it turned into a hail. My people were stoning me for sending my old uncle to hard labour. Their impotent wrath was falling on two teenagers. So this is the end, I thought. Dying ignobly as a thief at the hands of my people, after sending my lovable, old uncle to prison. What an end to a fool who dreamt of conquering the world and freeing his people.

The pelting of stones stopped as suddenly as it had started. With blood dripping from my face, I saw my mother weeping inconsolably and hugging the inert form of Kumbha. Fortunately, our citizens had yet to reach those heights of civilization when they stone women to death. Thank god for the small mercies he showers on our life. Slowly we were carried into our hut. My aunt lay unconscious and the twins were wailing. My neighbour, a fat, ugly lady, who had a heart of gold, but the tongue of a serpent, desperately tried to stop the wailing. It was then that I saw Vibhishana sitting in a corner and reading a book in Sanskrit and not even looking at us. I boiled with rage. So the guards had not buried him. The studious, good boy had come home and slept while we were getting thrashed. Then, when the uncle who was past his prime has been dragged to the oil mill to work with the bulls, the bastard was sitting and chanting some obscure Deva text like a frog.

I felt like murdering him there and then. I wanted to shove that book of the *Rig Veda* down his throat. I wanted to do so many things, when he caught my eye. He came and sat on the floor at my feet. I tried to raise my leg and kick his hateful face. Instead, a groan escaped me. Kubera's guards knew where to kick. Then Vibhishana broke down like a baby. He hugged my feet and oh God, it hurt like hell. But he would not let it go. The bastard wanted forgiveness. He said he was afraid and it took him the greater part of the morning to get the courage to tell my uncle. He was sorry for everything and wanted his big brother to forget and forgive and hug him. I wanted to get up and tear him in two. I tried to sit up. I made some gurgling sound which might have frightened my mother. She left Kumbha and came to me. Then she soothed my raging mind with songs of my long-past childhood. She sang as if I was a baby still in the cradle, searching her nipples for milk. She sang those old songs of Asura valour and the sad songs of long-lost glory. I slept, with love replacing the hatred I had felt for my younger brother. When I woke, my rage had gone.

I knew that my aunt had left the village the next day and a message came which said that that she had joined a weaver's guild. The pay was not good but the guild provided a roof and two square meals a day. Not the life for a former queen of a small Asura state, but certainly better than a hut with the night view of the stars and moon through the roof.

I was seeing my family after a long time, thanks to this old man with a cheeky smile, who thought nothing of handing over a pearl necklace for which his wife had sweated for seven years, to arrange safe passage for his sister's family; or about grinding sesame in a tyrant's prison so that his nephews could go free. The old rascal had lost a few more teeth, but looked healthier than I had last seen him, in chains. It seemed that he would outlive us all. He was forty-two now, but remained the same kind and jovial fellow. A king in his time, he will remain a kind-hearted uncle always ready to sacrifice his life to save those who he loved. I shall always remember that.

10 The Pearl Island Beckons

The Council had assembled under the Banyan tree. I presided over the meeting, with Prahastha as moderator, and the debate raged on. No one was making any sense. Everyone wanted to somehow take Lanka, but no one seemed to have a concrete idea how to do it. Kumbha wanted a frontal attack where we would cross the sea during low tide in bamboo canoes and challenge Kubera's army head on. I knew we would not last an hour. We were less than 2000 people and more than half were inexperienced warriors. They had the passion to fight but knew next to nothing about using arms. The best seemed to have only shot wood pigeons in the forest. A few others had been in various highway raids. There was no doubt that the only ones with any experience in real combat were Prahastha, Sumali, and Maricha. But that was years ago and military technology had changed.

Bhadra passed in and out of the meeting place, carrying refreshments. I felt uneasy in his presence as he was always on the verge of saying something. I didn't want a servant to interrupt the council of ministers and offer his unsolicited war strategy. I also did not want anyone to know I had spoken with him once in a while, when no one was around. Many of the things he said made sense and some of the ideas I put forth as my own, were actually his. It was surprising that no one, including myself, had thought about the fact that our army would not last long once we moved out of this forest, until Bhadra drew my attention to it. This forest abounded with game, wild berries, mangoes and jackfruit, so we never needed to worry about feeding the troops. Once we moved out, we were

sure to starve to death. After that, we started collecting jackfruits and drying them in the sun, making mango pastes, cultivating wild rice and bamboo shoots, and storing these meagre rations.

We also got our armaments ready and resorted to making wooden spears, swords and arrows, as copper or iron was hard to come by. Maricha had started a brewery for poisonous potions, which could be effectively used in spears and arrows. But this was all insignificant. The fall of Kubera had to be through a sudden, surprise attack. He had a standing army of 20,000 men, 4,000 mounted archers, 2,000 horse chariots, 500 elephants, and supplies to last two years. He had an effective navy with more than twenty ships patrolling the shores and two huge snake-boats, each rowed by sixty men. Sixty archers could be mounted on these swift and sleek snake-boats and they shot flame arrows with deadly precision. His training schools were famed far and wide and the swordsmanship of his soldiers was envied by other kings.

Of course, Kubera could afford all these things. He could hire the best talent from across the world, whether from China or Egypt or even the pale barbarians from colder lands. He could use the latest technology for his army and navy. It was even rumoured that he had developed a flying machine and was going to make fifty more, so that he could employ them to drop huge flaming balls or stones on enemy camps. It was also rumoured that only one prototype had been made and the technician who designed it had been poisoned. I forced my mind back to the debate.

"We need horses and have to get them from across the sea, so we also need ships, or at least large dhows. The question is, how many can we afford?" asked Prahastha. A debate ensued on the number of horses needed, the number archers to be deployed, the number of ships required, the timing of the attack. My mind drifted away again and it was then that I caught Bhadra's eye. He beckoned. I was irritated. Perhaps he thought that he had something better to offer than these veteran soldiers? I would have to put him in his place. But I thought it was better to hear him out first and walked away as if enjoying a stroll, towards the waterfall. The fall was huge here and the Poorna was almost 500 feet wide, where she fell a majestic 200 feet to meet the river and then flowed to the distant sea. On a clear day, one could spot the sea bordering this land of coconuts. All around was thick, evergreen tropical forest, with hundreds of colourful birds chirping and flying about. Dragonflies fluttered over the water. At night, when everyone was asleep except the sentries, I would listen to the forest. The occasional elephant herd rummaged through the forest; the distant roars of leopards and tigers; bears drinking from the stream. It was a different world out there. The drama of survival took place all around my camp, with life hunting or being hunted in turn. Violence was the very foundation of nature. Every moment something became prey to something else. The circle of killing went on. Could man stop it? Wars are inevitable, so is cruelty. Most animals are successful killing machines. The humble lizard on the wall is no less a hunter than a tiger.

"Your Highness, can't we go in as traders?" Bhadra's voice shocked me. I had not heard him approaching. He walked silently for a short and stout man.

"And what would we trade in?" I could not help asking.

"We could arrange for horses from the Arabs in Muzuris. We could get pepper from the hills, rubies from the east coast, and gold from the Greek camp in Muzuris. We could get some ships on lease from the rich traders… We could navigate around the peninsula and enter Lanka from the South-Eastern tip of India, where the sea is narrowest. Two ships would do, carrying about 400 people. . ."

"And you, fool, you plan to conquer Lanka with 400 nitwits?" I could barely contain my anger.

Bhadra waited for my temper to subside and then continued, "The ships could carry ivory and pearls back and about twenty men each. They could continue to the mainland and trade again. The rest could visit the king and ask to set up a guild on the coast, preferably near the Eastern gate of the Trikota fort, near the weavers' street."

I was warming up to his idea. "In six trips, we would have sneaked all the men onto the island. We could buy arms from the local market and hoard them."

"No need for six trips, Your Highness, that would take too much time. Once the first lot has been placed, we could send a few hundred in small canoes, ten or fifteen in each batch, as fishermen. The second trip of ships could unload more soldiers and they could form a second guild near the northern gate. If we carry on like that, we'd be able to place half our army in a month. In the third sailing, we could purchase horses and arms only and anchor outside the ports in the deep sea, at a distance of an hour, if the wind is advantageous."

I liked the plan. I needed just enough money to fill my two ships. I could manage that. But even for this, I would have to borrow heavily from Mahabali. I did not know whether the old man would agree. Otherwise, I would be left with no choice other than to plunder one or two ships in the high seas. It was a risky venture and we could encounter Varuna's ships, which ran a protection racket in these parts, or Kubera's navy. I doubted whether half the men in my army could swim, let alone fight in the seas. Most were inlanders and would see the sea for the first time in their lives. I knew the plan would be vetoed in the Council by Prahastha, and I would have to overrule him. I did not want any unpleasantness at this early stage.

"I want to go, Your Highness." I thought he was asking to go back to the servant quarters. I flicked my hand and became immersed in my own thoughts.

"I want to go to Lanka first, Your Highness." I was jarred and turned my head to stare at him.

"What made you think that?"

"I will be useful to you there."

He was going to be a spy. He made a funny figure as he stood there with bow legs, pot belly, curly hair, dark as midnight and without the least bit of respectability. He had a natural camouflage, he was common among common people. He would blend in like a chameleon. Was he going to desert the camp? Was he Kubera's spy and leading us into a trap? Suddenly, I felt paranoid. I told him he was not going anywhere. I wanted to talk to him at night and he could leave in the morning. He was rather uneasy and I could see that he was perturbed. *'I cannot leave you so easily, friend. There is something fishy about you,'* I wanted to tell him. Instead, I smiled at him. I was shocked at how easily I could lie.

Bhadra was confused. I thought something in my demeanour had set off alarm bells in his subconscious. *I had to watch this fellow carefully. He could be dangerous,* I warned myself. I walked briskly and he followed me with slow, deliberate steps. I could see him pondering his future action. I had my arm on my sword hilt, ready to draw and cut off his head in a clean sweep. I walked into the Council and presented my idea, actually Bhadra's plan, but by now I had started thinking of it as my own. It could have been due to my inborn leadership qualities that this stealing of a subordinate's idea and claiming credit for it, came easily to me. Those were still early stages and I could recollect whose ideas they were. Later, much later, I became a real leader, and then I was sure that all good ideas emanated from me and the bad and foolish ideas had some other father. The Council launched into furious debate. I raised my hand and it took a few minutes for them to notice and then they stopped. In those early days I had yet to acquire the quality of silencing people with a glance or by just raising my eyebrows.

Prahastha immediately raised an objection. "This is too dangerous. What if there is a spy among us? What if the very first batch gets arrested and executed? Moreover, it is a sly method. That is not the Asura method of fighting. We fight as men, prudence dictates that we wait until we gain enough means and men to fight. But when we do, we will fight like warriors. This is a stupid way of doing things, Ravana. I am surprised at you."

It was irritating when he took that patronizing tone. Also, he was not using the honorific and was calling me by my name in Council, forgetting that I was the king and he, a mere Prime Minister. Of course, he was my uncle and could call me anything in private. In public, he had to maintain decorum, or else the entire system I was trying to build would collapse like a pack of cards.

Maricha stood up and said, "No, Prahaṣtha, there is no other way. The plan the boy has shared with us is excellent and we should back that. We Asuras have always lost because we played by the rules, when nobody else bothered about any. But, we have to watch out for spies. That means we have to cut all communication with strangers. Still, I know someone could leave a small palm leaf in a tree hole for a contact to collect it later. But we have to take our chances."

I wanted to make sure my uncles did not patronize me by calling me a boy. It was demeaning. But these people were so valuable to me that I could not protest. Even if I had protested, they would only have become confused.

"Arrest this fellow. I want no execution, but only a detention. Do not let him out of this camp," I told them and clapped my hands. Two soldiers with long spears came running. My uncles looked perplexed and so did my brothers. The soldiers bowed low before me. One of them had the lace of his kurta tied wrong. *Oh God, how am I going to take these fools to fight, these slouchy beggars?* He saw my eyes darting down from his face and he crouched lower as if paying me more respect, but really to avoid my eyes seeing the sloppy way he had dressed. "Arrest Bhadra, but do not harm him. Give him the maximum security and watch him. Tell him the King has ordered this for his protection. Now go." I barked out the orders and they rushed out.

I had the vague feeling that I had done something wrong but pushed it away into a recess of my mind and tried to concentrate on the debate. Sumali agreed with the expedition. I noticed with pleasure that Prahastha was fast getting isolated. Then I saw Vibhishana stand up. He rarely spoke, so anything he said carried some weight in the Council. However, I had found that he usually spoke about unnecessary and uncomfortable things and was a pain in the neck. He gave a moral twist to things and made everyone uneasy. It was as if your grand consciousness was hovering over you and shaking its head in dismay at your slightest pleasure. Vibhishana was someone who constantly researched the right way to live, so much so, that he had forgotten how to live. He was a walking rulebook, with lots of obscure and utterly useless jargon and mumbo jumbo. I do not know why my hair stood up every time this pompous brother of mine spoke. It was duty to protect him. I loved him but somehow, his actions were irritating. He made me and the others feel small, as if he was the only son born of virtue and the rest of us were bastard children. Perhaps this was an affliction that came from reading too many of those philosophical books. If you read them a lot, you started believing, not in yourself but in the lifeless words of complicated arguments that lay between the pages. But, I also had a soft corner for my youngest brother. Vibhishana had yet to grow up. He believed that no evil existed in the world. Though I got riled every time he went on and on about *dharma*, my affection for my little brother always stopped me from being too harsh to him.

Vibhishana began, "I don't think we should cheat anyone. We should go and ask Kubera whether he is willing to give us a portion of his kingdom and some money to start our campaign against the Devas. We should put this money to good use and then, with our half-brother's help, we should start negotiations with the Deva kingdoms of North India..."

Kumbha guffawed at this suggestion. "We can also ask Kubera if he will share his wives with us. With them we can start a pleasure business to gain more money. Then we can negotiate with the Devas and ask them if they can put some investment, say their sisters or mothers, in our Asura brothel service guild, and then we can sit and calculate profit percentages. Eventually all the Devas and Asuras will share the same pit and become brothers and live happily after." Kumbha clutched his belly and rolled around on the ground. I could not contain my merriment either and laughed out loud. Even Prahastha could not hold back a smile and the grave Sumali's mouth twitched at the corners with the hint of a smile. Vibhishana stood there with a blank expression in his face, as if he had expected these silly comments from a boor like Kumbakarna.

"Please, please, can we at least stick to using civil language?" Prahastha was again the moderator and slowly the laughter died off. Vibhishana sat down in his seat and became immersed in his deep thoughts or at least he gave us the impression that he was deep in thought. Finally, after a lot of deliberation, it was decided that we would stick to the original plan of getting two ships. Prahastha, along with Dhumraksha and Vajradhamstra, were to go to Mahabali and ask for money to take two ships on lease from the merchants in the port of Muzuris. It was also decided that the destination would be kept a secret from anyone outside the Council, and that both ships together would carry about 1,000 people. Maricha suggested that the ships be redesigned to have secret chambers and a deck where the men and arms could be concealed. Messengers would be sent to get engineers from the Mayan's school on the east coast of India, to alter the ships. Maricha would lead that team.

Kumbha and Vibhishana were to accompany Prahastha's delegation and once the money was arranged, they were to buy the horses. Maricha was also to collect rubies and diamonds from the east coast, not real stones but fake gems shaped by the Mayans; a few gold bricks, again fake, were also to be obtained from the east coast. Maricha would accompany Kumbha and Vibhishana to Mahabali and take his share of the money for his purchases. Rudraka, Jambumali, and I, would stay back and train the troops. I respected Jambumali a lot. This man, who started as a billing clerk in a spice depot and had risen to the post of Governor of Lanka under Mahabali, deserved respect. I had to develop a second and third rung of leaders for effective combat. There was a lot of work to do. It was a big gamble we were taking, but we did not have any choice.

11 Traitor

Bhadra

Tears sprouted in my eyes. I cried like a baby by the time I reached my camp. They did not believe me. Worse, they called me a spy. The two guards who were on either side of me until I reached my camp, proved it. I was surprised to find my camp mates had moved out. I was imprisoned. The guards were quite nice to me – too nice for comfort. I cried for a long time. I wept for my wife and daughter, for my country and race. I moaned for the group of people who had followed my master, trusting him with their lives. I cried for the fact that I was no longer human, but a vampire thirsting for the blood of the Devas. I wailed for the dark depths my soul had fallen into.

I had to get out of this place. My King needed my service but he did not know that. I could not be kept chained like an old dog while my country prepared for war. I had to reach Lanka. I peered outside. It was a dark and silent night. Somewhere, deep inside the forest, an owl hooted. Was it a dark omen, a harbinger of things to come? It chilled my spine. The two guards were chatting. There were guards on the periphery of the camp as well. The roar of the waterfall was loud but it was just a background sound which we got used to. I had to take advantage of it. If I could reach the stream, I could follow it down by climbing the rocks on the sides of the fall. It would be slippery and dangerous but I was sure I could do it. I had climbed such rocks when I was younger, to gather honey. Of course, I was fitter then. But now, my need was greater. So it balanced out, at least I hoped so. Once I reached the river, I could use a canoe or a tree trunk and flow downstream. The swift flow would take me to the sea. By daybreak I'd have to leave the river and follow its course upland. I could once again catch up with the river by hitch-hiking to Muzuris and then taking one of the rice boats going to the port. But I had to act fast.

I made a hole in the tent with a small kitchen knife. I wanted to take my sword but it was too heavy. Bows and arrows were out of the question. I was not sure if some crocodiles would take a fancy to my plump body. But there were no crocodiles found near the fall. The swift current and lack of fish kept them away. I got out and looked around. My heart missed a beat. There was only one guard. Where was the other one? The tall, lanky fellow with the dirty kurta? I did not want to fight him. It would wake the others. Besides, I was not sure if I could win the fight. Then I saw him under a tree, whistling while he peed. His back was towards me but he would turn once he had finished his business. I prayed that he had drunk a lot of water or toddy. I ran. The rustling of dry leaves were like thunderclaps to my ears. Once I reached the woods, I looked back. The guard was standing erect, holding his spear, ready to throw it. He had heard something. The other guard had come and lit a torch. I could see both guards in the ghostly torch light. These guards were alert. One wrong move and I would dangle like a boar on their spear.

Then, I saw the shorter guard gaping at the hole I had made. Run! Every nerve in my body became taut. It took a few seconds for the guard to comprehend what had happened. Then he began to shout. His voice was agitated and terror gripped me. Lots of torches were lit. A small drizzle had started and I heard a change in the sound of the water. The flow had increased. The waterfall was more furious now and its sound drowned what the soldiers were saying. Then I saw the king coming out of his camp. He had his sword drawn. Should I rush to him and say that I was his servant and friend? I was tempted to do so. The tension was killing me. I saw his face in the flickering light of the torches. I was not so sure anymore. It was a cruel face, not at all kind, as I had imagined. He looked like a man possessed by the devil. The wind had grown stronger now and was howling through the trees. His dark curly hair flew like the mane of a galloping horse. He looked like a demon-king. I was afraid of him. I was also afraid of the surging waters of the river. Of the two evil forces of nature, I chose the river.

I ran, hoping that the sound of my running feet would not be carried in the howling wind. An arrow flew inches above my head. I knew that there was no time to clamber down the rocks. My life was at stake. On one hand it was sure death. My people, who I wanted to serve, were shooting arrows at me. On the other hand, my beloved river Poorna, was inviting me with millions of surging, frothing hands. I plunged into the river without a second thought. The freezing cold when my body hit the water was shocking. I could not keep my head up. The rain was falling like iron pins. I was carried away like a dead leaf on the swift current, sinking in the water, coming up, only to go down again. Then, suddenly, before I knew it, I was falling, descending and plunging into dark depths. There was a roaring, moving pillar of white water all around which kept me pressed down, not letting go of me. The Poorna struggled to swallow me.

When I opened my eyes I was floating on a log. The sky had cleared and the roar of the waterfall was distant. I did not know when and how I had got hold of the log. It was a miracle that I had escaped. I had a mission to fulfil and that was why the Poorna chewed me but didn't swallow me completely. Every single joint in my body hurt. I checked my head for any injury and found that it was slimy and warm. There was blood flowing. Blood! Blood would attract the crocodiles. I was in crocodile territory. Did they hunt at night? I did not know and did not want to find out either. I needed to get out of the water but the current was swift. I swam towards the shore without letting go of the log. It was exhausting. Suddenly, I saw something moving in the water. Had the crocodiles come for their dinner? For a late night snack of a poor, dark Asura? I was not sure if they could run and catch their prey on land but definitely land was safer. Safer as long as there were no leopards. I would worry about leopards and tigers and snakes if I reached land.

The dark moving thing came closer. I kicked hard. I had but a few feet to go when something hit my leg. This was it. This was the end. After escaping the Deva armies, the Asura arrows, and a mighty waterfall, I was going to end up as a late night snack for some ugly, long-nosed reptile. I waited for the powerful jaws to snap on my leg but nothing happened. I was too terrified to look back. Too frightened to swim and reach the shore. I hung onto my log and waited. A pale moon made its appearance in the wet sky. It could have been an hour or two or maybe even a few seconds, I do not know. But when I looked back, it had gone. Without a trace. I wanted to cry with joy. Then I saw it again. It was caught in the small overhanging branch of tree. It was no crocodile which had waited under my feet but a small canoe! Someone must have followed me and the Poorna had taken care of him. All this time I was worried about crocodiles, when I had men chasing me in canoes. I could have got the canoe when it was literally at my feet.

I swam towards the canoe carefully. I didn't want ripples to move it. I had almost caught it before a strong wind shook the branch and set the canoe free. I swam with all my might to catch it before it caught the drift. But it was too swift for me. I thrashed about, ignoring my pain and the rain which had started pounding me again. Finally, when I had almost given up, the canoe got caught in a whirlpool. After a lot of twists and turns, it miraculously shot towards me. It almost knocked my head off but I ducked underwater and grabbed hold of it before the canoe could go past. I clambered up and balanced in it. Then exhaustion overcame me and I collapsed on my back. As the canoe swirled and bounced on its way towards the great sea, I slept.

12 The wait

Ravana

Almost two months had passed but no one had returned except the search parties who were supposed to have hunted down the spy. That night we had lost three men in the swirling waters. The chief of the guards, a pale, burly, corpulent man, suggested that the river had swallowed Bhadra. The search party had found the bodies of two of the three guards a mile downstream, half-eaten by fishes and jackals. Perhaps the crocodiles had eaten up Bhadra and the other guard, whose name no one seemed to know. I hoped the spy was dead, but it was somehow difficult to believe that. He seemed immortal. There was something in him, some raw power that defied death. I was afraid he had betrayed our plans.

The endless wait was frustrating. Boredom had set in among my soldiers. Rudraka drilled the soldiers with a dedication bordering on cruelty. By late evening they were tired and slept like stones. It reduced the liquor-induced fist-fights and slovenly limericks. I separated 300 men who showed promise and selected thirty captains. I made the units as small as possible for swiftness and flexibility. Each team had ten members, including the captain. They were trained to use swords and clubs scientifically, free-arms combat, close combat with knives, and climbing walls. I also designed uniforms for them, with pitch black turbans and black *dhotis*. They were to travel light with a small iron club and a light-weight sword, a rope tied around their waist and a dagger hidden inside the rope. The men were physically fit even before the selection and after two months rigorous training, their dark bodies gleamed. They were good specimens to watch, the epitome of Asura manhood.

I had wanted Vajra to stay back but Prahastha thought Vajra had a better chance of getting Mahabali to lend us the money. Jambumali was a good administrator but in the kind of operation we were planning, his contribution would be limited. Men like Jambu would be assets when our kingdom had stabilized and then men like Vajra or Rudraka would become dangerous liabilities. I gave Jambu charge of the weapon kilns. He had to arrange enough metal and get swordsmiths and ironsmiths to make swords and arrows. The actual production though, was overseen by Rudraka. We discarded the heavy iron spears normally used by the Asuras. And the heavy, wooden clubs were exchanged for lighter ones with copper thorns jutting out. A single blow from a heavier club could splinter the skull but it was too clumsy and needed men of extraordinary physical strength to use it effectively and swiftly. A small light-weight club which could be lifted and swung like a sword, would be more suitable to carry and use in close combat.

Rudraka and I had sat together for hours under our Banyan tree, discussing new innovations in our armaments. I wanted to get rid of the six feet bow and heavy iron arrows. They were too unwieldy. Rudraka, as man with vision, was against the idea. He agreed that we could reduce the heavy archers as the forthcoming operation would require stealth and speed and not raw power. But he did not want them completely discarded. He explained that, in the not-so-distant future, when we had established a kingdom with forts for our protection, archers with heavy bows could shower arrows on attackers and even pierce the head of an elephant. I agreed with him after he explained the logic. But for the forthcoming raid, they would remain on the ship.

Rudraka was a man of vision, and his life was not just dedicated to warfare. He was married to arms-technology and had travelled far and wide and seen the huge catapults-on-wheels used by the Greeks. His attempts to recreate the same design had failed. But the genius of the man lay in his innovations. His catapult could not carry heavy stones for a long distance, so he decided they could be used to hurl oil-filled coconut shells, loosely held together with jackfruit paste. When the shells hit an object, the oil would spill out. This, followed by flame-tipped arrows, would ensure that everything that stood in its path would be engulfed in flames in a matter of seconds. He also redesigned the Naga *astra,* the poison arrows used by the Nagas, by drilling a tiny hole in the tip, where a small amount of poison could be stored, making it all the more deadly. Then Rudraka made arrows like those used by Varuna. They were poles actually, thrown by a machine from a ship's deck, which could sink another ship when it was struck. We were getting extremely confident about our engineering, but our supply was running short. Unless our envoys returned within a week, we would be stuck with a few thousand arrows, clubs and swords for about half my troops.

Rudraka had collected all the old, rusted weapons from the soldiers and melted them to make new arms. There was a lot of wastage and this annoyed Jambumali. There were frequent wars of words and I had to intervene. But I trusted Rudraka and he once again came up with a path-breaking idea which was brilliant in its simplicity. He designed bamboo arrows with copper tips. The bamboo shaft was filled with poison which was then sealed with a paste. On impact, the film broke and the poison penetrated the victim's blood system, killing him instantly. The idea was so simple that we were wondered why we had not used it earlier. Aborigines used bamboo arrows, but the Asuras and the Devas regarded them as toys. This saved us a lot of metal. Rudraka also used stones as hard tips for spears and arrows, which saved even more metal. By the time he had finished, we had more than enough weapons.

Then Rudraka decided to design armour for the few elephants we had captured and tamed. He sewed needle-sized, poison-filled iron spikes into the clothing which covered the elephants' head and sides. The elephants now resembled huge porcupines. Our elephants would prove deadly to any enemy elephant coming near them. Our army was reasonably well trained. The flabby men we saw before had almost disappeared. There were surprise attack drills every day and any lapse was dealt with severely. But what was worrisome, was the cavalry. We did not have a single good horse.

Even if my delegates brought back horses, we did not have enough time to train them. We had to attack immediately after the monsoon and the island had to be taken before the commencement of the retreating monsoon which would break over the island in less than a month. Once the retreating monsoon set in, the sea would become very rough and I was not sure if the leased trade ships would be able to withstand the fury of the waves. And only God could save us if we ran into Varuna and his fleet of ships en route. He would gobble us up in a matter of hours. So we waited for our ships and the horses. I worried about my delegation. But more than that, I worried about the traitor who had escaped. If Kubera has been forewarned, we could look forward to spending the rest of our lives grinding oil for him.

13 Lanka's welcome

Bhadra

I woke with the sun burning my eyes. My body ached and I felt nauseous. I raised my head and squinted at the slowly flowing water. It was slowly meandering about palm-fringed lands. There was a lot of activity on both sides of the river. I could see many barges and rice boats plying in both directions. There were paddy fields with farmers tilling the soil. A magical village tune floated through the air. In my previous life, I would have stopped and enjoyed the scenery. I would have jumped into the water and swum across the river. The toddy here would have been delicious. The girls more so. I could see seagulls and Brahminy kites soaring in the distant skies towards the west. I was nearing the mouth of the river. At any moment I would see the lighthouse of Muzuris; an ancient light-tower which had weathered thousands of monsoons and led travellers and ships from across the world to her wonderful city.

The river took a slow right turn and there it was. The port city of Muzuris, the timeless city, once Mahabali's capital, the centre of art and culture, the most cosmopolitan city in the world. Greeks, Romans, Syrians, Sumerians, Mesopotamians, Chinese, Arabs, Jews, Devas, various Asura tribes and Egyptians, had their own streets and places of worship. There were different trade guilds. Calico, peacocks, monkeys, pepper, cardamom, cinnamon, cotton, rice, clothes, gold, horses, precious stones, silk were exported from here. The ancient city was buzzing with activity.

I left the canoe and jumped into the water which was delightfully warm. I climbed ashore and walked to the nearest inn. People were staring at me. I must have looked a sight. It was an old shack, small but neat, with a palm-thatched roof. There were a few people loitering about, mostly sailors. I needed to take a bath and have a doctor see to my wounds. The inn-keeper was kind and I think he believed the story of my rice boat sinking in the heavy rain. It looked as if this inn was frequented by people who had survived the fury of nature. He gave me a set of new clothes and got a doctor's assistant to dress my wounds. I promised to repay him by working for him for a few days.

It was hard work and I had to draw water from a deep well, hew wood for fuel and sweep the floors. I was just happy to be alive. I hadn't forgotten why I had left the camp but I needed a rest. I thought I'd build contacts and then board a ship bound for Lanka. And it was at the inn that I found I had a talent. Quite by accident I discovered that I was a good cook. It was just something that happened one day when the cook of the inn vanished without a word. There were many guests and I volunteered to cook. In no time, I built a reputation. 'Bhadra's Fried Fish' became a must for evening revelries. They said my spicy fish fry went well with toddy. Soon I started getting invitations from captains of various ships. But I knew I had to be patient. I waited until I got a suitable offer from one of Kubera's ship bound for Lanka. It was a royal pleasure ship, a huge, sturdy vessel that was considered safe even in turbulent monsoon seas. It carried officers and their wives to the major ports of the world to shop. I was an instant hit with them and before I reached Lanka, I had employment offers from a dozen aristocratic families. But I had to choose my employer with care. I wanted to be inside the palace. I was, after all, a self-appointed spy. I wanted to collect as much data and send it back to my king. So I slyly struck up a friendship with one of the cooks of the royal kitchen. He was a lean, dark man of indeterminate age and wanted a helper to cut vegetables and dress meat and fish. He was sure that he could persuade the chief cook to employ me. I thought I would take a chance with him as this would get me into the inner circles of the palace. Wild plans had started racing in my mind.

I landed in Lanka after six days of travel. The ship had circumvented the peninsula and the northern tip of Lanka, before anchoring at the main port, near the capital of Trikota. I could see Kubera's glittering palace atop the Trikota hills. I saw watch posts with armed guards. The royal highway stretched from the port to the main gate on the eastern side, with beautiful gardens and trees lining either side. The western and southern sides of the fort had many shanty towns where the city's poor lived and worked in the trade guilds, that stretched miles to the north. Public parks and lakes adorned the beach in the north. The eastern side had inns for visiting sailors. There were houses of pleasure where pretty girls offered wine, toddy and their bodies, to men willing to pay. The royal guards patrolled the streets on fine Arabian horses. I had never seen a city like Trikota. Muzuris was bigger and busier, but it lacked the charm of Trikota. Muzuris was a city of intricate, narrow and winding roads, bustling with commerce and choking it. It was crowded and congested, like a collection of huge village markets. There were no visible exhibitions of wealth and of course, there weren't any shanty towns on the outskirts like in Trikota. I sensed that the poor were dumped at the outskirts of Trikota to present a clean and neat city in the commercial parts of town. Anyhow, the effect was nothing short of spectacular. Any visitor would have been impressed by Trikota and the palace atop the hill.

I was apprehensive about my welcome at the fort. I walked a few paces behind my friend from the ship, when I was gripped by sudden fear. A palace guard, astride a tall ,dark horse, was staring at me. It was as if he was trying to recollect something. I tried hard to remember his face. It was vaguely familiar, but I could not place him. I did not want to lock eyes with him. There was something sinister about him. My friend was chattering incessantly and occasionally turning back to urge me to hurry as it was nearing sunset and the fort gates closed then.

We reached the fort gate manned by four armed guards. They looked professional, with taut muscles and long limbs. I was taken aside and searched for any hidden weapons. I almost fainted when they found my kitchen knife in the folds of my *dhothi* and made me stand aside. My friend explained that I was a professional cook and it was required for my profession, but they shoved him out along with his other friends. I sat in one corner of the guard room and was left alone for a long time. I gathered that they were waiting for their superior officer to come and that I might be subjected to some sort of interrogation. As the moments passed, my fear increased. What where they going to do? I wanted it to get over with. It was almost midnight and I was nearly dead with fear, when a tall, dark man entered the room. Three guards stood behind him reverently. He was evidently their superior. He went directly to his table, and put his seal in a couple of palm leaves, and then called for the messenger boy. Once the courier was dispatched, he turned towards me.

It was the same man who had been staring at me when I was walking behind my friends from the ship. There was the trace of a smile on his face, which made him look hideous. My heart was in my mouth. He walked towards me and in one swift moment, without any warning, kicked my face. I was thrown back and lay coiled there, expecting more blows and kicks. I wanted to scream. He picked me up by my shoulders and peered into my eyes. The stench of cheap toddy mixed with his bad breath hit me. It was worse than his kick and I felt like vomiting in his face. He gave me a backhanded slap and I tasted the warm blood in my mouth. Then he threw me down. "I have seen you somewhere, you son of a swine."

I recognized him then. He was with the gang that had attacked my village. This was the man who had followed me when I killed the boy who splattered my daughter all over my wall. I did not know how he ended up in Kubera's service but it was nearly seven years. Much could happen in that time. "I have come to Lanka for the first time, Sir."

"I have seen you somewhere else." At that moment the door opened with a blast and a corpulent man entered the room. "You are getting out of control, you bastard. Just because you are an inspector of the royal guards does not mean that you can thrash my servants around. You're going to pay a price for it," the man screamed.

"Ah, my pleasure. Vikrama is grateful that Your Highness, the King of the kitchen, has placed his holy feet in my lowly office. But why isn't your

Highness copulating with a hussy under the kitchen stove? Why do you choose to be here at this hour is beyond my comprehension."

"Vikrama, you son of a drunken monkey, you will pay for this. You leave my servant alone. Else, tomorrow the King will hear about it and you will be breakfast for his pet tigers."

"Take your boyfriend and have a nice time. Just take it easy while you are at it. I do not want him to puncture your stinking arse and wake up half the city with the screaming." The inspector picked me up like a rag and threw me at the fat man. I fell at his feet and tried to get up. The inspector and the fat guy stared at each other.

Finally, the fat man turned and I hurriedly followed him. I could feel the inspector's eyes boring holes into my back. *He will get me, he'll surely get me one day.* I shuddered at the thought and walked faster, trying to catch up with my savior, who walked surprisingly fast for a man of his size. He did not speak a single word until we entered a huge complex. "This is the central kitchen. The entire army is fed from here. I am Suboga, the chief cook. I personally supervise the food for the royal household. For the others, there are about twenty supervisors and 300 cooks and helpers. Then there are the cleaning staff, servers etc. I was looking for someone who knows about fish and Arasu suggested I take you. When he said that you had been detained by that rascal, I came rushing out. But do not think I am your friendly uncle and will be always there to save the black skin of your backside. I came to get you because six people on the ship vouched for you. You can join Arasu's team. I'll try you out for a few weeks to see whether you are good enough for my kitchen. Your sleeping quarters are on the left."

I thanked him, relieved to have escaped alive from Vikrama. "And three coppers a week will be your pay," he shouted, walking towards the corridor which led to his sleeping room. I wanted to go and find Arasu, my friend from the ship, and thank him. But it was late and I thought I'd do it in the morning, so I entered the room. There were some mattresses spread on the floor. About a dozen people were asleep in various postures. I found a small gap and crawled in-between. Tomorrow I would start work. But now I just wanted to lie down and sleep for a hundred years.

14 Betrayed

Ravana

One by one, my delegates arrived. The mission to get the ships had been successful. Maricha was also successful in getting the head of the school of Mayans. He was said to possess one of the best engineering brains in the country and had come with twenty of his best technicians. He was a widower and had brought his daughter along. Did I want this unnecessary distraction in my almost all-male camp? But I did not want any friction at this stage. She was said to be a beauty but kept to herself. It was also rumoured that she was a prude, who observed all sorts of fasts and prayers. Not my type anyway, so I did not give her a second thought.

We had fixed the fifteenth of *Chaitra* as the day to start the expedition. Jambumali arranged to fill the lower deck with provisions to last a few days. He led a number of sorties to a deserted beach south of Muzuris, where the ships were anchored a few miles away. We carried supplies from nearby villages and even the city market, in small quantities, in order to dispel any suspicion and stored the supplies in a temporary camp in the woods near the beach. From there, they were transported to the ships by night. The altered chambers were filled with sacks of pepper and in them, weapons were concealed. About 300 men were hidden in a secret deck in-between. We were now ready to go.

There were many problems and initially it was chaotic. But slowly things fell into place. We decided to leave behind in the forest, a few hundred soldiers including my mother, aunt, sister, the engineers as well as the

Mayan and his daughter and proceed to Lanka. Jambumali was also left behind as it was too dangerous for him to go to the island. There might have been people who would have recognized the former governor of the province. There was even the chance that someone might recognize any of us three brothers. But we were nobodies in Lanka and decided to take the chance.

As the fifteenth approached, the tension and excitement in the camp became unbearable. All that was discussed was the forthcoming battle, war strategy, the glories of Lanka, the beautiful girls.... nobody wanted to discuss defeat and decimation. No one wanted to think about the eventuality of being encountered by Varuna's pirate fleet. No one dared to mention the possibility of Bhadra, Kubera's spy, pre-warning the merchant king and our being ambushed. We pushed such thoughts into the deepest pits of our minds.

Bhadra

A month had passed since I had become Kubera's employee. There was no trace of our ships. The monsoon had weakened two weeks earlier and the weather became balmier by the day, just as it should for the one month break before the monsoon retreated. Every Tuesday I'd go to the market to buy meat and vegetables for the kitchen. I would then sneak to the nearby spice market which overlooked the port, to look out for the ships or to spot a familiar face in the crowd.

I felt uneasy whenever I went on these sorties. It was as if someone was following me. It was a vague feeling but it persisted. I looked around, took sharp, unexpected turns into narrow market alleys and ducked into small eateries and emerged through the back doors of shops. But I could not find anyone. I felt naked. I was afraid of my own shadow. I felt morose most of the day and wanted to give up everything and go back to some unnamed village in my native land. I would wake screaming in the night. I kept seeing the splattered brains of my daughter, the spread, bleeding legs of my wife and heaving bare buttocks of those devils. I knew I had to stay and plot my revenge. Vikrama sneered at me in my nightmares. He sat crosslegged and licked his fingers, as if at a feast. He kept offering me some delicacy which invariably turned out to be my daughter's splattered brain. At those moments, I forgot about going back and the quiet life. All I wanted was to see the the Devas ruined. All I wanted was revenge.

Finally, I saw them one day, leading a few horses, laden with goods, through the streets of the spice market. They had spread into many small group but I could easily distinguish Ravana. I was horrified. He did not have the posture of a merchant. He rode like a king. And which king would be found in a market place? Ravana, with his mannerisms, would give away the whole plan. But I could have been wrong. Perhaps Ravana appeared to be a prosperous merchant to others who were unaware of the invasion. The soldiers, disguised as servants, were also a big give-away. They did not behave like servants at all. They did not chat among themselves. They did not linger in front of small shops selling sea shell necklaces and glass bangles or haggle over prices. Instead, they walked silently. Their cover could be blown any time. Then I noticed the two ships anchored in the distance. They looked so puny and small. I had to get near my king and warn him. But what if he did not trust me?

"So, this is what you came for, eh?" I was startled to hear Vikrama's voice. He was standing behind me and chewing a blade of grass, perfectly disguised as a petty merchant who merged with the surroundings. In one hand he held a small brown bag like those used by petty merchants and the other was behind his back. I was sure he had a dagger in that hand. Before he could do anything, I stepped on his toes and gave him a hard push. He staggered and fell flat on his back. He was quick to scramble up but I had taken off by then. I could see the dagger blade glistening in the sun. The crowd screamed. I weaved in and out of the crowd as fast as I could move, overturning carts of fruits, stepping over vermillion mounds, getting screamed at, abused, clawed and even hit, by the hawkers and sales boys. Ravana turned towards me. Confusion clouded his face. Then, as he recognized me, I saw pure hatred cross his handsome face. I saw men moving and circling us from all directions. Disguised guards were closing in on us. Vikrama was thorough and he had us like a lemon in his hand. And he was squeezing us hard.

"Get away!" I screamed at the top of my voice. I saw the glitter of a sword in Ravana's hand. And then I saw hundreds of swords drawn up in the crowd. Dust swirled in different corners of the market as Ravana's men struggled to escape. I reached the King's horse and cried, "Take me, my Lord, take me with you."

Vikrama was very near. At any moment I would be killed or taken prisoner.

Ravana roared, "You traitor, son of a scoundrel! Go rot in hell!" The kick I received on the bridge of my nose did not hurt half as much as those words. I nearly fell on Vikrama, but he dodged me adroitly and went for Ravana. He got hold of the horse's rein and tried to stab the king. Another powerful kick from Ravana left Vikrama sprawled on the floor. I saw with relief that Ravana's men had succeeded in breaking the ranks of the guards. The king was hacking and thrusting his way out of the crowd and shouting commands for a retreat. Soon he rode out of the market at full gallop with his followers behind, some on horses and others running to catch up. This small group left the market with a few guards half-heartedly following them. The blood from my broken nose had formed a pool. I tried to stand up but got a sharp kick on my face. Vikrama was red with anger. He kicked me hard, again and again. I wanted to get up and flee but Vikrama's kicks landed like rain. I had almost lost consciousness when someone half-lifted, half-dragged me towards the palace. I was bleeding all over by the time I reached the small cell of Vikrama's office. There he started his act all over again. I wished I had died before I had got to his jail.

Ravana

Ruined. Ruined, because of a bastard. Months of planning, struggling for arms and supplies, training and living under the sun and rain. Everything ruined because our good-for-nothing guards could not get their hands on that short, stout farmer. I could grind him with my bare hands. But I knew this kind of anger and frustration would only make our lives more miserable. Prahastha was asleep under a tree and Sumali and Rudraka were discussing something after drawing maps in the sand. Kumbha and Vibhishana had vanished into the woods. The war was lost even before a single encounter with the enemy. I wanted to take Lanka head on and go down in a trail of glory. I wanted to lead my soldiers to Kubera's palace and die valiantly. But Prahastha thought it was suicidal. A more efficient way to die, he thought, would be to jump off the cliff on which we were now perched. That way we would not bring misery to the civilians. So we were stuck in this hellhole. We were on top of the Subela hills, overlooking the sea on one side and Kubera's palace on the other. In the valley between, Kubera's army waited for us. We were besieged. They could come up and finished us off at any time. They were certain we would starve to death. The Subela Hills were bare and the woods had little game. It would not support 300 people for long. We saw our ship, modified by the Mayans, the ship to glory and the rebirth of the Asura kingdom, sunk like a leaf boat by Kubera's navy. All our spare weapons found a good storage place at the bottom of 200 feet of water.

Only Maricha took things lightly. The old man was always cheerful. He devised games to amuse the soldiers and told them stories of olden times, when things were not modern and complicated, when thoughts were pure and men had the time to enjoy life and the world was a better place to live in. Huddled around a fire, we imagined ourselves living in those unhurried times when our forefathers lived and breathed fresh air. He always ended his tales lamenting how things now were when young men no longer respected elders, people cheated and lied all the time and hurried through life. But he maintained that things would be better in the future. Maricha, you're such an optimistic human being, such a wonderful man. What would we have done without you?

The retreating monsoon started. We were soaked, sick and frustrated to be alive. Half the soldiers were down with fever and we were starving. I waited under the dark sky, with monsoon clouds swirling above me. Claps of thunder resounded. I had fought with Prahastha again and again about staying here and dying like flies. He was adamant that we remain where we were. We'd walk into Kubera's trap if we moved. I could sense revolt within the ranks and see that their confidence in me had ebbed considerably. There were no cries of, "Long live the King!" whenever I moved about. Fewer men attended the morning parade and drill. I had the nagging doubt that Prahastha was counting on a rebellion in the ranks to take over as leader. I spoke about it with Kumbha. He thought it was my imagination but promised to keep an eye on Prahastha. I waited for deliverance and hoped for a lot to happen. That Varuna would attack the island and offer us a respectable path for retreat. I hoped the sea would swallow the island. I hoped Kubera would be killed in a palace coup and then I, his half brother, would be invited to rule the island. I knew none of these things would ever happen. What was sure was the vultures circling high in the sky, waiting for us to fall and die one by one.

Then one day, unexpectedly, my wishes came true.

15 Poisonous brews

Bhadra

I was surprised that I was still alive. They had plucked the nails from all my fingers and toes. They scalded me, poked me with spiked rods, sprinkled pepper powder on my flayed skin, hung me upside down and lashed me. I lost count of what was done to me. My wounds became infected and flies circled to settle on them. I retched and curled up naked on the mud floor. Fleas and ants came out of mother earth to eat me alive. Vikrama came once in a while and poked me with his sword tip, sometimes thrusting it a bit too deep, all the while taunting me. Then he laughed his devilish laugh. I lay without a thought. I became numb. It might have been two weeks or two years. I did not know and I did not care. I just wanted to die.

Then one day, suddenly, I decided to live. Vikrama had either grown bored with me or was too busy. I didn't see him too often. The guards felt sorry for me and brought a doctor to my cell. He inflicted even more pain while examining my wounds. But after a while my wounds healed and my body got stronger. A guard named Suka, became rather close to me. During his work shift, which was usually midnight, he talked about his village on the southern coast of the island, his wife and six young children, waiting for him to come back, and the debts he had pay. I listened because I wanted to escape. I heard him patiently because I wanted him to trust me. I feigned attention as I was sure that I would murder him one day. He nursed me, soothed my bruised soul, and entertained me with his stories. I was afraid that I would start loving him, so one night, when he was talking to me, I feigned weakness and leaned on him. He carried me and put me down on the torn mattress that was my bed. From the corner of my eye, I saw the prison door was ajar. This was the chance I had been waiting for. I strangled him. I still remember his face when he understood that I was killing him. His face, with its trust in humanity draining away as fast as his life ebbed, will remain etched in my mind.

I placed him on the mattress and said a silent prayer for his soul. For a moment, the thought of his faceless and tired wife with her six children, waiting in a far-away southern village for this man, flashed through my mind. It lingered for a second or two but then I remembered that there were other guards outside. It was not safe to linger, I had to get out. I peered out. It was past midnight, to judge by the absence of sounds from the street beyond. One guard dozed near the door, two others chatted by the wall lamp which cast a ghostly light on their faces. The lamp flickered in the breeze and made the shadows jump in a macabre dance. I froze near the door and thanked my stars that they had detained me in the temporary prison attached to the guard house and not in the notorious town prison with its high walls and the moat with marsh crocodiles. It would have been quite a task for Vikrama to walk every day to the town prison to torture me. Here in his office, he could torture me whenever he wanted to. There were two other cells. I prayed they would be either empty or the prisoners fast asleep. The sleeping guard stirred, murmured something and went back to sleep. I crept on all fours towards him. I wanted his sword which hung behind his stone desk. The wall lamp went out and I heard the guards near the door swear. The sleeping guard awoke and looked for his sword. I quickly grabbed it from the hinge and unsheathed it. I tried to squeeze through the narrow gap between the table and the wall but collided with a guard.

"Take care, you fool!" he said. Then I saw him freeze and heard the scrape of his sword being unsheathed. I was sure he would not use it but I did not wait. I plunged my sword into what I thought was his throat and felt warm blood splash on my face. I pushed his weakening body down and ran towards the grey rectangle of light filtering in from the street. I could hear the guards stumbling over each other. Any moment they would ring the huge bell and the city would become one huge beast hunting me down. Mounted patrol-men would assemble at the guard house and Vikrama would arrive. I looked to left and right, deciding which way to run. The sharp pealing of the bell ended my indecision and I ran left, towards the palace.

I ran like a mad dog. It took me a few minutes to realize that I was running through the royal highway. I could come face to face with the mounted guards at any time and I could hear the sound of hoofs. Abruptly I turned right and entered an alley. It was dark and the street lamps had gone out. A rectangular window of light made patterns on the farthest corner of the alley. As I walked towards it I could hear conversation. A woman was arguing with a man who was obviously drunk. I was nervous and needed a place to hide. The door suddenly banged open and I quickly stepped back into the dark shadows. A bulky man in his undergarments was pushed out. He stumbled a few paces, hit a lamp post and fell face down into a gutter. A stream of abuse followed him. The man did not stir at all. This was surely not his home. No decent lady would swear like that. It could have been one of those dance houses or a house of pleasure. Before she could slam the door I stepped out of the darkness and put my foot in the door.

She was shocked for a second. I noticed that she was about eighteen or twenty, with hazel brown eyes and straight jet black hair. She was fair like a Deva woman or a cross breed. She had on a silk blouse that barely covered her breasts and a silk *dhothi* tucked inches below her navel. A diamond on a thin gold chain lay wedged in her cleavage. I entered the house before she could scream and closed the door firmly with my left hand while pointing my sword at her throat. I knew there would be guards in the house. Such places needed them and they were more brutal than the palace guards.

"Take me to your room," I said, aware that my manhood had started rising on seeing her sensual body. A smile played on her lips. She looked at my face. I felt inadequate and ugly. She settled her eyes on my crotch. Restrained and long-forgotten emotions tried to break through the shackles. She burst out laughing and I felt like throwing the sword away and covering my shame with both hands.

A loud knock on the door broke the spell and I grabbed the knot of her *dhothi* and pulled her towards me. I whispered death into her ears and she understood. Her breasts brushed against my bare skin. She pushed me away firmly yet gently and said that she would take care of things. Freeing her, I moved behind the thick curtains while she opened the door. There were guards outside. I heard them but could not make out what was said. I was sure she had betrayed me and at any moment the guards would enter and drag me back to prison. I waited for the first guard to enter and felt the sharp edge of my sword. I decided not to go down without a fight. I would not be gifted back to Vikrama. But with astonishment and relief, I heard the steps moving away. She came in and closed the door.

"Come out, you coward" she taunted and then burst out laughing. I felt like grabbing her and kissing her mouth. I felt like plunging my sword between her breasts and puncturing her heart. I felt so many things as I stood there with my sword hanging limply in my right hand, my left hand twisting the drapes of the curtains and my legs shivering and unsteady. "Follow me," she said and walked confidently towards a flight of wooden stairs. I followed her like an obedient dog.

I awoke in the morning to see her sitting in a chair near my bed. I tried to reach for the sword but it wasn't in its place. She smiled and said that she had it in safe custody. She was wearing a pale blue blouse and a white cotton *dhothi*, which made her look even more beautiful. The diamond was missing; she had taken bath and applied a small sandal paste *bindi* to her forehead. I remembered that last night she had led me to this room and closed the door from outside. I had slept with frustrated images of having sex with her and not rising to her expectations, of Vikrama cutting my balls off and offering them to this woman. I was not sure whether I was a prisoner or a refugee.

"So, let me hear your story." Her lovely mouth was inviting enough for me to narrate my life story. I told her about my childhood, of the games I played, about the fast currents of the Poorna, of the huge rosewood trees I climbed to get honey. I told her my story over breakfast, over fruits and nuts we had together, over lunch, while walking in the small garden in her backyard, before we made love, when we made love, and after we made love. I took more than a week to narrate my story. As I spoke, my childhood became picture perfect, my village became heaven, the Devas who had attacked it became the worst kind of devils. My adventures became bolder, my role with Mahabali's army important, my position with Ravana high, my culinary skills perfect. And my torment under Vikrama unbearable. I exaggerated and she realized I was exaggerating, adding frills to the humble life of a common farmer. I knew she understood and somehow it did not matter.

She was a dance girl. She did not know her name. People called her Mala and she called herself the same. She sold her body and earned a good living. But it took a long time and practice for her to establish her reputation. She had no remorse and said this unabashedly, as someone who says she is a good dancer or a doctor or an actor. Her clients were rich merchants and high officials and she lived alone with no guards or a protecting madam. She told me that Vikrama was a regular and that he was lousy in bed. Somehow this gave me a perverse satisfaction. I fell in love with her. She served her clients and I waited in my upper chamber for her to come to me. I was jealous at times, but thankful also to get her back. Slowly, I told her about my life's mission. She was disinterested at first, but after two weeks of my conversation, she started taking some interest. Then she caught my enthusiasm and I taught her hatred. She gave me love and I gave her hatred instead. I wanted her to be on my side. I plotted with her. I corrupted her by giving her my love which was nothing but pure hatred towards anyone not like me.

One evening, she came to my room and said that Vikrama was her client for the night. I burnt with jealousy but it was time for us to put our plan into action. I hid behind the thick curtains and waited with trepidation. I saw Vikrama enter the room. Mala stood up and walked towards him and planted a kiss on his lips. I burned hidden behind the curtains. He walked to the tall bed and removed his gold brocade footwear and tucked his feet up. Mala stood a few feet away and removed her blouse. She fell on Vikrama and with her breasts rubbing his bare chest, tied both his hands to the bed pole with a shawl. Then she removed his dress and hers too. She stood there naked, elegant and beautiful. Vikrama was lying prone, his tough muscled pale body twisting in anticipation. She took off her *dhothi* and tied his legs too.

I walked out slowly to Vikrama. Mala withdrew and picked up her clothes and started putting them on. Then she left the room in a hurry. "What the hell. . ." Vikrama's face flushed with anger and then it dawned on him. I was death coming. He froze. I put on my best smile and walked deliberately towards him, measuring each step. He struggled to get up but Mala had tied him nice and tight. I pulled out his nails one by one. With the clinical precision of a good butcher, I deposited then in a plate after emptying the mangoes it contained, onto the floor. He screamed and screamed. I told him he didn't have to worry, he would not die for another four or five hours and I would continue to work on him till then, or even after he died. I broke his bones, emasculated him and then I took pepper powder and spread it over his wounds. He screamed and screamed but he did not die. Finally, about two hours before daybreak, he died.

I was not happy or satisfied, it was not enough, but I had learnt the hard way that life does not satisfy you completely. So I stopped and picked up Vikrama. I dropped all the pieces into a sack and called out for Mala. She entered the room, saw the mess and vomited on the sack. '*Serves him right,*' I thought. '*Carry the vomit of a whore on your head to your grave, you devil.*' It took half an hour to console her, but I think she was happy to see me glow with happiness.

We carried the sack to the back garden and burnt it with sugar, which would not leave any trace of the body. We hoped no one would notice the acrid smell of flesh burning. I went out and killed two stray dogs and put them in along with the burning corpse. That would put off any nosy neighbour. Thus ended Vikrama, chief of the palace guards.

I had managed to take the keys from his pocket and I wanted to get into the fort. I had to do it before the chief was missed. As I walked towards the fort. I could see the lit palace in the distance. I was still a wanted man and it was dangerous to move about, but I did not have a choice. There was a separate entrance to the fort for security officers and I decided to use it. I was dressed in Vikrama's clothes, which were a bit too big for me. I tried to walk like a man used to authority but was not sure if I could fool the guards. I was too tame for a guard. As I neared the palace I saw two guards stationed near the security entrance but I walked past them with an air of authority and they snapped to attention. They were looking at the distant horizon, where the sky was turning orange. I could hear my heart pounding and was afraid the guards would hear it and look at my face. My hands trembled as I turned the key. Nothing happened. Beads of sweat fell from my brows. Dawn was painting the eastern skies pale.

"Let me, Sir." The taller of the guards took the keys from my hands, put the right one in and turned. With a clank, the door opened and I stepped in, thanked the guard and quickly closed the door behind me. I checked the small mud vessel I carried with me. It had taken me more than ten days to prepare the thing. I removed the chief's uniform, made a bundle and shoved it under a bush. Then, dressed in my own clothes, I walked into the royal kitchen, where I had worked earlier. About twenty cooks were busy preparing food for the army. I hoped they had not heard about my arrest and detention. Perhaps Suboga might have known, as Vikrama would have not let go an opportunity to get even with the fat cook. But the chef's ego would have prevented him from telling his subordinates.

"Hey Bhadra, where were you? Suboga said you had gone to your native village on the mainland. You've just returned?" Kriman, a loud-mouthed fish cutter, shouted from the other end of the kitchen. All heads turned towards me and many smiled. I could not see my friend who had got me the job here.

"If you are looking for Arasu, he was sacked. I think some captain complained about his cooking and he was sent back to the mainland. These beggars in the army think they are Gods." I felt a knot in my stomach. So Arasu got the boot for helping me. The bastards! I could not blame Suboga. It was his head he had to take care of first. "You have to first go and meet Suboga or he will get angry" old Mupra said "Is that his instruction?" I asked knowing all too well that Suboga didn't think I'd be back at all.

"No. . ."

"Then I will join you now and see him later, after we have served breakfast."

I entered the vegetable chopping section and started working. After I had

moved close to the stove to pass on the chopped vegetables for the third time, I took out the mud pot and emptied the contents into the boiling rice. The soldiers prefer different curries, but everyone ate rice. I was counting on that. I waited with bated breath. Bullock cart after bullock carts arrived and carried baskets full of rice and different curries to the various sections of the army. Boats would carry them to the ships moored at sea, if they were stationed near the capital. A number of things could go wrong. A small bit could spill onto the ground, a crow could eat it and fall dead, and my secret would be blown. Or, a few soldiers could die or fall sick and the army would stop eating the food and start an enquiry. I would be caught. I prayed and fretted at the same time. Yet I smiled as I continued to work inside the steaming kitchen.

After an hour, I heard a commotion outside. They were bringing in soldiers upon soldiers, men retching, and men in the pangs of death, men twitching in agony. Bullock carts and horse-drawn carts were bringing men from all corners of the city and dumping them in the palace grounds for the palace doctors to examine. I ran out. Nobody noticed. I wanted to reach my master. I wanted my King, Ravana, to come and take over the city. I ran amidst falling soldiers vomiting, with their heads buried in drains, men grabbing their stomach, twisting in their death pangs. I grabbed the reigns of a horse from a soldier who was clinging with one hand to the horse and vomiting on the other side. I kicked him, mounted the horse, and galloped towards the Subela hills. Ordinary citizens started to assemble on the streets, peering at the dying soldiers. A country was being released from the tyranny of a merchant king.

I galloped through the pouring crowds, running to watch their tormentors dying. As I climbed the Subela hills, I remembered to tear off a portion of my white *mundu* and tie it to a staff. I did not want to die in friendly fire. As I neared the camp, I could see archers forming a circle around their king. They were ready to shoot and a slight movement of the kings' brow would have ensured that I ended up looking like a porcupine. I slowed down and waved my white flag. Tears welled in my eyes. My words seemed stuck in my throat, "Your Highness, the city is yours. I have finished Kubera's army. . ."

"Arrest him." His voice shattered my heart. Images of my nails being pulled out, filled my mind. My body ached in all the places where Vikrama had performed his art. I fell on my knees and howled like a wounded wolf. Soldiers from the side I had always believed to be my own, surrounded me, ready to kill.

"Ravana, just hear him out." I could see the old, aristocratic figure of Prahastha walking towards us. Maricha also came, pushing the soldiers back, and lifted me up. He hugged me and patted my back. I sobbed like a little baby and I could feel Maricha's tears wetting the bare skin on my back.

16 The pirate's seige

Ravana

I took some time to realize that Bhadra was not a traitor but a friend. He was the saviour I had been waiting for. With renewed vigour, we clambered down the hills and marched with as much dignity an army of starving troops could muster. As we entered the Royal Street, we could see thousands of people standing on either side, cheering us. I was elated. This was the moment of triumph I had anticipated. Unknown amounts of wealth awaited me. I could build an army with the great resources this kingdom possessed and then take over the entire sub-continent. Moreover, I could throw my half-brother onto the streets, which he deserved, and with a flick my hands, throw him a few gold coins. I could look at my father's face and jeer. I could do so many things. I was the King and the Emperor. Ravana, the Emperor of Lanka, sounded good. Ravana, the Emperor of India, sounded even better. Was I getting too ambitious? No, no, I was always self-confident.

Cheers erupted from all sides and I raised my sword. The crowd went mad. There were cries of ecstasy. People danced on the roads. Drums beat with full vigour and pipes and horns blasted the sky. I was in dreamland. Then, suddenly, I felt bitter. This victory was empty. It was gifted to me on a platter by an ugly farmer, a coarse, uneducated villager, a sly serpent. I looked back and saw him carrying something heavy on his shoulders. He was bent over and Maricha was lifting a corner of the heavy load and talking to him as an equal. I tasted mud in my mouth. How could he demean himself by associating with such a lowly being? Maricha had been a king once and he was now the uncle of a king. True, Bhadra helped us to victory. But was it done the right way? It was against all the principles I had learnt as a child. Would an empire built on deceit and slyness last? Was I creating an empire of truth and *dharma*? Doubts lingered in my mind. I looked at Prahastha. He looked serious. I was not sure if it was because he thought like me or because he wanted my seat. Kumbha was dancing with a crowd of drunken, young men, to the tune of drums and was infinitely happy. Vibhishana was morose, but that was nothing new. Others smiled and acted happy.

As I entered the palace, the image of a poor woman and her four children standing before the merchant king with a begging bowl, flooded my mind. The derisive glance and the flick of Kubera's hands fired the flames within me. Butterflies fluttered in my stomach. I saw the cow pen and glanced back at Maricha. He glanced at it and then smiled at me. I loved him just for that smile. Kumbha was oblivious, in an advanced stage of inebriation. I wanted to see Kubera's face as he came out to surrender. I waited outside the palace, waiting for its golden gates to open and the King to come out and lay his crown at my feet. That was how they surrendered, wasn't it?

We waited for a long time, but nothing happened. I wanted to barge in and take the palace by force. At least that would quench my conscience. Then, suddenly, the gates opened. An uneasy hush fell upon the crowd. An old man came out and read from a parchment. "Kubera, the King and the God of riches, the richest King of the world, merchant *par excellence,* wishes to convey his regards to his dearest younger brother, Ravana and says, 'I wish to tell you that I was always willing to pass the kingdom to you my brother, had you ever asked for it. I am sad that you have used deceitful methods, unworthy of a nobleman and unworthy of a brother, to secure this tiny island. I feel great sadness that, instead of fighting with my army as a man and soldier, you chose to poison them. I am ashamed of the fact that you used deceit to gain your brother's riches, spurning hard work and honest means. You have failed both as a soldier and as a brother. I leave the kingdom to you, but I hope the Gods will forgive me if I curse you that your rule also will end with betrayal and slyness by someone smarter than you. Adieu, my brother and rule well and long li--"

I jumped into the room and grabbed the parchment from the old man's hands. "Where is he?" I shouted at him. He stared at my eyes for a full minute and then pointed his finger to the distant, blue sea. There, with Kubera's golden flag at half mast, I saw a huge ship leaving port. Victory dissolved in my mind. I wanted to murder Bhadra. The crowd had slowly started to disappear. I looked at that sailing ship tiredly. I had missed the bastard! The next day I would be crowned the King of Lanka. I declared a public festival to last seven days to mark the occasion and dispatched a boat to bring my family and the others. Everyone was running around to make it a grand occasion. I searched for Bhadra but he was hidden somewhere in the crowd milling around as if they were contributing to the arrangements, but were in fact only hindering the progress.

I sat on the verandah on the first floor and watched the sun set. The western sea was purple and the ships in full sail were beautiful. The breeze was refreshing. Thousands of birds made music in the garden below. But there were too many ships in the sea. Something was troubling me. Something...

"Your Highness, Varuna's fleet is approaching our shores." I was shocked out of my lazy thoughts by a panting messenger, standing a few feet from me and wheezing like a mad dog. The whole palace stood still. There went my coronation! I ordered an end to all celebrations. Our Council met to discuss the emergency. We did not have any army to speak off. Kubera had taken most of the navy with him. The rest were poisoned, many dead, and many more violently sick. So we were left with only 300 odd soldiers to fight the pirate king. I gained a kingdom without any bloodshed and this bothered me. I wanted to fight with Varuna; I wanted a war with someone. I just could not accept that I had become a King without any heroics. A kingdom gained through the leaky bowels of a cheated army. Disgusting! The victory was hollow and I wanted to legitimize it. Crushing Varuna would increase my prestige and set my mind at peace, or at least that was what I hoped. But a fight would be disastrous. Varuna would swallow us and swarm the island like a tidal wave. It would be like trying to dam the sea with our bare hands.

Prahastha, as usual, was his irritating self. He spoke all sorts of uncomfortable truths and made everyone uneasy. I had started to hate this fellow. He was no pompous prude like my Vibhishana, whose spurts of moral preaching I had learnt to ignore. Prahastha made sense. His logic was always crystal clear. But he behaved as if he were a thinking machine, like Mahabali had wanted me to be, a walking brain with the necessary accessories attached to keep it functioning. Prahastha argued prudence. He pointed out that there wasn't a reasonable army to fight the pirate. If Varuna chose to leave his ships and enter the city, there would be large scale plunder and arson, mass rape and butchery. So the only course of action left was to buy peace. Surely peace would be costly but the cost of war would be more. I kept my mouth shut. I wanted to say so many things but nothing sounded right. I did not want to go and fall at the feet of a third rate pirate. Finally, after an uneasy consent, Prahastha was authorized to negotiate with Varuna. I wanted to go with him but he curtly refused. I did not like his brusque tone and reminded him that I was the king.

"It was for that very reason that I do not want you to come with me," he said. "If Varuna took you hostage, Lanka would fall into his hands."

"If Varuna wanted to take Lanka, he could have done so by now," I countered. But Varuna was a long-term thinker and a steady stream of riches year after year as ransom was more to his taste than quick plunder. By agreeing to pay him ransom, we were falling for his game.

"So, what is the alternative?" asked Prahastha.

I did not have an answer so I reluctantly let him go. He had the indulgent smile of a parent who had got rid of a stubborn child. I was left fuming when the small boat carrying Prahastha and his two aides left for the fleet of ships dotting the distant horizon.

I was edgy and irritable throughout the evening. There was no feeling of accomplishment, no happiness at the thought that I had come this far in life. I wanted to change the world. I wanted to make it a better place to live. I was afraid that I had misplaced all those gilt-edged dreams somewhere along my journey from that hut on the edge of a cliff, to the palace of Trikota. To my horror, I started behaving like an ass. I shouted at my servants, threw hot water on the face of a poor woman servant who thought my parched throat needed it and fetched it without my orders, and I slapped a bodyguard who was not standing in his assigned posture. I was behaving like petulant two-year-old. No one dared complain, no one dared to come near. I knew that my behaviour was odd. I had no right to kick around people who had been willing to die for me a few hours before. But strangely enough, I enjoyed the role I played. *It was good to be a king. Even if it was just to kick people's butts.* The servants might even expect to get thrashed. It was natural and what Kubera used to do.

A servant came to my room and bowed before me. I saw that his knees were trembling and felt a sudden urge to see his head rolling on the ground. I had visions of severing his head with a graceful sweep of my sword and then kicking his head with my left foot, before it touched the ground. With great difficulty I restrained myself.

"Your Highness, Mayan seeks audience." The last thing I wanted was an audience with someone who made a living counting numbers and taking measurements with a stick. But before I could dismiss the servant, Mayan walked in with a sheepish grin. He looked like an owl, with a sheep in some remote ancestral line, but more like an owl than a sheep, I decided. The servant withdrew discretely. Mayan came and sat in a chair across from me. He looked around the hall with approval. At times, a frown creased his forehead when his eyes met some garishly designed ceiling carvings added by that idiot Kubera. He made a noise with his tongue and then shook his head disapprovingly. He started blabbering, "Actually Ravana, they should not have used lime on the ceiling. It fades to yellow with the salty sea breeze. If they were particular, they would have used coconut milk and honey while mixing the plaster. Ideally the slate found. . ."

I watched in astonishment, the old, bald man was chattering like a monkey about various technical details of architecture and engineering. And I noticed that he called me Ravana. The last thing I wanted was an unsolicited master to give me a crash course in engineering. I wanted to get up, hold his head down by the scruff of his neck and rub his nose on the ground. Instead, I asked with all the civility I could muster, " To what do I owe the pleasure of your visit?" I hoped my tone did not betray my emotions and that I had said the right thing to the venerable old professor and architect.

"I just walked by and thought I'd have a word with you." Five minutes passed and I stood there while the old man muttered to himself, jotting down certain things, punctuated by exclamations and cries of anguish or joy. I imagined all sorts of things happening to him, like the huge pillar falling on his head, like Vishnu with a mask of a lion jumping from his hiding place in the pillar; like Mayan falling and breaking his remaining two teeth. Then it struck me. He was supposed to be with my mother and sister and that rigid daughter of his, on the mainland. How had he reached here? More importantly, where were my mother and sister? Had they fallen prey to Varuna? If anything had happened to my mother, I would flay Varuna alive, negotiations and peace treaties notwithstanding, irrespective of our relative strengths and Prahastha's diplomacy and his intricate web of politicking.

"Shiva, Shiva, have you not told him yet, Mayan brother?" The knots in my stomach untangled as I heard my mother's voice. I was relieved to see her walking in with her aristocratic bearing. *'When was your mother an aristocrat, Ravana?'* I asked myself. The last time I saw her, she was a poor woman dressed in shabby rags. Now she was dressed in a pure white cotton dress. My sister beamed behind her. I also noticed the very stiff lady standing behind them, her gaze unwavering, meeting my eyes and not flinching. I had yet to attain the steely all-freezing gaze of a king. *'Keep practicing, Ravana,'* someone inside me mocked. She looked into my eyes as if assessing me. Mandodari – the engineer's daughter! Stiff as a rod, with straight-jacketed morals and thoughts, or that was what Soorpanakha told me, yet beautiful like a statue.

"What a gentleman, that Varuna. It was an absolutely delightful voyage," Mother said indifferently.

Mayan turned back and said, "Yes, yes, an absolutely fascinating ship. The workmanship was superb."

"Brother, the rickety boat uncle Jambumali arranged, nearly sank in the middle of the journey. It was Varuna's ship that rescued us. Oooooo. . .it was a fabulous ship." she cooed.

"So where is Jambumali? and why did you start before I could send someone to fetch you?"

"Jambumali is still on Varuna's ship. Varuna was quite happy that you have taken over Lanka. They say he is a pirate, but he is a man with exquisite manners and he asked me to convey his regards to you for a long and illustrious reign."

"Prahastha has gone to talk to him."

"I will leave politics to you men. Son, you are at a marriageable age now. Some might say you are the most eligible bachelor around. So how about getting married?"

"I don't think I am ready for it, mother, I have a country to rule. I have just started," I protested.

"So. . . I asked Mayan if he would be happy to give his daughter, Mandodari, in marriage to you."

I was flabbergasted. The last thing I wanted was to get married to a stiff rod. I looked at her and there was no coy smile, no shyness. She met my gaze with an intensity that shocked me. Her eyes were dark, sharp, with heavy eyelashes. She was beautiful in a stiff sort of way. There was a kind of haughtiness in her. It was as if her father had used a chisel and a measuring tape while making her.

"Fortunately he agreed, so I have asked the astrologers to fix the time for the auspicious occasion." When did you succumb to this purely Deva custom of asking astrologers for everything, mother? "I think we should give you some time to get acquainted with each other, so shall we elders move out into the garden?"

Saying this, she went out without meeting my eyes. My sister lingered with a sly smile on her lips. I wanted to run out, jump through the window and vanish. Mandodari, now what kind of a name was that? Mayan, you could have done better than that. There is no point in making engineering marvels if you do not know how to give a nice name to your daughter. She stood there without moving, her eyes boring into me. I felt naked. I was uneasy. *'Hey, isn't it the girl who is supposed to be nervous? Get a grip, Ravana, you are a King, albeit through a revolution of indigestion,'* I reminded myself.

"Mayan brother, I have something important to talk to you," my mother called out from the garden. "And you Soorpanakha, go and unpack your things. Hurry."

"Sure, sure, the garden layout is marvellous, but the watering systems need some modification. . ." I watched in horror as Mayan stumbled out mumbling something. My sister gave me another of her knowing smiles and vanished in a fluff of swirling clothes. '*Don't go away. Stay here old man, I like you, I love you. Wait and we shall discuss the intricacies of Gandharva architecture or a Vanara temple design. Stay and let us talk. What was that you were saying about the ceiling pattern? Don't go away; stay here and talk. . .*'

"This room has a nice view." she said. Like father like daughter.

"Yes." said I. After that she remained silent and I searched my mind for something to say, a single thing to say. '*So this is how your family life is going to be Ravana? She will stare at the wall and you will stare everywhere else like a dumb ass. Should I ask her about the things she has studied or should I ask her to sing a song? Does she play an instrument? What if she declines to talk or does not answer my questions? What if I break one of those intricate social customs by asking the wrong question?*' The room was getting increasingly stuffy and humid. This was the wrong way to get married; I was convinced of that by now.

"Well. . .er. . . I learned archery under Brahma and I love music. My hobby is to find a cure for children's ailments and. . ." I stammered and stuttered and stopped.

She turned, crossed her arms and looked at my eyes steadily. "My father told me you are going to be my husband and as I am an obedient daughter, I agreed. I know all the *Veda*s of the Devas, and I have studied Deva and Asura history. I have also studied engineering and architecture under my father. I write poetry and I paint. I love hunting and I am a sharp shooter."

No one asked whether I was ready to marry a walking encyclopaedia. She stopped and I waited to see whether there was anything more. She might know Chinese, might even know how to build ships but was being modest and not telling me everything. On the first night she might say, 'Surprise! I actually know how to recite the *Chandagyo Upanishad* backwards, but kept it a secret when we met in that nice room with a view. But now that we are so intimate, I feel we should have no secrets. As an obedient wife, I will also tell you that I feel the *Atharva Veda* has many tribal and Asura elements in it.'

I felt small, uncultured, unaccomplished. I knew I was a good warrior, but so were the 300 soldiers trained under Rudraka. I was trained under Brahma but I had rejected most of that formal education. I wanted the interview to end. I was worried about the treaty Prahastha was going to sign with that pirate and how we were going to cope after coughing up the princely ransom. Then I got a shock. Mandodari started singing. It was a melodious song, glorifying the rule of Mahabali, and she sung it very well. Her voice was rich and her rhythm perfect, rising and ebbing at the correct places. It was flawless but lacked soul. It was too perfect to have soul. There was no passion. Mandodari did not mean what she was singing, it was just an exercise, mechanical, emotionless, passionless, but perfectly rendered. No maestro could have faulted her singing but somewhere it jarred.

As suddenly as she had started, Mandodari stopped singing. An uneasy silence came up between us. I did not know what to do. Should I compliment her? Applaud her singing? Pat her back and feel the smooth texture of her skin? Or just smile? Maybe I should sing a song in return? I was confused and stood there miserably, waiting for someone to appear and rescue me. Earlier I had been irritated by all the idiots passing by my room and coming to talk to me. Now I desperately prayed for someone, even old man Mayan, to come and get me out of this.

"So you have got acquainted. Next Sunday is your marriage and I have sent messengers to invite those of our relatives who can be reached. The rest we will inform later." Mother had come into the room and the engineer was standing at the door and tut-tutting at the ornamental pillar near the window. My sister was at the doorway, beaming at her future sister-in-law.

"But moth--" I was cut short by the sudden noise of shuffling feet and the room went quiet. Prahastha entered with Jambumali and Maricha walked behind. I was annoyed at the sudden intrusion into what was essentially a private affair but was relieved at the same time. Seeing my mother, Prahastha bowed with folded hands and enquired about her health. Maricha went straight to my mother and with a twinkle in his eyes said, "So sister, the match-making is over, eh? And see, how he is blushing."

I wanted to strangle him. Prahastha stared straight at the ocean and Jambumali suddenly found it convenient to start a conversion with Mayan. Mandodari stood staring at me with an intensity that made me stutter. Kumbha and Vibhishna came running into the room and Kumbha hugged me, his two-day stubble scratching my face. He reeked of toddy.

"Hmm. . . if you don't mind, will you ladies please leave us poor men to tackle some important affairs of state?"

My sister went out with a pout, and my mother came and planted a kiss on my forehead before leaving the room. I turned red as I saw a smile twitching at the corners of Mandodari's mouth. Mayan lingered as if he wanted to stay and admire the architecture, but Maricha took the professor out of the room with a kindness which only he could show. We sat there, the silence building, and finally when I thought Prahastha might go mad and start singing raunchy songs, Maricha walked in, rolling his eyes and shaking his head.

"If your antics are over, Maricha, let's start doing some work," Maricha smiled at Prahastha's attempt to get even. "It was a tough bargain. The pirate is a tough negotiator. I know you are not going to like it but we need time to build our strength." Prahastha paused. I grew pale. I did not want to hear what the terms were. I was itching for war. But reason told me that foolhardy heroism would not take me anywhere. Many Asuras perished that way and now come to life only in country ballads.

"And what have you conceded?" I asked.

"Spare the accusatory tones for later. You are speaking to a Council and I was fully authorized by you to negotiate as I deemed fit."

"You wind bag! Have you forgotten there is no Council now? I am the King and you are my Prime Minister. If I ask you questions, you answer them without showing off your superior education." I was trembling with rage and had drawn my sword. Prahastha stood there cool and unflustered, an arm resting on the hilt of his sword. It was like he was baiting me, daring me to make a move.

"Please let's be civil with each other," Jambumali said. Maricha was staring at me, an ugly scowl crossing his otherwise, smiling face.

'Why do I say things like that to a man old enough to be my father?' I slowly put the sword back and sat down on my chair. *'Your throne, Ravana, your throne,'* I reminded myself.

Prahastha also sat down and when he spoke I noticed that he had lost that tint of righteousness which always irritated me. "Two lakh gold coins, 20,000 gold coins every third month, seven of our best ships, one third of our total pepper produce, one fifth of cardamom and cloves, and a quarter of our revenue from the customs we collect from our ports."

There was total silence in the room as Prahastha read the signed parchment. I heard Maricha swear under his breath and Kumbha shifted his legs uneasily.

"What do we get in return for these small favours?" I hoped my sarcasm would not provoke another reaction from the old nut. *'Only you react, Ravana, only you rave like a lunatic. Prahastha, he's an aristocrat.'* I clenched the armrests of my chair so hard that it would have hurt them.

"We are in no position, Your Highness, to demand anything." Prahastha continued in a dry, flat voice, "He offered us protection from all forces. He offered to police the seas to make it safe from pirates."

A derisive laughter followed this remark and even Prahastha smiled before continuing. "He will withdraw the siege as soon as he receives the two lakh gold coins. He has promised not to attack the city. The coins have to be delivered to the ships he chooses. His delegates will inspect our warehouses and granaries to assess the present produce and assist our accountants in computing the share."

Again an uneasy silence followed. Everyone computed the settlement in their minds. None of us was sure how much we would have to give. We had no idea how much the state treasury held, how much our warehouses and granaries had, what the tax collection was, the toll collection, or anything else. We warriors considered such things beneath our notice, best left to those inferior creatures called accountants. The room, with the exception of Jambumali, did not contain any experienced administrators. I did not know that ruling a country would be tougher than capturing it. I did not know why Prahastha agreed to all the terms without having any idea of what we possessed.

"You might wonder why I negotiated all this without actually knowing how much we have in the first place. It was tough. I assumed Varuna had spies in the government, who would have been regularly supplying information to him about our country's economy, even during Kubera's time. So I thought that Varuna would make us an offer which would be stiff but manageable. I negotiated from there." Prahastha looked up as he said that.

"So you assumed the pirate would be generous enough to give us an affordable settlement." Kumbha was baiting Prahastha.

"I think that was the best anyone could have done given the circumstances. Now let's start our work of appeasing the pirate," Jambumali intervened, before Prahastha could react, and I gave him a grateful look before I stood up and brought the meeting to a close.

Prahastha walked towards me with long, easy strides. "Ravana, should I arrange for your coronation? Would you like to combine it with your marriage?" he asked me in a whisper.

'And save some expenses in the process?' I managed to nod my head in assent.

"Your Highness, we will sit and study our position." he said loudly and the conversation stopped. "Perhaps you would like to retire if you feel tired, Your Highness."

"No, I will join you. Get the officials who are in charge of the treasuries." I said and saw Maricha smiling.

17 The silver-tongued

Bhadra

I was sitting near the kitchen, waiting for someone to come and take me to my master. The day passed, with people moving in clusters through the street, busily chattering with each other, discussing politics and their future. I wanted to go and join the crowd and gain information about the general mood of the man on the street. But I was afraid to move lest I miss the messenger who would surely come to take me to my master. My master was going to come himself to meet me. He would hold me close and thank me for all that had been done. I would say that it was all Shiva's doing. That I was but a small pawn in his game. I dreamt and dreamt but no one came. I sat there, sweat pouring down my face in two channels and soaking my chest. Yet I dared not move. My king had already forgotten me. I could not believe it. No, he was busy, he was waiting for his family members to disperse and then he would call me. But by evening I was not that sure. I was afraid to go and show my face. Who was I? A lowly creature, a small worm. I felt like spitting on myself.

There was no point in waiting. I felt betrayed. I had risked my life, had been tortured, and now I lay here forgotten, thrown out like a curry leaf after use. I tried to push the thought from my mind and walked without direction. I heard that Varuna's fleet had surrounded the island and there was going to be a war. So what? It did not concern me. Let the princes and warriors bother about it. What I wanted was a drink. Suddenly I remembered Mala. It was possible she would be sleeping with someone else now. If so, I was going to drag him out, kicking and screaming, and throw him out.

I lost my way in the labyrinth of streets and it was quite late by the time I found her house. I was quite drunk by that time, having stopped at three toddy shops en route. A mangy dog was sleeping on the doormat and I kicked it with all the viciousness and strength I could muster. It vanished into the night, howling with pain and cursing me in doggie language. I pounded the door and peppered it with a stream of abuse. By the time she opened the door, I had already reached her great, grandparents' habits in detail. Some heads had popped out from the neighbouring houses and I showered them with some choice vocabulary.

Mala opened the door and poured a pail of water over my head. The coolness of the water stunned me and she dragged me inside by my waist cloth, dripping wet. By the time we reached her bed, I was crying like a baby and she was cooing meaningless words. I slept with my head buried in the cleavage of her heaving bosom, with her fingers tracing paths through my hair and her heartbeat in rhythm with my snoring. Later, when the palace bells tolled twice in the early morning, I woke and reached for her. I slept again, fulfilled. I woke much later with a hangover. The street was busy with vendors shouting, pushcarts zig-zagged between pedestrians and bullock carts. Through the open window, the smell of sweets from a nearby shop rushed in and I vomited. I watched the puddle forming designs on the expensive silk sheets of Mala's bed. Then she came, cursing me, with a pail, a wooden mug and a coir brush. A million needles exploded in my head.

I slept the whole day, except for a few minutes when I was force fed some gruel. About midnight I woke to find Mala lying beside me nude, sleeping like a baby. I caressed her and slowly succeeded in arousing her. Then, with a sudden force which made her cry out, I entered her. Images flooded my mind. Scenes of torture by Vikrama mixed with the roaring sound of the waterfall of the Poorna, the taste of blood in my mouth, the eyes of Ravana, that thankless bastard, all mixed to form a collage which was frightening and fascinating at the same time. To my shame I found that my organ had shrunk and was lying limp like a decaying old banana. Mala sat up and looked at me with open contempt, pity and horror. I tried entering her again, but she shoved me away and stood up. I felt ashamed of my nudity, my impotence, and ran out of the room covering my groin.

Somewhere on the outskirts of the city, a lone jackal howled a painful cry and I felt like joining him. You impotent, good-for-nothing bastard. Bhadra, you fool! You wanted to dine with kings and change history; you wanted to give up your life for your race; for the life you irrevocably lost on the banks of the Poorna. This is what is left of you, forgotten and cast away.

"Get inside." Her voice was soothing as her fingers ran through my hair. I stood up slowly, unashamed of my nakedness, not caring if anyone else saw me and walked like an obedient puppy into her home.

Three days after I entered her life again like a lost dog found, she suggested we go to the local vegetable market. We walked towards the sea, towards the smell of fish, rotting vegetables, cow dung, sweets and snacks frying in oil. The setting sun coloured her smooth cheeks a bright orange and her eyes laughed when she spoke. A small drop of sweat swayed precariously on the tip of her nose. I wanted to lick it then and there. My eyes wandered and touched her eyes, brow, tresses, small straight nose, full kissable lips, the cleavage between her round breasts and further down, her exposed navel. I locked my hand with hers and looked into her smiling eyes and at that moment I knew that I had fallen in love.

I stood behind her, holding the basket while she haggled with the hawkers. Lost in my daydreams, I did not register the implication of the arguments and opinions of the people in the market. As we walked back, the happy and easy romantic mood vanished as she grumbled about the prices. I felt irritated and snapped at her to keep quiet. She reacted with surprising ferocity and began cursing me and every man in the world, "Politics, politics, why can't you men stop ruining our lives with petty politicking and fights? It costs twelve sovereigns for a dozen bananas. He has fleeced us but says it'll go up again. The new king has imposed further taxes and additional tolls on the highway which adds to the cost. Damn politicians, damn the king."

"Hush Mala, you cannot speak about the king like that. If someone hears, we could get reported." A few heads turned and stared at us. I was not amused and was afraid. I did not want to be reported for treason.

"You keep your mouth shut. I do not care for any king. They all are the same. What is so fancy about the new one? Deva, Asura, Gandharva, half castes, they are all the same. They only worry about how to glue their fat asses to the throne and screw the people. They talk big, like the emancipation of the Asuras, getting even with the Devas, preservation of culture, and all that humbug. But finally it boils down to the same thing. Screw the people, enjoy a luxurious life in the palace and cling to power."

"What do you understand, Mala? Don't you know there is a siege?"

"What siege? Why can't your King put Varuna in his place? He is a coward, your Ravana. He got his kingdom because someone poisoned Kubera's soldiers. Spineless cowards – that's what your people are. He is not ready to wage a war with a bloody pirate and he claims to be the saviour of the Asuras. Shiva help the Asuras if Ravana is an example of the kind of hero the Asura race can expect to produce today. King indeed! He's just a spineless rascal."

The intensity of her frustration and disillusionment was unsettling. I winced at her reference to the poisoning. I did not know it would create such a big slur on Ravana's victory, but I was sure I would have done the same thing even if I had known. What use would it have been if Ravana had bravely fought Kubera and died valiantly? Between glorious martyrdom and deceitful victory, I would always choose the second. Too many Asuras had become brave martyrs and the addition or deletion of a Bhadra to their ranks would not make the slightest difference. I had a grudging admiration for the Vishnu clan, that devious clan which had produced many great Deva generals. They had raised deceit to the heights of the divine.

We walked home in an uneasy silence. I was surprised that I had thought of her house as our home. Sometime earlier I had realized that my attraction towards her was not merely physical. Nor was I sure how she felt. Perhaps, I was just one among the scores of lovers who frequented her house. I was jealous. I wanted her completely. She was a whore but that did not bother me. I was beyond such moral shackles. I was sure I was broad-minded enough to ignore such small details.

As we turned the corner, I saw an affluent man caressing the manes of his horse in the courtyard of her house. As we approached, he turned towards us and smiled. I saw Mala's face light up and in a trice she handed me the basket she was carrying and ran into the waiting man's embrace with a yelp of joy. I stood there in the growing darkness, too stunned to move, as the couple smooched without any shame. I was still standing there with my hands full of vegetables, when they walked into their nest and closed the door. I saw the horse jeering at me. I was angry as I had never been in my life. I wanted to kick open the door and drag the man out of our home, with his head banging on the steps. I wanted to thrash Mala black and blue for behaving so shamelessly in front of me.

As emptiness filled me, I thought how foolish I must look, standing in the middle of a street, in front of a whore house, with both hands full of vegetables. I felt a wave of self-pity wash over me and anger and frustration at the unfairness of life. I imagined the horse watching me again, his jaws systematically chewing the grass with an expression of disdain. I walked towards him and emptied the vegetables in front of him. I watched with satisfaction as he started munching them with evident pleasure. I felt small and mean, foolish and ridiculous as I played out my frustrations as the spurned lover.

I walked towards the market. The curfew had been lifted and there were no restrictions like those imposed during Kubera's time. Anyone could walk freely. As I neared the market, I suddenly felt I needed a drink. I wanted to get drunk, but not because I had lost my lover. She had never been a lover in the first place, just a whore. I passed many people in various stages of inebriation. It was funny to think that each drunkard who passed me had once had Mala, the celebrated whore of Lanka, the great Asura slut – I spat on a wall. I imagined what Mala would be doing now with her lover in bed, my bed. I badly needed a drink so I entered the inn on the street corner and walked right into the middle of a fight. A tough-looking man was sitting at the counter, chewing pan and watching the fun with an impassive face. He might have been used to drunken tiffs. I approached him shyly and he raised an eyebrow in response. I searched in my purse and discovered some copper coins. I could not remember where the coins had come from, perhaps they were my pay from Kubera's kitchen.

"What are they fighting about?" I asked but did not expect an answer.

"Politics. They do not have anything better to do than fight about it, lazy idiots. What will you have, palm or wine?"

"Er...actually what I want is a job." I had not intended to ask that question and my thoughts until that moment were only on getting a drink. Before he could reply, I hastily added, "I am Bhadra, and I used to work in Kubera's kitchens, they say I am a good cook."

"Your fancy preparations will be useless here. If you can cook up simple dishes like fish curries or chicken fries, you can expect a temporary position. By the way, I am Ilango, and my family has been running this inn since Mahabali's time, when this God forsaken island was a colony of the Emperor."

So I joined Ilango's inn and soon found it was a hot bed for political discussions which usually ended in a bloody fight. The proprietor never took part in any discussions but gave tacit encouragement by not barring anyone from talking politics. The sly Ilango had decided that these discussions were actually good for his business and he quietly added the expense of repairing or replacing any broken furniture, to the bill of the customers responsible for the mess. Between serving and cooking, I listened to various customers debating heatedly about the affairs of state. This was the voice of the common Asura people, who were incapable of changing things, but who were forced to bear whatever burden the ruling class dumped on their backs. The crowd visiting Ilango were ordinary folk with significantly little education or money. I suspected that the upper middle class of merchants or government officers, considered the present regime boorish. The poor and lower middle class seemed to hope that Ravana would bring about change for the better. Many identified with the poor boy who had risen from poverty. They were sure he would not just concentrate on trade and traders as Kubera had done, but dole out goodies to the poor as well. Many of the older men remained skeptical as they seen many regimes and palace coups. They claimed that things would get worse. Usually, there were several fights between the pro-Ravana men and the pro-Kubera gang. But there was eager anticipation regarding the new government's policies.

I was fascinated by the discussions and wished that an optimistic view would prevail, but knowing Ravana better than all these people, the future didn't seem so bright. The pangs of love I still had for Mala and the frustration I felt because of her blatant betrayal, added to my already miserable view of life. I wished to return to my past and live a simple life on the banks of the river Poorna, tending my cows, farming my small piece of land, loving and fighting with my sweet fat wife, playing with my daughter and walking with my friends to the toddy shop or dancing at the temple festival. I missed all that I had known. But I missed Mala the most and kept an eye on her house. It enraged me that the tall, handsome man frequented it often. Once I tried to follow him but he lost me somehow. I wandered through the labyrinths of the bazaar and was late getting to work. I got a mouthful from Ilango and lost half a day's pay in the process. The man was an enigma. He looked confident and strong; he had the stride of a warrior; and easily appeared and disappeared at will; but to my eyes, he appeared to be constantly on guard as if he had something to hide. I had decided he was the villain of my story and vowed I would find him and do the needful.

Slowly but perceptibly, public opinion changed. I could feel the tension in the streets; in the inn and in the way people walked. Jambumali, the new minister of finance and trade, had imposed fresh taxes. He sent messengers to all the trade guilds and shops and even addressed a joint meeting of the guilds to explain the dire necessity of increasing tax percentages. Everyone was implored to bear with the government. They were assured the taxes would be withdrawn once Varuna was paid off. No one believed him.

Soon Jambumali became the most hated person in the whole of Lanka. The road toll was increased three-fold and farmers were brought into the tax net. The salaries of the armed forces were cut by half and many government servants were literally thrown out of office. Prices soared sky high. Because of the trade embargo, trade came to a standstill. It was rumoured that Prahastha had sold Lanka to the pirate Varuna. The regime became the most hated in the long history of the island. But only a few hated Ravana. He was the innocent, romantic, young man who had established an Asura kingdom, but was in the grip of a vicious coterie. Three months passed in a state of tension. There were small riots in various part of the city and in one instance, a mob lynched a tax collector to death. The Government reacted swiftly and brutally. The army, under the personal leadership of General Rudraka, swept the residents off a street, most of whom were innocent bystanders, and dragged them into the torture chambers. Rudraka became the image of fear. He rode his black horse, surrounded by heavily armed bodyguards, and imposed a reign of terror.

The business at the inn also fell and I had a lot of free time. Once I visited Mala but found her house locked. I was told she had vanished a few days ago. I felt sad and relieved at the same time. And there ended a chapter in my life, I thought despondently. To add to the woes, the retreating monsoon failed. The harvest was poor and people from the neighbouring villages thronged the temples of the capital, where free food had been provided since time immemorial. But there were no longer any patrons and many temples fell into disrepair. The king had announced that his marriage with chief engineer Mayan's daughter, had to be postponed to avoid hardship to the people. Except for a few derisive laughs, it did not draw any positive response from the populace. What the king did was his private affair, as long as he did not spend any public money, or so it was said in the Asura's unwritten code of governance. Like so many codes and laws, this too was meant to be violated.

By the end of the winter, a trivial incident sparked large scale rioting in the city. No one would have thought that Mayan, the unassuming bumbling professor, now chief engineer of the regime, would be the reason for rioting. But the professor touched a raw nerve in the highly-strung, tense and starving populace, when he chose to show his engineering skills. It was a clear winter morning when I was surprised from my sleep by a hullabaloo in the street. I struggled from my cot when the uproar became unbearable. There was a strange whining noise outside. Sleepy and irritated, my long-drawn yawn was cut off in the middle by the sight of Mayan inside a *vimana*, a flying machine. He was doing sorties in the sky and was quietly enjoying it, quite oblivious to the rage he was generating below. The huge crowd was shouting at him in awe and horror.

It was *Pushpaka,* the famed flying machine made by the old Mayan, the present one's grandfather. I had only heard about the existence of a prototype developed by Kubera, with the help of some earlier Mayan, but his untimely death in a horse race, led the millionaire merchant-king to shelve the project. Kubera had spent a fortune trying to develop something like this but he could never get the thing to fly. As I watched in astonishment, the *Pushpaka* made a graceful turn and vanished towards the palace. Then the murmurs started. People started saying all sorts of things. It was then I saw him – Mala's lover. He was standing on top of a wall, shouting something. I wanted to hear what he was saying so I wove my way through the crowd. The noise subsided slowly, except for occasional murmurs and whispers and some hissing. There was an air of expectation. Then my rival exploded in fury.

"*This is absolute nonsense my dear brothers! Do we deserve this? While we starve, your King rolls in luxury…*" The crowd roared in approval. "*Ravana is your nemesis, do we need such a ruler?*"

"No! No! No!" I found myself joining the chorus.

"*While your children starve, the jokers inside the palace choose to fly.*" He stopped and looked around, waiting for silence. "*He defies the Gods. Not even the Gods fly and the king doles out money to mad scientists to make flying machines.*" The crowd booed. "*When your children die of hunger, when your fields are littered with the corpses of your kin, when your cattle die of thirst, your ruler will fly above the waste you have become and take an aerial view. Why?*"

"Why? Why?" a thousand voices echoed his question.

"*Because he is afraid of you. He is afraid to come down and mix with you common folk. Shame on Ravana*!" he roared with a powerful punch to his own chest.

"Shame! Shame!" the mob echoed and did the same.

"*He says it's because of Varuna that your life is miserable. Who is this Varuna and what right has he over the people of Lanka? He is a pirate. It is your misfortune, nay, your weakness, that you have a coward like Ravana as your King.*"

There was movement at the rear of the mob and I jumped up and down to see what was going on. It was a small scuffle but nothing of importance and I turned back to the speaker. "Did we invite Ravana here? Did we ask him to come and rule us?"

"No! No! No!" the crowd roared.

"The old king was a rogue but he was a brave rogue."

"Hear! Hear!"

"He kept pirates at bay. He robbed you, but he robbed with a conscience. He bent you but did not break you. After all his luxuries, he left something for you to eat. This coward Ravana, earned a kingdom through deceit, then he imposed his devilish rule upon you. He will rob the milk from a baby's mouth. He will drink your blood. He will sell your wives if he thinks that will subsidise his luxurious lifestyle. He is weak, cruel and above all, a coward."

I was mesmerized by his oratory skills. He was perfect, his voice rising and falling with perfect timing, his gestures powerful, and I could sense the crowd swaying with emotion.

"Arise my fellow countrymen of Lanka. We Asuras do not want cruel weaklings as our rulers. Let us remove this imposter and dump his coterie into the sea. Then we will fight Varuna and teach him his place. Let us march to the palace and drag this demon from his throne. Let us mar--" There was a sudden silence and I saw him fall forward slowly. His chest became crimson and it was then I saw the blunt end of an arrow jutting from his clutch after he had removed it from his chest. As the crowd watched in horror, horsemen entered from all sides and started hacking the crowd. There was a widespread pandemonium. I saw Rudraka at full gallop, his black horse trampling everyone in his way towards the fallen orator. I wanted to run from danger but was drawn towards the centre of the drama. I wanted to see the end of my rival and ran, ignoring the pain as many running in the opposite direction collided with me. By the time I neared the wall, my feet had been stamped on many times. I saw Rudraka was trembling with rage and frustration. There was no bleeding man lying prone. Rudraka hit a soldier

with the hilt of his sword in frustration. Ignoring the blood which sprayed from the wounded soldier, Rudraka barked instructions to his other men to find the rebel. He could not have gone far. I was disappointed. I fervently prayed that the arrow had done its job and the man would die in a few hours. But I knew I could not count on it. I was never lucky in my life. Then I saw flames rising in different parts of the city. Lanka was burning. And it would not be the first time the island city would burn.

18 Brother's brother

Ravana

"There are reports of riots in the eastern side of the city and some rogues have burned the artisans' village and hacked the chief artisan to death. Many lives have been lost. Rudraka has managed to curb the riots in the northern and western sides, but the riots have spread to outlying villages as well. Temples have been torched, granaries looted, women raped. The situation is grim in the central district. The tribes of the southern forests have joined the looting and have committed widespread arson in the southern parts of the city.

Rebels hold sway in the south and Vidyutjihva has proclaimed himself king. He has started collecting a major part of the farm tax. Sumali and Malyavan have rushed to the south to curb the rebellion and if possible, capture Vidyutjihva. We have also dispatched search parties to find the whereabouts of the missing prostitute, Mala. We are awaiting confirmation to see if the man who visited Mala, was the same spy Bhadra, who escaped from us earlier. Rudraka is sure that he sighted Bhadra during the commotion, but he vanished. It appears that Vidyutjihva, Mala and Bhadra are conspirators in a well-rehearsed scheme to topple the government. Permission is sought from the King to impose strict and ruthless measures to curb the rebellion. Orders may be issued to the army to proceed to the southern forests and take back the territory lost to the rebels."

Prahastha stopped reading and stared at me as if expecting a ready solution. He looked as if he was almost happy at the turn of the events.

Maricha, Jambumali and I sat in silence. A decision had to be taken. I did not want to use excessive force in curbing the rebellion. I wasn't even sure if it was as serious as Prahastha made it out to be. I was hurt that my own people had taken up arms against me. Why did these idiots not understand that governance is not simple? That the government needed taxes to run the State. Was I not supposed to be the saviour of the Asuras? Unless they allowed me to do so, how could I consolidate the kingdom and recover the lost Asura pride? My people spent more time fighting each other than the common enemy. These nitwits could handle change. I wanted to run a model state and build a kingdom where everyone was prosperous, a strong Asura state which could take on the Devas. I want to drive the Devas out of India, and do many great things for my people. And these thankless rabble go and rebel. The stupidity of the people was astounding. Didn't they know that the present difficulties they were facing was for a brighter future? Why did they not comprehend that I had to buy time to garner enough strength to take on Varuna? Why did they not remain patient and give me some time?

"Crush the rebellion with force. No traitor shall be spared." I looked away towards the sea as I pronounced damnation on my own people. '*For the greater good, of my people,*' I consoled myself. Then it started, the bloody voice inside me. '*But then, that is what every tyrant in history has told himself. Ravana, I know you are a fool, but you still surprise me. So, for greater good, you will do some lesser good, like chopping off a few heads, splitting some families, and endorsing wholesale slaughter. Bravo! You have become a real ruler.*' How I want to squeeze the breath out of the mocker within me.

"I want full authorization to curb the rebellion, your written approval with the royal seal on the order. And I do not want to answer any silly questions of the Council during the operation. I shall submit a report after I have finished the job." Prahastha's demeanour was irritating to say the least. I was getting tired of the whole exercise. It was as if the Council did not believe I would stick to my decision. It was frustrating, more so because I was afraid they were right.

"You will have whatever you want." I prayed this meeting would end. Prahastha made me an elaborate bow. There was a smile playing about the corners of his mouth. One by one everyone left the room. I felt lonely, very lonely. '*You were born lonely, Ravana, and you will live and die so.*' I could see smoke curling towards the distant, bleak, grey sky. There could be lives burning there. My sense of fairness and righteousness that I believed I possessed, were going up in smoke all around me and my palace. I know it was too early in my career as king to feel a sense of loss. I had a long way to go, many more people to torture, lives to ruin, more justification to give myself, and more terrible things to do. It was too early to play the suffering hero in the grip of remorse. Was a vacancy for shipping clerk in any of Varuna's ships still available?

"Ravana, I want to talk to you about something important."

"Yes mother, what is it?" I was irritated and did not want to be disturbed but at the same time I was relieved that I had someone to talk to.

"I want to talk to Mayan."

"So talk, why you are asking my permission?"

"Stop playing the fool, you are the King of Lanka now."

"Thank you mother, for reminding me, I keep forgetting."

"You do not like Mandodari?"

"Does it really matter?"

"Perhaps not to you, but it may matter to her."

"Then ask her."

"I'm fixing the marriage this fortnight. If you want any special friends, you should invite them."

"Do kings have friends?"

"You are the first King I know, so I don't know the answer to that."

I glared at her and then stared outside. I could hear her walking out swiftly. I should have been elated over the match or perhaps wary about it. But there was no emotion. My mind was blank. Darkness had engulfed the city which stared at me with a hundred eyes. Slowly, a sense of inadequacy swept through me. I had no control over things happening around me. Not long ago I had thought of controlling my destiny, even holding the destiny of others in my hands. Now I had been left in the grip of a thankless kingdom which wanted to crush me. A cold salty breeze from the sea blew past and made the small lamp in the room flicker and die out. I could hear the waves breaking against the shore. The fog over the sea slowly lifted. The lights in the distance looked as if they were dancing, Varuna's ships perhaps. A plan formed in my head. I wanted action. I could not sit and let others plan my life. I turned away from the window and. . .

"Who is that?" I drew my sword drawn from its sheath. A small figure stood silhouetted against the grey light of the door frame. It moved into darkness with a rapidity that threw me off as my eye struggled to adjust to the light. I jumped into the corner, waving my sword around. With my back to the wall, I had to guard only the front. I didn't have to worry about a back thrust.

"Your Highness, it's me."

"Who are you?"

Silence.... If it was a foe, he would not have spoken and given away his position. I relaxed, but only a bit. "I won't hurt you. Come into the light." I told him as I heard the shuffling of feet. Then as I watched the door frame, where I expected him to appear, a firm hand gripped my wrist and whispered in my ear, "Forgive me your highness. . ." The voice continued as he blocked my kick aimed at his groin, "I'm not your enemy but your servant, believe me."

I relaxed a bit. I could have shaken him off and delivered a punch to his nose which would have left him unconscious. But something in his voice made me trust him. Perhaps, if Prahastha was here, he would have told me that a king should never trust anyone, not even himself. My sword flew from my hand and hit the wall with a clank and dropped to the floor. I was surprised by the sudden kick which had knocked the sword from my hand. Blasted Prahastha – I think he was right as usual. But the hand which held my wrist had gone and I stood with my nerves taut. My body assumed a combat posture and the lessons learnt in Mahabali's forests, were sending signals through my nerves. I heard my sword moving and aimed a kick in that direction. Pain waves shot from my toes as they made contact with the walls. But I was back in combat position in a trice, ignoring the pain. Then I saw him in the flickering light of the corridor. The face was oddly familiar, like that of a snake – a hooded cobra, ready to strike.

"Bhadra. . ."

"At your service, Your Highness."

"How dare you?!"

"Forgive me your Highness but please hear me out."

I stood there, contemplating what to do.

If I had killed him then, history would have been different. Ah history. . . it would always be different for different people and take its own course. Perhaps nothing matters one day. On this battlefield where I lie bleeding to death, I assume I have created a great chapter in history; lived a hero's life; and died a villain's death; or vice versa. But I might have been only having illusions of grandeur.

This war with a small prince, Rama, and his monkey men, which devastated my life and laid waste to all the things I had achieved, could be too insignificant in the history of mankind. When did I start bothering about history? History starts with me and ends with me. Perhaps the jackal eating my limbs might be surprised to know that he is swallowing a part of history. How does it matter? How does anything a poor man like me, who played Emperor and buffoon intermittently and sometimes together, did or had forgotten to do, matter in this indifferent, cruel world, which has existed before and shall exist long after I end, dissolved in the earth.

But, I was too young to know then as I am too old to care now. So I heard him out. I heard as he took me through the dark lanes of his past and the tangled by-lanes of his present. When he wept, I became indifferent. When he accused me of disowning him after I had conquered Lanka, I was really surprised. Was it not my own plan which had succeeded? What had this man to do with any of it? But I felt some sympathy for him, like I felt for a puppy which was run over by my step-brother's chariot and kept howling through the night. I could keep this man as a puppy dog, just to spite Prahastha. The thought was pleasurable. I smiled and that idiot Bhadra thought I had relented at last. He fell at my feet and started kissing them. I was aghast. Why would a man demean himself so? I tried to pull my feet back but then it was strangely pleasurable. I felt a twinge of happiness within. But suddenly, guilt washed away that tiny bit of pleasure and I shook him. I felt contempt for him and myself.

"You are my personal servant. Not a royal aide or anything fancy, just a plain, personal servant. You will do what I bid."

"I will serve you like a dog, Your Highness."

Something inside me snapped. Did he read my thoughts? Could he have felt the contempt brimming inside me? My puppy, my plaything, Bhadra. I felt small in my own estimation. No, I would treat him as a friend, as an equal, well not exactly equal, but almost. A slave with equal rights as his master? I would die laughing. 'But Ravana, look at his face, look at those frail arms and pot belly, is he your equal? Bhadra is the scum of the earth, the lowliest of the creatures you are destined to rule.' No, he is the representation of my poor Asura race. He is my bridge to the common man. He will bring me the views of my people and I will rule with, well, justice and prosperity for all.

"You may go now." He elaborately bowed and slowly left the room.

What I needed was action. I went over the plans I had left halfway. I chewed over the details and somewhere in-between, I fell asleep. I woke to see dawn breaking over the hills. But I did not want to get up from my bed to another weary day. Another day in which accounts of death and arson would be presented by pompous clerks, a new day where I would see the people I had vowed to protect, killing each other and praying for my death. Another day in which I would learn some more irritating administrative lessons from the likes of Prahastha. A day in which I would be pestered by my mother to marry that, what was her name – the daughter of the nutty scientist – Mandodari or something.

A lone soldier paced at the palace gates. How I envied him. He just had to walk to and fro until noon and then go home, eat his lunch, sleep or possibly make love to his wife or mistress, get drunk in the evening and then go to sleep like a hog. Life was simple and sweet. But perhaps it was not that simple. He could have an unfaithful wife, a drunkard for a son, even a nagging mother, and a sick father, to take care of. But I loved the sensation of being jealous, so I preferred the first version of his story. I wanted to call the watchman and give him an impossible task. Just to wreck his life. Perhaps the power that kingship brings, is just that, the ability to wreck other people's lives. That was its only pleasure.

"Your marriage is fixed for tomorrow." I was startled from my joyful reverie about wrecking the watchman's life. It took a few seconds to recognize my mother.

"Why not today mother?"

"You are dripping sarcasm. You have never spoken to me like that. This kingship has gone to your head. It was I. . ."

". . .who struggled to raise us, who went hungry to feed us, who went na-- no a son should not say that, but, hmm, will it be okay if I say deprived of good quality clothing, to clothe us. . ."

"Enough. Your majesty, you are forgetting a poor mother. . ."

". . .who carried me nine months in the womb and delivered me through pain..." She stood there sobbing. I was shocked that I had spoken to her like that in the first place, without any provocation. I took her face in my hands and she looked at me, challenging me with those burning black eyes to defy her love. "Please make the arrangements for the marriage mother.

The burden of the kingdom is now getting too heavy for your poor son to carry and I was not myself when I spoke to you."

"You have just started son, and I hope you will not become worse than this. Tomorrow evening, as I said. Good day son." She walked out with unfaltering steps and before remorse and shame could strike me in waves, I called for Maricha. He was too old to fight in the street and so he was the only senior officer available in the palace. Besides, he was the one I loved and respected. He never thrust his opinions on one, unlike the know-everything Prahastha.

"You called me, Your Highness?" As I waved him to sit, he sat down directly in front of me.

"Uncle, call me Ravana, at least in private."

"Okay. Kumbha has returned. "

"Let's call him."

"Before that, I want to say something important, Ravana. Your brother is not who you think he is."

"What is wrong with Kumbha? Or are you taking about Vibhishana, the pious one?" I asked, feeling affectionate about my youngest brother.

"I will talk about Vibhishana some other day. The oaf is a matter of immediate concern." I laughed at his reference about Kumbakarna. "It's no laughing matter, Ravana. He has picked up bad habits. He has a weakness for girls, we all know. As long as he is discreet, it should not worry us. He visits taverns and drinks country liquor like an elephant and he never bothers to pay."

"The boy is just having some fun. Send someone to clear the debts and charge it to my personal account. I mean, whatever is left from the account which we collected before launching the attack on Lanka. I do not want my brother's drinking habits to be subsidized by the State."

"It is not only that, Ravana. He has taken to drugs. He has a group of friends who make things out of *bhang*. They also process jellies from the *Soma* plant. I think Kumba was enticed by them. . .I sent two of my best officers to track what Kumbha was up to. They have confirmed what I had suspected for the past few days. Ravana, most of the time the idiot is knocked out."

"He makes friends fast." But then, Kumbha had always been a friendly soul, rather like a big dog waiting to be petted.

"I don't know whether they can be called friends. They are using the oaf. And the idiot doesn't know it."

"So what do you want me to do, Uncle?"

"Give him some official post. Give him something to do."

"I don't want to be accused of nepotism."

"Don't speak nonsense, Ravana. Most of the people holding official posts are your relatives, like Prahastha and me."

"That is different. You have long, administrative experience and have ruled kingdoms once. Kumbha and Vibhi are just children."

"And you want them to remain just that? Don't you want them to grow up? Ravana, are you saving the posts for your children? Are you afraid that your brothers will be a challenge to your dynasty?"

"Now you don't speak nonsense. You know I'm not like that. I'm not interested in ruling forever. I have ideals and principals. . ."

"The throne you are sitting on has a way of twisting the principals to suit the occupant, my son."

"Why is everyone accusing me of becoming corrupted by power? What power do I have? Just because I have a city to rule, and half of them want me dead, it does not mean I have to prove I'm not the ignoble Asura despot they want me to be." '*But why I should share the power with idiots like my brothers*?'

"If you are sure you are not and will not be corrupted by power. . ."

"Stop talking like Prahastha. I called you to discuss a plan I want your opinion on and I want Kumbha also to be with me. Bhadra. . ." The speed with which Bhadra appeared surprised me. Was he listening outside? How far could I trust him? "Go and fetch. . .er. . .Prince. . .Kumbhakarna."

"Why are you taking such creatures into your personal staff?"

I laughed at Maricha's scornful tone as Bhadra ran out. "A king has his own reasons."

"Your personal spy, eh?"

"Why not? He is ordinary, can merge into any crowd. And he is ruthless to the point of sadistic cruelty. He seems to have suffered much and has nothing to lose."

Maricha suddenly asked, "Hey, he was supposed to be the traitor who had started it all, isn't it?" But before I could answer, Kumbha entered. He was looking drunk.

"Kumbha, you look a little forlorn. What's wrong with you, son?"

"Why do you ask that? I'm not the king and don't have to please anyone."

"If you want to sit here and play the neglected, poor, younger, brother of the rich, cruel king, do it as long as it pleases you. Uncle, let's go out and have a stroll in the garden and leave this melodramatic idiot."

"No, no, Ravana, I was just joking. This uncle of ours would have sung many songs about my debaucheries to you. Just a little fun, that's all, my brother. What's your plan?"

I told them my plan. There was total silence.

"But tomorrow is your marriage. It will be risky." I looked at Maricha's deepening frown and for the first time felt apprehensive about the sanity of the plan.

"I just love it. It's brilliant." Kumbha pranced around the room.

"How many would you need?"

"Just the four of us, Uncle, you, Kumbha, me and Bhadra. . . and perhaps a dozen good swimmers."

"It's just too risky." Maricha said shaking his head, "And how far we can trust Bhadra."

"We have to take the chance."

"But why do you want to? Do you want to prove something to us? We know you are brave, but I would prefer a living coward than a brave dead fool as the Asura king."

"He's trying to prove that he is every bit a warrior. When we won the kingdom, I never thought life would be so dull. I too am longing for action. Let's not waste time. Tomorrow is a good day." Kumbha was itching to leave.

"Are you leaving?"

"Why, are you afraid that I'll go and get drunk and tell everyone about it?"

"Stop it, you two. Let us sleep over it today."

Maricha left before Kumbha and I felt a tinge of anxiety mixed with frustration. Kumbha was my dearest friend, much more than a brother. Now every time I spoke to him, I had to think if I was hurting his already fragile ego. "I'm sorry, brother. . ." But he had left before I could tell him anything.

19 Pirate troubles

Ravana

Later that afternoon, Rudraka came to report he has arrested over 3,000 rebels and had ordered the destruction of most of the southern tribal villages. The situation in the east remained tense.

"How many were killed?" I wanted him to say, *"Just a few."*

"About 800 of our soldiers."

"And you call that a law and order problem? It's a bloody war out there. Will removing Jambumali solve the issue?"

"Maybe, but I'm no politician to comment on it, Your Highness." It was amusing to see him struggle to say the last part. I was sure he considered himself better qualified to be king of Lanka. And maybe he was right. "Actually, it seems you did not understand my question properly. When I asked how many were killed, I did not want the count of only our soldiers."

Silence.

"I hear that more than 10,000 have died."

"Maybe."

I exploded. "*What do you mean*? You're supposed to be the army chief and what I get as a reply is a pathetic 'maybe'. Who ordered you to massacre women and children? And old men and women?"

"Did that scum, Bhadra, feed you these opinions? *Your Highness*."

"*Don't you dare talk to me like that*! I choose my company. What I want to know is who gave you orders to butcher civilians?"

Silence.

"Answer me."

He stood there and said, "I believe it was authorized by the Council."

"*Council*? *What Council*? This is no Asura *panchayat* and I am no petty *sarpanch*. I'm the King and I give orders. I take responsibility for any fiasco. Now you have gone and wiped out a couple of districts with your sword, and it is I who feel the anger of my subjects. *Now answer me, who ordered this genocide*?"

"If you want me to resign, Your Highness, I shall." A small smile twitched at the corners of his mouth.

That threw me off. I didn't want him to resign. He was doing a fine job. But his ruthlessness was worrying me. I just wanted him to go a bit easy and curb the rebellion in a civilized fashion. I could have ordered his immediate arrest and risked a rebellion among the soldiers. I closed my eyes in an effort to calm down. "See here Rudraka, it hurts me to think I'm responsible for the murder of innocent people. It's not that I'm afraid of battle. But this is just monstrous. Do we need to go on like this?"

He wore an amused look on his face. I was losing this battle too. I tried to put on a brave face, but I was sure he saw through it.

"Your Highness, I was made to believe that you had given written orders to Prime Minister Prahastha, to do everything to curb the rebellion. Do you think I enjoy killing babies?"

I looked out the window and saw Varuna's fleet blobbing up and down in the sea. The sails were drawn and the sea breeze occasionally carried odd notes of merriment to the palace. I closed my eyes. I was too tired to think about anything. I was beginning to think this confrontation with Rudraka was quite unnecessary. Had I exposed myself? My doubts, my indecisiveness, my weakness? What was I afraid of? That my men thought me a coward who stole a kingdom from my half-brother and then used my soldiers to perpetuate mass murder on my subjects? Perhaps everything would change tomorrow. I dismissed Rudraka with a wave of my hand. The same arrogant flick of the hand that my brother Kubera used when he sat on the same throne. *'Ravana, you are a fast learner.'* I knew I was getting arrogant but it was an enjoyable sensation.

Bhadra updated me on the happenings in the city every four hours. I took a stroll in the palace gardens and saw Mandodari under a large Banyan tree. I was rather embarrassed and she stared at me for a few seconds. I stammered and coughed and cursed myself for taking this path. I was thankful when she did not start a conversation with me and I quickly walked past. I saw my sister smiling at me but ignored the jibe in the smile and continued walking.

I was relieved that the situation in the city had eased somewhat by the evening and sat down to dinner with my mother and sister. Bhadra, who had been trying to make himself indispensable, ran to and from the royal kitchen, shouting orders.

My mother spoke first. "You may leave us alone. What is this evil looking fellow's name, Ravana?"

"Bhadra, wait outside." I said, ignoring the sharpness in my mother's voice. Bhadra left reluctantly but I was sure he would have his ear to the keyhole.

"I hear you blamed Prahastha for all the excesses." I was rather shocked when she said this without lifting her head from her plate.

"No, it's just. . ."

"Ravana, you are still young. These people are experienced in governing.

You abide by their advice. Let it not go to your head that just because you have become king of a puny island, that you are the lone saviour of the Asuras. You have a lot to learn and be thankful that you have able advisors around you."

"Mother, you are treating me like a child! I don't want any advice from idiots who have managed to lose their own kingdoms, honour, wealth and everything they inherited, to the Devas. Whatever experience they had by ruling handkerchief-sized kingdoms and living in perpetual fear of Deva raids, has neither served the Asuras nor these bunch of pompous know-it-all buffoons, well. You know that better than me."

"Why are you speaking to me like this?"

"Now, don't start narrating your tale of suffering. I know it by heart. Mother, I love you and respect you, but it does not mean that I will always remain your toddler. Leave the ruling to me."

My sister was shocked by this outburst. She stopped eating and sat looking at me, her eyes filled with tears. My mother stood up. "Enough! There is no point in talking. Power has gone to his head."

Anger got the better of me. I pulled the tablecloth off the table in one quick movement. Vessels, plates and everything on the table tumbled to the floor. Servants rushed in from all sides to clean up the food splattered around. Mother stormed out of the room, dragging my reluctant sister with her. And I walked listlessly to my room, anger slowly oozing out of me. I wiped my hands on the silk curtains, ignoring the stains I was making and then threw off my footwear and lay sprawled on the huge bed. What wrong had I done to these people? I had just begun to live my dream and it had already gone sour. Why did everyone find me overbearing, arrogant and tyrannical? A servant came with a lamp but I waved him away. I found the darkness cozy and comfortable. Perhaps Prahastha might have had a theory to explain my new-found fondness for darkness – perhaps the reflection of a dark soul?

I had to put an end to this nonsense today. I cannot live like this forever–

with my ministers talking behind my back; my subjects cowering in fear; the nagging of my mother and the irritating self-righteousness of Prahastha. What I needed was action. Ravana was no coward and I jumped from my bed and shouted for Bhadra. He appeared surprisingly quickly. Had he been waiting outside? He made me an elaborate bow and I felt he was mocking me, but I chose to ignore it. Maybe he was just showing his sycophancy. We Asuras – always ready to bow low. But then, how I would have felt had he not bowed? Would I not have taken it as a mark of disrespect?

"Bhadra. . . How many warriors you can arrange? I mean, within the hour?"

"You want good swimmers, Your Majesty?"

"How do you know I want swimmers?"

"You want soldiers who are expert in martial arts, who can swim in a rough sea, and storm a fleet of ships. I think I know the people and can arrange about twenty of them, Your Majesty."

I was silent for a moment. It was eerie the way he read my mind. What sort of a creature was he? A wizard? Even I was not sure that was what I wanted. The plan was sheer madness. Taking on a fleet of ships with a handful of soldiers was the height of foolishness. And I was no soldier of fortune now. A king could not afford to be so reckless. I imagined Prahastha's face when he learnt that the King had departed at dead of the night with a motley crew of half trained soldiers, to take on the most fearsome pirate in the world. I almost smiled at the thought. Just to spite Prahastha, the suicidal mission was worth it.

Bhadra made another elaborate bow and left the room silently. I looked out at the pirate fleet. The merriment had died down and the lights in the ships were turned off. I hoped that the pirates were drunk and fast asleep. I was not sure which ship housed the pirate-King, Varuna. The biggest factor would be surprise. My kingship depended on it. I knew it was a huge risk and if I was captured by the pirates, the doors of Lanka would be left wide open to their marauding hordes. I was also afraid. It was a numbing, paralyzing fear. The stories of torture meted out by the pirate king to hapless souls who fell into his hands, were legend. His cold heartedness raised him to the league of the Deva Gods. I tried to rationalize the fear I felt as concern for my countrymen and relatives.

Then it came, that ugly inner voice, '*You could even fool yourself, Ravana. So noble, so brave! The great Emperor of a tiny village, so concerned about the fate of his subjects. How many kings are as noble hearted as you?*' When would I ever silence that voice? I know…I am more afraid about my own safety. My vivid imagination painted pictures of the torture I might endure. I am afraid of Varuna. Would I be able to withstand the pain? More than that, would I be able take the shame of being dragged naked through the muddy lanes of Lanka? Why couldn't I be satisfied with a simple peasant's life?

In the stealth of the night, we would launch the canoes and paddle slowly towards the ships. The decks were at least twenty feet off the water. How would we climb up to them without any sound? Which ship should we attack first? The key would be to capture or kill Varuna. There were six ships at anchor. The pirate-king's ship – a floating palace – was visible from a distance. But Varuna, the small-time fisherman, did not become Varuna, the pirate-king, by being predictable. There was every possibility that he would be in one of the smaller ships, anticipating such a move from the Asura army. Without intelligence about the enemy position, it was a fool's war we were going to wage. Prahastha would have a heart attack when he heard we had gone on such a reckless mission without sufficient information and military back-up. Should I abandon the mission? My legs trembled and I was horrified to see my hands shaking.

I was startled to hear a cough behind me and turned to see the repulsive face of Bhadra. This guy could assassinate me without my being aware of it. Had he got the paws of a cat?

"Your Highness, your people are at your service." Translation, twenty people, including this creature, were willing to die at my orders. But why did I not feel like I did when I led an army into battle? My first war was electrifying. I could compare it to what I felt when I took my first girl into the bushes when I was fourteen. But I could sense the excitement building in the men. In the hot, humid air, the smell of their sweat mingled with the smell of Jasmine flowers from the garden. The moon had hidden behind the clouds. I could smell blood on my hands, and fear. I prayed to some unknown god in whom I did not even believe, that these men, who also appeared so brave, should not smell my fear.

Silently I walked out of the room trying to hold my head high and my shoulders straight. I tried to walk confidently and appear like the warriors of old. Had they been as afraid as I? Perhaps, if I came out of this alive, after thousands of years, there would be stories told about me too. The voice inside me started its tirade. '*Ah, Ravana, you are just a tiny speck in the universe and it does not matter a bit if you die or win today. Your death is less valuable than a worm's death. A worm becomes food for a bird or manure for the soil. If you die, your body will be burned, adding only empty fumes to the atmosphere. As far as nature is concerned, your struggles and trials, your triumphs, your very birth and death, are all irrelevant incidents. They are small stones crushed under the wheels of time. If you live, you will just be one day closer to the inevitable end. If you die, then the universe will still remain the same. Ravana, what a fool are you. . .*'

The waves crashing onto the rocks woke me up from the numbing lullaby of the depressing inner voice. Bhadra and another man of slight build, pushed three canoes into the sea. One by one, the men waded through waist-deep water and got into the canoes. I stood transfixed, staring at the heaving ocean and the sure death which awaited us. Varuna's ships were anchored close to the shore, yet now they seemed to touch the edge of the horizon. I stepped into the waves and was immediately submerged. The waves rolled me back to the shore. Sputtering and swearing, I stood up and waded towards the canoes again. I chose to ignore the grin on my soldiers black faces and jumped into the first canoe. Immediately the crew started rowing the canoe towards the ships, with the other two canoes following. Thunder sounded in the distance. A sword of lightning silhouetted the pirate-King's ship against the dark horizon. The sea became rough. The other two canoes fell behind, but rowed furiously. Slowly, fighting the rolling swells, we reached within a few yards of the ships.

Another streak of lightning illuminated the sky and the rolling waters.

Removing all my clothes except for my loin cloth, and clutching my sword between my teeth, I jumped into the freezing water and started paddling towards the ships. I could hear the soft paddling from the soldiers who followed me. The ships heaved in the rolling waters and I found it quite impossible to stay near them. I swam towards the ship I thought Varuna would be in. As if on cue, two soldiers climbed the ship's vertical side towards the deck. It was amazing to watch them as they used special claws to dig into the wooden boards to get a grip. They climbed up fast, almost like lizards. But it seemed an eternity before two ropes came snaking down. I jumped and grabbed one of the ropes and started climbing.

Bhadra followed on the other rope. Quickly, the others followed. I reached the deck first and the sight I saw chilled my heart. The two brave men who had climbed up first, lay there slain – their bodies sprawled on the deck.

"*Get out*! *It's a trap*!" I shouted. Then it started raining, a sudden storm raged and the ship swayed precariously. Some of my soldiers fell into the sea, but others joined me on deck. There was silence, other than the deafening noise of the howling wind. We stood there with our swords drawn. It was ridiculous, standing there almost naked and completely drenched, waiting to be killed. The rain washed away the puddles of blood. And it washed away the false courage I had built up. '*Oh God! What had I done?*'

Then the darkness resonated with devilish laughter. In a flash of lightning, I saw we were surrounded by heavily armed pirates. We were seriously outnumbered and there was no chance of escape. With a mighty effort of will power, I jumped and thrust my sword into the guts of a fearsome pirate. This electrified my troops and a battle ensued on the swaying decks. I was reckless and astonishingly my fear deserted me. I fought from my heart and lost count of how many I butchered. The wooden deck was slippery with blood and the dangling ropes of the sails added to the danger. I was wounded thrice and bleeding profusely, but that was the least of my worries. I slowly realized that we could take over the ship. To our dismay, we found that the other ships had closed in. Pirates were jumping into the raging sea and swimming like mad men towards our ship. If they reached us, total annihilation would be inevitable.

Where was that bastard Varuna? If only I could lay my hands on him! The first pirates from the other ships started climbing onto our deck. I kicked one in the face and saw him fall into the raging sea. Perhaps Varuna was in the lower chamber. I kicked open the door leading to the stairs and jumped down to the lower chamber. The ornate door were closed and a faint light came through the cracks. Ghastly shadows played on the curved walls of the ship. The sounds of the battle on the decks reached me faintly. Was Varuna inside?

I kicked open the door and swung my sword in a sweep. The room was empty. I drove my sword into the flying silk curtains. Like a sniffer dog, I fell to the floor to see whether the coward was hiding under the bed. Then a cold, steel blade touched the nape of my neck.

"Well, the Emperor of the Asuras is paying a royal visit to this poor fisherman's chamber. I am grateful, Your Majesty."

I tried looking up to see the face of the hated pirate-king, but with his wooden shoes, he kicked my face. Blood oozed from my nose and formed a pool on the floor. My fear returned. Trapped! This was the end.

"You surprise me, Your Majesty. You visit your guest's chamber in your loin cloth? Is it an Asura custom from the mainland or are you making a new fashion statement for your subjects to emulate?"

With an agility which surprised Varuna and me, I kicked at his ankles and in that second of surprise, I rolled onto my feet. I was burning with anger. If only I could kill him or better yet, capture him, I would not only retain a kingdom but also my shattered pride. I tried to hit him a heavy blow with my sword, but he easily blocked it. Fuelled by my frustration and pent-up anger, I started fighting. But Varuna, who was almost forty years old, parlayed my strokes and thrusts with an ease bordering on boredom. His swordsmanship was beyond compare and he resembled Mahabali at his best. My twenty-something youth and energy was no match for the quiet confidence and poise of the veteran.

"Oh good, good. . .but you need more practice. . .no, not that way, try swinging from the left – there there, that was better – but you need to exert more power. . ." His monotone was irritating and made me feel like a child being trained in the martial arts. He had drawn blood many times and I had not been able to touch him even once. My wounds started bleeding again and I felt dizzy. All was lost. I was desperate.

"Varuna, you pirate, hold on or lose your blasted head!"

I turned and saw to my surprise, two archers framed in the doorway. It took me a few seconds to recognize my uncle Maricha, and my brother Kumbakarna. They pointed their arrows at Varuna and for the first time I saw him lose his calm. Before I could react, he tried to jump into the sea through the open window. I grabbed his legs and he fell with his face flat on the floor. Before Varuna could shake me off, Kumbha was on him and together we pinned him down and tied his hands behind his back with the silk curtains Maricha had torn down and handed to us.

"How the hell did you people arrive in the nick of time?" I could not stop wondering at this fairy tale arrival of the redeeming heroes.

Maricha was out of breath but that did not stop his tale. "When you discussed the plans with us this morning, I kept thinking about it. The more I thought, the more reckless and foolish it appeared to me. I came to your chambers to warn you not to undertake this idiotic mission. But you were missing. One did not need to be a genius like Prahastha to guess where you had gone. Certainly not for a late night stroll. I woke this oaf, then ran like a mad dog and blew the war bugle. I could assemble only a few hundred soldiers. Half of them were dead drunk. These Asuras… Then we paddled like crazy to watch the entertaining circus you had set up on the high seas."

"Did we lose any men?"

"Do you think we were warmly welcomed with betel leaves and sweets into Varuna's ship? We lost a few dozens and half of them died not because of battle wounds but drowning in these turbulent waters. I heard you also lost some men."

"The count was six when I started my interesting chat with the great pirate-King."

"I'm sorry, but I think your pet Bhadra drowned. Vaystha, the head soldier saw him fall over and no one has seen him since. In these rough seas I think he would have reached China by now."

"Brother, what shall we do with this pirate?"

"Throw him with his legs and arms tied, into the sea – a fitting end for the king of the seas." Maricha said without a moment's hesitation.

"That would serve him right. No, hold on. Let's take him to Lanka. Let's drag him through the streets in his loin cloth.' I was getting enthusiastic. "Let the people of my kingdom see the man who was responsible for their miseries."

"And let them also see King Ravana, who freed them from their misery. Ravana, the slayer of the pirates and the King of the seven seas," Kumbha added with a smile.

Maricha stared at both of us. Then as an afterthought he added. "It would be better if you gifted the King of pirates to the mother sea."

I ignored this piece of advice. But, if I could rewrite my life, I would perhaps start from that moment and ask Maricha and Kumbha to lend me a helping hand to lift Varuna and fling him overboard.

20 Wedding bells

Ravana

I had to enter my royal chamber but I did not dare to. She would be there, waiting for me. I was married today. Of all the people, I married that frosty Mandodari. I knew it was inevitable but I wanted to postpone it as long as possible. But when the royal procession entered the streets of Trikota, I was beyond myself. Victory can make one foolish. And this week many things happened so swiftly that I was barely able to think.

The word had gone ahead of us that the mighty King of Lanka had caught the pirate-King Varuna. The pirates were stripped to their loin cloths, smeared with mud and dirt, spat upon, brutally beaten up, and then made to walk in a macabre procession behind their fallen King. Thousands lined the streets, shouting triumphantly. I walked in front of the procession hoping I looked sufficiently heroic. Once in a while I raised my sword to the cheering crowd and it seemed to electrify them. I was their hero-king who had saved Lanka from the clutches of the dreaded pirate. My heart swelled with pride. I hit Varuna across his face, drawing blood from his nose. Ah, that felt good. I hit him again and raised my sword. The crowd started shouting, "Long live Ravana, long live our King". Some poor soul came and fell at my feet. One of my soldiers kicked him and the crowd laughed. Someone near me booed. I stared into the crowd and the entire section cowered. I could smell their fear. The same people who wanted a revolution to throw me out were now afraid of me. Success can be so sweet. People bowed down to me.

I looked back and suddenly my soldiers who had been shouting and laughing, stopped. I stared at them and they too lowered their heads. I looked at Kumbha and he smiled at me. I did not return the smile but caught Maricha's eye. He shook his head sadly. *'Why does this fellow not bow to me?'* I began to simmer. Varuna, with his blood-stained face, caught my eye and gave a devilish laugh. I dreaded his laugh, but more than that, I dreaded myself. *'What sort of a demon was I becoming? Why was I treating my people like this? Why was I getting angry even at Maricha, when he did not show respect?'* Suddenly, I wanted to run and hug him and say I was sorry. But something held me back. I increased my pace and entered the palace gate.

Standing at the far end of the long corridor, waiting for me, was Prahastha. There was a frown on his face and a faint air of disapproval. I wanted to dance round Prahastha. The idiot had kept advising me to be cautious. Fat good caution had done him and his bunch of Asura jokers. As I reached him, I slowed and looked into his eyes. He was staring at me. A staring contest. What did he want now? If he started to lecture me about statesmanship and diplomacy, I would catch hold of him by the scruff of his neck and rub his nose on the floor. Thankfully, he kept quiet. Perhaps he practised what he preached – prudence.

"Call the court, I would like to speak to all my ministers." I ordered him as he stood there with his frowning stare.

I was busy hugging my sister, and Kumbha, when Prahastha spoke again. "Shall I send a message for withdrawal of the army from the southern sector of the city?"

"Do what you think is right. You are the Prime Minister." I dismissed him with a wave of the hand and he made a slight bow and left. As I watched his steady, departing strides, my eyes looked into those of the chained pirate-king. A smile played about his mouth. Had the wily fox sensed the political tension? It did not matter as long as he was chained like a mad dog. As far as I was concerned, he could keep his amused smile until some lowly soldier from my army saw it and decided to wipe it off his face with a good hard knock. I could hear the festivities outside the palace. Just another reason for the Asuras to get drunk. Let them celebrate. My heart went out to them. Finally, I had lived up to the expectations of my people. I did not want to remind myself that sharks would have been eating the last of me had Maricha not turned up when he did. . . So much for my brand of heroism.

"My hero, have you finished your day's quota of heroism?" My mother was smiling at me and I went and hugged her.

"You fool! What if you had got killed?" I could feel her tears dripping onto my bare shoulders. I hugged her tighter. She held me at arm's length and peered into my face. "You look like your father, Ravana."

I went stiff. He was the last person I wanted to look like. I would have preferred to look like a cat run over by a chariot. I think she sensed that too. There was a thick silence. I took a few steps forward and stopped dead. There was Mandodari, leaning against a pillar and looking at me with that same toneless, featureless, emotionless, intense look. I did not know what to say. *'Go, go and kiss her on her lips. That is what heroes are supposed to do after their bouts of heroism. Kiss the heroine and if a horse is handy, lift her up and ride into the sunset.'* Instead, I fumbled.

"What is this, a lover's meet? Silent communication with the eyes?" my sister, Soorpanakha's devilish voice broke the spell. I turned and caught hold of her by the ear and she howled.

"Any more nonsense from you and I will marry you off to the first Asura drunkard I see today," I cried out in mock anger. I was relieved to have escaped the ordeal of striking up a conversation with Mandodari. I sneaked a glance to see if she was blushing or feeling shy. Nothing of the sort. Just that stare. That piercing stare which went through my soul. Could she read my dark secrets? *'Oh God, if I married this creature, she would stare and stare and one day I would go up in smoke.'*

Suddenly I felt my privacy violated. I had forgotten about the pirate-King. He was standing there with that arrogant smile playing on his lips, drinking in the scene unfolding before him. Chained and almost naked, he did not seem bothered about his plight. Why hadn't a minister or officious bureaucrat, dragged this prisoner away to his dark cell? All the useless Asura fools were enjoying their King's victory and had forgotten about their king and his captive. I shouted at the top of my voice. It was another five minutes before someone appeared and made an elaborate bow. I wanted to kick his black arse but it would have been unfair to punish this efficient Asura for his promptness. I asked him to drag the pirate-King to one of the dark, underground cells where Kubera used to keep his detractors.

The deferential way in which my guard was treating the pirate-King almost made me gag. Except for his chains, Varuna looked as if he was on a state visit. My biggest challenge would be to discipline these Asura clowns. They behaved like children. Images of the twenty odd soldiers who had risked their lives a few hours before, believing in me totally, flashed through my mind. How many were dead? How many widows had I created? How many children in those huts sprinkled beyond the city walls would fall asleep crying for their fathers, for many days to come? Tomorrow I would visit the huts of my soldiers who had gone missing or been killed. I would ensure their children would not starve; nor the widows dragged into the vicious net of prostitution. I owed them that much for trusting me and sacrificing their lives. *'What a great man I was. But what about the civilians that Rudraka and company had butchered during the past few days? How about the orphans created by the efficient and ruthless curbing of the civilian revolution?'* How would I ever feel happy if this joker inside me kept throwing such ridiculous thoughts into my mind? I had the right to feel noble and great, at least once in a while.

And where was Bhadra? The guy was an enigma. Could he have died so easily? I felt responsible for the death of my beloved servant. The sun climbed up and everything looked fresh and washed after the previous day's shower. Birds chirped in the trees and dragonflies buzzed around the flowers in the overgrown garden. I looked out of the window and could see kites hovering over the swaying coconut palms. Crows cawed and the distant sounds of women washing clothes, kept rhythm with each other. All was well with the world and it was one of those wonderful moments when all thoughts ceased and a pleasant emptiness filled my mind.

"Pray. Pray for your soul and the men you have killed. And peace shall be yours, my King."

"Shut your mouth, you. . .don't tell me what to do. . ." I did not know Mandodari was standing near by, watching me with those intense eyes. I was startled to hear her voice. I had been so absorbed with nature. Now I wanted to grab her throat and squeeze the life out of her. Had I asked this prude for her advice? How dare she enter my world and talk rubbish? She had gone pale and a sob quivered in her throat. I was embarrassed at my outburst and felt the anger drain out of me. I had never been in such a situation and did not know what to do. Should I apologize? But she had deserved it. I felt my anger return.

"I'm sorry. . ." she said.

"Alright, alright. . ." I wanted to add that she had had it coming but I prudently kept quiet.

"Your Highness, the court has assembled," the guard shouted at the top of his voice. I was thankful for the break and walked past, my mind racing through the probable questions Prahastha and others would raise and how best to deal with them.

The court was in full assembly and the dozing guard at the door snapped to attention when I went past him. It bothered me a little that I had to cough and let him know of my presence before he showed his version of respect. I wanted to kick the guard and drive some discipline into his wooden head. But then I would have ended up kicking my entire army. Besides, I had more important things to worry about than being a drill sergeant to my soldiers. Now the priority was to emphasize my authority and not let the Council take over. I knew Prahastha would be scheming behind me as he was livid at my spectacular victory against the pirate-King Varuna. He might even thrust forward his hare-brained opinions about how to treat the pirate and quote from some obscure books on the Asura code of conduct. I decided that if he quoted some ancient Asura sage, and said that I had to leave Varuna with full state honours as a visiting King, I would ensure that the pirate-kings would be demeaned to the maximum possible extent, dragged through the streets and flogged in public, and finally left to an agonizing, slow and painful death in public. I was worried and unsure how the rest of the Council would respond. I had to get rid of this farce of a Council. Why did I need them to give me advice on how I should conduct myself?

As I entered the *durbar*, I looked around. The ornate chair at the end of the room had a decorative umbrella over it. Pearls and diamonds of various shapes hung from its frill. There was a huge diamond on the chair back. It was the royal throne of the king of Lanka. I felt a little perturbed that it had not come naturally to me to think of it as my throne. Yes, it was the same throne which had supported my half-brother's fat bottom. Where his pompous Highness sat dispensing his version of justice. I stood transfixed. I had came a long way, a very long way, from the day when I had accompanied my mother and siblings to beg before Kubera, who had been sitting on this same throne, and he had thrown a few coins at our feet and dismissed us like beggars, with a wave of his hand.

I climbed the steps to the throne.

"*Stop*!" The shout echoed inside the large *durbar* hall. I turned back hastily and my steps faltered. Then I saw Prahastha standing with his arms crossed behind him. Blood shot into my veins. Instinctively I drew out my sword. The ministers who had been sitting, stood up in their seats. '*Why were they sitting in the first place? Were they not supposed to stand up when I, the King, entered the room?*' My lips trembled and I was sure my eyes had turned blood red. I had never felt angrier in my life. Prahastha, my prime minister, had stopped me from touching my own throne. Had I been blessed with prophetic vision, I would have thanked him and walked out to the freedom waiting outside the palace. I should have gone then, leaving the governance to those who were learned like Prahastha, and pursued my true interest in music. Instead of bringing death and damnation upon my beloved people, I could have presented the world with hours of pleasant memories with the *ragas* I could have composed. But the magnetic pull of that golden throne is not matched by anything else in the world.

I stood rooted to the spot and then slowly raised my sword and pressed the sharp tip against Prahastha's chest. I raised an eyebrow and glared at him. He stood there without flinching. I could sense the tension in the room. Many hands had gone to daggers and swords.

"Your Highness, your official coronation ceremony is not done. Until then you cannot touch the throne. You cannot sit on it without your royal crown. Our custom dictates that." Prahastha addressed me evenly. The tension in the room eased and I felt like a fool. I felt like slapping my own head. I looked around and caught the eyes of Maricha. He had an uncharacteristic frown on his face. Rudraka had a sneer and Jambumali and Malyvan were discussing something with Sumali. Dhumraksha and Vajradhamstra were standing near the round pillar on the farthest right corner and looking at me with unconcealed hatred. I did not know what I had done to earn their hatred. I searched for a suitable chair to sit on and to my chagrin, there was only a battered old wooden chair left. With some reluctance, I pressed myself onto the seat, half expecting a bug to bite me. Maricha noticed my predicament and tried to lift his chair and bring it to me. I waved him away and sat down in the creaking chair.

Immediately, Prahastha called out in his tough harsh voice, "Council meeting commences."

'Wait a minute, had I not dismissed this stupid Council? Then why was this idiot acting as if we were going to sit here for the whole day like the olden days and talk and talk and do nothing? Council, my foot! If I did not act now, I would become the Sarpanch of the Asura race and not its king.'

"Has it escaped you that the Council was dismissed long before we ever set foot on this island? Next time I hear any of you talking about the Council, you can catch the next ship to the mainland and join the old Emperor in his mad pursuits. That is, if I'm in a good mood. God forbid if my mood is bad. Then you can expect to end up as a crocodile meal in the moat around the palace. Do I make myself sufficiently clear?"

"But. . ." Prahastha had gone all red and Jambumali was trying to say something.

"And I do not care if it violates a dozen Asura codes and customs. I make my customs. I will act according to the rules I make. I am sick of these thousand-year-old traditions. Just to prove my point, I am going to sit on the throne Kubera has left. I do not care for any ceremonies. I owe the kingdom not to any Asura superstitions. This is a new world, a modern world, and let the beliefs and superstitions of the old India not tangle our march towards progress."

Before I could lose steam, I deliberately took the old wooden chair and threw it at the nearest wall. It broke with a loud snap and I thought it was symbolic. I turned swiftly and marched towards the throne. I could hear the shocked intake of breath from my Council…and my ministers. I sat down with a flourish. I felt some trepidation, and then a shiver and thrill passed through me. I slowly leaned back until my head touched the headrest. My hands played with the contours of the huge diamonds on the armrest. A cold breeze blew in from the sea and streets sounds came in from outside the palace. All was well with the world. And the world went on whether Ravana sat on a gaudy chair with some ceremonies or without. The strange sense of elation I had felt a moment ago, drained away to be replaced by a sense of emptiness. The images of my men drowning and the heart-wrenching scenes in their homes, disturbed my mind. *'Was this two-feet thick cushion worth it? What had I become? A pacifist? My ambition was to conquer the world. I wanted to be the Emperor of India, the saviour of the Asura race, the benevolent ruler who would bring prosperity and happiness to his subjects.'*

I wondered why my ministers still stood. *'Ah this was good. They were waiting for permission from me.'* I gestured for everyone to be seated. Prahastha continued to stand. He struggled to say something. I deliberately crossed my legs and started massaging my left heel. I balanced my leather shoe and swung it with my toe. I thought I should get a cobbler to stitch a few pearls on my footwear. It would look good. My gesture of superiority was not lost on any of my ministers. I was happy that they were learning fast who was the boss. But I could not meet Maricha's eyes. It would have been embarrassing for both of us.

"Your Highness," I noticed there was a small lisp in Prahsatha's voice, "the first point we would like. . .that is. . .you should take a decision on is the fate of the pirate-king Varuna."

I should have pointed out to him that a prime minister should not use words like 'you should'. I did not want anyone to speak to me in ornate sentences with a hundred nuances. I had made my point and I did not want to press it any further. All said and done, if any of these ministers resigned, I would have been hard pressed to find a suitable replacement.

"What is your advice, Prime Minister?" I was sure he would suggest that the pirate should be treated with full honours and given a royal reception befitting a visiting royal dignitary or be sent free with lots of gifts. He would back it up with some stories of some Asura king who may or may not have lived a few thousand years ago, and who had treated his captives with great respect. I would have liked to know what happened to that magnanimous king a few years after his splendid display of chivalry. Most probably the let-off captive had come back with more might, conquered this king, and then rendered the most inhumane punishment possible without a passing thought about chivalry. But no one learns from history. Whether the Devas or the Asuras, there are enough fools to add new chapters to this mutually destructive competitive chivalry, though I must admit the Asuras do it more often, thanks to the learned men like Prahastha. When that learned man voices his wooden-brained opinion about chivalry, I was going to blast him.

Meanwhile, Vibhishana stood up and gave a long speech about Asura chivalry and the humane treatment of prisoners-of-war. He managed to bore and irritate all those present. I had already decided what punishment should be meted out to the dreaded pirate. I waited. The ascending waves of murmurs and the heavy cloud of anticipation had created a surreal quality.

Finally, after what seemed like an eternity, Prahastha began, "Your Highness, we believe that the pirate-King should be executed. He is too dangerous to be let off and he might turn against us when we are weakest. Prudence dictates that he should be given the harshest punishment in order to send a lesson to other enemies of the State and the Council. . .that is, we ministers suggest that he should be summarily executed."

I was stunned. This was quite unexpected. I saw Sumali, Vajradhamstra and Malyavaan furiously discussing it amongst themselves. Kumbha and Vibhishana were debating, while Dhumraksha sat in a corner, morose at being ignored. I was sure I was in a fix. If I let off Varuna, it would be like siding with my brother Vibhishana, and if I executed him, it would seem I was being controlled by Prahastha. Oh boy, what a mess!

Prahastha's steely glare bored into me as if challenging me to contradict him. The pirate-King was standing there unfazed. Not an emotion crossed his impassive face. I almost admired him for his coolness. The man was brave, definitely much braver than me. I had ended up in a deep mess. It would have been easier to abide by the Council's wishes and execute Varuna. But then, I needed to assert my supremacy over them. At the same time, I could not let off the pirate-King with great honour and respect; I could not let him walk free.

"I am not going to execute him." The murmuring stopped suddenly. After a few moments of stunned silence, my ministers stood up one after the other. "I think I owe you an explanation. It is not my intention to let this pirate go free. I've ordered that his entire fleet of ships be confiscated and added to the royal navy. The pirates must be given proper military training and absorbed into the navy. And as for the pirate-King. . ." I walking towards Varuna. He towered over me by at least half a foot. I stared into his eyes and through my teeth I said, "I am going to drag him through the streets, shave his head partially, and then take him around the city on the back of an ass. Then I am going to conduct the marriage of this pirate-king with a pig. This will be at the expense of the royal treasury, a state sponsored wedding. It will be conducted along with my marriage."

A small smile twitched at the corner of Varuna's mouth. He matched my stare and said, "Ah the day when all pigs will get married."

I hit him across his face, the laughter of my ministers burning my ears. Then I also caught the humour of Varuna's repartee and started laughing.

Only Prahastha remained still, without the trace of a smile on his aristocratic face.

"Your Highness, if you will not execute this prisoner, may I suggest that he be imprisoned for life in a dark cellar, and no further insults be meted out to him in public?"

"I will do as I wish. You have given your opinion. Keep your council to yourself." I snubbed Prahastha and the matter ended there. Or that is what I thought. I walked out of the *durbar* with my ministers following me, while Varuna was dragged out so his head could be shaved partially and for other abuses and tortures.

Maricha and Kumbha caught up with me on my either side. "I thought you were going to execute him, Ravana." *'That was before I entered the durbar.'* I could see surprise in Maricha's eyes but I did not reply.

"I have a suggestion." Kumbha struggled to catch up with me. "Why not make Varuna our admiral?"

"And what's the guarantee that Varuna will not attack our ships once he is out of Lankan territorial waters?" I asked him.

"At heart, Varuna is more of a businessman than a pirate. If he is offered favourable terms, he will stick to them. Of course, we should always remain alert and not trust him too much."

"And what do we gain by striking a deal with a pirate?"

"A secure trade route, ports free from pirate attack, revenue from security for foreigners, and plenty of goodwill with the outside world."

"The idea doesn't excite me." I was bent on insulting the pirate-King. His jeering laugh during his duel with me inside his cabin, still rankled.

"I am with Prahastha in this matter," Maricha intervened. "It is too dangerous. I don't know why you took such a stupid decision." I remained silent. How could I say that I too had wanted what Prahastha advised, but took an idiotic decision just to assert myself?

Mother was standing at the end of the corridor. The fumbling professor Mayan, was also there, scribbling something furiously on a palm leaf. "Maricha, please leave the children and come with me. We have important things to discuss."

Maricha gave me a wink and disappeared with my mother and the professor. I knew what they were going to discuss. So this was it. My bachelor days were about to end. It was almost noon. Outside the palace, the market was slowly emptying as the city prepared for its afternoon siesta. A few kites circled high in the sky, again and again and again. Somewhere outside, a fishmonger yelled in a last ditch attempt to sell off his day's basket of fish. The sea shimmered in the sunlight and reflected the afternoon sun in a thousand little mirrors. Clouds were forming on the distant, western horizon. The humidity was intolerable and the air hung like a thick, wet carpet over the city. Standing at the balcony of my palace, I reflected on my life.

The wedding was fixed for Friday, four days hence. I personally supervised all the arrangements, not for the marriage, but for the meting out of the greatest possible humiliation and torture to the pirate-King. I could not help admire the courage of the man – he took it all without a murmur. With blood-caked lips, Varuna smiled, showing off his broken teeth, when he saw me. I raised my hand to hit him, looked into his eyes, and stopped. I was disgusted. What sort of a hoodlum was I?

The marriage preparations were like a constant toothache. Hoards of Asuras landed from the mainland in boats and motley ships. I had never suspected that we had so many relatives. Where were these mobs when we were starving? Obese uncles and aunts sailed into my bedroom just to see how 'our boy Ravana' had grown up. One even dared to joke that the last time he had seen me, I had looked like something the cat had chewed out. I promptly called my guards and threw the old man out. Children ran around breaking crystal vases and smearing the walls of the palace, babies howled in the night, fat black Asura women lay on the floors, sofas, beds and steps – anywhere they could find a place. They woke me just to tell me how very lucky I was to have achieved so much and what a fine lady I was marrying. Some came with their good-for-nothing sons and demanded employment for them in government. Food was free and wine flowed like a river.

21 Happy family

Ravana

My sister fluttered around showing off her newly made jewellery and escorting all and sundry to Mandodari's chamber to show off her new sister-in-law. For once I pitied the professor's daughter. I had to keep my temper in check and smile at everyone and act as if I was the happiest man in the world. The strain of keeping a smiling face when I was seething inside, started telling on my nerves. By Friday morning, my smile was almost a grimace. I looked in the mirror and felt sorry for myself. What kind of marriage was this? There was no love, no romantic courtship, no whispers under the moon, no stolen kisses; in fact it was clinical. Not even my fertile imagination could conjure up a romantic relationship with Mandodari.

I was woken up at some godforsaken hour on Friday morning and almost dragged for a ritual bath at the palace lake, amidst peals of laughter. Gaping men and women; elders commenting; girls giggling around corners; a cacophony of noises; the aroma of flowers, sweets, fried meat, fruit and rotting garbage in the streets of Lanka; milling crowds outside the fort jostling and screaming and getting fried in the humid tropical heat; cow dung – fresh, old, dried, burnt; incense; spices; fish; the sickly smell of the creek, and a million other things, assaulted my senses. I was led to a room where, like a girl, they applied *mehendi* on my toes and palms. Old women sang suggestive songs – old women who were shrivelled like sun-dried betel nuts, sang about the pleasures in bed. These came from the depths of the human soul and glorified an eternal truth – procreation, the only tool for the survival of human beings. I should have tried not to laugh at them.

I was escorted to the palace hall where a stage had been erected. It was gaudy and yet beautiful. Garlands of marigold and jasmine hung all over. A huge painting of Shiva and Parvati formed the backdrop. And of all things, three Brahmin priests sat croaking like frogs around a fire. What was this? That was a Deva custom, Asura marriages were always simple affairs. I did not know whose idea it was. Then I saw my father had come and was sitting in a huge chair. My mother sat on the floor, massaging his feet. My brother Vibhishana was also reverently standing by. All my ministers, except Prahastha, were present and standing in marked obsequiousness, as if paying obeisance to a visiting Emperor. Soorpanakha was desperately trying to impress our father, who was barely listening. The old lecher's eyes were roving over the body of the maid watering the plants in the garden.

"The proud father meets the great achiever. Aha! What a melodramatic scene." Kumbha was grinning.

"So you did not join the grand reunion?" I could barely conceal my anger.

"I chose to give it a miss. I think I forgot the lines of the family song." Kumbha was laughing now. The smell of country liquor hit me like a blast. I eyed him with contempt. Fat, ugly, with a huge beer belly, he looked forty and not twenty. I screamed, at him, "How dare you drink like this?" I grabbed his hair and banged his head on the wall. "You good-for-nothing. You scoundrel. . ." I kept banging his head and he ineffectually tried to parry my blows.

Hearing the ruckus, the family reunion broke up and they all came running into the room. Kumbha had collapsed on the floor like a heap of manure. Blood dripped from his nose and he moaned in pain. Maricha held me back. Soorpanakha screamed at the sight of the blood. *Smack*! My ears burned, and I saw with astonishment that my mother had cut her hand on my ear stud. She had hit me – in front of my ministers, my servants, and now the story would spread through the country like wildfire – a king who walked in the shadow of his mother's *pallu*. A king who was treated like a baby by his mother.

I pushed Maricha aside and saw him fall backwards and hit his head on the floor, from the corner of my eye. I could not have cared less. I grabbed my mother by her hair and dragged her out of the hall. The sight of Prahastha standing with his hands folded behind his back, staring at me, stopped me dead. The grip on my mother loosened and she scrambled up. The horror of the crime I had committed hit me like a thunderbolt. I was both shocked and shattered, but in some corner of my mind, satisfied and happy.

"The prisoner is ready for the punishment, your Highness," Prahastha said, with a slight bow. For a moment I went blank. Prisoner, which prisoner? It seemed the Varuna affair would follow me to my deathbed.

"First you finish with me. I'm your first prisoner!" yelled my mother behind me. "Shave my head and make me ride round the town naked on an ass. Why did you stop? You scoundrel son!"

I hung my head in shame. My mother's screaming had tuned into hysterical sobs. My hands trembled. I could not face anyone. Someone put a hand on my shoulders. "Kaikasi, he has not changed. I'm ashamed to say I sired this demon. I thought I would grace this occasion and brought my learned friends to perform this devil's marriage. And this Satan hits his mother and almost murders his brother in front of my friends!"

I felt the anger rising in my veins. I held onto the balustrade of the verandah with a deadly grip. Where was this good-for-nothing Brahmin when we were hungry? Where was he when my mother begged for food and clothes? Where was he when held precariously to live in our tiny cottage, swaying in the monsoon squalls? And all the while this lecherous Brahmin had perhaps been sowing his wild oats in the brothels of the mainland

"I should not blame him alone. He is, after all, an Asura. A more blighted race I have yet to see. Debauchery, sodomy, avarice, you name any evil and this devilish race can easily claim monopoly over it. Black-skinned, ugly creatures. . ."

"If we are so bad, then why did you marry my sister?" I turned in surprise at the sound of my uncle Maricha's voice. He was cool but I could feel his anger.

"Shut up, you stupid Asura, I'm talking to my wife and son and I do not answer to anyone like you." A drop of red betel nut juice oozed from the corners of my father's mouth.

Maricha looked at him with contempt and then turned to me. I drew to my full height and stepped menacingly towards my father. He began to cower. I towered over the poor fellow by almost two feet. I was angry enough to kill him with a blow but I was still ashamed at what I had done to my mother. My mother understood this was the decisive moment and stepped between us. She put her hands on my chest and shoved me back. I looked at her face and again the shame of hitting her struck me.

My mother spoke. "I am leaving. Your father, brothers, sister and I, will never again step into your home. We do not want to see you again. And when we die, do not come to see our dead bodies. Power has made you into a demon. You. . .you. . .will never find peace. . ."

I staggered back and grabbed the pillar in the corner of the room to stop me from collapsing to the floor. I saw my mother grab Soorpanakha's hand. She was sobbing as my mother tugged at her. My sister looked at my face and saw the tears flowing down my face. Slowly, deliberately, she freed herself from my mother's grip. I could see the shock in my mother's face. Mother walked to Kumbha, who was sprawled on the floor. He had passed out.

"Kumbakarna, Kumbha, wake up! Wake up!" But all my mother's screaming could not wake Kumbha from his drug-induced stupour. I almost smiled. "You have murdered him, Ravana. You have killed your own brother."

The situation now bordered on the hilarious. "He is not dead, mother. Your son is dead drunk. You could ask your fair and handsome husband to carry him on his shoulders." I laughed out loud as I imagined the fat buffoon carrying his jumbo-sized son on his shoulders.

"Vibhishana, do you want to go with this great Deva gentleman, this learned Brahmin?" I asked my younger brother, as I walked towards him

"No no brother. . .I mean. . ." Vibhishana stammered. I came so close to him that I could smell the sacred ashes he had smeared on his forehead. He was sweating.

"Why will you not accompany your Brahmin father? He could teach you all sorts of *mantras* and make you into a high class robber. You could perform all your usual mediations and have Vishnu or Indra or some Deva God as your personal protector. He could teach you all that and more." I walked towards my father, who was now ashen with fear. I saw the Brahmins had stopped chanting *mantras* and one of them was actually packing whatever he could lay his hands on. The greed of that Brahmin for other men's possessions was greater than his fear of death. I laughed out aloud. One of the Brahmins jumped out of the window with two of my good brass lamps held to his chest. The other one had a few vessels with him and tried to sneak out. I grabbed him by his top knot. He fell at my feet and started mumbling something. I thought he would take out his holy water from his jug any instant and curse me and I'd be hopping around the garden as a toad.

It took some time for me to register that that he was praising me. By Shiva! I had to pack this joker off before he spewed a mega poem in my praise, delivered extempore, and that too from the extremely difficult position of being sprawled flat on the floor. I kicked him and he scrambled up and ran for dear life. My father wanted to utter some curse, but because of his fear, he was unable to even open his mouth. My mother, with whatever dignity she could muster, took my father's shaking hands in hers and in her best melodramatic style, proclaimed, "I will not step into this hell even when I am dead. I will not allow you or any of your siblings to see my dead body. And because of the insult to your parents, you will pay. I do not know in this world or the next, but you will surely pay dearly for this."

She walked out of my palace with my father trailing behind. The onlookers and palace servants, the dregs of society who had assembled to peek and secretly enjoy the palace drama, moved over aside to allow this motley procession to pass. The two Brahmins and a few servants joined them. There was a muffled cry from the corner of the room and I saw my dear sister, sobbing uncontrollably with her face in her hands. Vibhishana stood awkwardly before her. I went to her and put my hands on her shoulders and she fell onto my chest and hugged me tight. Had I failed her? Had I wronged her? Something pulled at me. '*My dear, dear sister, what have I taken away from you*?'

"There. . .there. . ." The words sounded meaningless even to me, but I kept repeating, "There. . .there. . ." Maricha came and touched my shoulders gently. Prahastha stood like a pillar, with his eyes fixed on some unknown point in the distant horizon. I lifted my sister's chin and said with all the love a brother could muster, "Soorpanakha, whatever happens, whoever walks away from our lives, I will be there for you, as a brother, a friend, a father, and mother. Don't you trust your dear brother?"

With tears glistening in her eyes, she smiled at me and nodded. I felt afraid. Would I be able to keep this promise? I did not want to shatter her innocence, so I kept running my fingers through her hair and held her for a moment longer. Then my pride came back, my anger returned and I was myself again. Slowly but firmly, I walked out of the room. The guards at the door bowed. I knew they were sniggering inside, but I ignored them and walked past to stroll in the garden. An epoch in my life was over. I was sad beyond words. The image of my mother and her struggles to keep us fed and clothed, our struggles to stay alive, the inspiration she had been to me, all these, like indigested food, came up and choked me.

But a small bubble of joy started growing bigger and bigger and then it filled my whole mind. Free at last! Free from the protective wings of mother bird. Now what was there to stop me? No morals of a bygone era, no voice of a strict mother, no one who I really respected, to tie me down with the ropes of tradition. Ravana was no longer a boy. Kingship, from then on, would not be a burden to carry. It came naturally to me. I enjoyed being the King, the Emperor, the Lord of the world. That morning, on the day of my marriage, Ravana was born again.

Like all my dreams, this one too, was also shattered by none other than Prahastha. He said the bride was waiting to be married and the prisoner to be punished. Wearily I stood up and went to finish off my chores. In the days to come, I would dream and dream again. I had found the elixir of youth. The elixir was never exhausted as long as I kept dreaming on a grand scale. And my dreams became my story.

22 Revolutionaries

Bhadra

I fell into the mouth of death, into the howling ocean. Just as I was about to give up, my head bobbed above the heaving waters. I spluttered and coughed as another huge wave took me under. It hurt in a hundred different parts of my body. It would have been so easy to let go and sink deeper into the bosom of the sea. But the images of my wife and my girl butchered by the Deva devils, danced before my eyes. It gave strength to my arms and power to my legs. I started kicking again. As I came to the surface again, I could see the heaving ships like dots on the distant horizon. I was being lashed by the tropical hurricane. Sheets of water fell on my face. I tried to keep my head above the waves but did not know where to swim to. I bobbed helpless in the pitch dark, howling, heaving sea, with a threatening, grey sky covering this boiling and bubbling pot of rage.

Something was floating a few feet away. I swam towards that and was horrified to see a slain soldier drifting like a log. I swam away as fast as I could and tried staying afloat on my back. After a while I saw an old log floating at a distance of a few hundred feet. I was afraid to swim towards it lest it turned out to be another dead soldier or pirate. Finally, I decided to take the chance and swam towards it. It was an old tree trunk and I climbed on. I was dead tired and clung on with all my strength. Twice I was knocked over by rogue waves, but the sea was evidently calming. The rain weakened to a drizzle and the stars came out in the inky sky. I took off my turban and tied myself to the log and slept. When I woke, I stared at a once-familiar face. I tried to recollect the face but my head throbbed.

"Will he live?" I heard a deep voice asking.

"I hope so," a female voice answered. It came to me in a flash – Mala! Mala, my mistress, my forgotten sweetheart. I tried to sit up but she shoved me back. I wanted to ask her why she left me for that traitor. I wanted to scream at her, tear her hair and kick her. I wanted to kiss her, and feel her rounded hips. But, the impotent man I was, I just lay there, a tired and beaten Asura.

A shadow moved behind her, towards the lone burning oil lamp and half the face was lit in the flickering light. I thanked Shiva for not letting me open my mouth. It was none other than Vidyutjihva. Had he recognized me, I would have been long dead. Anger and jealousy hit me with a force greater than the hurricane I had escaped. The bitch was living with him. He was sleeping with her. The tall, fair Asura with the flowing mane and aristocratic nose, the deep, black eyes and broad shoulders, the brilliant orator and master strategist, the hero of hundreds of people, and the rival of my master, Ravana, stood there with a contemptuous smile playing on his lips. I pitied myself. I could now understand why Mala chose him over me. I was a nothing, a black pot-bellied Asura with crooked, yellow teeth and curly hair, short and plump. Could I expect a beauty like Mala to choose me over this hero? '*But I will get you man. One day, you will fall at my feet and beg. Then I will make you pay for that contemptuous smile.*' With the dreams of my grand revenge, I slowly faded back to sleep.

When I woke again, it was almost afternoon. There was some cold gruel on the crude, unpolished wooden table near the bed. I removed a dead housefly floating on the surface and drank the gruel in quick gulps. Everything was still outside. I was surprised to find the door was unlocked. I stood outside the thatched hut and squinted in the blazing white sun.

"Where were you? I thought you had gone back to the mainland." Mala had come from behind the house and stood with a pile of washing over her left arm. Water dripped from the clothes and formed curious designs on the sand.

"I worked here and there doing odd jobs, trying to make a living." I did not want her to know what I had been doing. I smiled. "And what were you doing?" Sleeping with that bastard, I wanted to ask, but looked away. I could imagine them together. She sensed what I was feeling and came near me and said coldly, "You left me and only he was there."

I tried to think of a dozen repartees that would sting her but could not come up with one. Instead, I smiled like a fool.

"Besides, you always treated me like a whore, just a thing of pleasure, even though I tried to love you. He treats me like a real woman."

"I'm poor man and not a handsome hero with ambitions of overthrowing the king. So. . ."

"Go ahead, Bhadra, talk about all your shortcomings. You get some perverse pleasure in talking about yourself like that. I've heard all this a hundred times before from you."

I wanted to grab and hit her till she was black and blue. She walked past me, beads of sweat gleaming on her back. I moved towards her and put my hands around her waist. The clothes fell from her hands and she hugged me. For a moment there was an animal passion between us. I pressed myself against her firm body and our lips met. With a hurriedness that comes from deprival, I tried touching her everywhere at once. Two hands were not enough. I almost bit her lips and she returned my kiss with equal passion. Then all of a sudden, she pushed me back. I tried to grab her again, but she pushed me back again. "No. . .no. . ." she sobbing hysterically.

Anger, jealousy and sadness, washed over me in waves. I felt like tearing her apart. Suddenly I was seized with a sense of utter helplessness. I left her there and walked towards the cliffs. I felt like jumping off and finishing everything there and then. I felt so lonely, so unwanted. I sat on a rock, afraid to jump and afraid to go back to life. I could see the golden flag of my King flying above the castle, flapping in the wind against a dark, black storm cloud. I sat there for hours until the first drop of rain hit me. Then I walked back to my life. By the time I reached my hut, I was wet through but too tired to care. I lay on my bed and watched a lizard waiting to pounce on a fly, when I heard a soft rap on the door. Before I could stand, Mala entered the room. I watched her with mounting irritation but before I could give vent to it, the tall figure of Vidyutjihva came in.

"Be seated, be seated," he told me. "Mala says you are looking for a job. This is a fighting organization and not a trade guild. There is no specific job defined for each." He became animated and walking to and fro, his arms moving in an exaggerated fashion. "We are here to create an equal and just world. There is no place for tyrants like Ravana in the world we want to create. Everyone will be equal. There will not be kings or landlords. There will not be any exploiters of the people like priests, magicians or traders. All people will be equal in the new world I create." He paused for breath and the subtle change from 'we' to 'I' did not escape my notice.

"The evil of the caste system will be wiped off. I will abolish trade guilds. A council of people will determine what each one of us should have. I will not accept any form of exploitation. Blood-sucking leeches like Kubera, will be killed. The Ravanas of the world will be crushed. There won't be any Gods. The Indras of the world will be vanquished. There will be no Godmen, nothing called money. People will serve each other and be happy. The world will belong to people like Bhadra, ordinary, common folk. I will create a paradise for people like you, Bhadra. Join us in this final fight for an ideal world."

I do not say that I was not moved. The idea of owning the world was appealing. I did not even own two pieces of good clothes, let alone a brave new world. But then, the idiot that I am, I never believed him. I acted as if I was excited by his idea, but deep down I knew he was just another tyrant in the making. My limited intelligence refused to grasp the great man's vision. I felt he was a hypocrite like all the others, like me, like Ravana, like every human being I had ever seen. Mine was a cynical view of the world, a far cry from Ravana's vision of a grand revival of Asura civilization, or Vidyutjihva's dream of an equitable social order, where he could play God. The philosophy of the common man, in Vidyuatjihva's words, could be summarized in six words, *What is in it for me*? I was all for an equitable world. Or even for a grand Asura civilization, if I could benefit from it. I wanted my revenge, two square meals, sex, and if possible, a chance to acquire wealth and position so that I could continue to treat other common men in the same way they were treating me now – with contempt.

I smiled at my own philosophy and Vidyutjihva took it as agreement. He slapped me on my shoulders and hugged me, careful to keep our bodies apart. All men may be equal, but not that equal. "Come over to our training class. Mala, see that he is fed and clothed properly. And ask him to bathe." Vidyutjihva went out with his silk robes flowing behind. His equal, Bhadra, stood there with his mistress, Mala. Is mine bigger than his or is it equal? I kept wondering.

"You do not believe him?" Mala asked.

"Do you?" Mala let out a sigh and went out. I followed her, curious to know the training the rebels were imparting. I was handed over some bathing herbs and a towel, by another equal of Vidyutjihva's, a puny Asura with sores on his bare toes, who wore torn clothes. I walked towards the small well to bathe. I scrubbed the places Vidyutjihva had touched. But the stench of equality stuck. Soon, I got used to that too.

23 Revolution comes home

Bhadra

I had become Vidyutjihva's confidante in a matter of days. News kept coming in from the palace from the rebel leader's spies. I learnt Varuna had been captured. After punishing the pirate-king, Ravana had let him take charge of protecting the Lankan coast and any territory Ravana might capture in the future. I doubted the wisdom of making the pirate-King the admiral of the royal navy, but the learned ones knew better. I also learnt that the King's mother has left the island after a spat with her son. Prince Kumbakarna was now a total addict to drugs, *bhang*, alcohol, gambling, and women, not always in that order. Ravana had extended control over all of Lanka, except the small north-eastern tip, which was wild country and where my new master's sway was not strong.

I had yet to decide who my master would be, whether I should hitch my fortune to Ravana or Vidyutjihva. For now, the chances favoured Ravana, and I should have gone back. But something kept telling me that my future was linked to the charismatic rebel leader. Moreover, he seemed gullible, and except for his grand ego and fantastic theories about social equality, he was the better person to be around. Even though his attempts at treating us all as his social equals was just play acting, the cadres went along with it as no one had even pretended to be like this. Once in a while, I would sneak kisses with Mala, though I had yet to share her bed. This added to the appeal of staying put with the rebel leader.

One day, Vidyutjihva called me to the beach. It was late evening and there was a full moon. The sea glistened silver and there was the fragrance of jasmine in the air. A song drifted lazily from the camps, a song of love lost and found and the ecstasy of reunion, which men yearn for when their stomachs are full and their bodies healthy. The leader was standing on a rock jutting over the sea. I climbed up. I was afraid. Had he found out I had kissed his mistress?

"Are you ready for a night cruise?" I could not see his face, so I could not decide whether he was angry.

"Yes." I mumbled. He pushed me aside and started down the rough-cut steps to the beach. A small country boat bobbed up and down in the water. He jumped into it and I stumbled in behind. With broad sweeps of the oar he cut across the waves. After a few minutes, he motioned me to take over. I started pulling the oars and steered the boat in the direction he pointed. As we approached, I could see the dark silhouette of the castle on the cliff. Mist had crept over the higher slopes of Trikota hill. In the night, the palace looked eerie. It was as if it was haunted by demons. All the old stories about evil spirits and *Rakshasas* began to play tricks in my mind. Slowly the boat reached shore.

"Stay here till I come." Vidyutjihva moved towards the rear gate of the fort. He walked with the confident gait of a man who had done this a hundred times. I was in my old master's palace, with the rebel leader. If I got caught, death was certain. Instinctively, I moved towards the shadows of the rocks. It was getting cold and I rubbed my hands together. The water was comparatively warmer. It was almost an hour before my master returned in an expressive and joyous mood, humming a song. The tune haunted me long after we had reached our shore and my master had retired to his cottage. I took the song to my bed that night.

I accompanied my master again on his nightly sojourns. I grew more and more curious about what was happening. I wondered how he entered Ravana's fort undetected and came back unharmed. It was obvious that an insider helped him. But it was big risk to take. The King's entire army was searching for him dead or alive, and here he was, roaming around the King's grounds with impunity. The audacity of the act was awe-inspiring.

I was called once more to be his oarsman. I wanted to put an end to my burning curiosity and decided to follow him. I waited for a few seconds and then started behind him. He walked fast, without looking back, not even caring to keep to the shadows. As he reached the fort gate, he turned left. I was perplexed. As far as I knew, there was no gate or entrance there. As I got closer, I saw the answer – a rope dangled down the sheer wall. He climbed up and vanished over the high wall in a trice. I went close and examined the rope. It swayed and I tugged it to see whether it would hold my weight. It was a foolish thing to have done since I had seen it take the weight of a giant like Vidyutjihva.

I climbed up with great difficulty. By the time I reached the top, I was drenched in sweat and puffing and panting. I cursed as I slowly dropped into the fort compound. The silence was total and frightening. Somewhere an owl hooted. Instinctively I reached for my dagger but I had forgotten it. Cursing myself again, I tried to get my bearings. Odd rays of light flickered through bushes in the garden. The sky was overcast and heavy. There was a noise like the rustling of clothes and a muted whisper somewhere nearby. I slowly moved towards the sounds. In the darkness, two shadows were embracing each other and kissing passionately. I could see the tall figure of Vidyutjihva. The woman seemed familiar, but I could not place her. I watched for a few minutes and then the woman moved back. Princess Soorpanakha! Cozying up to the arch enemy of the State! I was shocked.

A plan formed in my mind. This was the chance to do away my rival. It was at that moment that I chose between my two masters. By the time I reached near the palace, I was bubbling with joy and enthusiasm. I would kill many birds at once. I would eliminate my rival Vidyutjihva, enter the good books of Ravana, own Mala, and ensure that the Asura clan would not be divided between two charismatic and powerful leaders. Vidyutjihva had foolishly entered Ravana's fort alone, unprotected, unguarded mentally and physically. This was my chance to strike. I needed to see the King privately and pass on the news.

I was not sure where his chamber was located. Surely it would be heavily guarded? The only thing I could be sure of was the basic lethargy of my race. It was late and the guards would be asleep or drunk. The ferocious Asura of daytime battlefields was a different creature from the fun-loving, woman-chasing, brawler of the night. This could have been one of the Asura's best kept secrets. To defeat the Asuras, attack late at night. This could be why the ancient Asura code insisted on *Dharmayudha*, where war was based on ethical principles and the most important thing was that no battles were fought at night.

I went around the palace once, keeping to the cover of the hedges, to see which was the best access point. I scrambled up a mango tree and hoped that the balcony windows would be open. It was hot and humid. Somebody coughed and I froze. I could hear my heart thumping. I stood still for a few minutes and then moved again. All the windows opening onto the verandahs were closed. I cursed. Time was running short. If Vidyutjihva returned to the boat or the princess saw me on her way back, I could start my last prayers. One window was open. I moved near it. Someone was sleeping on the bed inside the room. I wasn't sure if it was the king as there was no bride beside him. But his profile resembled the king. I hesitated, but I knew time was running out. A small oil lamp burned near the bed. The face lay in shadow.

I entered the room and whispered, "Your Highness. . ." There was no response and I moved closer to make sure it was Ravana. Suddenly, like a pouncing tiger, the man jumped on me and seized me by the throat. I was too frightened to speak. With his other hand, he brightened the lamp. To my horror, I found I was in the wrong room. Not to say that the treatment would have been different had I been in the right room. But it was terrifying. The man holding me by my throat was Vibhishana. Of all the people in the palace, I had ended up in the room of this pious rascal. I was more afraid as he was unpredictable. I trembled with fear. He slowly loosened his grip and set me down and I collapsed onto the floor. He towered over me with his sword drawn.

"Don't kill me, my Lord, please do not harm me." I cried.

"Bhadra, you scoundrel, you were trying to murder me. You are either a ghost or you refuse to die!" It appeared that he was also confused. Taking advantage of his predicament, I continued to plead. He stamped his foot in anger. I stopped whimpering and crawled back to the wall and curled into a ball. I was still shaking. His anger was unnerving. I had always suspected that he was a dangerous man and his characteristic calm and poise was just a mask, but seeing him with his sword poised to thrust into me and the mad gleam in his eyes, I was certain. I was sure he was the most cunning and ruthless of all men I had ever seen. He would go to any extent to achieve his ambition. He was unlike his brother, Ravana, who, though an egomaniac, was a nice person with compassion in his heart and a sense of justice and righteousness. This man was the devil incarnate. He was passionless and his piety and humility were all pretence. He would not hesitate to kill, maim or serve anyone if it served his purpose. He hid his ambitions well, but in the flickering light of the oil lamp and the ghastly shadow it produced on the opposite wall, I could see through his soul. Perhaps I saw the evil shadows of the future also. What the great learned ministers or all powerful Ravana did not even suspect, Bhadra, the country bumpkin, knew. One day, if an opportunity presented itself, this bastard would sell his soul for a piece of land or some gold coins. I fell at his feet again.

"What are you doing in my room?" His voice had a sinister edge.

"Sir, I was afraid to tell His Highness. You know his anger. But you take decisions with a calm mind and do only what is right. . ."

"You idiot, how dare you enter the palace at dead of night? Did nobody stop you? Where are the palace guards?" His voice rose each moment.

"My Lord, my lord. . .please. . .This is a matter of utmost importance and secrecy. Please do not call the guards. . ."

He kicked me and I groaned.

"Why should I not call the guards? You should be hanged."

"This involves your sister. She is meeting with someone. . .please do not kick me. . ."

He stopped and raised me from the floor by my throat and whispered in a malicious hiss, "What have you got to do with my sister, son of a swine?"

Between the choking and coughing, I managed to say with some satisfaction, "Vidyutjihva, the rebel king and traitor your people have been hunting for the last few months, is with your sister now, in the garden." I completed my words with a smirk. *'Take that, you blue blooded Asura bastard.'*

He threw me to the floor, but I could feel his strength had ebbed. He sat on the bed tired, not knowing what to do. My time was running out and I had to think fast. "Shall we call Lord Maricha, Sir?"

"I will go. Are they still there?" He slowly stood up and put the sword back into its sheath and belted it round his waist.

I could not resist adding, "They couldn't have finished by now." He glared at me and I expected another blow, but he simply walked out of the room. I followed in his wake. Maricha slept on the ground floor, with his family. We descended the wooden stairs. He paused for a few seconds before Maricha's room, and then knocked softly. There was no response for some time and so he knocked again. After a few minutes of silence, we heard the rustle of clothes and someone walking with heavy steps on the wooden floor. The door creaked open. Maricha stood with sleepy eyes and was visibly irritated.

"Uncle, we have a problem with Soorpanakha." Suddenly Maricha was alert. He closed the door behind him and came out. Vibhishana explained and when he mentioned me, Maricha's eyes expanded with surprise. He heard everything and went back into the room. When he came out, he was fully armed. We moved out of the palace past the snoring guards. When we reached the garden, I pointed to the place where his sister was and slowed down to hang back. The two warriors approached from either side. Suddenly there was a piercing scream and I saw the princess run into the palace. She was almost nude. Then there was the noise of a scuffle and

Maricha, seeing that the princess had reached the palace safely, shouted for the guards. Vidyutjihva fought bravely and would have murdered Vibhishana, had not scores of armed guards arrived and captured him. The guards were sleepy, drunk and slow, but numbers did matter.

At last I was free! Now I could have Mala for myself. I did not have to share her with wooly-eyed aristocrats with illusions of grandeur. I wanted to howl and dance and sing. But I remained hidden in the bushes. In the event of Vidyutjihva doing some heroic act and escaping or becoming the top dog in the scuffle, I did not want to be caught on the wrong foot.

24 Death of a revolutionary

Ravana

I lay and tossed on my bed. Sleep eluded me. Today too I ended without sex with my wife. I had always thought I had a tremendous sex drive. But my marriage has been a disaster from the first. On the first night, my frigid wife refused to even undress. She submitted to my half-hearted caresses with an immobility that bordered on death. She tried to be a model wife as far as other things were concerned. She took care of me like a small child, which irritated me to the core. She was kind to all and sundry, and tried to run the palace like a village housewife. But three times in my four months of marriage, when I attempted to get close, she was like a wooden block. I lost arousal, both sexual and mental, in a few seconds. After that, I did not dare attempt anything. Night after night, I spent hours on my bed irritated with myself, my wife, and the whole world, while my wife slept soundly beside me, fully covered like an old woman, without any concern that her husband lay wide awake, hating her every moment for her indifferent attitude towards him.

There were noises somewhere out in the garden. Wearily I got up from my bed and went to the window. It was closed. Even in the hot, tropical nights, my wife did not allowed me to open the windows. That was another thing that irritated me. I prised the window open and the sounds became clearer. Some scuffle was going on. Blasted Asuras, some soldiers must have been fighting after a good drinking session. Someone knocked on the door. Before I could reach the door to open it, the knocking became louder. I opened the door, glancing back at the queen. She slept like a baby, unmindful of all the commotion around. Uncle Maricha was standing outside, fully armed, and before I could ask anything, he gestured for me to remain silent, grabbed my left hand and dragged me out.

"We have a problem." Maricha whispered in my ear. I braced myself to hear the news of an imminent attack by some Deva army or Varuna turning against us. I never imagined it would involve my sister. And of all the rascals and goons on earth, I did not imagine Vidyutjihva would be the person involved with my sister. In growing surprise, then in dismay and anger, I listened to the licentious story of my sister's nocturnal adventures. She had shut herself in her room and refused to come out. The only good news I heard that night was that the biggest rebel and my rival, Vidyutjihva, had been captured. And surprise, surprise, it had been my pious brother, Vibhishana, who had done a worthwhile act for once in his life.

I did not even bother to put on my sandals or my shawl. I asked Maricha to call all the ministers to court and immediately commence a trial. I walked as fast as I could towards the *durbar*. I was sure my wife would not even have heard the door banging shut. Bless her.

The *durbar* was dark and the guards were sprawled on the floor, fast asleep. One was snoring. I kicked him in the ribs and he scrambled up with a curse. Then, seeing me, he blinked like an owl for a few minutes. Recognition finally dawned and he promptly fell at my feet. I did not have time for his antics so I kicked him again. He ran out and the other buffoons also awoke and ran. I stood in the dark till my ministers arrived. My servants had not lighted the lamps or torches and we stood in the centre of the *durbar* hall as the idiots ran hither thither like rats. After overturning two chairs and breaking a good vase, the room was finally set and the assembly began in earnest.

Prahastha, with his characteristic emotionless voice and precision of thought, managed to irritate everyone. He advocated the beheading of the rebel the next morning, in the main market place, to set an example to all those who nurtured intentions of rising against the State. For once, I found myself in agreement with Prahastha, but was unwilling to conclude the proceedings immediately after his speech. No one stood up to contradict him. I saw Maricha fidgeting and on the verge of saying something. Vibhishana was uncharacteristically silent and we were all spared the heavy dose of morality and ethics which he usually shoved on us at every possible opportunity. He must have been gloating over the fact that he was instrumental in capturing the rebel and did not want to lose his glory. As silence ruled, I stood up to say that the execution would take place the next evening. Prahastha had suggested early morning, so I felt good about contradicting him. Wearily, I dismissed the meeting and returned to my room.

My wife was still sleeping and a silver beam of moonlight illuminated her face. She looked so angelic and innocent that I was moved by the sheer poetry of her face. I had a sudden urge to kiss her. I sat beside her, grabbed her face, and kissed her on her lips. She mumbled something and turned on the other side and continued to sleep. Denied again, I wanted to grab her by her hair and bang her head to pulp. But then, unknown to me, in the past four months of marriage, a seed of love had been planted inside my soul. Against my wishes and determination, I found myself madly in love with my wife. I lay down, careful not to touch her, and started thinking about Bhadra, how he had come back into my life, and then my thoughts drifted to my sister. She was someone who had been denied everything in life. As a child, she had been denied every comfort, love and affection. It was no wonder that she fell into the trap of love. I had cornered the lion's share of my mother's love. Then, when we grew up, I had been so much in love with myself and my ambition, that I had forgotten to even acknowledge my sister's existence. She had always been a lonely child. Not beautiful to look at, a dark and somewhat plump girl, her existence had been dreary and dull until suddenly she became the princess of Lanka. Then there were many suitors. I had been so immersed in governing that I had not kept an eye on her. I had the feeling that she had become more bubbly and happy, but put it down to her sudden elevation in status. Now I understood why she appeared so happy. She was in love, or she believed she was in love. Whether the feeling was reciprocated by that bastard, I did not know. How daring of him, to court the King's sister when there was a price on his head. Was he using my sister as a bait? I would ensure he paid a price for his audacity. Rudraka will have a good time tomorrow.

I kept tossing on my bed as sleep eluded me. Finally, giving up any attempt to sleep, I got up to perform my morning chores. My wife slept without a worry in the world. I envied her for a while and then without disturbing her, I went out of my chambers.

My ministers were waiting for me when I reached the *durbar*. I was late and I hurried to my throne. I could feel the tension in the air. And then I saw her. I did not like it. I did not like it a bit. Soorpanakha was standing there, hair dishevelled, eyes red and sore, in an angry mood. The last thing I wanted was emotional blackmail. I hated it when my governance became mixed with personal affairs. I was in a no-win situation here. I was sure she was going to use all her tricks to persuade me to let her lover off the hook. I was already angry by the time the murmuring settled down in the *durbar*. I looked around and caught Maricha's eye. He was shaking his head and I braced for the worst. Prahastha sat with his hands crossed at his chest, his determined chin up, and a look of supreme arrogance and defiance in his face. Kumbha drooled in his seat and Vibhishana was busy going through some palm leaves. All my ministers sat in various postures of defiance.

"I wish to marry Vidyutjihva." There was perfect silence in the room and Soorpanakha came a few feet forward and looked me straight in the eye and repeated, "I will marry him and you can have him hanged after that. And once you murder him, I will commit *sati* on his funeral pyre."

Inadvertently I flinched. The notion of an Asura woman committing the custom of Deva widows, would have been shocking, even if she was not my sister. The entire clan would become a laughing stock. "Don't try to blackmail me." I shouted at the top of my voice.

Then she started behaving hysterically. She began hitting her head with her hands, tearing her hair and screaming at the top of her voice. It was quite a scene. I could see the servants and guards trying hard to stop laughing. I became pale and was totally clueless as how to handle the situation. It was most embarrassing. I looked at Maricha but he was concentrating hard on a small spot on the opposite wall, studying it intently. Soorpanakha called me names and dared me to behead her. The entire palace was silent except for my sister's insane howls, screams and curses. I felt helpless, angry, tired and confused. But more than that, I felt guilty for not being a good brother, for not caring enough for my family, for separating my siblings from our parents, and for being so nakedly ambitious. I knew I was weakening inside.

I saw Kumbha rise from his seat. "Brother, this is a family issue and we should deal with this in private," he said ponderously. I was grateful to him and stood to denote the dismissal of the meeting. Then my favourite friend stood up. Prahastha, in his most pompous and grating voice, said, "Your Highness, this is no longer a family issue. This concerns the entire Asura kingdom. This is about an enemy of the State and how firmly we deal with terrorism and treason. This is about the future of a nation. The fact that the rebel is a lover of the King's sister, does not change anything. Rather. . ."

I cut him short with a grunt and then exploded, "Stop your lecture, Prahastha. I know what it is and how important it is to our race and civilization. But have some patience and pity on the poor girl. . ." My voice trailed off. Had I become so weak that I had to ask for pity from my own minister?

"I do not have anything to say in private. I want to be hanged by this heartless monster." Soorpanakha started screeching again.

Prahastha stood up, bowed and left. One by one, all my ministers left, except Maricha, Vibhishana and Kumbha. I sat on my throne with my head buried in my hands. A splitting ache had started throbbing deep inside my head. Maricha came near me, patted me on my shoulders and asked me to take a decision according to my conscience. From there things went out of my control. Vibhishana and Kumbakarna argued that nothing was more important than our sister's happiness. They insisted that if we could not make our own sister happy, the kingdom was not worth it. I wanted to protest that I could not let a man accused of treason go unpunished, just because my sister wanted him. I, as King, could not set a bad example. I had many arguments why Vidyutjihva needed to hang but I am ashamed to say, I kept quiet. I allowed them to convince me that Soorpanakha needed to be married off to her lover. So, against my better judgment, against my minister's advice, against what was right, moral, ethical, and even practical wisdom, I allowed my sister to marry the enemy. I retired to my chambers, a broken man, leaving Vibhishana to convey the news to my sister.

25 A little worm

Bhadra

It had been six months since Vidyutjihva had become Ravana's brother-in-law. My life, as usual, continued to be miserable. I could not show my face in the palace since Vidyutjihva would have ensured my death. I was also not sure about Ravana. Now that they had become relatives, I did not know what my position was. I hid in the forest for a few days and when hunger chased me out of hiding, I tentatively came out to the streets. For a few weeks I lived in mortal fear of getting caught. Every time I saw a soldier or heard the noise of the police chariots rumbling through the streets, I hid. Then slowly my fear ebbed. I was too small for kings and the relatives of kings to be bothered about me.

After a few more weeks of loitering about the streets, I moved in with Mala. At first she was glum and did not want to have anything to do with me. The entire revolutionary cadre had been dismantled with the disillusioned idealists returning to the villages on the mainland and the opportunists, who were the majority, joining Ravana's army and holding positions of power. Mala was a subject of ridicule as her hero lover had left her for the dark and ugly princess. On the first day she did not allow me inside her house and abused me. I grinned as I knew I had won. Finally, at midnight, I was allowed in and I had a real meal after months. Then we made love and slept, but in the morning she was sour again. I ignored her mood and kept humming that old Asura folk song which I knew irritated her. The song was about a plump, dark Asura girl who chased every man in town. It was a rowdy song and I paused and rolled and cooed at the appropriate places to make sure she understood who the heroine of the song was. She went out after showering me with more abuse, but nothing could dampen my mood for many days to come. That was until I found out that she was meeting her old lover on the sly.

I was so mad with the slut that I wanted to murder her the night I found out about her trysts. Instead, I ended up between her legs panting and puffing. I was angry with myself for being manipulated, angry with her for treating me like this and I plotted revenge. With each thrust, I imagined my dagger piercing that man's bowels. She pushed me back with contempt and went outside the hut to wash herself near the well. The image of her standing stark naked in the moonlight made me feel weak but I turned and closed my eyes. I could hear her coming into the room, but I did not turn. I could feel her naked body beside me, but her contempt erected a wall thicker than that of any fort. I wanted to turn and grab her, but I could not. I lay there with my heart beating furiously, my thoughts of erotic adventures mixed with physical violence, anger mixed with lust, and a hundred other emotions, all coiled together like cobras. I developed a headache and lay there helpless and naked, with the growing realization that I was nothing but an impotent worm in the greater order of things in this big, bad world.

When I woke, I felt irritable. I stood up lazily with a towel around my waist and walked towards the well. I could smell the toddy on my body and I was disgusted with everything. I stood for a long time gazing at the reflection of my black face in the glistening well water. I wanted to jump in and end it all. But there was only two feet of water. Slowly, a plan formed in my mind. I had to meet Ravana somehow.

I came back to my room and dressed to go out. My crumpled *dhothi* smelt but I did not have a spare one. I looked like a beggar. I combed my hair with my hands and put ashes on my forehead. Then I walked towards the palace. By the time I reached the main gate, there was a huge crowd outside. I was curious about the commotion. Lots of sweet vendors and groundnut sellers were moving about among the general hustle and bustle and a gang of teenagers were trying to break into the crowd. I asked one tall, black, bony young man what the matter was.

"You don't know?" His large eyes bulged in surprise.

"Hell! How should I know?"

"It's alright, you are too old and so you need not bother." he said.

I was irritated. I was only thirty-five, but perhaps, to a man of nineteen, anyone above twenty was an old man. Hiding my irritation as best I could, I asked him, "What are those buffoons fighting about?"

"You old rascal, we are all going to become soldiers of our Emperor."

"Emperor, what Emperor?" I stopped in mid-sentence. Perhaps the king had promoted himself. I was alright with Emperor or Maharaja or whatever, as long as he did not bother me.

"The Emperor needs a large standing army, which is why he needs idiots like you." I could not for my life imagine what this lanky child was going to do in the army.

"By Shiva, you are really a country bumpkin, uncle," his companions snickered. "Our Emperor is planning to attack north India. We Asuras are going to have our revenge. We will teach the Deva bastards a lesson they will never forget."

Almost at the same moment an electrifying thrill swept through the crowd. And huge cry rose in waves. I could see a tall, glittering figure on the top balcony of the palace. Cries of "Long live our Emperor! Victory to the Asuras! Death to Devas!" rang through the crowd. Bejewelled and bewitching, the tall figure of Ravana, with his sword drawn, shouted "*Har Har Mahadev*! Hail Shiva!" And the crowd picked it up. Cries of *Har Har Mahedev* rang through the crowd. The crowd swelled and I was almost in the middle now. Soon another, more attractive figure, joined Ravana. The spectacularly dressed Vidyutjihva, joined his brother-in-law on the balcony. He was followed by the portly Kumbakarna, and relatively diminutive Vibhishana. Then one by one, Ravana's commanders and ministers joined the Emperor on the balcony. The crowd was in a frenzy. Drums were beaten. The sounds of *chenda* and *timila* created a huge din and the atmosphere was electric. Battle horns blared and conches were blown.

I was thrilled. The secret wish I had nurtured in my heart, revenge on the Devas who had shattered my little daughter's head and raped my wife, possessed me. This was the moment I had waited for. I cried at the top of my voice, "*Har Har Mahadev*! Death to the Devas! Death to Indra! Victory to Maheswara!" I was joined by many and I soon became the caller for a group of about fifty, who repeated whatever I said, with much energy and enthusiasm. The portly Asura closest to me, tried to outshout me but a well directed, secret, kick on his foot, silenced him for the day and my leadership was ensured, at least for the moment. Vidyutjihva tried to say something but nothing spoken from the balcony reached the crowd.

Many small circles had formed in the huge crowd and each group tried to create the maximum noise. A few fought each other, but the general enthusiasm was unbeatable. This went on for more than an hour. The sun was almost overhead and thousands of black bodies glistened. The smells assaulted my senses as did the heat and humidity. A sore throat bothered me but I kept up the cries, lest someone else take over the mantle. Then suddenly, a hush fell over the crowd. The dignitaries had left the balcony as the sun's rays now beat down mercilessly. They had retired to their cool chambers inside. Someone in the rear picked up the cry, once more hailing Shiva. I could see men on horseback entering the crowd. There was a big stir near the horses and food packets were thrown. Thousands of black hands went up to catch them. I too pushed forward and fought my way through to get a food packet. It turned out to be stale meat, some rice and a very spicy fish curry, wrapped in dried banana leaves. I gobbled it up. By late afternoon, the crowd dispersed, leaving the palace grounds littered with banana leaves, fish bones and food crumbs.

I walked along the main street thinking about a way to get into the palace. The lanky Asura and his other teenage friends were sitting on the steps leading to the Shiva temple and ogling the girls passing by. Such an uncomplicated life! The lanky teenager waved to me and as I had nothing better to do, I moved towards him. He swept the step near him with his hand, sending a puff of dust flying, and motioned to me to sit down. I walked to the boiled-peanuts vendor under the Banyan tree and used my last change to buy a handful of steaming peanuts, wrapped artistically in plantain leaves and then went and sat with the teenager, offering my peanuts to the gang. They passed around the packet and by the time it reached me, only a few nuts were left.

"I thought they were going to war today." I said nonchalantly, and the teenagers burst out laughing as if I had told them a great joke. I grinned tentatively and the lanky teenager slapped my back. I grinned wider.

"This has been going on for the past few weeks. Even we are impatient. We just want to go out and beat the Devas." the boy said casually.

"They say the Deva girls are very beautiful." An ugly Asura boy with protruding teeth, added with some hope.

"Oh they have fair complexions and breasts like mangoes," another Asura boy stated dreamily.

"But they smell like rats." said another intellectual-looking boy.

"Oh you have smelt them then?" asked my lanky one, and everyone laughed.

"But why do you want to join the army? Do you have any personal grudges against the Devas?" The question I asked sounded stupid, even to me.

"They have killed lots of Asuras, haven't they? They destroyed our temples. They do not respect Shiva, do they?" The boys looked rather confused.

"My mother says the Devas have horns and also tails. They hide the tails in their *dhothi* folds."

"Old women's tales," the intellectual one hissed, "they are just uncivilized barbarians."

"I suppose you people just want to roam the world." I said.

"Ah, but we will die for our race." The lanky one stood up with his fist

clenched and added dramatically, "Our bodies for the earth, our lives for the Asura race." The other boys cheered and continued chatting animatedly.

I envied their youth and innocence. I feared what war would bring to these poor children. *What do these simpletons know of war?* I felt very old next to them. I felt I did not belong. I was too grown up for my own good. I sat there for a long time and when the sun slid behind the tall coconut palms and the evening sea breeze caressed my tired body, I wearily slipped out of the chattering gang and made my way home.

Wafts of evening prayers and the jingle of temple bells mixed with the jingle of bangles of pretty girls moving up the temple steps. There was an air of gaiety and life brimming over from all sides. Yet, I felt a cold fear that this beautiful evening would fade away like the mist. I was mortally afraid of what the darkness would hold when it emerged from the folds of the mist. I could discern the faint smell of blood and smell war and death. But above all, I could smell a terrible treachery and decay. The dream of our poor, blasted race, had begun to turn sour.

I dragged my feet to the palace and requested an audience with the Emperor himself. The portly gatekeeper looked as if I had escaped from a mad house and promptly shoved me out. I waited outside in the garden surrounding the palace, under an Ashoka tree, hoping the Emperor would see me from his balcony or window, and grant me audience. This just proved that I had yet to learn my lessons. I slept under that thick tree that night, and in the early morning, when it rained, I walked back to my hut. Then in the evening, I walked back and waited under the Ashoka tree again.

26 The untouchable king

Ravana

The day faded slowly. It was so hot that the island was like a damp cloth just washed in hot water. I was tense and nervous. The preparations for war had been going on for the past few weeks. It was a sort of pilgrimage for me. I had never crossed the Narmada, except for a brief trip to the Himalayas through the forest trails and I was eager to see the legendry cities on the banks of the Saraswathi and Indus, which the Asura civilization had built at its peak. Not that much remained standing now. The rising tides of the Indus, the slow drying up of Saraswathi, sieges and raids, had turned those cities into the biggest graveyard of our race and civilization.

An entire civilization and its people had been crushed and their spirit annihilated. A great race had been taught to think of themselves as inferior creatures, to hate the colour of their skin and believe that fairness was equivalent to greatness. But now, the time of reckoning had come. From a remote island on the southern tip of this vast land, a man with no royal blood or great ancestry, a half-bred Asura, was going to claim the lost lands of an old civilization. I felt the thrill in my veins. It was a new dawn. When history spoke of Ravana, it would be with awe and pride, about a man who, against all odds of poverty and opposition, led a spiritually crushed and vanquished people to glory. By Shiva, the Asuras would rule this vast country again. That is if everything worked according to plan.

I entered my private chamber and spread out the cloth with the hand-painted map of the sub-continent. If I had to begin an attack, I would have to follow the eastern coastline, smashing the smaller Asura kingdoms and then reaching Alakapuri. My step-brother held fort there and he, with his genius for business, had rebuilt his business empire. Now his ships sailed east instead of west and he chose to avoid the islands altogether. And he was once again one of the richest men in the world. To fund my campaigns, I would have to loot my brother once again.

But, more than funding or war plans, what worried me was the fate of my little one. Her birth was difficult and we did not dare hope she would survive. When I held her little, tiny body in my hands, hardened by years of warfare, I felt deeply content. I felt I owned the whole world and nothing else mattered during the hours I spent watching my wife cooing to the baby, feeding and bathing her. I could have gone on with that life for ever. But then one day, everything changed. An astrologer, who claimed to be my father's friend, came to the palace, looked at my daughter and proclaimed in front of everyone, that she would bring destruction to the Asuras. From that day onwards, all my family members, the palace servants, my ministers, began to behave in a strange fashion. They showed great reverence and love when my daughter was in my arms or with Mandodari. But I could feel the hatred and fear they felt for her. The Asuras were always so superstitious. I was afraid to commence a campaign leaving my daughter behind. She was hardly a few weeks old and the Asuras were capable of anything. I feared for her life. It would be hard to convince Mandodari to allow me to take my daughter along. But I would find a way. It was ridiculous to carry an infant into war camps, but it was better than having her poisoned or stabbed while I was busy building my empire. I could keep a watch if she was with me. Perhaps I could ask Bhadra to keep an eye on her. But could I trust him?

Ideally, a small army of dedicated troops would have been a better bet and more effective if our small group could strike repeatedly like lightning in the night and vanish. That way, we could break the peace and morale of the enemy. Only Karthiveerarjuna, on the west coast, and Bali, in central India, would be dangerous for a small army. Their kingdoms spread away from the sea and we would have to undertake pitched battles inland. The swamps of the Narmada were too shallow for the bigger ships of the Asura navy and reaching the rugged middle India on foot, through thick shrub forests, would be tricky. But smashing the barbarian Deva tribes of the Gangetic plains might not be such a problem.

I was about to retire when, in the dying light, I saw a lonely figure limping slowly away from the palace. There was an odd familiarity to the small, dark figure. A sudden flash of lightning lit up the entire area as if it was daylight and I clearly saw the figure as it looked up in fear. Bhadra! The fellow never seemed to die. I did not know what feelings surged through me, was it relief or hatred or pity? But then, why did I call my page and ask him to bring the man into my chamber at that godforsaken hour?

BHADRA

The siege of Alakapuri was the bloodiest battle I had ever fought in. By the time we reached Kubera's kingdom, the Asura ranks had swollen to a few lakhs and the ravaging army left many smoking villages and fallen cities in its trail. By then, over sixty small and large kings and tribal chieftains had accepted Ravana's suzerainty and joined the victorious army. In many cities the Brahmins were hunted down and hanged. The idols of Vishnu were smashed and trampled upon and the Shiva *lingam,* installed in their place. It was a restoration of Asura pride. It electrified the whole country which rose as one against the Deva oppressors. Ravana led from the front with inspiring bravery which at times bordered on dare-devilry or outright foolhardiness. But nothing inspired Asuras more than a leader who was contemptuous of death.

Soon suicidal squads stormed the smaller forts and captured them one after the other, sometimes with boring ease but at other times, after bloody, pitched battles. Prahastha, Rudraka, Vajradhamstra, Maricha, Vidyutjihva, Kumbakarna, Dhumraksha – were all Asura heroes making a name for themselves through their ruthless execution of Ravana's strategies. They thought nothing of the loss of a few thousand Devas or Asuras. They sought glory and achieved it through blood and gore. A few dead Asura boys were incidental and inconsequential. The lanky Asura lad who had been so eager to participate in the war, was dead within the first hour of the attack on a petty south Indian kingdom on the west coast. I had a strange desire to touch his headless torso, but before I could move, whatever remained of his body was trampled under the marching elephants.

Finally, the army halted on the outskirts of Kubera's capital, Alakapuri. Our army camped in the farms outside the city and we looted the countryside for provisions and meat, and needless to say, we did not spare any woman. The countryside was fertile and rich, the men strong, and the women lovely and doe-eyed. So it gave us great pleasure to slay the men and take the women. Sometimes I felt we were no different from the rampaging Deva army which had trampled my village. But then, peer pressure is something which even great men find hard to resist. It was easier to succumb to temptation than raise oneself to the chivalrous act usually heard about only in legends and fairy tales. After all, they were just Devas and deserved to be hated, irrespective of their social standing. Like any other Asura, I too was quite sure of that.

We were getting desperate. It had been more than two months now and there was no sign of Kubera surrendering. The monsoon was approaching and we had stripped the entire countryside of everything it could offer. It was then that Prahastha saw stray dogs emerge from a hole in the ground, a few hundred metres into the jungle. Intrigued, he kept a watch at the spot and was surprised to find that at dead of night, men with supplies removed some earth and entered a secret chamber. Prahastha returned to the camp with the news and soon half our army was busy digging. Within minutes we found a huge, circular, iron door. We prised it open and one by one, thousands of soldiers entered the secret corridor which led to the fort.

I was among the first brave fools to enter. We took Kubera's army by surprise. They fought well but our army had swarmed the fort from all sides. We inched forward until finally, when the first rays of sun streaked across the eastern sky, Kubera's army was either butchered or had fled. When we reached Kubera's chamber, it was on fire. We cheered, thinking the King was dead, but Prahastha, after examining the scene, declared that it was just a ruse and the King had escaped. Then we found another secret chamber leading to the jungle, but we were too late. Kubera had got away.

Hoofprints pointed to where the King had mounted his horse and galloped away. Our sentries searched the countryside but they were in no mood to continue as their colleagues were busy looting the palace. The treasures we plundered from Alakapuri helped swell Ravana's ranks.

After the fall of Alakapuri, things went back to the routine. We smashed and ruined Deva kingdoms; burnt Vishnu temples; erected Shiva temples wherever possible; and religiously followed all the usual itineraries of war such as arson and rape. We dragged Brahmins out and sent them to Vaikunta, the Deva heaven and abode of Vishnu. It was amusing to see them quiver in fear and curse us. When they saw their curses only drew derisive laughter, they prayed to Vishnu, then to Shiva, and finally fell at our feet to beg for their lives. Needless to say, we butchered them and took their women.

By the time we reached the petty kingdom of Ayodhya, on the banks of the River Sarayu, the monsoon ended. The river swirled black with rage. At a distance, we could see a few hutments and rundown buildings with a torn flag flying. It had the emblem of the rising sun, but going by its condition, it would have been more appropriate to call it the city of the setting sun. Ravana sent a messenger to Anarnya, King of Ayodhya, asking him to surrender. But six days passed and there was still no reply. Impatient, Ravana ordered us to cross the river and attack the city. But what a shock awaited us when we entered the city. Of all the places I had seen, this was surely the worst. The streets were filthy and urchins ran around naked. Flies buzzed over the rotting carcasses of street dogs. Pigs fed on refuse. People lived on the road, pissed and relieved their bowels where they lived. The streets were narrow and winding. It was a dust bowl. Had it not been on our way, it would not have been worth entering this hole. There was nothing here to plunder. There was no defending army to greet us. Instead, a swarm of beggars with outstretched arms rushed to meet us. We were confused and dug through our pockets for some change. Our army marched through the narrow streets with urchins cheering us and semi-naked women staring. When we reached the palace gates, there were only two old guards. The gate was made of rotting wood and the guard carefully pushed it open and allowed the invading army in.

Vidyutjihva was our Commander and he handed over the palm leaf reiterating Ravana's command to King Anarnya to surrender. The geriatric who appeared to be the head of Ayodhya's army, stared at the letter for a long time. I could see Vidyutjihva getting tense. Then I realized that the enemy captain was holding the letter upside down, staring at it and then at us, time and again.

"The fellow does not know how to read." the soldier near me sneered derisively.

"What is this?" the old captain asked Vidyutjihva in a feeble voice.

"Just go to your king and say that the Asura army has come to his town." Vidyutjihva hissed.

"The King is at his prayers." The old captain blinked a few times.

"Ask the buffoon to get here right now." Vidyutjihva sounded almost desperate.

"Yes, yes. . .sir, but the King is praying." The old captain looked at Vidyutjihva condescendingly and spelt each word as if talking to a dim-witted child, and added for good measure, "If you have an appeal, you should come tomorrow. Today is Tuesday and the King is praying."

The situation had become comical and we were all laughing when Ravana entered. He jumped off his horse and asked the old captain for his King. The old captain was having a bad day for sure. He had just tried to convince a dim-witted chap about the impossibility of seeing his King on a prayer day, when yet another came along asking the same thing. But Ravana was not a man for niceties. He pushed aside the captain and walked into the fort, unsheathing his sword at the same time. All of us followed.

After the luxurious palaces of Lanka and Alakapuri, it was a shock to see this dilapidated palace. Floors crumbed under our shoes, pillars were moth-eaten, curtains dusty, and there were holes in the roof. An old man sat cross-legged before an idol of Vishnu, mumbling. Ravana waited for a few moments and then tapped the old man's shoulder. For a few seconds, nothing happened. Then slowly, the old man turned and stood up falteringly. Ravana extended a supporting hand to the old king but he shook off Ravana's hand and shouted in a voice that belied his age,"Do not pollute me, you untouchable Shudra."

We were shocked. A mighty king, who now had suzerainty over almost half the known world, stood facing a frail, old man, who shamelessly called himself a king of a dilapidated town. Instead of cowering in fear, the old man had commanded the other not to pollute him. I stared at my King. He was taken aback for a moment and mumbled something which sounded suspiciously like my father, he is also a Brahmin.

"You untouchable, if your mother is casteless, so too are you." The old man was almost shouting.

Anger flared in Ravana's eyes and he got hold of the old man by his throat and pressed the blade of his sword to the nape of his neck. "I don't want to kill an old man who cannot fight. Surrender and I shall spare your life."

"I will not surrender to a Shudhra."

"I am not a Shudhra, I am an Asura." Ravana almost pleaded. The old king laughed derisively."Then fight us, you old rascal," Ravana bellowed.

"I will not demean myself by fighting a Shudhra."

"Then die at the hands of a Shudhra." Ravana roared.

"You Shudhra, I curse you in the name of Vishnu. My descendants will take revenge for polluting me. They will destroy your city, your clan, the honour of your wives, your sons, you. . ." With a clean sweep Ravana cut off the head of Anarnya, King of Ayodhya. He held the severed head of the old king above the idol of Vishnu. Blood dripped from the head and flowed onto the head of the idol.

"Scourge Vishnu, drink the blood of your devotee." He kicked the head like a ball and it landed with a dull thud at the foot of the idol. The blood soaked lips of Vishnu smiled mockingly at the Emperor. With a mighty blow using the hilt of his sword, Ravana broke open the head of Vishnu.

As if on cue, the army fell on the small temple of the dead king and demolished it methodically. We found rubies hidden inside the idol and the garlands that decorated the idol, were made of pure gold, studded with diamonds. The dead King's insult, that our mere touch would pollute his body, kept us enraged enough to plunder the dead Gods and their buxom consorts. But, in some corner of my heart, a monster clung tenaciously with its piercing tentacles. It was the Emperor mumbling, almost apologetically, to the Deva king, that he, Ravana, the mighty Emperor and saviour of Asuras, also had a Brahmin father.

27 Love at last

Ravana

I left the dilapidated palace for my army to plunder. There wasn't much to plunder except the old temple in the palace. While his subjects died of hunger, their king was decorating his God with rubies and diamonds. And the rascal had the nerve to say that my touch would pollute him. But then, why did I try to seek his approval by saying that my father was a Brahmin? I wanted to kick myself for that. What did that mean? Was there a racist devil lurking inside me? Or was I uncomfortable with my Asura identity? Prahastha, in his one of those professorial moods, might have said it was because I still yearned for my father's love. I hated my father and all that he represented. I hated the Brahmins, the Devas and their culture or the lack of it. I hoped no one had heard. I was their leader. These poor people had left their homes, their wives, children and old parents, to follow me in my quest for glory. And what did I give them in return? I ought to have been ashamed. Never again, never again would I consider myself a Brahmin. I hated my fair skin. I hated my height. I was an Asura, the proud inheritor of Mahabali, Hiranya, Hiranyaksha, and scores of mighty Emperors who had shaped Indian civilization.

People moved away from me as I passed through the market place. I thought at first that it was due to the respect accorded to a conquering Emperor, but then I realized it was because I was a Shudhra. I was polluting their grand city. Even the sight of us was polluting. I saw Brahmins in filthy clothes, thumping their walking sticks sharply on the ground to drive away any polluting castes. People conducted their business in the market place with elaborate rituals so no one would touch or pollute each other. But they also spat red *pan* juice all over the street and walked over it. People openly defecated but were still scrupulous about not touching each other. Had it not been so pathetic and ironical, it would have been comical. Some culture this! I thought that the burden of civilizing these people had fallen on our shoulders. If I did not stop this nonsense, this extreme form of caste practise would spread throughout India. And if it did, we could say goodbye to our freedom.

A few of my soldiers were busy looting the shops and I did not have the heart to stop them. After all, they were only taking what was originally stolen from our people. The irony was that the natives were more afraid of being touched by the Asuras than of being killed. It was truly an area of darkness. Another strange thing I noticed was that there were fewer women than men on the streets. And they were veiled and did not look the men in the eye. They walked with their eyes fixed on their dusty feet. I had never seen such submissive women in my life. This was a different culture, an exotic civilization which was centuries behind anything I had seen in any kingdoms of the Asura, Vanara, Yaksha or Nagas.

I had had enough of Ayodhya and rode back to the palace, which looked even more desolate after the looting. Some members of the royal family had escaped to the neighbouring jungles and Vajradhamstra asked for orders to follow and kill them. I ordered the army to leave this place and forget about petty kings and their pale, ghostly wives. According to Prahastha, that was bad strategy, to let the members of a conquered palace escape with their life without a proper treaty or their accepting to be our subjects. I did not have the time nor the inclination to check the veracity of such quixotic theories so I overruled him and we continued our eastward march.

Our army marched out of Ayodhya and I promptly forgot the name along with the other north Indian dustbins our army had marched through. Later, much later, a prince from this miserable place would turn my world upside down. Perhaps, had I followed Prahastha's advice and hunted down the royal family and finished them off, things would have been different. Maybe, our race would have been saved; our country retrieved from the clutches of a religion which discriminated against its own people. I was quite sure this darkness from the north would spread over my beloved country, splitting people, not by language or race or affluence, but by the subjective views of a set of Brahmins who decided what was pure and impure. But who could predict such things then? I had crushed so many kingdoms, so many princes, any one from those hundreds could have been my enemy. Or perhaps, I was not a good king. I never went by the book. People who played by the rules did not commit such silly mistakes, even if they did not come as far as I had.

After a day's journey, we came to a small village market place bordering the jungles belonging to a tiny Deva kingdom called Mithila. I was bored with the whole expedition. Unlike western and southern India, the villages in these parts were desperately poor. There were no big cities to plunder. There were no majestic Shiva temples. There were only old wrinkled Brahmins who terrorised the people and followed a rigid caste system. We wanted to go back to the balmy heat of the south. The ocean beckoned us. But I wanted to find a way back through the eastern seashore to Mahabalipuram and then to Lanka.

I was taking a well deserved nap when a scuffle outside my camp awoke me. I went out and stopped dead in my tracks. There were four or five Asuras trying to grab a woman. I was furious. Taking a girl was accepted when you had conquered a city after a bloody war, especially if she was a Deva girl. But there was a line. Where were my bodyguards? And then I saw them among the Asuras fighting for the lady.

"Leave her!" I bellowed. Three of the Asuras, including one wallowing in the mud, scrambled up and ran away. The other two vanished when they saw me unsheathe my sword. It was then that I noticed the quarry over whom they had been fighting. Her veil had fallen from her face. And what a face it was. Dark eyes burned like fire, deep curved lashes gave her an innocent look. Her lips were full and red under a small straight and sharp nose. Curly, dark hair fell onto her forehead. Her skin without blemish and a pout gave her a coy look. I stared at her. My eyes became transfixed on a small mole on the right cleft of her deep cleavage. She had full breasts and a flat stomach. I saw her blush as she recognized the passion in my roving eyes. She was the fairest woman I had ever seen. She exuded feminine charm and softness. I wanted her.

She adjusted her dress and I averted my eyes. Even though I had never stopped anyone from raping or taking any women when our army conquered a city, I myself had never done anything of the sort. It was against my upbringing and I ensured that children and old people were spared from abuse. But I wanted her. It was not like the acquired taste I had developed for my wife, Mandodari, whom I had almost forgotten now. Was it desire at first sight? This woman generated an animal passion in me. I moved towards her and grabbed her wrists. She pulled her arm back and I tried to grab her again. Then she slapped me hard. Right across my face. My cheek stung. I was shocked. When I grabbed her again, she promptly slapped me again, this time causing my nose to bleed. She was one spirited lady. I turned as though giving up, but then quickly spun round and lifted her off the ground. Ignoring her scratches and screams, I carried her into my tent. I was angry, but more than that, I wanted her. I threw her onto the bed and when she tried to get away, I slapped her across her face. She spat at me. I grabbed the silk sheet and tied her hands and legs and bundled her onto the bed, suffering three more bites and numerous scratches.

Then, puffing and panting, I fell into the nearest chair. She was lying with her back to me; her rounded hip again stirred waves of passion in me. Her waist was bared and I wanted to kiss the folds. Her thighs were shapely. I just wanted to run my fingers over her soft, fair skin. I imagined her naked in my arms and slapped the arm of the chair in anger and frustration. *'Why won't she have me? I am the Emperor of India. The mighty Asura king, Ravana.'*

After a few moments silence, I tried to turn her towards me. "What is your name?" I asked her and immediately felt stupid. She slowly turned up her face, her curly, black hair making designs on her forehead. Her eyes bored through me and I was afraid. A shiver went down my spine. *'This is a historic and fateful moment on which my fate and that of my race and my country hung.'* I shook off the idiotic thought and recalled my anger.

"Do you require a girl's biography, before you rape her?" she asked.

I didn't know what to say. A corner of my mind found something humorous in the statement and I wanted to laugh. But then, I foolishly stood up, lost for words, not knowing what to say. I coughed, stammered, and moved away from her.

"Once you have finished with me, please leave me alive for a few minutes. I want to see your king, Ravana, the great Asura," with these words she spat on the ground.

"But.. I am Ravana." my voice trailed off.

An animal cry rose from her. I was startled. How could such a lovely creature make such a hideous sound? She was struggling to free herself but finally gave up and dissolved into fits of sobbing. I stood watching from a distance. After some time, I moved near her. I wanted to touch her but my hands trembled as I hesitated and then slowly put an arm on her shoulder. She stirred and looked at me with hatred. I withdrew my hand.

"Do you know how a Deva widow lives?" she asked in a whimper. I remained silent. "Do you know the choices a Deva widow has... How should you know? You are the conqueror. Why should a few lives bother you. . .?"

I was moved beyond myself. But I was from a different culture. I had heard of the plight of Deva women but it was so horrible that I had thought they were stories spun by the Asura or Naga spin doctors to discredit the Devas.

"Your people killed my husband. He was a poor man. . . a Brahmin who did no one any wrong. . . Why did your people kill him?"

I was stung. '*What was I doing with a Brahmin widow? Was it because she was a Brahmin that I was attracted to her? Did her fair skin trigger the lust in me?*' I felt disgusted with myself. But then, I had known she was a high-born Brahmin woman the moment I saw her. Why did I choose to be shocked when she spelt out her lineage?

"We can live a slave's life in the house of our inlaws... with our heads shaven... hands and throats unadorned... purposefully made unattractive... a living corpse... no bindis for us... no bangles... no coloured saris... only coarse white... no life... an unpaid servant... a living corpse... "

I was moved. I could not imagine such a life for an Asura woman. If the husband died, she would mourn for a decent period and then find another life partner and move on with her life.

"You are a mighty King...ha.... You know I could jump into my husband's funeral pyre and become a Goddess... the virtuous *sati*. Then the same people who would have treated me no better than an animal in life... would erect temples and worship me."

"What is your name?" I asked her. I moved closer and lifted her chin. Tears swelled in the dark eyes and made them glitter. I saw my own reflection, so small that I felt my own insignificance. She stared for a long time at my face. Finally, the hint of a smile lit up her face. I dissolved.

"Vedavathi." she said simply and I promptly fell head over heels in love with this Deva Brahmin girl.

28 An asura princess

Bhadra

When the guard shook me from sleep, I cursed him and his forefathers. He prodded me with the blunt end of his spear and told me that the Prime Minister wanted to see me, so would I please pull up my *dhothi* and get going? I felt heavy from the previous night's drinking binge and was not in the mood for barrack humour. I cursed him again and tied my *dhothi* tightly and washed my face in the sluggish stream nearby. I smelt of country liquor so I gargled once more and dragged myself to the prime minister's camp. Why was I being summoned? The last few months had only brought disaster on our race. Most of the camp was thoroughly disillusioned with this campaign. We had been camping in the forest across the river Narmada, eating wild berries and the occasional monkeys that were foolish enough to stray near our camp, drinking badly brewed liquor, and waiting endlessly for some action.

The wise men, the great men, the royals, like Prahastha and the others, were huddled together, talking in whispers. But our great King, the mighty Ravana, had it coming. He was busy wooing an adamant Brahmin girl without a thought for all the fools who had started with him on this campaign. He refused to meet his ministers, stopped his inspections of the ranks, and even his inspirational speeches. She would sit cross-legged near the river, meditating or sometimes vehemently cursing the Asura King for what he had done to her people. The King, like a love-struck teenager, would coo nonsense to her and grovel before her, pleading for her love. He had even forgotten the little daughter he was carrying along and not even the hungry cries of the little one aroused Ravana from his love stupor. The Brahmin lady was immune to all his charms and this made the King desperate. Why he did not take her forcibly, was beyond my comprehension.

The campaign drifted on aimlessly, avoiding the bigger kingdoms, mostly skirting jungles and occasionally raiding some village barns. Finally, after many months of loitering, we reached the banks of the mighty Narmada, when our King decided to impress Vedavathi with his swimming prowess. He stripped and entered the swiftly-flowing river, and got drawn into the strong current. At least that was what the woman told the Council. Our mighty Emperor had sent his bodyguards away, so no one else saw what exactly happened.

A few days later, we received a messenger from King Karthiveerarjuna, claiming that he held the Asura King as his prisoner. The entire army was held to ransom. For three days the great Asura Council was shut up inside the Prime Minister's camp, deliberating. In the meanwhile, the camp split into two. Vidyutjihva's followers spread rumours that Ravana was already dead. They argued that it was better to return to Lanka.

The other group under Rudraka, proposed storming Karthiveerarjuna's stronghold and teaching the half-castes a lesson, even at the cost of our King's life. He had supporters like Sumali and Malyavan, who argued that Asura pride was at stake and an all-out war with a decisive outcome was needed. Of course, these were only speculations started by guards standing outside the camp where the Council met.

All the great men were seated in their cushioned chairs when I entered the tent. I bowed low and kept my hand over my mouth, my eyes staring at the floor, my spine bent, avoiding any eye contact. The King's throne stood vacant but Prahastha was seated just next to it. There was an uneasy silence. Then Prahastha spoke, "Bhadra, we are assigning you a special task. We feel only you can do it."

My heart jumped. '*At last! Here was the moment I had been dreaming about, a chance to become a hero, an opportunity to become a legend and escape from the mundane.*' It was not that I had always yearned to do courageous and brave deeds, but I had sometimes wished that fate would give me the chance of a lifetime to somehow save my King and become his favourite and the hero of the entire race.

"It might be disgusting but you have to do it." Maricha walked up to me and put a comforting hand on my shoulder. My ears burned. *'What were these people talking about?'* The dreams of my heroism disintegrated in a million pieces. It wasn't going to be a heroic rescue of our Asura King. That would be done by these nobles surrounding me.

The job is. . ." Maricha was finding it difficult to spell out. Vidyutjihva moved towards me menacingly and I cowered. I wanted to stand up and stare at his face, but my body remained bent. "You will take that Deva woman and dispose of her." he sneered. "And also that ill-fated little princess."

I recoiled from the shock of what I heard. I had never liked the woman but our King loved her. I might not love Ravana but I stuck with him because I believed that finally, he would outrun all these buffoons. And that would serve my purpose. And now, when he was in danger, perhaps due to his own folly, his supposedly good friends were plotting to finish off his love and his little baby girl.

"Should we kill her? And the little princess. . ." Maricha mumbled.

"Pshaw!" Vidyutjihva spat out. "We have had enough bad luck with the King running around this woman shamelessly. And have you forgotten the predictions? That little girl of Ravana is an ill omen to the entire Asura race. She will bring death and destructions to us and our King thinks all these are stupid beliefs. I do not want to take any chances."

"Enough!" Prahastha's voice was calm and clear, which made it more frightening. He looked uneasy and indecisive. "I need not tell you this but I believe that knowing the reason for this decision will help you do your duty to our race, with a clear conscience."

Maricha's voice was barely audible, as if he had swallowed something and was trying to talk at the same time. "Our war campaign has reached a critical point. We are on the verge of a total rout. Our King has been taken prisoner and we fear we will end up paying a king's ransom to Karthiveerarjuna. Morale is low among the troops and the Council has, in all its wisdom, taken a decision. We feel that the lady was a major distraction to our King. I won't go to the extent of saying she is a spy planted by the Devas, but I know many people who would vouch for such fantastic theories. Notwithstanding the veracity of such conspiracy theories, there is no doubt that she has become a millstone around the neck of the entire Asura race." Maricha paused and looked intently at my face. I was sure he could sense my intense hatred towards all these great men. He sighed and put his hand on my shoulder as he towered over me. I felt like a puppy looking up his master.

Prahastha moved towards me, then stooped from his great height and whispered darkly in my ear, "Take her and dispose of her."

Vidyutjihva moved nearer and hissed, "And do not forget the little one."

I stood still for some time and then, with the utter helplessness of the lower class of Asuras, I bowed from the waist. 'Your wishes are my orders, Guru.'

I was dismissed with a wave of the hand by Prahastha and went out with a heavy heart, Vidyutjihva's jeer burning deep within. I went to my camp and fell onto my ragged bed. I was tired of being a dog to these people. *'Who gave these rascals the divine right to ride over poor people like me?'* I felt anger and indignation rising in me, but then, at the precise moment when it was about to brim over, a soldier entered and put a plate full of delicacies on the floor beside me. He banged down a metal glass and poured fine wine. I sat up on my bed and watched the ritual with faint interest.

"You grovelled before them did you? Well, you are being fed well," he sneered and left.

All that we had got for the last few days had been a few spoons of rice and a watery gruel. There was never enough. But for the important ones, there was always enough and more. When you did what they wanted, they sometimes fed you a few morsels from their table. I stared at the plate for a long time. Suddenly I felt very hungry. I wiped my hands on my *dhothi* and eagerly ate my special treat. For good measure, I licked the plate as well. Then in one sweep, I swallowed the fine wine and threw the metal tumbler out. It landed somewhere in the darkness outside and registered its protest with a clang.

It was still dark when I was shaken awake from my drunken slumber. I had a searing headache and hangover. I could hear the noise of the ox cart getting ready. I went out and washed my face in cold water, shivered, and then stretched. I could see the tall figure of Maricha approaching me. Quickly, I went in and changed into some decent clothing. Then, fumbling with my clothes, I went out to meet him midway, bowed, and remained bent at the waist. He was in a dark, pensive mood. He silently came near me, stretched out a hand to touch me, but then decided against it. After a few moments silence, he said, "Bhadra, I'm sorry about the task we have entrusted to you. But do it anyway, for our race, for our King."

I remained silent. Somewhere a cock crowed before its time. "I hope what we are doing is the right thing. . . I feel sorry for the girl. . . and of course, for the Brahmin lady. Godspeed Bhadra. . .do your duty and do not trouble your simple mind with anything. Leave the worrying to us." And with a swirl, he turned on his heels and left.

I stood there bent for a few more moments. '*Simple mind indeed.*' I felt blood on my hands. When I stood erect, I prayed for strength and inner peace and waited for the exhilaration to sweep me, knowing that I was doing my duty. Nothing came to me except a sense of dread, self-pity and disgust. In that mood I walked to the kitchen. The clerk at the counter smiled when he saw me and handed over a bundle of food. The bustling activity in the kitchen at such an early hour surprised me. When I walked back, a drizzle had started. I tossed the bundle into the cart and climbed onto the driver's seat and waited.

The east had streaks of light when they brought her. She was drugged and being carried by two men. Her dress has become dishevelled and a large part of her white breasts were exposed. The men carrying her were ogling at the rare treat and sniggering. They dumped her in the back, winked at me, and left. After some time, Maricha came, carrying with a little bundle delicately in his hands. He kissed the forehead of the baby girl and slowly

deposited her near the woman. He turned back, trying to avoid my eyes. I saw a tear drop on the baby's thighs. She stirred a little, smiled angelically in her sleep and was at peace with herself.

I whipped the oxen and with a jerk the cart started its swaying journey. The sun had already risen and painted the world saffron when I reached the swelling Narmada. The drizzle had turned golden in the morning sunlight. There was a huge rainbow on the distant horizon and I turned away from it. The cart swayed and jerked its way through the narrow forest path towards the kingdom of the Devas. My quarry was asleep in her drug-induced world. The beauty of the forest cheered me and for some time I was able to push aside my dark thoughts. I enjoyed the cold drizzle on my face, the fragrant wind caressing my skin and I forgot what I had been entrusted to do. I was a simple-minded person, wasn't I?

It was dark and the sun sinking below the distant hills when I stopped for a rest. She was still sleeping. I felt the stirrings of sexual passion arising in me. Her breasts were still half exposed. I wanted to remove her dress completely and see what remained hidden. As I reached a trembling hand towards her, the baby near her stirred. It jerked me back and I felt ashamed. Then the anger came back. She was mine to do with as I pleased. I had been entrusted with her disposal. I was surprised I had brought her so far. I could have gone a few miles away and finished her off and come back in a few hours. The story to be spread was that we had been taking her and the princess to a village doctor a few miles from camp, as they were suffering from forest fever, but both had succumbed to the illness.

By now I was miles away from camp. Who would know if I had her? Perhaps the Council would appreciate my act. I moved again and had my hands firmly on her clothes. I tried to unknot her breast cloth. But in my excitement I found it difficult. I had almost got through when she opened her eyes and stared at me like a cow. I cowered, stopped my fumbling, and stood up. Tears brimmed in her eyes and a small drop fell and wet the red silk cloth on the floor of the cart. I felt ashamed and turned my face away. Then she howled – an animal cry of agony, pain, and abandonment. It startled the birds around. The little oil lamp I had carried had toppled over and spread oil stains on the silk sheet. I tried to put it upright but my hands were trembling in fear.

"You uncouth Asura," she screamed in a high pitched voice. 'How dare you touch me?" The baby had woken up and started wailing.

"Your master never even tried to touch me and you…scoundrel. How dare you?"

I had regained my anger. She was all alone in a forest and I had been instructed to kill her. I moved towards her as she tried moving away. She attempted to get out of the cart but the flickering oil lamp which had spread oil stains over her clothes, burst into life in the wind and her dress caught fire. Instinctively, I tried to smother the fire but she slapped me hard and ran towards the river, a ball of fire, screaming in pain and anger. She never managed to reach it. I ran behind her, trying to catch her, if possible save her. She screamed and screamed, but continued burning. She had fallen a few feet from the bank and was beyond any help. I gave up trying to save her. Afterall, my job was to finish her off. Yet, she refused to die for a long time. Lying there near the river, a mass of half-burnt flesh, she looked ghastly. She kept cursing the entire Asura clan. She screamed that Ravana had brought her to this and that she would return in the next life to haunt him. I watched her die with an indifference bordering on boredom. Before she died, she howled that she would enter the body of the little Asura princess as a spirit and ensure that the entire Asura clan was destroyed, and the prediction of that astrologer would come true through her wrath, through her chastity and such nonsense. Finally she died when the sky was turning faintly red in the east.

The baby had stopped crying. I ran towards the cart. She looked at me and there was a flicker of an innocent smile. I did not know what to do and thought of smashing her head on the nearest rock. Then I saw the image of a small girl's skull splattered in my own house by the Devas. Did I want to do the same thing to this baby? I lifted her and her small fists tightened against my little finger. I could not. I could not at all. I collapsed with the baby in my lap and wept.

I sat there for a long time and drifted off to sleep with the baby crying in my lap, until other sounds woke me with a jolt. A large hunting party appeared – I saw hundreds of armed men on horses and on foot. They were erecting a camp in a clearing by the river. The baby lay limp and almost blue, perhaps dead. I had to get away from here. The hunting party made enough noise to wake a whole village and I was afraid the baby would awaken and cry. The party looked like Devas, though there were many black-skinned among them. The last thing I wanted was for them to discover the dead Brahmin woman, and me with the baby... I had to get away.

But when I turned to go, I tripped and fell in the undergrowth. The baby slipped from my hands and rolled a few feet into a slime-covered ditch and let out a howl. To my horror, one of soldiers turned in our direction and I saw him alerting the others and pointing in our direction. They came towards us to investigate. I had clambered up a big Banyan tree, hoping they had not seen me. I was fortunate that the guards did not look up. I saw more soldiers coming and then heard a distinct cry of alarm. They had found the dead Brahmin woman, lying burnt near the river. I saw one of them running towards their main camp. There was some general agitation and I could see them trying to get the baby out of the slime. It was not a deep ditch but the baby was slowly sinking. The soldiers knew that the moment they stepped into it, they would sink into the quagmire.

A squat man with an air of importance came and the entire party bowed to him and started talking in excited voices. He peered into the ditch and ordered one of his minions to fetch a plough, which he carefully used to lift the baby out of the ditch. He felt for the baby's heartbeat and on his orders, his servants scattered to fetch various things. After a few minutes, the baby began to cry again and everyone cheered. I also felt like cheering from the canopy of the tree but held back the impulse. Hidden among the branches, I watched them cremate what was left of Vedavathi and learnt from their conversations, that the scholarly-looking man was Janaka, the King of Mithila.

That afternoon, the men assembled about their King, and with Brahmin priests chanting, the King bent to whisper the name he had given the baby. The entire camp erupted into cheers and the name of the baby, Sita or 'the one got with a plough', filled the air. I was happy for the baby. Instead of being eaten by some wild animal, she would now be a princess in a palace. This was a lucky baby and I hoped she would carry that luck through her entire life. She was my master's daughter, a princess of Lanka, an Asura princess, but born with a curse, a death warrant for her blasted race.

Later, after their partying was over and most of them were dead drunk or asleep, I slipped down from tree and entered the camp quietly. I stole some food from the kitchen and drank some wine from the half-empty jugs scattered around. It was then that I had the irresistible urge to see the Asura princess again. I entered the most luxurious looking camp and in the dim light of the flickering oil lamp, I saw the little bundle snuggled coyly in a white silk sheet, near the loudly snoring king. I went close to her and peered into her beautiful face. I stooped and gently planted a kiss on her cheek. Perhaps the vile fumes irritated her, because she pouted and then sucked her lips a few times. I stood for a few minutes, watching her tiny hands and legs. Then, with great reluctance, I slipped away from the camp, tears streaming down my cheeks and my legs weak with emotion.

As I reached the clearing, I looked back once more. I felt I was leaving my own daughter there and prayed to Shiva to keep her happy. I prayed she would grow into a lovely princess and marry some good Deva prince who would keep her happy forever. This King seemed to be a gentle sort and learned and wise. As I walked back through the jungle to the Asura camp, I wanted to take her back and adopt her as my own. I wanted to give her back to my King and confess the truth. I wanted to do many things but I was confused.

When I was sufficiently far away to think clearly, it struck me. I should have killed the baby. I shuddered at the thought, but had the premonition that she would come back one day. She would return to her clan and be the cause of the destruction of everything her father had fought for. I did not know how I knew, but these thought kept coming back. I prayed to Shiva for deliverance, but deep down I knew that even Shiva was helpless. Perhaps that would be her revenge – the revenge of an Asura princess on a proud and heartless race that wanted her dead even before she had a chance to know life. She would change the history of mankind. But I am running ahead of myself. I doubt whether I knew so much or was so clairvoyant then. All that would come later and consume us all, condemning my country to darkness for many millennia to come.

29 Let her live

Ravana

I did not want to face anyone. Like a bull in a market, I was exchanged for goods. My people bought me back by paying whatever we had gained from our campaign. The humiliation was complete. In one stroke, Karthiveerarjuna neutralized my army. We did not have anything to take back to Lanka. We had to surrender all our arms, except our personal swords, the horses, the elephants and the gold. And what we got in return was my worthless life. I wanted to die, but then again, the entire sacrifice would have gone to waste. What was even sadder was that I could not put up a fight.

Vedavathi challenged me to cross the swiftly flowing river and the fool that I was, I dived into the ravaging Narmada. I felt like a teenager trying to impress his girlfriend. But I underestimated the swiftness of the current. And before I could recover from my ill-timed dive, my head hit an underground rock. I almost drowned and then got swept away by the current. When I opened my eyes, I was in a dungeon, chained to an iron bed, like a mad man. Initially, I was angry at myself, at Vedavathi, at the Asuras, and at Karthiveerarjuna, who I guessed was my captor. But soon anger died in the damp dungeon. When the door opened for the stale food which was thrown in, a glimmer of hope gleamed. After a few days, even that died. I soon lost count of the days, the time, and forgot even my ambition, dignity and pride. I was just a rat, scurrying around the dungeon to survive

They had unchained me after a few days. My spirit was broken, but I kept myself sane by counting the footsteps of the guards outside. I tried to escape and failed miserably. I was beaten by the lowly guards. I would not have minded so much had Karthiveerarjuna come to supervise my torture. I had practiced the words to shock him with. I wanted him to see I could endure anything and that my spirit could never be conquered. But he did not come and I think that hurt me more than anything else. I wept like a child in that dark dungeon; I cried for my lost glories, my freedom, my ambitions. Sometimes I thought of Lanka and my almost-forgotten wife, Mandodari. I yearned for the fragrance of ripe mangoes. I relived the taste of yellow jackfruit, the spray of water from the gigantic falls of the Poorna, near Muzaris, the lapping of waves on the white sands, the swaying of coconut palms on a moonlit night, the smell of jasmine. . .

Then one day, when all hope was dead, buried, and turned rotten deep within me, the door to the outside world opened. There was a jeering crowd of motley soldiers and the servants of Karthiveerarjuna lined up outside the dungeon to see me off. The brightness of the day hurt my eyes and I kept my eyes shut. Like a blind man I stumbled out to freedom. I should have vowed revenge at that moment, planned and plotted, with my mind in a frenzy, to get even with my enemy, but sadly, my only thought was to get hold of a razor. My beard had grown and I badly needed a shave. Even now I feel ashamed for having had no other thought at that moment.

They ignored me when I arrived back at camp. I was a King no more, at least in their minds. I searched everywhere for my lover and baby. I was afraid to confront any of my ministers. They were all too busy supervising the packing for the journey back home – empty-handed. Desperate, I finally cornered Maricha, first demanded and then begged, for information about Vedavathi.

"Brace yourself, son." His words confirmed what I had feared since my ignoble return and I sank to the ground.

"How and when?" I managed to ask.

"Many people fell sick in these forests and there were so many deaths. She fell a victim to the sickness around and so did the little princess. They were taken to a country doctor, some distance away but both succumbed to the forest fever." He looked away.

I wept. I didn't have to pretend anymore. I did not want a kingdom, or glory, let the Asura race take care of itself. Prahastha or Vidyutjihva or whoever wanted the kingship, could take it. I blabbered on and on. I felt Maricha's tears hot tears fall on my shoulder. Then a gnawing suspicion raised its ugly head. *'No, it cannot be true. At least Maricha was my friend and he would not have let it happen.'* I jerked myself free and confronted him."Who took her to the doctor?"

Maricha's eyes were listless. He stared at a spot on the wall and mumbled, "Some soldier or the other. . . I will enquire and let you know but son, you have to put it behind you. . ."

"No!" I shouted. "Tell me who took them to the doctor." I shook him and I could sense the fear in his eyes. But his lips were pressed together and he avoided my gaze. "Was it Bhadra?" I cried out aloud, dread filling my bowels as I uttered the cursed name.

Silence. . . then he started again, "Ravana, please. . . let it go. . ."

I almost knocked him down and ran out. I had my sword unsheathed and shouted for Bhadra. A few soldiers who were engaged in a game of chess under a tree, turned their heads towards me. When they saw the sword in my hand, they stood up swiftly. One of them ran out and returned in a few minutes, bowed and whispered, "Your Highness, Bhadra is on the way." His use of the honorific somehow soothed me a little. It had been a long time since someone had addressed me as a king. Perhaps the naked sword in my hand had done the trick. *'What am I thinking? Am I so obsessed with power that the instant a lowly servant shows me respect, I stoop to forgetting my lover and my baby's death?'*

By the time, that sly Bhadra came, I was struggling hard to regain my anger. I felt uneasy as he stared at me with the eyes of a serpent. I turned and ordered him to follow. I could feel his fear and was secretly happy to know that people still feared me. As soon as I entered my camp, I caught Bhadra by the throat and pressed the blade of my sword hard enough to draw a drop of blood. He was afraid and started rambling incoherently. "What have you done to my Vedavathi and the little one?" I shouted.

He began to sob and beg my forgiveness. He told me what had happened to Vedavathi and my baby, as I stood there like a pillar, shocked at the ghastliness of what had transpired. I had feared they were dead, but what I heard grieved and shocked me deeply. I wanted to kick the fellow wallowing at my feet, but he held me in a python-like grip. Despite the constant ramblings and incomprehensible sounds he made, some of it filtered into my mind and I tried to make sense of it. Slowly, very slowly, it dawned on me. *'My daughter was not dead. She had been adopted by a kind King, a Deva King, but still a King, and was now growing up as a Deva princess.'*

For a fleeting moment I was happy. My daughter was alive. But she was now a princess of the enemy. A new energy rushed through me. I would assemble my army and march to the kingdom of Janaka. I would smash his armies, plunder his kingdom, and reclaim my daughter. She was an Asura princess and no Deva king could take her away from me. She was the princess of Lanka, she had to grow up as an Asura princess. Then I grew afraid. I had to regain my strength, to get her back. *'Was my army strong enough? Did I have an army in the first place?'* Even if I succeeded, how could I be sure of her safety when vipers like Prahastha or Vidyutjihva, roamed freely in my kingdom? I felt helpless and frustrated. I kicked Bhadra hard, drawing blood from his nose. *'Despicable creature.'* Sometimes I felt there was some logic in the caste system followed by the Devas. How could he and I be equals?

Thoughts of my little daughter came rushing into my mind. *'Did she look like me or did she resemble Mandodari?'* The thought of Mandodari brought back memories of the glowing evenings spent on the banks of the Poorna and Kaveri, the fragrance of the flowering trees, Mandodari's fair, smooth skin, the smell of jasmine, the feel of the cool breeze on our naked flesh, the buzz of hundreds of bees and the chattering of squirrels, as we lay in each other's arms, our soft love for each other...

I wrestled myself from the grip of the lowly Asura and dragged my feet towards the river. I wanted to be alone with my memories. My wants dissolved in the sobs of my soul.

30 Lanka lost

Bhadra

We returned from central India empty-handed. Everyone was furious with our King, the army, our ministers, and with each other. It was worse for me. Vidyutjihva, along with some of the ministers, had left long before the King was released from captivity. I was sure Vidyutjihva would have renewed his affair with Mala and I was jealous. I was stuck with a foolish King while Mala was welcoming a cad back home. Thoughts of Mala had troubled me through the campaign, but it was when Vidyutjihva finally left for Lanka, that I grew even more concerned. Added to this was the sense of failure, the taunts waiting for us from the folk in Lanka, for returning in this beggarly fashion. The frustration of being blamed solely for what had happened to Vedavathi, made me feel depressed.

We added another humiliation to our record on the way back to Lanka. At the southern foothills of the Vindhyas, the mighty half-breed, Bali, ruled. He was disparagingly called the monkey-King and his subjects monkeys. They were a mixture of both the Asura and Deva races, but were shunned and despised by both. They led a life on the fringes of both civilizations. That was until Bali squelched their inter-racial quibbles and united the monkey race. With their capital in Kishkindha, the monkey race or Vanaras, became a threat to both the Deva kingdoms of the north and the Asura kingdoms of the south. As they restricted themselves to the forests of central India, we had not come into contact with the Vanaras during our northward campaign following the coastal route.

The fact that Bali's younger brother, Sugreeva, was an enemy of the monkey-King and that great and reputed warriors like Hanuman, had deserted Bali to join Sugreeva's camp, might have spurred on our King, desperately looking for some success to redeem a modicum of respectability. It was not that Ravana had become a beggar but his position was precarious. He lived in perpetual fear that Prahastha or Vidyutjihva would take over. The fact that they had left for Lanka ahead of him, made him suspicious and jumpy and so he decided to attack Kishkindha, hoping to win back his lost prestige.

The dispirited group attacked on a moonless night and was promptly routed. We surrendered easily. The next morning, when the monkey-King came to see his prisoners, he was surprised to learn that it was the Asura army that had attacked him. His comment that he had thought us to be country bumpkins out on a night raid, hurt us more than any wound from our numerous battles. Even more insulting was the patronizing way in which he dealt with us. He treated all of us with equal respect and even apologized for the inconvenience caused. Then he fed us like honoured guests. We gobbled down enormous quantities of food and got dead drunk. We danced till morning to the beat of wild monkey drums. By morning we had forgotten our shame and had become bosom pals. We swore eternal friendship between the Vanaras and Asuras. Later, when we left the monkey kingdom, we witnessed curious scenes. We saw Ravana hugging the monkey-King, who was seen giving advice to the Asura king. We all left the place in high spirits and I overheard that an eternal friendship treaty has been signed with the monkey-kingdom and that Bali had become our King's friend, philosopher and guide. It was curious to say the least, but then such matters were beyond a simple-minded person like me. My main concern was my next meal.

It took us almost a month to reach the southern shore of the mainland. We all wanted to cross the sea and reach our beloved island quickly. But Varuna's ships, which had ferried us to the mainland, were not to be seen. We waited for a fortnight, growing more restless with each passing day, until Ravana decided to take charge. He ordered us to cut down trees, and we soon had a few boats. It was a daring plan, but Maricha was restless.

Finally, he suggested that only a few should venture to Lanka. He had the gnawing suspicion that our king was no longer the king and that either Vidyutjihva or Prahastha had taken over Lanka. As the preparations were made, we saw a fleet of ships coming towards the port at the mouth of the river Kaveri, where we were camped.

Ravana ordered us back into the jungle and we lay hidden, watching the ships anchor. They were the ships of the pirate-king but they did not anchor in the usual wharfs where cargo was loaded to be taken to the lands of the yellow men or white savages. These were battleships. We saw small boats lowered with men and soon they were furiously rowing towards the beach where we were camped. We waited for almost half an hour for the men to arrive. Then we saw Prahastha and a few guards, wading through the shallow water towards us. Ravana and Maricha stepped out of their hiding places with their swords unsheathed and walked towards Prahastha.

Prahastha, with his head held high, looked at Ravana with undisguised contempt and I saw Ravana look away. Maricha recovered quickly and stood between Prahastha and Ravana. To our surprise, Prahastha stepped aside and bowed low to Ravana. A huge cheer rose from all of us. Maricha was taken aback and pleasantly surprised. He hugged Prahastha. Forgetting discipline, we rushed forward. Prahastha was uncomfortable, but Maricha reassured him and then asked what had happened.

Reluctantly, Prahastha said, "I believe I made a mistake when I decided to go with Vidyutjihva, leaving behind Rav-, I mean, His Highness, and yourself. I had always suspected that rascal, but the depths to which he would sink were beyond my understanding. He was sweet and diplomatic till we reached Lanka, but as soon as we arrived, he began to press for a regent King until you returned. I insisted that in Asura tradition, even the concept of kingship was new." Here he glanced at Ravana, who averted his eyes. Prahastha continued, "But you all know he is a silver-tongued orator, and he bribed, threatened and cajoled other members of the Council. Only Jambumali and I dissented. I resigned from the Council in protest and would have retired from politics altogether, had the new King Vidyutjihva, not unleashed a reign of terror. Most of Vidyutjihva's actions were quite unnecessary. In three months, he wrecked the economy, increasing taxes and levies whenever he wanted. He gave the pirate-King a free hand to plunder and divided the loot. But now they have fallen apart. Varuna is waiting in that ship for Rav-, I mean. . .His Highness, to come and take charge of his navy. He is thirsting for revenge."

Ravana stepped forward and asked Prahastha, "But what happened to my brothers, my wife and my sister?" We could sense tension and concern in his voice.

"Your Highness, your sister is safe, though unhappy. She's still madly in love with her husband. I moved your wife to a hiding place in the hills and later sent her to her father. Our greatest concern is Prince Kumbakarna, who was the only man to raise his voice against the tyranny of his brother-in-law. He is courageous, my King, but pardon me for saying so, very impulsive. And he is gullible to a fault. He was promptly betrayed by his friends, captured, tortured, and sent to the kingdom of Yama. He isn't dead. He was sent to the dreaded drug kingdom on the eastern slopes of the Sahyas, deep inside the forest, where a brigand named Yama, brews poisonous potions, drinks, and smoke herbs and drugs. Vidyutjihva, was a disciple of the drug-lord Yama, and he has rewarded his guru with an Asura prince for his experiments.

Ravana was, by now, trembling with fury. Maricha put a soothing hand on the King's shoulder, but Ravana brusquely shook it off. "Assemble for battle. We will take on this imposter," he shouted.

There was sudden commotion. Now we had a purpose, it was not a meaningless war for the glory of a single man. It was to free our brothers and sisters, our wives and children, our parents, from the hands of a tyrant. I worried about Mala.

But Prahastha raised his hand and after a few seconds, there was perfect silence. "Your Highness, first we have to free Prince Kumbakarna. We do not know his condition after being subjected to their experiments."

Ravana waited for a few seconds before answering. Then with a slight bow he said, "I value your wise counsel, my Prime Minister, and I respect your wisdom. I shall be guided by you." Turning to Maricha, who was now beaming, he said, "Uncle Maricha, please send a messenger to our friend king Bali, for assistance to finish off the drug-lord Yama. We need his help." Maricha bowed and left, summoning our master runner.

Then, as an afterthought, Ravana asked Prahastha, "And what about our younger brother, Vibhishna?"

Prahastha, suppressing a smile, said, "He, your Highness, has shut himself inside a small temple he erected with his own hands. He prays to the Deva God Vishnu, for deliverance from this evil. Other than praying, he does nothing."

"Pshaw!" Ravana spat with contempt and many of us snickered.

31 Den of death

Ravana

We had stopped for a few days at Madurai, the ancient temple town of the fish-Goddess, Meenakshi, to get our supplies, horses and weapons. Varuna sponsored the campaign after I had agreed to return the amount along enormous interest, once I regained the throne of Lanka. I didn't like depending on the pirate but what choice did I have? Moreover, it gave me some confidence that the shrewd pirate-King thought I would regain my throne. He was not known to get his bets wrong. But I was well aware of our shortcomings. We moved from the city of the fish-eyed goddess and reached the valley of death.

Yama's fort stood at the top of a mountain, which almost touched the sky and three sides dropped down into near-vertical, rocky cliffs. It resembled my fort in Trikota, but was much more compact and perched higher. In the shrubs and small trees that surrounded this barren mountain on the east, and the lush green forests on the western side, Yama's soldiers lay hidden, intoxicated on drugs and hell-bent on defending their territory. Drunk on opium-laced potions, they seemed oblivious to physical injuries and insulated from fear. Somewhere inside that dark and forbidding citadel, in a dark dungeon, my beloved oaf of a brother, Kumbakarna, lay drugged, or perhaps dead.

We planned to attack on a moonless night. At dead of night, our army stormed the fort. It was the bitterest battle we had fought so far. Yama's soldiers were not just fearless, they were almost inhuman. It took us till dawn to effect a breach. By that time, hundreds from our side had been slain. The campaign in north India had been a picnic in comparison. Yama's soldiers poured molten metal onto our scampering army, catapulted huge boulders at us, and their archers rained arrows with deadly accuracy. The situation became hopeless. It was then that I heard the victory cry from Prahastha's battalion. It came from the west side of the fort and surprised me. We had not bothered about the west side. It was surrounded by impenetrable rain forests and was dangerously steep. Moreover, it would have hampered our progress and denied us the advantage of a night attack. So when the victory cry came from the west gate of the fort, I was surprised. After almost an hour's pitched battle, the other three gates were opened and our army swarmed into Yama's citadel from all sides. We hacked our way through. Our horses stamped over hundreds of mangled limbs and severed heads. It was grotesque and revolting. There was the smell of blood, flesh and excrement of both of men and beasts. I wanted to get out of this place.

Even as I kept stabbing my way through the swarms of Yama *kingaras,* my mind wandered. I was disgusted by the meaninglessness of all this. '*I want to free my brother and get him back. But do I really?*' Strangely, Prahastha's words, spoken many years ago, came to my mind even as my life depended on my fighting skill against the scores of Yama's soldiers who were attacking me on all sides. The words were cold, precise and unpleasant. To a twenty-four-year-old who had romantic notions about his duty to his family and fulfilling his destiny, and who was generally misty-eyed about world, the words were devastating, '*Do not believe anyone, especially your siblings, when aspiring for success, for they are bound to be your bitterest enemies.*'

It was as usual, unsolicited advice, and one more reason to hate Prahastha. And now, strangely enough, when I was staking my life to save my brother, this advice nagged at me. '*Could I trust my brother?*' Then, with alarming clarity, I understood. This battle was not about saving Kumbha, but saving myself, my shattered pride, confidence, ambition, and my destiny. Pulling myself up, I concentrated on driving my sword through the heart of a boy barely sixteen years old, thinking about his faceless mother, but with no feelings for either him or her.

Finally, by late afternoon, we had taken the citadel and the search was onto find my brother, Kumbakarna. I bled from a thousand cuts and sat dizzily on my horse. The place was eerily silent except for the groans and gasps of the dying men and beasts. We had become used to the stench of blood, so it did not bother us anymore. I saw Prahastha and Maricha and rode towards them. Maricha smiled, but Prahastha made me a curt bow and continued with his work of ordering the search parties. Suddenly, Maricha turned and said, "It was Prahastha's idea to take the fort from the west side. He had an ally inside the fort who opened the gate for us, and as soon as the battle started, we moved west. In fact, Prahastha had positioned many on the west side before the battle had even started."

I seethed with anger. I had been made to fight like a common soldier and my ministers had used me as part of their diversionary tactics. I was angry that I had not thought of the plan myself. Instead the thousand things that could have gone wrong occupied my mind. It was then that a big cheer arouse from the western end of the fort and I saw a group of soldiers dancing and carrying a huge man on their shoulders. As the sun was setting, I had difficulty seeing who they carried, though I guessed. As they drew near, I saw an almost-comatose Kumbakarna bouncing on the black shoulders of our men. It was comical. I smiled and turned to Maricha. He beamed. Prahastha stood beside him with his habitual, stern expression. I wanted to ask him why he had kept me in the dark and my anger came rushing back. I was about to ask when Maricha caught my eyes and hurriedly whispered in my ear, "We suspected there were moles among us. I wanted to inform you but Prahastha insisted you should not know. He reasoned that you would not otherwise give your best while leading the battle and the enemy would have suspected our ruse. So we left you to fight a brave battle, while we sneaked in from the rear."

I felt cheated. I felt small and manipulated. *'I was the King and these geriatrics were playing tricks on me.'* I wanted to yell at the old men and just as I was about to spell out what I thought of them, Prahastha turned his head towards me and smiled. Maricha also smiled.

"We won, Ravana, we won. If it wasn't for a great fight, we would never have done it." he said more loudly than necessary.

And our entire army cheered. Wave by wave, our soldiers raised their weapons and cried, '*Har Har Mahadev.*" "Victory to Shiva." "Victory to Ravana, the mighty king of Asuras." "Victory to Asuras."

My heart leapt with pride. I did not know what to do and also raised my sword. My army cried out with an electrifying voice. Suddenly I remembered, '*I owe these two oldies something big.*' But then I felt my resentment rising again and changed my mind and asked, "Uncle, where's the spy in Yama's camp who helped us?" I ignored his eyes that were widening in surprise. I had taken off my diamond necklace and said, "I wish to reward him."

"Ravana, are you mad?"

My irritation rose. "Either you tell me, or I find him myself." I demanded.

Maricha shook his head sadly and said, "Ravana, sometimes you surprise me. He was the first person Prahastha thrust his sword into as soon as we stormed the fort."

Seeing the shock on my face, he added, "Ravana, it is a fundamental lesson of politics. Never trust a traitor, even if he has done the dirty work for you. Tomorrow he may turn against you." After a pause, he added, "Anyway, don't worry about such things. We have won the war, though Yama has fled, and your brother is safe."

I now felt like an idiot, clutching my diamond necklace in my hand. I wanted to dispose of it before Prahastha turned his head and saw it in my hand. I would not be able to withstand his condescending smile. So I looked around and saw a soldier sitting with his back supported by the fort wall and legs spread apart. He was panting and puffing and looked hideous with a portion of his nose cut off. He bled from many wounds and I felt a surge of pity for him. This fellow had suffered for me; he had almost laid down his life.

I beckoned. For a few seconds he blinked uncomprehendingly. Then, a look of sheer terror crossed his face. He tried to get up but collapsed. Then he crawled towards me. I felt disgusted. He crawled to me like a wounded dog. I looked at the diamond necklace. It was far too precious for a dreg like this. So I fumbled with my pearl necklace, looked at it with some regret, but before I could change my mind, I threw it at the crouching figure. It fell a few feet short. The man blinked like an owl, unable to comprehend what had fallen in front of him. Then he grabbed it and smelt it like a monkey. *'The man does not appreciate my gift. How dare he?'* Then it entered his slow mind and he looked at me with shock and with what, at first, I feared was contempt. But then, with elaborate courtesy and a show of gratitude, he bowed to me and kissed the ground. I saw his body shivering and was afraid he was going to die. I watched fascinated. Slowly he raised his head and with tears rolling down his cheeks, he smiled at me. His two front teeth were missing and he looked grotesque. I felt repulsed, but a nagging thought told me that I knew this beggar. I wanted to take a closer look. I prodded my horse to move a few feet closer to the prone figure. Bhadra! *'Why does this blasted man intrude into my life always?'* I wanted to snatch back the necklace and give the ugly face a kick and whip his black hide. Then his expression of gratitude when he received the gift came to mind and I calmed down. *'It is alright,'* I pacified myself. He too, deserves little prizes. I felt happy and content that I had done something right.

Later, when the party was over and we had retired to rest, when I was drifting in and out of sleep, it was not Bhadra's grateful face that I remembered. I recalled instead, the look of utter contempt when he had first touched my gift. Tossing restlessly, I forced my mind away from dark, ugly, Asura faces, towards dreams of glory, ambition and the gold-paved paths of my destiny.

32 Patriot

Bhadra

We had returned from the mainland. Ravana had threatened to finish off Vidyutjihva and his cohorts, who were busy looting the country. Alarmed, Vidyutjihva brokered a peace, offering all of India, which Ravana himself had conquered, except the southern parts of Lanka, which he wanted for himself. Ravana wanted to take back the entire kingdom, but Soorpanakha's wishes stopped our King in his tracks. While both sides wined, dined and negotiated, the people on the street fought for food, water, medicines, or simply turned over and died.

Soon the dreaded summons came. I searched for the pearl necklace in the small box where I thought I had put it. *'Where was it?'* I had thrown it on the floor as soon as I had dragged myself to my bed at the camp that day. Now, if the king saw me without it, he could think I had not valued his gift, which truthfully I had not. I searched everywhere and then with sudden inspiration, I searched my roommate's box. He was a foul-smelling Asura, who piously bowed to a small Shiva *lingam* thrice a day and always quoted from long-forgotten scriptures on morality, truth, life, and other useless themes. He had gone out and I yanked out his box from under his bed and prised it open. I found the necklace, tucked away and wrapped inside his clothes. I cursed and kicked the box to one side before taking the necklace out. I put it on and looked in the hand mirror, which was one of my precious possessions, to see how presentable I appeared. With a part of my nose cut off, a deep scar running over my left cheek, and one and a half ears, I looked hideous. I grinned and the gap made by two missing front teeth, gave me a funny yet macabre appearance.

With an effort, I pulled myself up from the bed where I was sitting, combed my hair with my fingers, and walked to the Council camp. I entered and bowed as low as possible – a few inches more and I would have touched the floor. Inside it was dark and odorous. The usual thugs were there – Prahastha, with his stern, impassive face; Maricha, with his sly smile; Ravana, looking disgusted to have to deal with scum like me; Jambumali, with his fuzzy, clerical looks; Kumbakarna, with good-natured curiosity; Rudraka with contemptuous scorn; and Vibhishna, the pious rascal, busy saving the world with his mumbo jumbo, with his eyes closed in contemplation.

"Bhadra," It was the kind voice of Maricha. "Once again, the entire race of Asuras is depending on you. Your country and your King need. . ." He rambled on. It would have been better had he just told me what filthy job they wanted me for. All this talk of patriotism and race got on my nerves but I did not dare voice my contempt. Like most of my countrymen, especially the black-skinned, low-living, simple-minded, illiterate, and innocent millions, I too had learnt the art of appearing submissive, peaceful, and the obedient servant of the rulers, when actually a million mutinies seethed within me.

It took me some time to understand I had been designated the task of finishing off Vidyutjihva. My heart leapt with joy. I had perhaps judged the Council too harshly and quickly. This was a god-given opportunity. I bowed low and walked out without turning to show my back.

I had to wait till it was dark. The mission was exciting and dangerous. To get into the fort on the sly and assassinate Vidyutjihva, was no mean task. But my personal hatred for the man and my ambition to do something worthwhile, prodded me on. As soon as I returned from the Council, I took my dagger from its sheath and examined its sharpness. Then I searched my sack for the ingredients to make a poisonous potion. I arranged the seven herbs I needed in a straight line, then mixed and ground them in various proportions to make it deadly. Carefully, I rubbed the potion onto the blade. Then, taking a small, thin cloth, I dipped it in the poison and wrapped it over the dagger. The rest of the potion I buried in one corner. Then, stripped to my loin cloth, I put off the oil lamp and poured the oil that was left in the lamp all over my body and left for the fort. Strangely enough, it was not thoughts of death or danger that engrossed me, but that I looked hideous.

I had chosen the darkest hour before dawn for my mission and left the camp three hours before sunrise and waited near the rear gate. Two guards slept in position, but another, who looked boyish, eagerly marched up and down with his spear. He might have been a new recruit, full of enthusiasm to please his boss. I sneaked past him and tried to steal the keys to the rear fort gate, which were hanging from a ring on the waistcloth of one of the sleeping guards. As I fumbled in the darkness, my hands slipped and the key ring fell with a clang. I froze. The sleeping guard stirred but did not wake. I quickly moved back into the deep shadows thrown by the huge pillars of the gate. The boy was standing a few feet away, looking intently into the darkness where I had vanished. I held my breath. Tentatively he moved a few paces towards me and then stopped. He seemed to be in a dilemma, whether to wake his superiors or to investigate the noise himself. After what seemed like hours, he slowly moved towards me, trying to adjust his vision to the darkness. I had only a fraction of a second to act. I pounced on him with my dagger drawn and before he could react, I had plunged my dagger deep into the hollow of his throat. He fell silently to the ground.

I turned back fast and faced the other two guards, who were now awake, my dagger dripping blood. One of the guards blinked at me like a fish, a scream caught in his throat. I walked towards him and quietly slit his throat. The third one, who seemed to be the most experienced, reached for his sword. I pounced on him, but he was quick. He kicked me with a vicious force that sent me sprawling onto the ground. Then he raised the sword over his head to plunge it deep into my heart. I saw my end near, but I had nothing to lose. I threw the dagger at his face and he froze in a grotesque position. I was terrified that I had missed him. Then his disfigured face, with the dagger struck in his left eye, shuddered and his entire body collapsed onto me. His sword plunged into the mud, a few feet above my head. Being short had its advantages. I wriggled out from under the giant and carefully pulled out the dagger from his eye.

It was then that I heard footsteps. Other guards where coming to investigate. I frantically searched for an escape route and fumbled with the keys to open the gate. *'The lock would not open.'* In a sweat, my hands shivered with excitement and sheer terror. *'Which was the right key?'*

"Hey you!" someone shouted. I fumbled again. An arrow pierced the wooden gate two inches to the right of my neck while its vibrating tail sang in my ear. The next one came whining along and struck a few inches to the left of my shoulder. Its feathers caressed me. I could hear footsteps running towards me but the lock opened at last and I sneaked into the fort as a sword blade hit the copper edge of the door with a murderous clang. I pushed shut the door and once again fumbled with the keys. They were pressing the door open but using all my strength, I pushed back and finally managed to lock it. Then I ran for my life.

I could see torches being lit in various parts of the fort as I ran towards the palace and the King's chamber on the first floor. I scrambled up with the help of the vine that clung to the walls and landed on the verandah like a cat. I was quite athletic in my own way. The guards of the chamber peered over the balustrade to see what the commotion was about. I tipped them both over the balustrade with a timely push and then kicked open the door of the chamber. I waited with my dagger in hand but nothing happened. Nothing moved.

A dark figure slept on the bed and small oil lamp flickered. I closed the door silently and latched it. I walked stealthily to the lamp and tugged at the wick of the lamp to brighten the room. Princess Soorpanakha! *'Where was the bastard? Has he escaped?'* A sense of disappointment filled me. Every second I stayed I got closer to death. I wanted to scream in frustration when I heard a small laugh like the tinkle of a bell. It was faint but I would have recognized it a mile away. *'Mala! What was she doing here?'* I listened like a wild cat on the prowl. The laugh came from the adjoining chamber and suddenly it dawned on me that Mala was with Vidyutjihva. Frantically I searched for the door to the adjoining chamber. I could hear the guards searching for me and knew my chances of escape were dwindling by the second. Someone knocked on the door and the princess stirred. I pressed myself against the wall. She opened her eyes and looked towards the door. She searched for her husband with her hands and not finding him, frowned. The knocking got more urgent as I desperately felt for the latch to the adjoining chamber with my fingers.

"Who is it?" she asked.

"Someone has entered your room, your Highness," a voice cried out. My heart pounded in my chest. It took some time for her to register what had been said. Then she slowly sat up and after a few seconds hesitation, walked towards the door. *'I'm finished!'* I thought. The soldiers rushed in and brusquely pushed aside the princess. My hand touched a secret latch and I yanked it open. A door opened and I fell onto my back. Instinctively I kicked the door closed, scrambled up, and locked the door. In a flash I turned. Vidyutjihva was there with my lover, lying on his back with she riding him. They froze in terror. Outside, guards pounded the door. Any moment they would break in.

I smacked Mala across her face with the back of my left hand so hard that she hit the wall three feet away. I jumped onto Vidyutjihva and sat on his belly. I could not help smirking. With a viciousness that I never thought I possessed, I slashed him again and again across his handsome face with my poisoned dagger. He was long dead when I decided to cut off his penis. I did not even feel Mala tearing my back with her nails trying to save her lover or the sound of the guards pulling open the door. Only the scream of the princess brought me back to my senses. The guards were too shocked by the grisly sight to attack me. I was not sure whether the princess screamed for her murdered husband or his betrayal. I pitied her. Blood dripped from my body and I was exhausted. I had almost given up when Princess Soorpanakha screamed at the top of her voice, "Bhadra, Bhadra. . . my brother sent you to kill my husband. Ravana. . .why, why?" She slapped her head with both her hands.

I was shocked but when all the guards' attention turned to the screaming princess, I escaped. The window was open and I jumped out in a trice. The captain of the guards shouted as I fell. My fall was arrested by a sprawling Ashoka tree and I bounced off its branches and rolled onto the ground. I did not know it then, but I had broken three ribs and my arm in the fall. But at the time nothing mattered. I ran for dear life, exhilarated at the thought of having accomplished great things for my master, my race, my nation, and myself. Arrows rained from all sides but miraculously, I was never hit. I knew a break in the west wall, from where I could jump into the sea, provided I could reach it. I ran with all the strength left to me. A few more steps, a few more steps, that was all and the mother sea would take me safely into her bosom. As I reached the breach in the wall, I had a strange sensation – no one was chasing me. *'Was it a dream?'* I was afraid to stop and look.

Then I heard the conches blowing. Surprised, I stopped and turned back. A procession entered through the wide open main gate of the fort. Ravana sat atop an elephant, as befitted an Emperor, with his huge army of elephants, cavalry, chariots, infantry and musicians, all marching in with great splendour. *Chenda*s were beaten with great gusto, the curved horn trumpets were blown and cymbals clanged. One by one, the loyal guards of Vidyutjihva laid down their arms. *Jai Shankar*! *Har har Mahadev*! Hail Ravana! *'Victory. Victory at last!'* And I was instrumental. Pride swelled my chest and ignoring the pain in my body, I ran towards the procession.

As I neared it, I was suddenly ashamed. I was in my loin cloth. I was dark and ugly and bleeding from a hundred places. These were Asura nobles marching in full glory. As I stood there, right in the path of the procession, vacillating, two soldiers ran towards me and forcibly dragged me off the path of the victory march and dumped me on the pavement. I lay there in shame, a sense of betrayal pressing hard against my heart. I could hear the tinkle of the bell of the royal elephant approaching and lifted my head and caught Ravana's eye. *'Was it disgust, hatred or gratitude I saw there?'* I'm still not sure. In my charitable moods I felt it was gratitude, but sometimes I thought it was hatred. It was likely that Ravana had not even recognized me.

The procession passed. I raised my head when a shadow fell across my face and saw Maricha. There was pity and even some gratitude in his eyes. For the first time I sensed someone cared for me and tears welled inside. I tried to raise myself but collapsed. Maricha tried to get off his horse, then he froze. I followed his gaze. Prahastha, who was ahead, had stopped his horse and was staring back at the scene. Maricha got a firm grip firm on his reins and trotted towards the Prime Minister without looking back.

A bitter laughed escaped me. I collapsed back into the ditch, laughing hysterically. As the sun rose and the day progressed, becoming increasingly more hot and humid, I found some strength to totter back to my hut. The sounds of celebration could be heard all around. Some people had thrown a few coins at me as I lay in the ditch and after a few minutes hesitation, I collected them. I was not sure I could work for the next few days as the pain had intensified. Every coin would count. Celebrations erupted everywhere. Emperor, princes and nobles, everyone was in a gay mood. They had achieved victory. But I had a hut to go to, a hole to crawl into and lick my wounds, and an unfaithful woman to deal with, and also a living to earn. As far as I was concerned, these things were more important than the coronation of Emperors. So I kept walking.

33 Son of darkness

Ravana

She was hysterical. Soorpanakha flew at my face and tore my cheek with her bare hands. She tried to bite and maim anyone who dared to venture near her. With her hair disheveled, her face black with agony, she kept cursing me and all the ministers of Lanka, occasionally beating her breasts with clenched fists. She guarded the dead body of Vidyutjihva like a hound. She kept the priest at bay and anointed the dead body herself. She dressed it in new clothes, all the while cursing us, me in particular. I did not want to console her. True, I had wanted her husband dead and was responsible for the same. But he had had it coming to him. He had signed his death warrant when he usurped my throne. He had asked for trouble.

Bhadra had done it for me. The thing I hated most about this nasty business was the fact that I owed that stupid man. *'Or did I? He was a mere slave and had to do what I bid him. Period.'* I looked at the corpse of my brother-in-law. They had cleaned it, but still it looked grotesque. When I had seen the corpse for the first time, I had almost thrown up. One had to have a really perverted mind to do something like that. What sort of creature was Bhadra? Disgusting! A high-pitched wail shocked me from my reverie. Soorpanakha was banging her head on the floor. And behind her, wailing in a much shriller pitch, was my mother. I had not expected her to come so soon.

'Satisfied, you blood-sucking *Rakshasa*?" I went pale at this unexpected attack. "You've made your own sister a widow. I am ashamed that you were even born in my womb."

I clenched my fists to keep myself from exploding. With her every remark, Soorpanakha's wails reached new heights. "You tyrant. . .you dog. . .You've made my child weep like this and you'll pay for it...you'll pay for it dearly." She kept on in this vein for the next half hour, praising the various aspects of her son-in-law. It would have been comical had she not dragged me into the farce. "You are drunk with power, intoxicated with ambition. Kill me! Kill me also, and use my old body as a stepping stone to your political success," my mother said, hitting her forehead and breasts. Then she started pummelling my chest.

My father had come too and was sitting in a corner, busily discussing something with the two Brahmins who always accompanied him. I felt like grabbing his hair and banging his head against the wall. He was planning a Deva funeral for his son-in-law, with some obscure rites and gifts to the Brahmins. I just wanted to get it over with.

However difficult Soorpanakha acted, it was nothing compared to Kumbakarna. The imprisonment in Yama's dungeon had changed him for the worse and he was stoned most of the time. He slept for most of the day and created a ruckus when he woke. I was worried about him. I was worried about myself. We were a close-knit family and I enjoyed my siblings' company. '*What had changed between us to destroy the bond? Why did Soorpanakha go and marry my bitterest enemy? And when I killed him for self-preservation, why did she hold it against me?*' Even as the thoughts went through me, I felt for her, it was after all her husband who was lying dead. She had the right to feel the way she did about me. '*Poor girl. Perhaps I should not have been so harsh.*' I should have imprisoned her husband. I could have compromised.

Vidyutjihva's face had been gashed haphazardly. I felt a surge of deep and pure hatred towards Bhadra. '*How could he do a thing like this? This was an Asura nobleman who has been butchered like a wild animal and that too, by the lowliest of low vermins.*' I felt ashamed that I had entrusted the task to him. There was no heroism in this victory. '*I was scum, no better than Bhadra. Why did I listen to Prahastha. Self-righteous oaf. Oh Shiva, what have I done to my sister?*' Why did I take away even the small happiness she possessed? Was the empire worth it? Was Lanka or even India, enough to quench my ambition? And what was it that I was building on the corpses of my people? How many deaths would I feel responsible for? Were we not much happier in that precariously hanging hut over the cliff? The biggest tragedy of life was that we grow up and achieve our boyhood dreams.

A hard slap on my face shook me from my immature philosophical ruminations. The entire room swam before my eyes and I staggered and fell. I was blinded for some moments and my head spun. I tried getting up, only to be kicked hard in my groin. "You bastard!" I could hear Kumbakarna's shouts as though they came from a deep well. My head reeled as I tried to stand up, but was kicked back again. My eyes were swollen and my lips split. Somehow I stood up, holding onto a pillar in the centre of the room to prevent me from falling. Slowly, the scene cleared. Maricha and three soldiers were trying to reign in Kumbakarna. His eyes looked murderous and he was stoned. He tried to free himself and lunge towards me and kick me again but didn't reach me.

I turned and saw my father and the two fat Brahmins smirking and enjoying the show. My mother hit her head with her hands melodramatically and Soorpanakha stared straight ahead with a stony expression. A few guards were almost smiling but trying hard to keep straight faces. This kind of family drama was so exciting to the dregs of our society. By evening, the entire city would be abuzz with a much exaggerated version of what had happened. More than the pain of this unexpected attack, it was the shame that stung me more.

Seeing the growing darkness on my face, Maricha dragged my brother from the room. I would have killed him right there but guilt weighed me down. I stood there with shame and guilt burning through every nerve, but did not move a finger. Kumbha shouted about my ambitions, my exaggerated sense of self-importance, my selfishness, my contempt for people, my undeserving pride, and my real and imagined vices. He cursed me and wished I would die.

I could not stand it anymore and wanted to retire to my room and drink myself to unconsciousness. As I turned, I looked out at the garden. There, my pious brother, Vibhishana, sat cross-legged, his eyes closed, and a silly smile of contentment on his face. '*What was there to be so smug and happy about when the entire household was in tremendous pain?*' I wanted to walk towards him and wipe that wooden smile from his face but he was perhaps the most harmless fellow in our whole clan. The guy was without ambition, self-satisfied with himself, and always detached from life and its trials. After passionate Kumbha, Soorpanakha, mother and even myself, he was a welcome change. I had not been blessed with a simple mind and I envied my younger brother for his contentment and uncomplicated way of living. Perhaps, a life without ambition was a life worth living. I could never have become Vibhishana, even if I had wanted to, but I had never wanted to be anyone other than Ravana. I sighed and left my philosopher brother to his blissful stupidity and walked to my chamber. I wanted a drink. As I entered, I saw Mandodari sitting on the bed. She was dressed in glittering silk clothes and gold and diamond ornaments, and resembled a walking treasury. Her face lit up as soon as she saw me.

I was hit by a sudden sense of guilt and shame. Vedavathi's fair face was fresh in my mind and I could not help comparing her to my wife. Mandodari was beautiful in a stern sort of way, but she was not sexy at all. She was almost a saint and I was a rather nervous and afraid of her. It was like she was holding a mirror for my soul and it showed all my hidden, ugly scars and warts. I hid my nervousness behind a veneer of contempt and irritation. With surprise, I realized she had never been in my mind during my long campaign, not even when I was imprisoned in Karthiveerarjuna's dark dungeon or fighting life or death battles. All I yearned for was Vedavathi. And I ached to see my first born.

As I stood transfixed with awkwardness, she stood up with a sad smile. Her smile lit up her face and I could not face her. I looked out and my irritation increased when I saw my brother continuing his meditation. When I turned, she was so near that I could smell her. She smelt of fresh jasmine and camphor. Tears brimmed her eyes as she batted her eyelids. She looked almost coy and innocent. I felt like hugging her and wiping the tears from those lovely eyes but my limbs would not move. Something was holding me back.

"Woman, where have you kept the wine?" I sounded coarse even to myself and looked away. I could feel her hurt and did not want to look at her. I walked towards the chair and sat there looking at the ceiling. *'How was she feeling? How had Vidyutjihva treated her? Did she miss me?'* Hundreds of questions swirled within me, but I kept quiet. I wanted to boast about my campaigns, to tell her about the sights I had seen, the strange and exotic lands of the Devas, tales of the vanquished tribes, the pain of imprisonment, the rout at the hands of the monkey-King Bali, and even my tempestuous love affair with a Deva Brahmin girl – but I kept staring at the ceiling.

Mandodari poured the wine and retreated towards the shadow of the big bed. Without a word, I gulped down the wine and impatiently tapped my fingers on the stool. She hurriedly came back and poured me another drink. I kept drinking. An eerie silence engulfed the palace. Occasionally it was punctuated by the distant wails of my mother or sister. When I heard those piteous cries, I felt guilty and tried to drown my feelings in more wine. Then the drone of Vedic *mantras* rose from the hall where the corpse lay. Those Brahmins were preparing the soul of my brother-in-law to cross various kind of rivers made of butter, honey, and the rest, on its way towards the Deva heaven. Some lowly guard came to announce that they were taking Vidyutjihva's body to the cremation ground and were waiting for me to come and pay my last respects.

I stood up in anger and the wine glasses tumbled from the stool, spreading stains on the plush carpet. I yelled at the poor guard and threw a glass at him with such force that had it hit him, he would have died on the spot. The wine splattered and the guard ran for his life. I shut the door after him with a bang and shut the window also, though my brother had uncoiled himself from his ridiculous, yogic posture and vanished, perhaps to assist the fat Brahmins.

Then I turned towards my wife. She trembled with fear. I grabbed her by her waist but she pushed me away with surprising force and drunk as I was, I staggered and fell. "Do not touch me." she said in a low but firm voice. She almost hissed like a snake. Like a fool, I sat there on the floor blinking, taken aback and confused by the strength exhibited by such a meek woman. "Do not try to touch me in this drunken state." She stood there, her head raised high, defying me, daring me to touch her.

I stood up in great anger and tried to grab her again. She picked up the fruit knife from the bowl and pointed it at me. '*Ah, I liked it. She had spirit. I was enjoying this.*' Then, to my utter dismay, she pointed the knife towards her belly and said, "You make one move to touch me. . ." She broke into sobs that shook her entire body and I felt disgusted with the whole thing. I could so easily have overpowered her but no longer wanted to. Instead, I threw a tantrum, tore the pillows, threw the silk sheet from the bed and stamped on it. After a while, I felt foolish and left the room cursing my wife and banging the door shut.

I was in a murderous and helpless rage. It was unfortunate that a fair and lovely maid was sweeping the corridor at the time. When she saw me storming out of the royal chamber, her mouth opened in stupid awe and she dropped her broom and started to run. I had not even noticed her, but her nervousness caught my eye. I chased after her and almost dived to catch her by the waist. I muffled her screams with my palms and dragged her to a nearby room. Then I raped her. To start with, she was unwilling; perhaps she had thought I was going to murder her. But after a while, she became quite obliging. So while my sister cried over her murdered husband; my mother sat cursing me; my brothers lit my brother-in-law's funeral pyre; and my wife was sobbing her heart out, I, the King, the Emperor of India was busy with a low caste maid. And from that sin and guilt, my dark, fat and ugly son, Athikaya, was born.

34 Riot

Bhadra

It took almost a year for me to recover. My hut was gutted when the Asuras were busy looting and fighting each other. Not only my locality, but most houses and shops were burnt down during those turbulent days when Ravana and Vidyutjihva were performing their macabre dance for power. I was bitter for a few days. Mala had returned to the small shack I had put up under the huge Banyan tree on the side of the royal highway. Before that, I had made my own enquires about her and found that she was a minor maid at the palace. There were rumours that she was pregnant by the king and she had been made the second queen by Ravana. I was jealous and hurt. I wanted to murder her but she was far too high up in the pecking order now.

Then, one day, she came. She did not look like a queen at all. She looked plain and dirty and carried a bundle of rags on her shoulders, the traces of vanishing beauty making her seem more ugly. For someone who was the King's mistress, Mala's situation was pathetic. The anger I had felt at her betrayal had numbed to a dull pain. She might have been selling herself for some food and small pleasures, or that was the only way a poor but beautiful woman could survive among kings like Vidyutjihva and Ravana. I burned with anger, self-pity and jealousy, for few months after I returned from my heroics. But, by the time she came, I had cooled off. I was running a high temperature on that particular day when she returned to my hut, and without saying a single word, she began to nurse me. Whether she had begged or stolen some rice, I did not know but she made some gruel. She fed it to me that and inexplicably, I began to cry. She did not say anything but kept feeding me the gruel with a leaf spoon.

By the time, I recovered, it was too late to ask. I needed her and I believe she needed me, at least until the next great man beckoned her to satisfy him. Slowly I fell into a routine. It was a time of relative calm and peace and most days we earned enough to eat at least once. The beggars and destitutes, the magicians and snake charmers, the acrobats and gypsies, who frequented the city markets, the streets and narrow winding lanes of the city, the palace, the temples, the countryside, usually came to rest under the Banyan tree. It was the travellers' natural resting place. Out of sheer boredom, I began experimenting with various foods and shared it with the wayfarers. Mala helped me built our first thatched shop where we sold sweets and snacks. But occasionally, she did odd jobs in the palace and she also took her son, Athikaya, to the palace regularly. Though I hated her for it, it had been a long time since I had enjoyed the peace and pleasure of a full stomach and I did not want to rock the boat.

Mala took over the responsibility of cooking and serving the snacks and other food. I found I had another talent – for a small sum, I would wash the travellers' clothes. I knew which plant or seed cleaned the clothes well and I kept experimenting. A couple of times though, the clothes lost their colour, but I soon found the right mix and my reputation as a good washerman spread. The kind of patrons I had also changed and rich merchants started trusting me with their expensive, imported, silk clothes from China, or the rich calico or muslin from mainland India.

The wayside shop soon became a centre of gossip and merrymaking. Even though I had felt sad to be excluded from the great parties at the palace, I chided myself for reaching beyond my position. I had had enough of moving around with eccentric and egoistic kings and nobles, who were willing to sacrifice a person at the altar of their burning ambition. Here, life was simple and straight-forward and I was the master of the small thatched hut we had built with our own hands.

I heard that Princess Soorpanakha had left Lanka with her father and mother, for the mainland. She had vowed that she would never look at her elder brother, Ravana, again. It might have been an exaggeration but it was said that she cursed her brother and Lanka and the Asuras, with colourful vocabulary, until she boarded Varuna's ship. The ship had many coloured sails and swiftly took a smug Brahmin, an angry mother, and her widowed daughter, to the mainland. If the king was affected by any of this, he did not show it. She had called him *Rakshasa,* and curiously, the name struck, though no one dared call him that to his face.

The next great event was the marriages of Prince Kumbakarna and Prince Vibhishana. It was a big jamboree and the entire city participated. I too wanted to go, but I was bitter that no special invitation had been sent to me. I was too proud to go as an ordinary Asura beggar. On the night of the marriage, the nobles got drunk on wine imported from the cold lands of the barbarians, far across the seas, while we humble folk got drunk on palm toddy, which we brewed. My neighbours, the snake charmers and the street magicians and acrobats, earned a fistful of money for their performances, which they promptly handed over to me for my specially made country liquour.

The palace gossip was always juicy and we all revelled in the scandals involving the high and the mighty. The juiciest one involved a sweeper. She had given birth to an ugly and black baby whose features resembled King Ravana. It was rumoured that initially the king had raped her, but then she had become his mistress. These stories were told by traders and vendors and whenever this topic came up, I maintained a judicious silence. The rumour even went to the extent that whenever the pious and saintly queen was dispossessed for sex, either physically or spiritually, the king called for this sweeper. Soon many knew it was Mala and they flirted with her even more.

I tried to physically stop her from visiting the palace many times, but she somehow sneaked out. When she came back, I made her life hell, but she took my thrashing and kicking with remarkable forbearance. She finally confessed that Ravana had indeed raped her and that Athikaya was his child. But she claimed that after that incident, the King had never bothered her and had always treated her with supreme contempt. It was Queen Mandodari who summoned her to the palace often. It was only the queen's

love for Athikaya that took Mala to the palace. My thrashing her after her routine palace visits became a sort of ritual. And our marriage, if we could call it that, survived.

Almost a month after the birth of this illicit child of Ravana, the queen gave birth to a beautiful boy. As the boy was born on a dark and thunderous monsoon night, he was named Meghanada, 'the one with a thunderous voice'.

Soon, Prince Kumbakarna fathered a beautiful girl baby and Vibhishana also became the father of a healthy and robust girl baby. All these events were important for us, not because we were concerned about royal fecundity, but because they attracted people from the countryside of both the island and the mainland, and that was good for business. Slowly and steadily, the King earned the goodwill of the people. Perhaps, he had curbed his natural ambition or the birth of a son had quenched his thirst for war and acquisition of new territory.

Slowly the territories of India, including the island, started to regain the prosperity it had once enjoyed. Trade began to flourish again. The surprising thing was that people who I had thought were impossibly cruel, proved to be excellent administrators. Rudraka's move to post policemen and mounted guards on the highways and at ports, was initially resented by the people, for they thought these guards would turn oppressors and thieves. But Rudraka instilled such fear into his subordinates, and underlined that fear by publicly executing corrupt guards, that extortion came to virtual standstill, at least in the vicinity of the capital. Prahastha, as a Prime Minister, kept the entire crew of ministers under tight control and his personal integrity was respected by the people, though as a person he was never well liked. Jambumali, the bumbling clerk, matured into a mature minister of finance. Though we did not understand a thing about his taxation policies, the rich merchants who frequented my laundry, always sang paeans to him. He must have been really good as these Chettis were usually as stingy with their praise as with their money.

Maricha was the minister in charge of hospitals, educational and charitable institutions, and was well liked by the populace. The kindheartedness of the man even during turbulent times had been notable, so in peaceful times, he excelled. He personally visited orphanages and hospitals and was firm and kind at the same time. He started a school-cum-orphanage for the children of soldiers who had laid down their lives for Ravana's greater glory. Though it was a small thing, the very thought that a minister cared for the poor and downtrodden and that the government was grateful to those who had died, was refreshing and almost made the State seem humane.

The King's father-in-law was the minister of civil planning and administration and the subject of much ridicule. He drew plans of grand cities and majestic roads such as no one had ever seen or thought could be built. No one took him seriously. No one believed him but he was tolerated despite, or perhaps because of, his good-natured blundering and absent-minded ways. He could be seen walking through the highways and streets, mumbling to himself, followed by two or three reverent students from his institute on the mainland, occasionally stopping to draw complicated diagrams in the mud.

Often, street urchins collected around this curious group. But the good natured professor was too involved in his own world of complicated mathematical calculations to even know these urchins existed. Sometimes, he would just ruffle the dirty hair of some foul-smelling urchin and continue mumbling to himself and drawing imaginary pictures in the air, ignoring the hoots of the crowd. He was tolerated by the people as a welcome and comic diversion. That was until the King gave him the commission to build the majestic temple at Gokarna, at the northernmost tip on the west coast of his empire. Anyone who saw the temple, ceased forever to ridicule the bumbling professor. It was a wonderful piece of art. It stood on the shore where the sea breathed, as if a jewel had fallen from heaven, exquisite and majestic. But that, of course was much later.

Initially, Vibhishana was well liked. His attempts to revamp the forgotten street Shiva temples or those of other lesser gods, and his streamlining of temple administration, drew many admirers. But soon he began to commission small Vishnu temples and introduce strange Deva customs. He even brought some Brahmins and slowly, these people began to introduce the wretched Deva tradition of the caste system. Of course, there were idiots who admired Vibhishana and these people quickly adopted Brahminical customs. The elite began to convert in droves and wore the sacred thread which a Brahmin was supposed to wear always. They began to look down on anyone who did a useful job.

Initially it was funny, as these new converts to Brahmanism went to ridiculous lengths to avoid bodily contact with all others. Rowdy elements among us would rush and embrace, or at least touch, the pure Brahmins returning from their purifying baths. No sooner did one of us touch one of the super-pure Brahmins, the entire bunch would curse us and amidst our laughter and fun, would return to the *Ghat* to wash us off their bodies. Many a day we had lots of fun making them bathe more than a dozen times.

But then, the dimwitted idiots that we were, it was much too late when we found ourselves excluded from the mainstream. There was a secret campaign led by prince Vibhishna, to reserve all important government jobs for Brahmins. Within three years, almost all important trade jobs were in the hands of either the neo-converts or the Brahmins who had migrated from the north. Resentment built up. Fat and fair Deva Brahmins started arriving in hoards from northern India and soon Brahmin colonies sprang up in important towns and villages.

Merchants who did not accept the Deva ways were slowly excluded from the palace. Roads and other public contracts for temples, got allotted only to the neo-converts. Then the roads were closed to people like us. My shop witnessed angry and impotent resentment against the way things were being done in our own land. The grand, new temples which had been constructed, were barred to us. The old priests were thrown out of temples and filled hastily by Brahmins. People spoke longingly of the rule of Mahabali, when everyone was treated as equal. Dust accumulated over past glory.

The suppressed resentment finally exploded. It happened when a butcher was negotiating the price of an old cow with a farmer in the market. *Maha Shivaratri* was two days away and the market was crowded with people jostling for their holiday purchases. People were purchasing cows, chickens and goats to sacrifice and feast on. There were fat Brahmin missionaries exhorting people to desist from eating cows. When the butcher purchased the cow from the farmer, a group of Brahmin priests came up to him and exhorted him to leave the cow alone. One suggested that the butcher would rid himself of all his sins by simply gifting the cow to a Brahmin. Initially, the butcher was amused and argued with the Brahmins about their love for a lowly, stupid animal. The butcher, already drunk, hugged the leader of the Brahmins. The group of Brahmins fell on the butcher and began to kick and hit him.

Meanwhile, the butcher had taken out his knife and started to slash indiscriminately. Soon many people had joined the fight and ended only when the Brahmins took flight. Three Brahmins and the farmer lay dead in the middle of the market. The butcher, in his new found heroism, wielded his knife like a sword and shouted, "Death to all Brahmins". The crowd roared approval. Soon, people came out with anything they could lay their hands on – swords, kitchen knives, tills, axe, pieces of furniture, stones – and the group had swelled to hundreds by the time they reached my shop. I also rushed to join in. I wanted blood. I wanted to spit on the fat Brahmin faces. This was my country, my race, my King, and how dare they come and spoil our culture?

The crowd snaked towards the streets where the Brahmins lived in their fine houses. Somebody found a torch and soon, one by one, the houses went up in flames. Women and children ran out. The crowd butchered the children and took the women. The fat Brahmins escaped, leaving the women and children to our mercy. And mercy was a word the Deva raids had taught us to discard. When we were finished, somebody shouted for Prince Vibhishana's blood. The mob turned towards the palace. Many Brahmins had hidden there. We wanted to punish them for their arrogance, pride, the insults they heaped on us, for treating us as untouchables and destroying the little dignity we possessed. The mob swelled to thousands and we destroyed indiscriminately, torching six Vishnu temples, the public bathing *Ghat*, shops belonging to both Asuras and Brahmins, and kept marching to the palace. A group of mounted police tried to stop us, but the mob devoured them in seconds. An inspector was hung from the nearest tree. Three police outposts were torched. We were on a high. But something troubled me. *'Why was Ravana's army succumbing so easily? Why was there was no resistance? Were they so cowardly?'*

Then my neighbour fell. An arrow had pierced his throat and blood spurted on the row of people behind him. Soon it started raining arrows and I watched in horror. Thousands of mounted archers galloped towards us. The palace gates opened and the soldiers swarmed on us like bees. I could see Rudraka leading the charge, his sword swinging in all directions, severing heads. The mob panicked. I was pushed and shoved and nearly fell down to be trampled by thousands of hooves and feet. It was the hand of fate that protected me. I jumped into a drain on the side of the road and crawled under a stone bridge. I remained under the stone bridge for more than seven hours. When it was dark, I crawled out of my hole. The whole place was a mess. Would-have-been heroes of the revolution lay splattered all around in their own filth of severed limbs and flesh. The stench was unbearable. There was an eerie and oppressive silence. The scuffing sounds of rats nibbling the dead made it more frightening.

I walked towards my home. All along the road I could see houses torched, bodies hanging from trees, and severed limbs and heads lying around like ripe mangoes in the groves during summer. Many of the areas where the poor Asuras lived, had already been flattened by elephants. That so much destruction had taken place in seven hours was hard to believe. At the turn towards the river, I saw the dead butcher hanging from a lamp post. He had led us into this. In impotent rage I rushed towards his limp body, my knife in my hand. I clambered up the tree branch from where he was hung to reach for his face. I slashed across his face again and again till I lost some of my boiled up rage. I jumped down. Then, with a howl, I wiped my hands on my *dhothi*, and then in the earth, again and again. Wearily, I stood up and walked towards my home. When I reached, I saw Mala under the tree. She lay battered and beaten, naked and gang-raped, breathing heavily. Where my house and shop had stood, there was a gaping hole in the ground. Thin spirals of smoke lazily rose towards the heavens.

35 The Duel

Ravana

Sleep eluded me. Bhadra's dark, ugly face took on grotesque shapes in my mind, sometimes leering, sometimes piteously pleading. I lay twitching on my sheet. Tomorrow I would send Maricha to him. Perhaps a few gold coins would assuage my guilt. But I was also angry and embarrassed by the man. It had all started in a moment of weakness. How could I have stooped so low? My conduct had been inexcusable. But I could have forgotten about it and got on with my life, but for this gift from Shiva. It was beyond me how a single act of passion could produce a child, while my queen and I struggled for twelve years to give my son, Meghanada, a sibling. Akshaya Kumara was born after many years, but Meghanada already had a half-brother – Athikaya. Mandodari knew and hated him so much, that she showed the maid and her son extreme kindness. A few minutes in the darkness, anger at my wife, my race, and my life – that is all that it had taken to make this creature of darkness – Athikaya.

I could have made both mother and son vanish at my royal command. But something held me back – perhaps some humanity remained within me. Or maybe it was the memory of a long lost love and a small baby floating in a reed basket over a swiftly flowing river – or maybe it was the memory of a long lost love and a small baby girl fished out of a ditch by a Deva King. After all, Athikaya, black and ugly, with buck teeth, was also my son, and I had become older and wiser, or was too foolish, to commit such heinous acts. Like my daughter in the northern Deva lands, the son of my sin too, grew up quickly.

It was true that I had not been paying attention to day-to-day governance. My ministers were efficient and I was immersed in family life. My coffers overflowed and I had no ambition left for any conquests. I was in my fifties and content. I knew I was a good King and that people would talk about my regime long after I was dead. Like most rulers in their middle age, I was more interested in leaving behind a legacy. Death did not seem so distant now. I could feel its breath on my neck. I was no longer invincible or immortal. Strangely, I had begun to value life. I relished every moment and the little things like the pealing of a distant temple bell; the clang of swords as my beloved son, Meghanada, practiced his swordplay; my wife cooing to my younger son, Akshaya Kumara; the tinkle of bangles as my teenaged niece, Trijata, fluttered around the sweeping verandahs of the palace. . .the small pleasures of life gave me so much joy.

In the centre of controversy was Athikaya, my son from the maid Mala. I loved Meghanada more than anything else in the world, even more than myself. Whatever Meghanada was, Athikaya was not. Meghanada was so handsome that it hurt my eyes. Athikaya was a huge hulk of black flesh, so ugly that people gaped at him open-mouthed. Where Meghanada was as graceful as a pure bred horse, Mala's son was clumsy and bow-legged. Meghanada exuded intelligence and charm, while Athikaya surpassed himself day by day with his own stupidity. It was as if nature had blessed Meghanada with everything and had nothing left to offer Athikaya. It puzzled me that the same father could sire sons who were so different.

I hated Athikaya as much as I loved Meghanada. But the cursed son followed me like a puppy. However I tried to avoid him, he somehow attached himself to me. Often I was cruel to him, kicking him or slapping him in public, or shouting at him, yet he would grin stupidly, showing off his ugly yellow buck teeth. Meghanada, if he was around, would laugh aloud. Athikaya amused him. It had not occurred to me when I was younger, but I had come to recognize that I loved this stupid son of mine in a different way. It wasn't like the love I had for Meghanada, or Mandodari, or my brothers, or my scores of nieces and nephews. It was more like how one loved a street dog you fed once in a while but would never keep as a pet because of its ugliness and smell.

Had it not been for Bhadra, I would perhaps have got rid of the boy long before. Bhadra came back to me when I had grown too important to think of people like him. It happened after that pogrom, when Vibhishana crushed the Asura rebellion against the fat Brahmins. I was no fan of the Brahmins and was secretly happy about the riot. When Vibhishana came back to court with scores of bleeding and battered Brahmins, my first instinct was to laugh. But as usual, it was Prahastha who showed me the way. He was in his late fifties then. But he continued to irritate me with his discourses. We had our arguments but I had begun to depend on him. I let him handle the mundane affairs of day-to-day governance, but on important occasions, I used my veto power. We were not exactly friends, but I respected the old man. He was one of the few men who were not afraid of me and certainly no sycophant. True to form, instead of arguing with me in front of the other ministers on the day of the rebellion, he requested a recess and came to me quietly and told me that this was the chance we had been waiting for. We had to crush the rebellion with full force so that no Asura got any ideas about taking the law into his own hands. The King-Emperor was supreme and only his writ should run, Prahastha argued.

Since I was the King-Emperor, I had no problems accepting what he said. But I was uneasy about supporting the Brahmins. Then it struck me that I could kill two birds with one stone. So we let the city burn for a few hours and allowed the hooligans to do their job with the Brahmin ladies. Then we struck back. My soldiers, with perfect impartiality, hacked off the heads of Brahmins and Asuras alike. I let my soldiers loot the Vishnu temples. They did so with gusto and converted them into Shiva temples. The Brahmins fled in hoards towards the mainland and Varuna ferried them across, always charging a hefty fee. Varuna could make a profit whatever the circumstances. Rudraka did such a thorough job that I never faced another rebellion. It was true that Vibhishana sulked for a while, but that mattered little to anyone. However, I felt sorry for my brother and pacified him saying that I would not harass the Brahmins who had managed to remain. Slowly he came around and I thought I had contained my little brother's idiosyncrasies. Or that was what I thought then.

When Bhadra came to me, I sensed he was seething. I could also sense his helplessness. Suppressed frustration lay coiled inside him. But then, Bhadra was always that way. He stood and stared at me. I was amused. He appeared when I least expected him, when I was looking at my garden from the balcony, drinking in the smell of jasmine, listening to the cooing of the pigeons, unmindful of the bloodbath taking place outside my secluded palace unconsciously, my hands went to my sword. Like a small child I had named it Chandrahasa and was extremely possessive about it. It was a masterpiece created by a famed blacksmith and never left my side.

Then, inexplicably, Bhadra began to weep. His cries came in fits at first and then his whole body shook with his torment. He collapsed onto his knees and then fell outstretched at my feet. In earlier times, in a similar situation, I would have kicked his face. I could not stand weakness in anyone. But I saw that Bhadra did not weep from weakness but for his survival. It took courage to lose your pride and still survive. It took will power to suppress one's screaming ego and grovel before another man. It took determination to keep one's head down and act humble, when you were seething inside. Ultimately, the victories do not matter, nor pride or glory, only survival matters – one's life and successors, the clan, race and language. Other things were useless. But then I was what I was and he was what he had become. Neither of us could do anything about it. So I leaned down and helped him up.

"Bhadra." I looked into his coal black eyes. A flicker of hate came like a flash and went, to be replaced by a dead expression. I ignored the hate. I ignored the stench. Life was too short for such things. I almost felt noble. "Have you eaten?" I asked, with what I imagined was kindness. He shook his head. "Go to the kitchen and eat. I will send instructions."

He still stood there. It was an awkward situation. He did not speak and I had run out of words. His stench was overpowering. I tried to keep the kindness and pity I felt for the creature intact, but found revulsion creeping in. I fought against it, keeping my eyes away from his black, cracked skin, disheveled and matted hair, the sores on his legs, the protruding belly and unclean teeth. But the smell kept coming back. I wanted to wash my hands, it felt so impure. Involuntarily, I wiped my hands on a silk handkerchief and was embarrassed when his eye followed my movements.

It was then that three-year-old Meghanada came running into the room with peals of laughter. He stopped abruptly and his huge, lovely eyes registered surprise at the dirty, black Asura standing so reverently before his father, the king. I wanted to lift my boy and moved towards him, but then I did not want to touch him with the dirty hands that touched Bhadra. Once again I wiped my hands and a snigger emanated from the dirty fellow. Anger rose in me like a tidal wave and I turned back to him furiously. It was then that my illegitimate son, the dark, ugly, Athikaya, also came running into the room. Except for a loin cloth, he wore nothing. His three-year-old fingers were messy from a half-eaten, ripe mango. His eyes locked with Bhadra's. I do not know what registered in the mind of the three-year-old but he walked towards the half-starved Bhadra and offered him the mango. Before I could react, Bhadra took it and sucked it as though it was the last thing he would ever eat. Then to my horror, Meghanada extended his little hands and Bhadra stopped eating and dropped the half-sucked, messy mango into them. I kicked the hands hard and the mango shot out of the balcony. I struck Bhadra with the back of my hand. All my altruism vanished. *'How dare, this lowly one come into my palace and have the prince eat his leftovers?'* Bhadra fell down with an expression of glum satisfaction. I wanted to wipe it off his ugly face with a swipe of my sword.

The two boys howled. I took Athikaya by his shoulders and shook him hard. Meghanada tried to free his half-brother from my grip. He pummelled me with his little hands and then Mandodari came running in and pulled Athikaya from my hands.

"Ravana, are you mad? Are you trying to kill this child?" she screamed. She left the howling Athikaya on the floor and pulled Meghanada to her. My son wept on his mother's bosom. Athikaya saw this and howled all the more.

"Why do you allow Megha to play with this dirty urchin?" My words sounded hollow even to me.

My wife glowered. "It is your dirty urchin, Ravana," she said and picked up her weeping son in her arms and stomped out. I was shocked. *'How dare she speak to me like that?'* She used to be afraid to even come near me. But after a son was born, she acted as if she owned me. She was not afraid anymore. She was not afraid to call me by my name or scream at me and throw tantrums to get her way. I had mellowed, except for the occasional flare of temper. Some could say I was henpecked. Though I hid it with my acts of belligerence and shouting, she got her way most of the time. She used my love for her and my son as tools to control me, and quite truthfully, I was happy.

It took a few seconds to register that there was no noise. I looked around. Athikaya and Bhadra had vanished, leaving me alone. I went to the balustrade and looked down. I could see a limping, dark, figure holding the tiny hand of a dirty urchin, walking towards the kitchen block. A pleasant breeze came in from the sea and carried whiffs of their conversation. Tangled in their laughter, a word shot out like a dart and struck a soft spot in my heart. Athikaya, the son I had never wanted, in his innocent voice, called Bhadra his 'father'. I did not know whether Bhadra had asked the child to call him so or whether the boy felt like doing so. But it hurt me. I recovered when I thought that the ugly urchin would be out of my hair and away from my beloved son, Meghanada.

Though everyone knew Athikaya was my son, it helped that Bhadra had married the maid I had raped so long ago. So there was some sort of legitimacy to Athikaya and Bhadra's relationship. It had embarrassed me to know I had raped my servant's wife and given a child to that family, but I got used to the embarrassment. One can get used to anything, even embarrassment. As a special concession, I allowed the royal instructors to teach Athikaya also, after their lessons to the Princes. And I was surprised to hear that he was a fast learner in the use of arms. He must have inherited it from me. I thought he could be developed as a reasonably good combat companion for my son.

It was with great pride that I announced the graduation of my son, Meghanada. It was fixed for the full moon day of Shravan. My close friend Bali, was the state guest for the function. After the fiasco of my youth, our friendship had grown and I admired Bali and believed the respect was mutual. His wife Tara, and my queen, were good friends. Both Bali and I had errant brothers and that was a much discussed topic between us. Bali kept a watchful eye on my amoral sister, who had settled on the outskirts of his kingdom. He would say that she would bring disaster to everyone because she was so self-centered, but I ignored him, thinking Soorpanakha too insignificant to create an impact. She needed men and she took them indiscriminately. She was a blot on the family, but as long as she and my mother and my sly father kept away from Lanka, I cared nothing about what people said.

Bali was at the height of his glory when he visited Trikota for my son's graduation. His own son, Angada, a few years older than Meghanada, accompanied him. The boy was a bit of a rebel teenager but which teenager with spirit did not rebel? I felt my friend was a bit too harsh on his son. Children needed space to grow and it was difficult when their father was a huge Banyan tree. Nothing could grow beneath it. The boy was silent and brooding and many times was openly hostile to his strict father. Compared to Angada, my son was an angel. Actually, my son was an angel compared to anyone. I was always afraid of his friendship with Angada, but Meghanada stood up for the rights of the weak. I thought this was rather unsuited to the modern age we lived in. My son had the old-fashioned notions and morals of a bygone, classical age. Secretly, I was afraid for his future. But he always argued passionately that people were basically good and noble and that all men, irrespective of caste, race or religion, were equal. Values, truth, morals and right conduct, were eternal and no progress made by mankind could change them. I was proud and worried at the same time.

Unfortunately, I was proved right. Poor boy, what did he know about blue-skinned imposters who played God and justified despicable acts with obscure Sanskrit blabberings? What did he know of the treachery of brothers and friends, about hypocrisy, the ugly, dog-eat-dog world? Of course, I too had fantastic notions of changing the world and creating a great and prosperous society when I was his age. But then I grew up and out of such dreams. Meghanada was showered with luxury whereas the only thing I had at that age was hunger.

But I am digressing. The jackals have left me alone for now. Why do they not eat my feverish brain and put an end to this? There's so much I have to remember. Oh Shiva, please call me to your abode. That is, if you actually exist. I will soon know. But the images keep coming to me, so many of them. Prominent among them is the venue of my son's graduation. I could see the glum satisfaction on Mandodari's face. I knew it was not because of her handsome son, his glorious looks and dark flying mane as he rode past our seats, or the graceful way he held his bow and shot arrows at birds and fish while swiftly riding past them on horseback. She was proud her son had turned out better than that of her friend, Tara. Her son was much better than my illegitimate son, Athikaya. I felt proud too but Mandodari looked as if she had won the race of parenthood. When did parents become so competitive?

It was then that one of the most embarrassing incidents of my life happened. My son slipped from his saddle and the crowd gasped. Angada, who was seated between Bali and Tara, howled with laughter. My son regained his balance and gracefully continued his ride. I ignored the derisive laughter though I was seething. But what ensued was disaster. It almost drove my country to war and my kingdom to destruction. I heard the sound of a scuffle. *'Asuras! Always drinking and fighting,'* I thought. I turned to look at commotion and got the shock of my life. Angada lay on the ground. There was an uneasy silence. My son had halted his horse a few feet away. Behind our backs, the bulky and dark figure of Athikaya rose. Then, with slow deliberation, he scrambled away. *'What had the idiot done? This son of a lowly maid?'*

"Catch that idiot!" I roared, and hundreds of guards drew their swords and surrounded both Angada and Athikaya. Bali's face had gone red and I felt afraid.

Athikaya stood with his thick, black lips parted, strands of his curly hair puffing in the wind, looking positively bewildered. He looked like a stupid bull but I could see his hands were tense. Rudraka walked towards Athikaya, his sword drawn.

"He. . .He. . .insulted my. . .bro. . .I mean. . .Prince Meghanada." Athikaya stammered. A murmur rippled through the crowd. Meghanada's face showed amusement and love.

"Throw him into the dungeon. We shall decide his fate tomorrow." I shouted, stealing a look at the grim faced Bali.

"I'll deal with him." It was Angada who had scrambled up.

"Angada. . ." Bali's voice was chilling but his son defied his father's anger. What I saw in his eyes was the same hatred I had for my father. I sank back in my seat, knowing that matters were getting out of control. My only prayer was that Angada would finish this idiot Athikaya quickly and save the day.

"You fool. . ." Bali hissed, but Angada was beside himself. He theatrically waved away all the guards and Rudraka looked at me for instructions. I gave a curt nod and he ordered his guards back.

"He kicked me and I want to reclaim my honour," Angada hissed at his father. Then, at the top of voice, he announced to the gallery, "Citizens of Lanka, watch how we Vanaras deal with an ass who thinks he is a lion!"

Athikaya stood there stupidly, his eyes blinking like an owl. Meghanada dismounted and came to Athikaya. He took his hands and whispered something in his ear and then led him to the centre of the venue. *'Son of a sweeper, the curse born to erase my pride.'* I wanted to kill him with my own hands. As the son of my sin walked into the centre with my beloved Meghanada, the crowd roared approval. With that one gesture by the prince, Athikaya had become the gallery's darling. Meghanada drew his sword and threw it to Athikaya who caught it with such ease in mid-air that I was startled. The boy had flair. Now I was torn. I wanted Athikaya to be killed so that I could save my country and my friendship with Bali. But somewhere within me, my parental pride throbbed. I wanted Athikaya to win. After all, he was my blood.

Angada walked in circles. I could hear a few cat calls and hoots. Then the crowd began to chant, "Death to the Vanaras; hell to the Vanaras; *hai hai* Vanaras." I stole a glance at Bali and saw his hands tightly gripping his chair. The nerves in his huge arms were taut and throbbing, but his face remained impassive. The crowd began to abuse the Vanaras, calling them half-castes and monkey-men. Some abused the Vanara King himself. I searched for Rudraka. But to my amazement, Rudraka was intently watching the start of the combat with his back turned to me. The noise was deafening.

The first clash of swords broke through the noise. Then they fought – the bellicose son of my friend and the son of a sweeper woman. In the first few minutes, Angada drew blood many times. He was lithe and swift. Athikaya was clumsy at times, elegant at others, but he could not manage to even nip Angada. I began to relax, but also felt sad. The crowd had gone silent and tense. I could feel the hostility in the air. I could also sense Bali relaxing a little. Then, with a powerful kick in the groin, Angada send Athikaya flying to the floor. Athikaya crashed into the ground with a sickening thud. A huge gasp went through the crowd. Angada gave a loud laugh and roared.

Athikaya lay in a heap, unconscious, or perhaps dead. Angada waved his sword at the crowd. He could have thrust his sword into Athikaya and finished him off. But he did nothing of the sort. That would have been too tame for him. He was relishing the moment of victory of a Vanara prince over an Asura and wanted to savour every second of it. I could see the twitch of a smile on Bali's face and also a flicker of pride. I was sad but relieved. A crisis had been averted. But then I saw the tall, elegant figure of my son walking towards his fallen half-brother. Angada stopped his antics and stared with open hostility at my son. I prayed that he would not challenge Meghanada to a duel. My son would have to accept and the result, either way, would have been disastrous. As I watched, I realized that my entire body was trembling. '*The idiotic son of Bali, I could murder him. Why could not people bring up their children properly?*'

Meghanada took Athikaya's head onto his lap and then whispered something in his ear. There was an uneasy calm. Time stood still. It was a hot and humid day and even the breeze from the sea had stopped. Somewhere in the distance a goat bleated and was soon answered by its lamb. My back was wet with perspiration. A murmur rose from the crowd as Athikaya stirred. Then, with an arm over Meghanada's shoulders, he slowly tried to stand. He faltered twice and was strongly held up by Meghanada. Then he pushed Meghanada aside and took two faltering

steps towards Angada. He steadied himself and gave a roar. It was not human, that roar, it reverberated through the gallery and lost itself in the momentary silence. Then the crowd roared back with its ten thousand throats. The sound chilled me.

Meghanada took a club from Maricha and walked deliberately to Athikaya. Without looking at Meghanada, his eyes intently focused on his rival, Athikaya took the club in his left hand and passed it to his right. There he stood, with his legs wide apart, bleeding from a hundred cuts, his huge, left hand firmly on his hips, and his dark, ugly face scowling at Angada. Angada had no choice. He was bound by honour to put down his sword and fight with his club. As he took the club, the crowd with one voice chanted, "Death to the Vanara. Death to the monkey-man. *Hai, hai* Vanara."

The game changed altogether. Athikaya was clumsy with his sword. His bulky body could not move as nimbly or as fast as the supple Angada. But his huge weight was an advantage in swinging the heavy club. Angada was still swift and graceful and managed to hit Athikaya more often than the other way round. But Athikaya had such power and accuracy to his hits that the few he connected, injured his opponent. Angada's style was to thrust and dance away, far from the reach of his heavy rival. That was well in swordplay. But with a club, unless the blow was heavy and well aimed, it did not create much impact, especially on a heavily-muscled adversary like Athikaya who went from strength to strength as the crowd roared for him.

I felt proud of my sons. '*Did a half-bred monkey-man think he could come with his brute of a son and thrash our warriors?*' Then I caught myself. I was afraid what would happen if Athikaya won. I wanted to remain Bali's friend. He was a good friend, but good friends were dispensable. Bali was a strategic ally, who kept the barbarian Deva hordes of the upper Gangetic plain at bay. Such allies were not dispensable. Illegitimate sons were easily dispensed with. But he had my blood, this huge, stupid son of a maid, and the way he was going, he could make Bali my biggest enemy.

Angada fell, sprawled on the ground. Both his arms were broken and twisted impossibly. Athikaya was bleeding and a pool of blood formed under his left foot. He kept his right foot pressed firmly on the chest of the gasping Angada. Bali stood up from his seat, his fist clenched hard and face taut and tense. His queen's face had frozen with horror. The crowd shouted in a frenzy, "Kill him! Kill him! Kill the son of the monkey!" The roar could be heard everywhere.

Athikaya raised his club high above his head in an arc, the club almost touching his back. He would have swung it with mighty force and smashed it down on Angada's head. And Bali's son would have had been crushed in a second.

"Rudraka!" I shouted at the top of my voice. I was not sure whether he heard or not. It seemed like an eternity, but then Athikaya turned his face towards me. '*What was it I saw in those eyes – hatred, astonishment, pity or pure raw contempt?*' He stood for a fraction of second looking at me. The crowd went silent. The image remains frozen in my mind. Then Rudraka caught my eye and understood. He just flicked his hand and more than twenty guards rushed towards the centre. Athikaya stood there, peering into my soul, the son I never wanted, as twenty men hit him from all sides with clubs and sticks. But he stood there like a huge Banyan tree, unmindful of the raging monsoon of beatings performing a death dance. Angada lay still pinned under his huge foot. A dark figure darted from the crowd and almost reached Athikaya before the guards. But Rudraka hit a powerful blow with the hilt of his sword and the figure fell. Later I heard it had been the fool Bhadra. He was stamped upon by the running guards, wriggled for a few moments, and then was still. I could see Meghanada and Maricha trying to stop Rudraka. The crowd was too shocked to react. This was grossly unfair and I was afraid how the crowd would react once it woke from its stupor. I could hear Prahastha shouting instructions to the guards, positioning them for a quick evacuation. And to my horror, I saw my own uncle and my beloved son, fighting with my faithful commander and his troops, to save my illegitimate son. This was a nightmare. The crowd fought with the guards and a few fires began to crackle. There was a stampede.

Then I saw Bali running towards the centre. Maricha was fighting a pitched battle with Rudraka and Meghanada had almost got through the guards

when Bali hacked his way through the chaos. Meghanada turned against Bali and my hands went involuntarily to my sword. But before I could do anything, Bali, with one deft movement of his hand, caught hold of Meghanada's wrist and pried away his sword. Then, with a powerful kick, he sent Rudraka sprawling. He pushed away Meghanada and my son staggered for a few steps and fell onto his back. Next was the turn of my brave uncle. Bali lifted Maricha and threw him a good ten feet away. The other guards were too afraid to move and gave way. Athikaya had collapsed over Angada, wheezing hard. Bali lifted the huge hulk of Athikaya easily in his hands. *'He's going to slam him hard on the ground. How dare he come and kill my son?'* I thought.

The crowd bayed for Vanara blood and many broke through the security ring and ran to the center. I expected Bali to throw Athikaya down and finish him off before attending to his son. But, surprising everyone, Bali walked back with my son in his arms – my bleeding, thrashed, hacked, ugly, black son. And the crowd fell silent. The men who had run to the middle to fight, stopped in their tracks and watched. Tara sobbed and my wife joined her. But then, tears had welled in my eyes too. I wanted to hide them so I turned back and shouted instructions to my soldiers. But nobody listened to me. And my friend, that noble warrior, the fairest man I would ever see in my life, Bali, the only one who could be truly called great, came to me with my fallen son in his arms. His son lay there dead or alive, we did not know. But the man had the greatness of heart to be fair. What I had done had been ignoble and I was ashamed. I, the mighty king of the Asuras, cried that day, in front of thousands of my subjects. I hid my face from the world and cried. I cried for my son Athikaya, who had almost died; for my friend, his fairness and supreme sacrifice; for my son, Meghanada; and my uncle, who were brave enough to stand against me and Bali for what was right. And I cried for being such a scum.

They took Athikaya away to the court physician, and that idiot Bhadra too. They carried away the son of my friend who was half dead more from shame and fright than from Athikaya's blows. Their wounds would heal, but what about the wounds to our hearts? Would they ever heal? Could friendship survive such a magnanimous act from one friend to another? Friendship could survive betrayal, but could it survive such an extraordinary act of kindness and great heartedness?

The crowd dispersed but over the din of voices, I heard something that was a harbinger of things to come. That brute Angada hissed as he passed his father, "Weakling! I'll get back at you..." and so on, while Bali stood staring into the distance as if he had not heard anything. I saw Queen Tara look at her husband with unadulterated hate and I was afraid for my dear friend. At that moment, I was afraid that the world as I knew it, had changed. Our generation and its values was giving way to a new, unscrupulous, arrogant, young world of Angadas. I was afraid that people like us would be wiped off in the coming days. Our values were being lost and life was becoming too fast and unscrupulous for older men like me. I was growing old much too fast. Slowly I took my wife's hand and walked towards our chariot. That day my wife left me alone in my own world and I curled inside my darkness like a worm. Early next day morning, Bali and Tara left with their wounded son. And I never saw my friend again.

36 A country thanks its hero

Bhadra

It was almost dawn when they brought him home, bandaged and bruised. He moaned softly as they came. Without a word, they gently laid Athikaya down, and they left without a word.

Athikaya grew up in my arms. From the time he was three, he called me father. Initially I had been horrified. He was a prince, though an illegitimate one, and I was what I was. I had shouted at him, pleaded with him and even cried, to stop him from calling me so, but he had persisted. And in my heart, I wanted him to call me his father. He was now my son. No king could lay claim to him. He anchored me to the earth. Together we explored the city of Trikota and the jungles, backwaters and hills which surrounded it. I taught him to use arms. He was a prince in my humble hut. And he was my pride, my future.

It pained me when he was mocked; when he was dragged around like a puppy with the legitimate prince, that haughty, know all, Meghanada. But the boy carried a deep affection towards his half-brother. I was jealous of it and of the love he showed my wife, Mala, his mother. I tried to dissuade him from going to the palace but the summons came often, either from the King or his son. They needed someone to run around, to do odd jobs. He had a doglike devotion for the King and the Prince. He was such a simpleton, so innocent. He was strong in body but weak in his mind. He went out of the way to help people. But like other good natured people from the lower rungs of society, his goodness was mistaken for naivety.

Everyone considered him a fool. But I was sure that behind that soft and kind face, a tremendous strength of character lay hidden. At times, I saw glimpses of that hidden steel, but mostly Athikaya was just a young, gullible, innocent boy, who was taken advantage of by the cunning people of the world. Kindness, courage, morals, principles, sympathy, these were dangerous values to have for someone who belonged to our social position. It was unsafe to have a golden heart under a dark skin. Those were the luxuries of the rich, the noble, the high-caste, the fair-skinned, which they used when it benefitted them. My large-boned, black and ugly son, could do without them. But a bit of sycophancy, a dash of cruelty, a willingness to serve any master to survive, and the ability to hide seething anger and cower before those who were stronger, were survival tools in our world. But I could never convince foolish Athikaya about any of it.

The boy had a privileged life till now. Did the present generation understand the hardships we had undergone? Even Prince Meghanada has had a privileged life while his father built his kingdom on the flesh, sweat and blood of people like me and struggled to become what he was now. Perhaps, when we started, all of us had the same chance. Anybody could have become what he was now. He was nothing more than us. What did Ravana have that I did not possess? Was it the quiet confidence that he was born to rule? Was it plain luck, or because he was so ruthless and clever? If ruthlessness was the key, then Rudraka possessed it more than anyone else. If strategic and long-term thinking was the answer, no one could match Prahastha. If it was bravery, then there were scores of brave Asuras around who could have made it big. If charisma was the most important factor, then why didn't Vidyutjihva succeed? If cleverness was important, then why had Maya not made it?

I think it was the size of the dream and the willingness to act on it. Ravana dreamt big and strove ruthlessly to achieve it. And he got all sorts of people working for him to achieve his ambition. He crushed many underfoot. He used fools like me as firewood for his burning ambition. And so he now lived in the palace and I in a hut. I hated Ravana for it. Ravana could beat my son to a pulp; treat me like a cur; refrain from touching our ugly black, soiled, sweaty, stinking skin, and at the same time talk loudly about the equality of men; and pose as the saviour of the Asuras from Deva torments, but mark my words, we the meek would survive when the kings of all colours, had gone. Despite Ravana's arrogance, patronizing attitude and riches, we would outlive him. We may lick his boots; crawl on the earth in front of him and pay obeisance whenever his shadow falls on the earth, but one day his tribe would vanish, fighting his useless battles for vainglory. But we would survive and win the final war – of survival.

My son stirred and let out a moan. I was shaken from my fantastic and heroic mental flight. Cold reality crept up on me. What was I? A small-time nobody trying to make a living, betrayed by his wife, saddled with her illegitimate son, ruled by a selfish king. A poor, hungry, unhealthy, and beaten up, black, untouchable rascal. That summed me up. And I dared to dream of challenging kings? I laughed at myself.

It was very hot and I was getting pickled in my own perspiration. My body hurt as I slowly sat up. Hunger gnawed at my belly. I tried to stand but my head swam. I caught at the wall and stood there panting for a few minutes. Then I collapsed and lay still. A wave of self-pity rushed over me as I gulped down my tears and anger. I turned and crawled towards the kitchen. I could see holes on the rough floor. There was dust everywhere, which I had never noticed before. I was so close to the floor that I could smell it. *'Why couldn't that damn woman keep the house clean?'* I was angry with my wife. *'Let her come back and I would teach her proper housekeeping.'*

A large, black spider scurried away hastily as I entered the kitchen. I stared at it for a few seconds but realized that looks cannot kill spiders. I crawled to the hearth and managed to sit on the floor with my legs spread as I opened the lids of the pots and vessels one by one. Empty. Nothing. My stomach rumbled with hunger. A pot hung from a rope in one corner. Perhaps it had curd. Mala would have kept it high to keep it safe from the rats. Or perhaps jaggery or some other nice savouries. How could I reach it? I could not stand up. Then I laughed. Savouries here? In an untouchable's house? Some of Ravana's vanity had rubbed off on me too. I was dreaming too big.

'Where had Mala gone?' I heard the noise of a cart drawing near and stopping in front of the house. Was the King sending her home in a chariot now? I crawled towards the front door. There were hushed whispers and then a soft knock on the half closed door. I waited silently. A bejewelled hand pushed the creaky door open, throwing a trapezium of sunlight on the walls and floor. My son moaned again. A dusty breeze wafted in, ruffled the old clothes in the corner, and went out through the window opposite. I squinted into the bright sunlight, and saw the tall figure of Prince Meghanada enter. It was followed by Maricha's tall, jaunty figure. Two princes in an untouchable's humble hut! I could not believe it. Involuntarily, I tried to get up, but collapsed again.

Smiling, Maricha came forward and lifted me up gently and placed me on the lone, broken chair. I protested and tried to stand, but he gently and firmly pushed me back into the chair. *'Dear God, how can I be hospitable to these people?'* A prince in my hut. I was angry that they saw my poverty, my broken chair, my rags, my torn bed sheets, my cracked walls and floors, and my weak body. This was my house and I needed some privacy to hide my failure from the eyes of a cruel world lorded over by rich princes like these two. Then I grew afraid. Had they come to take away my son? Had the king decided at last that he had a brave son in Athikaya? Had my wife finally deserted me? Was she living with the king as his queen and taking away her son from me? Or had these people come to gloat over our misery? I sat there with a hundred questions scrapping like wild cats in my mind. I sat blinking like an owl, speechless.

"How are you Bhadra?" Maricha's voice had lost none of its kindness. *'Thank you sir, for the thrashing I received from your soldiers,'* I wanted to scream. But I sat there without a word. Meghanada sat on the bed, close to Athikaya, and examined his wounds. He spoke softly and Athikaya responded like a lost puppy which had finally managed to find its master. With disgust, I thought, *'If Athikaya had a tail, it would have been wagging.'*

"I know, Bhadra, we have wronged you." Maricha had his hands on my shoulder now and was so close that I could smell his rich perfume. I averted my eyes – I could not stand so much kindness. I was, after all, an untouchable, scum of the earth. I peered to see whether, like Ravana,

Maricha too had wiped his hands after touching my black skin. No, he had not. I was disappointed. Perhaps, he would bathe once he reached his palace.

"You should not think unkindly of our King, Bhadra." I looked back at him. Who was I to think anything and how did it matter? "He is the same Ravana. His whiskers have turned grey, but Bhadra, he is the same impulsive boy with audacious dreams and a will to achieve. I know, bad things have happened to people like you. Though the Brahmins have been banished, the bane of Brahmanism is slowly creeping into our society. It is so easy to believe that one is superior to all others. I know there are people who consider the poor, black, original Asuras, impure, and even refuse to touch you people. They think that poor settlements like this will defile our beautiful cities. I know, there are people who would like to banish the poor like you out of the capital, or if possible, out of the country. But believe me, Bhadra, it is Ravana's compassion that has prevented that from happening. He feels for the poor. True, we are far from the ideals of Mahabali, in achieving social equality. That is still a dream. But we are striving towards it. And he has sent us with a message that he will banish all caste or *varna* from his thoughts. The State will no longer discriminate among its own subjects. This is our solemn promise, and as a minister, I make it on behalf of His Majesty."

What a speech! But I was not impressed. The old man hugged me and I could see tears in his eyes. Perhaps he felt noble hugging me, touching me, and talking about elevated ideas to me. Let him enjoy his moment of greatness. Perhaps the years had hardened me. I could hear Athikaya sobbing loudly. The poor boy had been moved. He was lucky he still believed such tall talk. He had yet to become infected with the malaise that people of my generation suffered from – incurable cynicism. But the people standing inside my stinking hole of a hut were powerful and important. So I kept up the pretence. I acted deeply grateful and thankful. From the expression on his face, I could see the old fool had been taken in. Poor fool, one could easily deceive him. Then my heart went out to the old man. If anyone was really sincere amongst all the thugs who were our ministers, it was this hard, brown, nut, Maricha. He believed what he said and might have even striven to implement it in all earnestness. His King might do it for glory. But whether the conservative old guards like Prahastha, Jambumali, and the rest, would allow such changes, was still to be seen. And even if all of them agreed, Vibhishana, the disguised Brahmin among the Asuras, would see to it that such gestures were defeated. Vibhishana was an intolerant fanatic. Even then, I was sure that one day he would sell the entire Asura civilization to the Brahmins and Devas.

"As a token of goodwill, His Majesty has asked us to present this small gift to you. It will not recompense you for all the services you have performed or the privation you have undergone for the glory of our race and country, but please accept this token from a grateful King." Saying this, Maricha put a reasonably large cloth bundle that jingled with coins, into my lap. There was satisfaction on his face. He waited for my profuse gratitude, but I said nothing. I just kept staring down at the bundle.

Meghanada took leave of Athikaya and I heard my son saying to the Prince, "When you asked me to do it for you, I forgot everything else. I would happily die for you, Your Highness, I would die for you." And he kissed Meghanada's hands. Something inside me snapped. *'The idiot would die for the prince?'* This was our fate – to toil, to live, to strive, and to die, for the high and mighty. I once did it for the father of this same Prince, and maybe would be forced to do it again. Oh Shiva! Was there no escape? And now my son says he forgot his parents and himself and would have died for his master. Did these men boast that they could command worms like us to die? Did they think they could pursue their destiny by crushing a few black, irrelevant, cursed, puny people like ourselves, under their feet while marching to glory, riches and destiny?

I stood up. My head swam, but the anger that lay coiled inside gave new strength to my weak and battered body. "Get out! Get out you bastards!" I screamed. I threw the bundle of coins and it flew out of the open door like a missile. The cloth tore open and spilt its contents all over the filthy road and gutter. I saw they were silver coins. I couldn't even boast that I had throw away gold coins for the honour and dignity of my people. Had they been copper coins, it would have justified my belief that princes and noblemen were miserly and mean and I cared nothing for their presents.

But they were plain silver coins. They would not make me rich nor were they small enough to feed my deeply held prejudices. Urchins and beggars had gathered, but did not dare to touch the glinting coins. The presence of the Prince and a minister, and bawdy, old Bhadra shouting and creating a scene, was too fascinating to be distracted even by silver coins.

I had gone too far, so I decided to speak my mind. "You think you are doing me a great favour by visiting my hut? You nearly killed me and my son. Who wants your coins? Keep them for yourselves. The King is compassionate, you say," I spat for effect. "Does he know what it is like to be treated as though one had a contagious disease? Does he know the pain of hunger? The sting of failure? The throbbing ache of hopelessness? The agony of being homeless? He does not want poor, black Asuras to be treated as untouchables, he wants us to live in the cities. I know the reason for that too. You noble, rich, pseudo-Brahmins rave against us being unclean, our black skin, our smell. . .but you need us more than we need you. Who would carry your rubbish if we were banished? Who would sweep your streets, draw your carts, and die for you in your petty wars?"

I felt cold steel at my throat. I stared at Prince Meghanada's gleaming eyes and was afraid. I trembled as my fury fled and I came to earth with a thud. The horror of what I had said hit me with brutal force. My lips trembled and tears of fear and helplessness traced their way over my burning cheeks. It was over. The blade was pressed harder and I felt the warmth of blood trickling out. Surely I would die for my impudence.

"Let him be, Meghanada. I think he is drunk," I heard Maricha say. Slowly the pressure eased from the sword and Meghanada took it away and wiped my blood from its blade with his fingers and put the sword back into its sheath without taking his eyes off my face. I shivered and collapsed on the chair.

"Bhadra, we'll leave now. Take care of your health and do not drink so much. You might lose your head, literally." Maricha said with a smile, but I saw that his eyes did not smile. I could see contempt in those eyes. Meghanada went and hugged the sobbing Athikaya. Then the Prince and the Minister walked out into the sunshine. I heard the horses being whipped and the chariot drove away through the narrow, uneven street. I lay there, my mind blank.

Then I heard the noise of fighting men. It did not register at first. Then I realized they were fighting over the silver coins I had thrown outside. My coins. I tried to stand up, lost my balance and fell on my face. Then I crawled outside and jumped into the fray to get hold of my coins. Most of them had vanished. I clawed and fought my way through. I stamped two urchins and kicked an old beggar and received much the same back, but I was past pain. It was my money, my hard earned money. Finally, I managed to grab a fistful of soiled coins from the gutter. Though many tried to grab them, I held on tightly to my possessions through the kicks and blows. Finally, the beggars and my neighbours gave up and went away, cursing me and each other. I slowly got up from the gutter and counted the coins. There were twenty-one. Maybe a hundredth of what had originally been there. I stared at the coins for a long time. I had thrown away the chances that life had handed me many a time before too. Perhaps I deserved this. Anyhow, the tavern around the corner would be open now. There would be whores with breasts as big as pumpkins and plenty of country liquor. Ah, just what I needed. I stumbled towards it as the sun set, with the coins I had fought for. A good drink and some whoring – after all, that was what life was about.

37 A daughter's marriage

Ravana

I had been receiving disturbing news. I wished to concentrate on the mural I was painting but somehow, I could not focus. The colours and tones did not come through as I wanted. The news was disturbing and I wondered who I could share it with? But it was a closely guarded secret. Maricha? No, not even him. He was not at all sympathetic about that particular relationship and may not have been willing to listen to my ramblings and self-pity.

I felt old, both in spirit and body. I had seen her once, many years ago. She would have been sixteen or seventeen then. Only Maricha knew. It had been a dangerous mission and took place immediately after my son's graduation. The way I had treated Athikaya tore at my heart and I wallowed in remorse, when Maricha came and jerked me out of it. He was cruel and candid and said I had no business to feel sad. After all, I was the one who had cruelly cast away my first born.

I went mad and reminded him that it had been his wise Council of Ministers who had done that. He retorted that I hadn't done anything after that. That stopped me dead in my tracks. I dismissed him haughtily and went back into my shell. I shouted at my wife and even threw Meghanada out of the room. In the middle of the night, I woke up in a cold sweat. I had seen a ghost. I would have laughed if anyone had said that there was a ghost inside the palace of the Emperor of the Asuras. Until then, ghosts were something that lurked with a silly leer in

childhood stories. But that night I saw one clearly. It was a woman with a veil over her face. She looked familiar as she stood at the window peering at me intently. I couldn't move a limb. I could smell my own fear. The face gradually became clear and I wanted to touch Mandodari and wake her. But my hands would not move. The face became clearer by minute and I waited with horror and anticipation for the final revelation. An owl hooted in the garden, piercing the thick silence. And in a wisp of breeze, the veil fell. It was Vedavathi!

My throat went dry. All the emotions I had buried in my soul came rushing back and lodged in my throat. Vedavathi broke into hysterical laughter. Then slowly, she dissolved into the mist. I lay immersed in my fear. Images of my unreciprocated love and the tragedy that had followed, choked me. Slowly, painfully, I moved my limbs and got off the bed and searched for my sandals in the dark. I stood for a while without any thought or emotion, watching the still leaves of the coconut palms awash in the silvery moonlight. Then I knew what I had to do. It started as a small thought, but soon possessed me. I hurried out, leaving the door open. I ignored the snoring guards and ran through the corridors to Maricha's chamber. I banged on his door, shocking the guard who had been dozing with his head resting on the door. Ignoring the scoundrel who mumbled something, I kept banging on the door till the old man opened it. A curse died on his lips as he saw my face.

"We have to go now. . .I have to see her now." I told him.

"Who?"

"Dress and come quickly. I want to see her now and you are coming with me."

"Who?"

I pulled him out of the room. The guard bowed with alacrity. I pushed Maricha into the garden and said, "I saw her. . .Vedavathi. . ." I continued, ignoring the confusion and shock in Maricha's face, "I wish to see my daughter now."

"Are you drunk?" Maricha struggled out of my grip.

I stamped my foot impatiently and asked, "Who keeps the key to the large shed?"

"Ravana, come to your senses. You want to go Mithila now? To Mithila, deep inside Deva country, and you want me to fly with you in your mad father-in-law's contraption? When was the last time you flew that thing?"

"Get me the key and wake Mayan up!" I was almost hysterical.

Hearing the commotion, the guard came running and I shouted at him to fetch the key of the shed where the flying machine, *Pushpaka Vimana*, as my bumbling professor of a father-in-law called it, was kept. He ran to do my bidding while Maricha stared at me.

"We are going now." I said with finality. Maricha shook his head and walked away. "Where are you going?" I got angrier by the minute. How dared he walk away without an answer?

"To change," he shouted back and banged his chamber door shut. I smiled at the old man. I stood there thinking about what lay ahead. As Maricha said, it was a mission fraught with great danger. For one, I had not flown the *Pushpaka* in a long time. I did not like flying. Man was not supposed to fly, otherwise Shiva would have given him wings. So a flying machine was a challenge to God. I also questioned the emotion which made me want to see my daughter. I had kept a tab on her as she grew up but after my sons had been born, I rarely even read the reports sent to me by my spies. Mithila was too far away and too small to be of any consequence to my mighty and ever-growing empire. Since she was so far away, I rarely thought of her. Soon she was as good as dead to me. Or worse, as if she had never been born. So a dangerous intrusion into enemy territory without my army, was foolhardiness.

"Ravana, son, I am so happy. . .so happy. . ." My father-in-law stood panting before me like a happy child. The old man had come running with the keys jingling at his waist. I had begun to like this absent-minded professor. Before he had undertaken the construction of the mighty temple at Gokarna, I had never taken him seriously. Since then he had built scores of similar structures on the banks of our sacred rivers. He was a master-craftsman and engineer.

Sprightly old Mayan ran like a teenager to the shed where the *Pushpaka* was kept. He fumbled with the keys and then opened the door wide. I had always admired the smooth contours of this strange machine. It had huge wings that did not flap but whirled round dazzlingly fast. It looked like a bird, yet it also resembled a fish. It had some levers, the use of which I had mastered over the years. I was not a good flier, but nevertheless, I could handle the machine reasonably well. Mayan rambled on about the use of the various levers and the sail once the machine reached a certain height, so it would float in the air. But I was barely listening. '*Should I tell Mandodari*?' It was a journey of over 2000 miles and could take three days. Eventually, I left her a note to say I would return in a week. Then I hesitated for a moment and guilt made me add that I loved her.

By this time Maricha had arrived and packed my clothes, some food and wine, as well as my weapons, along with his things. He threw the entire lot into the back of the flying ship and asked hopefully, "Ravana, do you really want to go?"

I jumped in as he shook his head and followed suit. I was apprehensive at first, but then, with a silent prayer to Shiva, I pushed the lever and the machine rolled out slowly. I pushed another lever and the fans whirled faster and faster till, with a jerk, the *Pushpaka* lifted into the air. I could see Marciha clutching the metal rails in front of his seat. I was afraid as well but pushed the thoughts of the thing stalling in mid-air, out of my mind. It was frightening to think of us falling like bird droppings, to be splattered on the face of the rocks below

Lanka faded away below us, a green teardrop island in an ocean that was silvery-black in the moonlight. There were thousands of stars splattered over an inky black sky, as if the Gods were peering through the holes of their blankets. Wispy clouds swirled beside us. My mane flew in the howling wind. I imagined how impressive I'd look to an onlooker and smiled to myself. Maricha had also relaxed a little. I howled with pleasure as we flew over the mainland and Maricha joined me. I tried to remember the raunchy songs of my teenage days. And we flew to the barbarian lands of the north with naughty Asura songs on our lips – an old man of nearly sixty and a middle-aged man of forty, like two teenagers with no worries in the world, on their first picnic without elders.

I had unfurled the sails and we cruised at a steady speed. The fans would only be needed to land. Below, India lay sprawled with her riches and sorrows. There were towering mist-filled, steamy jungles, almost touching the sea to the west, and wide open plains, broken by small hills and hillocks, to the east. There were estuaries and backwaters with coconut palms standing tall like sentinels, broken only by the temples that stood even taller. Silvery rivers snaked through the land and a million moons reflected from the blades of swaying paddy leaves. It was immensely beautiful. My heart filled with pride when I saw the prosperity I had brought to the once-parched countryside. It was my India, my empire, the ancient land of the Asuras.

I knew that by tomorrow night I would be flying over unclaimed territory, a no man's land of shrubs and jungles and mazy sand dunes of central India, that separated my kingdom from the barbarian Deva principalities on the banks of the sacred Ganga, Yamuna and Saraswathi Rivers beyond. I felt sad that I had not extended my kingdom to the abode of Lord Shiva. The Himalayas too belonged to the Asuras, as did the Ganga, that flowed from the manes of an Asura God – Shiva, the supreme God of gods, Parameswara. Why did I stop the campaign? I should have extended my kingdom to the whole of our ancient land and thrown the Devas into the wilderness beyond the Saraswathi and the Sindhu. I had started with such an ambition, but somehow, over the years, I had lost my ambition and my dreams had shrunk. I was too happy making half of India prosperous and wealthy. Perhaps it was a wise decision.

Maricha had grown silent and was dozing. I looked down again and wondered at the sheer size of mother earth. I felt humbled. All the dreams of glory, all the wars I had fought, all the kingdoms I had gained – it all seemed so small in comparison. The earth was eternal, everything else perished. How many men had dreamt ambitious dreams like me, and achieved them? How many had built their fortunes? How many kings had this earth seen and how many more were yet to come? Ultimately, did their toil matter to mother earth? She remained aloof from the petty travails of man.

Men cheat, betray, love, strive, struggle, fail, fall, get up, and repeat the process to die and vanish forever or be reborn. But the earth remains aloof, distant and unchangeable. I was just a speck floating in the mighty universe. Tomorrow, or perhaps the next minute, I would be gone. Would it matter to anyone? A few perhaps would be sad and others happy for it, but it would only be relevant for a while. Over time, my achievements, my birth and death, would be irrelevant. So the size of my empire was irrelevant and there was no need for any more bloodshed. Life was too short for fighting wars and too sweet to throw away on silly things like ambition. I wanted to believe that I was not afraid to die. One day everyone died. That was the way of nature. You had to give way to the next set of living things. Mentally, I had never been afraid to die. But then, how could I ever leave this beautiful life? Wind whistled past my ears and I took a deep breath of the cool morning air. I breathed life.

The east turned red as the clouds floated by like red-dyed cotton, on the eastern horizon. The west was still dark, with a pale, white, setting moon. Maricha stirred in his sleep. I looked at the man who had been more loyal to me than anyone else. I looked at his greying hair and balding head, his still strong arms, and felt sad. Life was rushing past all of us. One day he would be gone and I would be alone.

'What would she be doing now? Who did she look like? Perhaps like her mother?' Something snapped in me when I thought of my long-lost love. Was the empire worth losing her? Perhaps it was. Mandodari was an ideal partner. Vedavathi had been too spirited to be a wife or a queen. I longed to see the face of my daughter more than anything else. I had not read the reports from the field for some time but I vaguely remembered reading about the marriage arrangements being made for her. These northern people had a strange custom. The father of the prospective bride would announce a contest among eligible suitors. I found it boorish. Was a bride a prize to be won in a contest? I had even heard of Deva men selling their wives as slaves, mortgaging them, or using them as wagers. It was terrible but what

could one expect from a semi-civilized, nomadic tribe? Women were treated by the Deva men as nothing more than commodities. Perhaps I was prejudiced as I belonged to an entirely different culture. But I had always believed a society could be called civilized only when it treated its woman and downtrodden people, well. Caste was rigid. The condition of people belonging to the lower rungs was beyond imagination. By such standards, the people of the dusty, northern plains, were almost sub-human. Of course, the Asuras had problems of their own. The Asura men loved material things. Asura woman were aggressive and almost amoral, but then, our girls were brought up almost exactly like our boys. There were social differences like the caste system among the Asuras too, but it was not based on birth or skin colour. Anyone could reach a position of power through hard work and luck. I was the best example of that.

I hoped to reach Mithila by the time the contest for my daughter began. I felt restless. *'Which boorish Deva was going to marry her? How different would her life be?'* I had a premonition that her life would not be easy. I couldn't explain it but the feeling kept nagging at me. I vividly remembered Vedavathi's hysterical laughter. Her curse haunted me. What if the astrological prediction that my daughter would bring death and destruction to the Asuras was true? What if Vedavathi's curse as she went up in flames, found life? This was utter nonsense. I was hallucinating. Perhaps the guilt I felt in abandoning my daughter and not doing anything to get her back, along with last night's drinking, must have brought it on. What would happen if I claimed my daughter? What right did I have to bring her back to an alien culture? Would Janaka oblige? Or should I have attacked Mithila and brought her back? It would have been half a day's job. Mithila was a small kingdom but I did not want any bloodshed. I had had enough of wars. I was also afraid of how Mandodari would react. She did not know of my yearning for Vedavathi, and I did not want to bring it up. My straying days were over and I had found peace and happiness in marriage. Athikaya was an embarrassment. I did not want to add another.

I was getting close to the Narmada and thought wearily of another day's journey still before us. The excitement of the flight had worn off and the plains below were dry and uninspiring. I dozed off many times. I had wanted to take a detour to Kishkindha to renew my friendship with Bali, but with my ego hanging round my neck like a millstone, I took a route that avoided Bali's kingdom. We halted for a few hours on the banks of the Tungabhadra to relax and eat, but I hurried to be in time for my daughter's *swayamvara*.

38 The time has come

Ravana

We landed near Mithila early in the morning. I had selected a secluded and uninhabited place a few miles away from the city. We hid the *Pushpaka* with plants and shrubs, changed into Deva costumes, and walked towards the palace. Many people were going in the same direction. Hundreds of vendors, selling all sorts of things, jostled with the pedestrians and cows that roamed about freely. I observed that the streets were narrow and winding and that there was no drainage system to speak of. The houses looked rustic and the palace looked like the large house of a middle-class farmer in Lanka. I was not impressed but I had not expected much. These were backwaters, culturally and economically, and yet this was supposed to be one of the better cities in the north. Most of the people had brown hair and a sickly fair complexion, but many were dark skinned too. I found many dark-skinned men and woman at the palace. They had perhaps used some other road. These, I guessed, were the untouchables. The better dressed, fair ones, avoided these pathetic figures and the semi-human untouchables patiently waited for the great men and women to pass. What sort of culture was this? Would such a thing ever happen in my rule? Janaka was one of the few enlightened kings and yet, even he was not free from this malice. I was a far better king. Only Ravana had ensured a prosperous and just society.

It was with a mixture of pride and contempt that I entered the assembly where a curious shaped bow lay at the centre. *'It's too heavy to be of any use.'* I thought. Many dignitaries were seated and on a raised pedestal, in what appeared to be a wooden throne, a man of my age sat with immense dignity. On a balcony above him, I could see veiled figures. My heart leapt. One of them could be my daughter. I frantically tried to catch a glimpse. *'What would she look like?'* I cursed the blasted Deva custom of keeping woman under a veil. People conversed with each other. I was amazed. *'How could they talk while their King was present?'*

King Janaka stood up and everyone waited for his pronouncement. His voice boomed across the large hall. "Mighty kings and princes, today is an auspicious day. Today is the *swayamvara* of my beloved daughter, Sita. Only the mightiest, the bravest, and the most skilled among you, will win the hand of my beautiful daughter today." He paused. I looked around. Many pot-bellied or scrawny men were also sitting around in anxious anticipation. "The rules of the contest are simple. The heavy bow here has to be lifted and strung. Gentlemen, it is not an easy job. The bow is called *Triambaka* and was once used by Lord Shiva himself. The one who is able to lift and string it, will win the hand of my daughter."

I nearly choked with laughter. *'How did these people get hold of Shiva's bow?'* Shiva's bow, my foot! Perhaps it gave them a thrill to imagine that someone would be able to lift the bow of Shiva, the primeval Asura King and God.

"Kings and Princes, behold my daughter." Janaka's voice stopped me short in my musings. I waited in trembling anticipation. A hush fell on the crowd. Then a door with lots of bells on it jingled open and a tall, bejewelled figure walked out with a trail of maids in her wake. I gripped Maricha's hands tightly. I could feel the muscles of my face become taut while my heart pounded wildly. She stood there in the middle of hundreds of men, trembling, while many lusty eyes greedily assessed her – the prize of a stupid contest. One of the maids came forward and slowly lifted her veil and the crowd gasped. She stood there so radiant and lovely that I almost wept. Sita. She resembled her mother, but her skin was dark, the colour of honey. She had long, black tresses. She was my daughter, an Asura princess.

I noticed that the princes and kings assessed her like they had come to a cattle market and have found their prize cow. I burned with anger. What sort of custom was this? An innocent young girl in her prime exposed to the lustful eyes of old men who could win her in a contest? What about her feelings, her loves, her dreams and wishes? Any ruffian who has enough strength to lift that stupid bow could marry her. She would know none of the joy of courting her husband, there would be no whispered words of love, no pangs of separation and the sweet wait to see her lover on a moonlit night. Maricha held me firm. Initially I had resented my arranged marriage to Mandodari and cursed my interfering mother many times. But we had known each other and spoken many times. This was uncivilized.

I could not take my eyes off my daughter, Sita. She demurely lifted her head and scanned the lusty crowd that had assembled. She did not pause for more than a few seconds on any one face. When she stared at me, my heart skipped a beat. She stared at me intently and I was afraid. Something tugged inside me. Was it guilt or fear? I don't know and quickly looked away. When I looked up again, I saw her peering intently at a young man of about eighteen. He was no prince. He wore quite ordinary clothing, but had a bow thrown over his shoulder and had his hair tied in a knot. He was tall and well toned and there was something arresting about his appearance. He looked composed and at peace with himself. For a young boy of his age, his composure was remarkable.

I saw my daughter's eyes lock with the boy's. She blushed and her dark face lit with a dimple. She looked down quickly, turned, and walked away. I watched the dark-skinned boy intently. I felt a strange jealousy and hatred rush through my veins. He might have sensed my feelings for he turned to look at me and smiled. I recoiled. I do not know why or how, but I knew this man was dangerous. I was sure he was going to win my daughter. I was afraid for my daughter and for myself. I wanted to rush and protect her from harm. I wanted to whisk her away and take her to Lanka, away from these barbarians and their boorish customs. But I stood rooted, alone in my fears and apprehensions, and prayed for a miracle to save my daughter.

An old Brahmin with a flowing white beard stood near the boy. Another young man, with a perpetual scowl on his face, looked at me. When my eyes met his, he gave me such a look of pure hatred that I winced. *'How did the young muster so much confidence and arrogance so early?'* I too, had been young once but I had never had this kind of confidence or arrogance. I had always been humble and deferential towards my elders.

The contest began. One by one, the contenders came forward, tried to lift the heavy bow, and failed. After watching a few of them, I realized that the bow had different weights on either end. The correct way to hold it had to be thought about first and then attempted. Soon, all the invitees had tried and failed. There was a disturbing silence in the room. But I was relieved. No brute could marry my daughter now. It was time to reveal my identity to Janaka and claim my daughter. I would take her to Lanka and give her a life befitting an Asura princess. She would marry who she loved or I would find a good match for her. I would confess to Mandodari and ask for her forgiveness. Only I could atone for all the follies of my youth. I stepped forward.

I felt the crowd staring at me as I walked towards the king. But then I realized my mistake. Everyone thought I too was a contender and Janaka looked at me hopefully and then frowned. He must have thought I was too old for his daughter. I was only forty-six, but in a society where girls were married at six, I was ancient. I stopped when I was near the bow. I was curious. I touched it, running my fingers over its curves. I gripped it. It had poor workmanship and I was sure this bow could never be strung. It would break if anyone was able to lift it. Shiva definitely could not have used this inferior product. Janaka must have picked it up from some school of armaments were trainees practised making bows. This was an imperfect sample and these people were conducting a contest to sell off my daughter with this?

"Sir, if you want to try, you should hurry," a minister called out. I stared at him evenly. *'What would I do if I lifted it? Marry my own daughter?'* Then the dark and handsome young man came forward and bowed to the king. I looked up. Sita had removed her veil and sat waiting in anxious anticipation. A part of my heart wanted this young man to win. My daughter would get a husband she liked, if not loved. Another dark corner of my mind kept telling me that Sita would never be happy with this man. I was certain that even if the young man succeeded in lifting the bow, it would break if he tired to string it. If that happened, Sita would be spared, at least temporarily. I waited for him.

“Your Highness! I am Rama, Prince of Ayodhya, first born son of King Dasratha.” The young man bowed to King Janaka. *‘Ayodhya? hmm. . .where had I heard that name before. . . possibly one of those small and irrelevant pastoral principalities that dotted the dusty northern plain.’* Then it struck me. King Anarnya. . . and my campaign. *‘Oh God! That dreadful little one-horse town, not even half the size of Mithila.’* I remembered how primitive the place was. I had finished off the last king long ago, hadn’t I? These plains sprouted kings like mushrooms!

I moved back. Rama walked around the bow two or three times, observing it keenly. I was impressed. This chap was intelligent and resourceful. He had not rushed in to show off his strength. He measured the bow from one end to the other with the tip of his middle finger and thumb. Then he found a spot three fingers above the middle and with one smooth motion, lifted the bow. He almost staggered with the weight but got back his balance quickly. I began to perspire. *‘Would he do it?’* The bow should break, if my knowledge of arms was to be trusted. It could not be strung. I looked at Sita. She was tense, with her palms together in a silent prayer.

Rama took the string from the bottom and tried to tie it to the top. His muscles were taut and his face showed the stress of the effort. I watched fascinated. *‘This boy was a good warrior. Maybe almost as good as Meghanada.’* The bow bent and Rama wound the first round of string. I could feel the tension in the air. Everyone watched the young man perform the impossible. Miraculously, the bow held. I could not fathom how. *‘Is my knowledge so rusty?’* I looked away from the taut figure of the Prince of Ayodhya to my daughter, and in that instant I heard a small creak. I turned back quickly. My heart raced. I knew that sound. The next instant the bow broke into two with a whip-like crack. Rama looked confounded for a minute. Everyone was too stunned to speak. I was ecstatic. No one could string the bow. I could now take Sita away to Lanka. I looked at Maricha, but he sadly shook his head. I was confused and raised an eyebrow in question.

Then a deafening cheer rose all around me. I watched in dismay and shock as my daughter approached the Prince of Ayodhya and garlanded him. From that moment, Sita and Rama were husband and wife. Tears welled up in my eyes. I looked at the young couple and could see the happiness and pride in Rama's eyes at the unexpected victory, and the prize. It upset me. *'You do not deserve her, young man,'* I wanted to shout. Then I saw pure and innocent love in Sita's eyes and felt helpless. What right did I have to destroy the happiness she felt? *'Daughter, I have failed you.'* I hoped she would be happy with the man she love so much. I hoped he would treat her with love and respect and reciprocate her love. I hoped he would be worthy of her. I had no rights over my daughter, but I prayed for her happiness. Something told me that the man she had chosen, or more correctly the man who had won her as a prize, would only make her sad. I hoped I was wrong. But I would keep a protective watch over her from now on. She was the daughter of the most powerful Emperor on earth. If I ever found that the man was not worthy of her, I would whisk her away to my palace, my bosom, and protect her from all harm. I turned and pushed my way out through the thronging crowds. I emerged sweating and tired, unable to control my tears. I tried to push Sita from my mind and cursed myself for having come on this trip.

I retraced my steps to where we had hidden the *Pushpaka*. I was tired of this Deva kingdom and their strange practices. I wanted to get back to Lanka, to my wife, my sons, and my people. I reached the hiding place and only then realized that Maricha was not with me. Maricha came a little later. I was still worried about my daughter. *'At least her husband seemed to be a capable warrior. Let's see how things turned out.'* I could not shake off the dark premonitions I felt as I climbed into the *Pushpaka* and motioned Maricha to follow.

"Tell our entire network to keep a watch on them, Maricha. Keep an eye on the boy. Watch him closely," I told Maricha and he nodded gravely.

"We shouldn't have waited this long to take her home," Maricha said. I felt the same. But there was no use thinking about that now.

We reached Lanka in two days. I confessed to Mandodari my affair with the Deva Brahmin woman. It was difficult but I told her everything. I told her about our daughter and the fear I felt for her. She wept at my betrayal, but forgave me. I had a feeling Mandodari had known about it all along but had not brought up the subject. My confession was good for both of us. I had the feeling that from that day on, she respected me more. Mandodari told me she yearned to have our daughter back, but since she was already married, it would be better to leave her with her husband. I finally slept peacefully.

As promised, I watched Sita closely. I learned with dismay that Rama had thrown away his inheritance because his step-mother wanted her own son to be king. She had extracted a promise from Dasaratha that he would send away his eldest son to the wilderness for fourteen years and make her son, Bharata, king. My son-in-law, the fool that he was, volunteered to abdicate his claim and vanished into the wilderness. Though the people of Ayodhya wanted Rama to be their king, he ignored the wishes of the masses to satisfy his henpecked father. I hated Rama for his false ego and eagerness to prove his self-righteousness to the world. I would never understand his logic. And how could his father have made such an unfair promise? A king could not act like that. It was against *Raja Dharma*. As the heir, it was Rama's duty to rise against the king who had acted unjustly. He should have overthrown his father and assumed the kingship. Instead, he abdicated in favour of his step-brother. And his other brother, Lakshmana, followed him into the wild. And now my beautiful daughter had been dragged along with them.

I instructed my soldiers to protect the trio from enemies and keep me informed. I learnt that Rama roamed all over India and many times my spies saw Sita crying silently, all alone. I suspected that Lakshmana was an uncultured brute and was always afraid he would harm my daughter. But my fears were misplaced. Lakshmana appeared to be devoted to his brother and sister-in-law. Meanwhile, Lanka prospered and I introduced many reforms. But Sita continued to occupy my thoughts. I was worried. Then one day, Soorpanakha came running to my court. The time had come.

39 Return of the Asura Princess

Bhadra

I am almost fifty now and I had grown bald and lost the strength of my limbs and my mind as well. Each day was like any other day. It dawned, I woke and did my chores, ate, imagined the beautiful girls I had seen at some point in my life, brooded over the way things were going, drank, complained about the affairs of the world, bored listeners with the real and imagined feats of my youth, and collapsed onto my bed at the end of the day, to wake again the next day. And the cycle continued. Ravana's revolution had given us nothing. We were perhaps slightly better off. Maybe even more civilized. But we had been put in our place and quickly learnt how to behave. There were the nobles, and then there were all the others. There were the privileged ones, and then us. As long as we kept to our place, we could live. But many among us, through enterprise, luck, and a great deal of sycophancy, had managed to rise. Most of my earlier companions in the army continued to be dirt poor like me. But a few had become really important.

The most irritating thing was how the Brahmins had grown in recent years. After the failed coup and the butcher incident, there was a temporary halt to Brahmins coming south. And there were fewer followers for their religion. But not long afterwards, they began seeping back in. Ravana had by this time developed his own ideas about how a great king should behave. A group of Brahmins, led by their holy man Agastya, requested asylum in the Asura kingdom. Prahastha opposed giving them refuge and there was much resentment among the public as well. But Ravana, in his kingly wisdom, decided to grant them asylum.

For a few years, Agastya and his herd of Brahmins stayed out of the cities and led a quiet existence. They kept to themselves and gave us no trouble. Agastya would go and plead with Ravana to allow them to set up villages inside our kingdom, almost every day. Vibhishana also threw his weight behind their request. Eventually, they built villages on the west and east coasts of south India, including on the island of Lanka. It started as a trickle. The fair-skinned, plump, Brahmins slowly formed their own little islands in all the major towns and cities of the empire. And before we knew what had happened, they had occupied all the important positions in the civil services, taken over the temples, and effectively pushed out all others from lucrative and important positions.

Ravana believed that to be respected in the world, he had to be a secular king and treat every religion with respect and tolerance. The ideals for which many Asuras like me had fought, were forgotten. He went to the extent of saying that the minorities had equal rights over the country's resources, and as King, he was duty bound to protect them.

The people fumed. After fighting for Asura glory and sacrificing everything in quest of the ideal Asura empire, was this what we deserved? It seemed that only the rights of the minorities and their religious feelings mattered and ours did not. Thanks to the Brahmins, beef, a staple food of the Asuras, was banned. Brahmins could enter our temples and abuse our simple Gods, or worse could take over the temple, if the money collection happened to be good. Eventually they wouldn't even allow us to enter our own temples. We were, after all, impure. The rights of the minority became an obsession with the ruling class. There were many conversions from Asura to the Deva religion, even when obstinate pigs like me refused to be converted.

After that incident when Athikaya and I were almost beaten to death at the duel, I no longer wanted to go to the palace. I was tired of being a doormat. I wanted to start my own business again but the place no longer existed. They had widened the road and gardens had come up where my old

Banyan tree had stood. Trikota expanded on all sides and we were driven further and further away. Men who travelled said that the city was more beautiful than the main port city of Muzaris. But for people like me, things had not changed. We were still eyesores and had to be hidden from people who mattered. But they needed us too. After all, who else would have tended their gardens; become their maids and nannies; drawn water and hewn wood for them; swept their streets; and carried away their night soil? So, while they did not like us, they tolerated us. We learnt how to become invisible. Most of us would perform our chores and vanish before the city woke. And life went on. It had been almost fourteen years since they had beaten my son and me.

When Trikota expanded and grew, I moved with my wife to a small hut many miles south of the city, and tried my hand at farming. I cleared some jungle and decided to cultivate pepper and cardamom. I did not have seeds, so I took some on loan from the local money lender. And then we began weaving our dreams of becoming rich. After some time, those dreams were diluted to dreams of living comfortably. Later, we only dreamed of making ends meet, then of eating at least one meal a day. We dreamed of somehow getting free from the tangle of debt. Finally, we gave up dreaming altogether.

But the nobles continued to prosper. They dazzled the world with their wealth which they showed off with pomp and pride. And it was said that under Ravana's reign, the Asura kingdom prospered at a great rate. It was true. The elite prospered, so the country prospered. Did it really matter if the majority struggled or farmers committed suicide to escape the usurers? We were the invisible people and did not count. I took solace in the fact that my country was one of the fastest growing countries in the world. Not that it filled my stomach, but it helped me to brag and it tickled my ego. I had many friends like myself. We got drunk every day in the local, shabby haunts and raised toasts to the prosperity of our King and the Asura empire.

That day was just like any other day. Hot, humid, dull and boring. It was a breezeless evening and I had almost passed out from drinking countless pitchers of palm toddy in the local toddy shack. I did not want to go home.

It was comfortable here. Forget the money lender and forget the crops. Also the King and the nobles and all the Brahmins. If I could manage to sit here a while, some fool would drop in and buy me a drink. So I sat there, listening to spicy tales about the princess Soorpanakha and her sexual adventures and the insult she had suffered from some renegade forest dwellers, who were rumoured to be Nagas or Vanaras or Devas, who had cut off her breasts and nose after raping her. People also said Ravana was going to wage a huge war to avenge the insult meted out to his sister. It was then that we heard the deafening sound of the flying machine. We all ran out. There was a huge crowd looking skywards. I jostled for a vantage point as people pushed and shoved all around. The traffic on the streets had come to a standstill. Was the mad professor Maya at his aerial acrobatics again?

Then a huge gasp went through the crowd. I could see the profile of a grim-faced Ravana, concentrating hard to control the complicated machinery, as the huge iron bird swept over us. But what made my hangover vanish, was the sight of the huddled figure of a woman, with her head bend, and evidently crying, as the iron bird swept over the howling crowd. In the red glow of the setting sun, the lovely face of the lady was clear. A shudder passed through me. It was a face from my long-forgotten past. Was it Mandodari? She looked exactly like the queen had when she was young, but possessed a much darker skin tone. She looked exactly the same all these years later. *'What was the King up to this time?'* I did not know. I only knew the fear that crept over me from my toes. Instinctively I knew there was going to be trouble – big trouble.

40 Adieu Maricha!

Ravana

Maricha was dead. Actually, he had been brutally murdered and I was responsible for it. I had failed him. It had been a foolish scheme fraught with danger. Like an adventurous teenager, I had recklessly jumped in and lost him in the bargain. He had advised me against it. I took away my daughter from Rama, but sacrificed my beloved uncle. Thinking back, the entire mission was foolish. I had instantly reacted to the sight of a breastless, noseless and screaming Soorpanakha, at my *durbar*, the previous evening.

The entire assembly had been stunned. For some minutes we did not comprehend what she was blabbering about. She had been hysterical and in a state of shock, and took almost half an hour to make some sense. When I understood what she said, I burned with rage. *'How dare that insignificant man lay hands on my sister?'* And she looked so pathetic. She had never been a beauty, even in her youth, but now, in her late thirties, with her nose cut off, she looked hideous. She rambled about how she had found a lovely woman roaming the jungle with two men and had merely asked whether the lady would be willing to be the wife of her brother, the Asura Emperor. At that, the younger man had pounced on her and done what was visible to everyone now. She howled until I lost my temper and hit her across her face. Then she stopped dead. I tried making amends by putting my hands on her shoulders, but she stormed out, cursing me and lamenting that she had such a spineless brother.

I smarted from the insult to my sister. But more shameful was the fact that I had a sister like her. I had kept a watch on her when she had moved in with our distant cousins, Khara and Dushana, who were two of my vassal kings whose petty kingdoms bordered the northern Deva lands. Initially I had been amused at the number of men she bedded but was later disgusted. It was not a crime according to Asura social law, but the times had changed. Some Deva-like tenets of morality had brushed onto me as well. It had probably been while chasing a man, that she had come across the two men and the woman, who I was quite sure, were my daughter, son-in-law and his brother. Soorpanakha was, of course, unaware of the relationship, else she would have told me a different lie.

Another thought worried me. *'How safe was my daughter with these dangerous men?'* I was in no mood to continue the *durbar* so I dismissed the assembly and retired to my private chambers. I called for Mandodari and told her my decision. It was not easy. She was not happy when she heard what I planned to do. But I told her that I could not leave our daughter with men who cut off a woman's ears and nose. I was concerned about her safety. Then Mandodari advised to declare war and capture Sita. I laughed at the idea of waging a war against two insignificant men. It was too much trouble and too expensive. I knew what I was going to do and there was no turning back.

I told Maricha the plan. He didn't think well of it and told me that I was being emotional and childish. I was livid. I could see the hurt and pain in the old man's eyes, but he continued to argue with me. I was so furious that I decided to carry out the mission alone. Finally, he agreed to go along with my plan and we took to the skies in search of my daughter.

While we were flying north, Maricha tried to dissuade me again. I ignored him. "You could kill Rama and his brother and bring Sita back after telling her the truth about her birth." he said. But I did not want to kill Rama. My daughter was devoted to him and I did not want to cause her any sorrow. I only planned to keep Sita in Lanka till Rama's voluntary exile was over. She could then join him when he assumed the Kingship of his petty kingdom. Secretly, I hoped that once I had brought her to Lanka and she had seen her father's dazzling home, she would persuade her husband to stay with us. It wasn't that I had suddenly developed a liking for the man, but I was willing to accept him. I was even ready to give Rama a portion of my northern empire

But things started going awry right from the start. When we reached the place where Rama had camped with his brother and Sita, it was early in the morning. The forest looked idyllic. Had it been any other occasion, I would have forgotten all my worries, sat down with my brush and palm leaf and copied the lovely secrets the jungle held so close. A soft curtain of mist hung over the trees and every blade of grass glistened in the soft, radiant sunlight. A small, thatched hut sat perched on a gentle incline which led to a gurgling stream. Thousands of butterflies of all hues fluttered about. Golden sunlight drizzled through the little holes that appeared and disappeared as the tree canopies gently swayed in the cool breeze. Birds and crickets, buzzing honeybees and dragonflies, all added to the pleasant cacophony of the jungle. Antelopes grazed lazily, while hares sniffed suspiciously at the glistening edges of grass and darted here and there aimlessly. And on a rock, like a Goddess of the forest, Sita, my daughter, sat lost in some dream, her hands crossed lazily at her navel, the smooth dark skin of her legs glistening with the droplets of water that the stream had playfully thrown up.

A tap on my shoulder by Maricha broke the enchantment. Then I saw the scene for what it really was. This was enemy territory. The enemy would be near. If I encountered Rama, I would have to kill him. Contrary to what my spies reported, Sita seemed happy enough. *'Those cowards! They told me what I wanted to hear.'* They must have guessed that I was interested in the girl. I could hear snatches of conversation now and looked in the direction Maricha was gazing in. Two men appeared from the woods. They looked like hunters and with a start I realized they were Rama and his brother, Lakshmana. The brothers had grown darker and older since I had last seen them almost fourteen years ago. To my eyes they looked dark and ugly, though Rama's face still had some inner radiance. *'How could Deva princes be so dark-skinned? Even I was fairer.'*

"I will distract Rama, away from the princess. I think you can handle the

younger one," Maricha whispered in my ear and vanished into the woods in a flash. I wanted to tell him that I could handle them both, but he had gone. That was the last time I saw him. As I said, it was a foolish and hasty plan, quite uncharacteristic of a thorough man like Maricha. And it wasn't as if I lacked experience either. But that day, call it destiny, call it fate, but mistakes kept piling up. I had been waiting for almost two hours and was getting impatient. *'Should I rush in and knock them down and take my daughter away?'* I had almost decided to do this when I saw a sudden flash of brilliance on the other bank of the stream. I watched fascinated. It was a golden deer. Only it's front and curved horns were visible, but it looked like a creature from paradise. It gave a soft, melodious bark and vanished into the bush.

The two men and Sita quickly turned and looked at the source of the noise. There was perfect silence in the jungle apart from the rustle of the leaves in the breeze and the chirping of birds. Then the golden deer sprung up again and vanished into the bushes. Sita let out a cry of joy. I saw that Lakshmana had drawn his bow, the arrow pointing towards the bush. For a few moments Rama and Sita watched fascinated. After what seemed to be a very long time, the deer peeped out again. An arrow sprang from Lakshmana's bow and pierced the tree under which the deer had been a few seconds ago. The embedded arrow vibrated. I looked at him with new respect. *'He may be uncultured, but he is a good archer and has been well trained,'* I thought. I almost laughed aloud. I knew it was Maricha who was the deer and that he was too good to be shot. Maricha must have killed a deer and skinned it and was hiding behind it. It was a brilliant and simple camouflage. I could see Sita chiding Lakshmana and then beseeching Rama to catch the deer for her. I saw him hesitate for some time and then start towards the deer's hiding place. As he was about to reach the opposite bank, the deer darted away at great speed and Rama scrambled to the other shore. He shouted to Lakshmana to take care of Sita while he went in pursuit of the deer.

I thought of taking Lakshmana with a well aimed arrow. I was sorely tempted, but that was not how real men fought. Hiding behind a tree and shooting an unsuspecting enemy, was a eunuch's way of fighting. I was an Asura and an Emperor. Such acts were not part of my character and went against my sense of fair play and justice. But had I known then what levels Rama and his brother were capable of stooping to, I would have surely finished them off there and then. I was a fool and should have taken the opportunity while it presented itself. So I lie here now, betrayed and cheated, bleeding and being eaten by rodents, slain by lesser men who used dubious means to kill and win. Perhaps I deserved this fate, for fate had handed me the chance to finish off these two men and I had frittered it away to feed my ego with talk of fair play and justice. I had the wrong mentors in my life and that was my failing. I had men like Bali, the epitome of justice and integrity, and Mahabali, who threw away an empire for the sake of truth, as my gurus. So I too met the same fate as them. Had I finished off those two then, I could have saved the tears of many men and women who had put their trust in me and believed that I would protect them from evil.

When my hands trembled that day, I knew I had failed in life. But lying here, bathed in my blood and that of my kinsmen; having lit the funeral pyre of my beloved children and lost whatever I had striven for over a lifetime; I knew that if the same situation were to arise, with Rama and Lakshmana as easy targets and I stood hidden behind a tree with poisoned arrow drawn taut, I still would not shoot them, or any one else. That was the coward's way. Perhaps that was why I was fated to die now, but I would so with my head held high. I felt nothing but sorrow for the man who had stooped so low to attain godhood. '*Rama, was it worth it?*' The blood you have shed will haunt you and this country for years, long after after all of us have gone. You keep the godhood you gained through unfair means and I'll keep my manhood and die a warrior's death.

As I sat there debating with myself whether to finish off Lakshmana or not, I heard a blood chilling cry. Lakshmana and Sita heard it too and we were all shocked. I recognized that voice. But I did not know then that it was the death cry of my beloved uncle. I froze, not knowing what to do. I tried to reason that it must have been part of the plan. I heard Sita cry out and then Lakshmana's raised voice. I saw him set off in the direction his brother had taken. Still I hesitated. '*Should I follow him and rescue Maricha if he is in real danger*?' But Maricha was a veteran. He could take care of himself. I moved fast then. I hid my weapons as I did not want to frighten her. I removed my jewels and bundled them in a knot at my waist. With the parallel ash marks already on my forehead, like any devotee of Shiva, but without my royal ornaments, I knew I looked like a hermit seeking alms.

I was close to her when she turned and looked at me. With those lovely, dark eyes focused on me, a lump formed in my throat. I wanted to touch her and take her in my arms. 'Sita, my daughter! Sita, my little daughter.' I turned away and stood with my eyes closed. I wanted to kill myself. '*Why had I forsaken her? Why had I forgotten her? I had lost her entire childhood. Why had I not attacked Mithila and taken her back?*' Perhaps if I had told Janaka the truth, the bloodshed could have been avoided. Janaka was one of the noblest of the Deva kings, learned and wise, he may have returned my daughter to me. But I did not trust her husband. I could not forgive what the two brothers had done to my sister. Sita was not safe with them and an Asura princess and the daughter of Ravana, could not waste her life roaming about in the forests, living the life of a beggar. All I had achieved and earned, the golden Lanka, the entire Asura empire, was hers. But what if she spurned my riches, my kingdom, my love? I was afraid of the deep devotion and love she cherished for her husband. I was afraid I would unleash the supernatural powers of that astrological prediction of long ago. I was afraid of the dying words of Vedavathi.

Then, as suddenly as they had come, the unnatural feelings vanished. With a prayer in my mind, I turned back, only to find that she had vanished. She had gone into the hut to bring me alms. She came towards me and looked for my bowl. But I pulled her towards me, circled her narrow waist with my hands, lifted her over my shoulder, and ran to where I had hidden *Pushpaka*. Sita was too shocked to react in the initial moments, but after a few seconds she started to cry out and fight me. She scratched my face and back with her nails. I could feel blood trickling down. I felt a strange elation in thinking that I deserved it all for having abandoned her, for believing in some unscientific prediction and being afraid of my own daughter, and for the things I had not given her as a father.

Finally I dumped her into the flying machine and bolted the door. Then I waited for Maricha. I waited till the sun had almost travelled three fourth of the distance in the sky towards the west. Except for the sobs escaping my daughter and the wild cries of birds and animals in the distance, the forest gave out no other sound. I did not want to leave her to go in search of Maricha. Finally, with a heavy heart, and dreading facing my aunt, I got back into *Pushpaka* and began the journey back to Lanka

The journey back was hell. A big bird, a huge vulture, became entangled in the huge fans that propelled *Pushpaka*. It was a terrifying moment. The machine started losing altitude rapidly as the fan stalled and we hurtled downwards like a stone. The earth rushed up to hold us in her deathly embrace. The bird struggled for its life and got even more entangled. In stupefied fascination, I watched death rush up at us. Sita's scream woke me from my stupor and I drew my sword and tried to hack off the bird. The *Pushpaka* wobbled. Then suddenly, the machine tipped and somersaulted and began to fall, upside down. Sita slid down and almost dropped to her death, but I grabbed her waist with one hand. My sword had fallen free. Another turn and it would have cut either of us on its way down. Sita hung out of the *Pushpaka* as the wind screamed past. I pulled her in with one mighty tug and the machine wobbled some more. All this happened within seconds. Then I fastened my hands around the my daughter's narrow waist and pulled up my *Chandrahasa* with one leg. With the sword in one hand, I hacked the bird with desperate abandon and saw pieces of it falling down. The earth approached fast and I could clearly see the leaves of the trees. I hacked at the bird with all my strength, while the machine swung wildly. If the sails came lose, we would have to leave this life.

Finally, the bird, or what was left of it, fell off. We were sprayed with its blood. I stretched and desperately pulled the levers to level the machine. The fans were not rotating. I pushed and pulled, but it had stalled. The tall trees were so close I could see the birds fluttering away in fright of the approaching giant, iron bird. *'This was it,'* I thought, *'an ignoble death in the middle of nowhere, that too, when I have got my daughter back!'* my life flashed before my eyes. I watched helplessly. A sudden sob from Sita startled me. *'No, I cannot let her die. She is young, at the prime of her life. Did I rescue her from her husband only to get her killed?'* With all my might, I jerked the lever up and down and finally the fan sputtered. I pulled and pushed once more, and with a shudder, the fan started rotating. I closed my eyes in relief only to open them again in sudden terror. *'No, it was too late! The blades were chopping the treetops. Would we make it? Oh Shiva!'* Slowly, so slowly, the machine gained altitude. We were a few feet above the tallest tree. I kept pushing it up. Ten feet. . . twenty. . . and just when I thought we had made it, I saw a huge rock looming ahead. We were heading straight into it. *'Would we clear it?'* I sweated profusely and my fingers ached. The boulder was only twenty feet away now, but I still had to gain thirty feet to clear the top. The fan almost touched the rock. And just as I thought we would crash into it, *Pushpaka* cleared the rock with inches to spare.

I kept gaining altitude and when I finally reached cruising height, I folded up the fan and set up the sails. I fell back exhausted and relieved. My daughter sat like a stone and I felt sorry for her. Then I remembered Maricha. I had lost him. It hit me like a bolt. In our own silent worlds of grief and loss, father and daughter, so near and yet so far, flew to Lanka.

I could see the wide-eyed surprise in Sita's face when the first sight of Lanka caught her attention. For a moment she forgot her grief. My heart swelled with pride. I wanted to show her what glories I had in store for her. *'Sita, my daughter, behold your Lanka!'* There was the golden palace where she would dwell. I wanted her to look at the gardens and smell the fresh sea; the glittering markets and green paddy fields; the swaying coconut palms and spice gardens; my wide royal boulevards and towering castles and palaces. Let her see it all and compare it with the measly home her husband called a palace. But I was silent. I just watched her eyes filled with wonder, as the setting sun reflected off the golden dome of my palace and I directed the iron bird into an uneventful landing. Before the fan could completely stop, I jumped out, forgetting all about Sita. Mandodari had come running, followed by Trijata and Meghanada. They were curious to see our guest.

My aunt searched for her husband but I averted my eyes. The dreaded moment had come and I did not know what to say. I felt numb. Maricha was dead. That was the naked truth about my ill-fated adventure. Somewhere deep inside the forest, the old man lay dead. I had left him to the mercy of those two barbarians. At the time, I had not thought of him, or the selfless love and the sacrifices he had made to make me into what I had become. I had heard his cry and yet I did not move. I heard Rama's arrow pierce the tired old skin and knew that even in the final moments of his life, he had been thinking of me. Yet I did not move. His cry for Lakshmana had been so like the voice of Rama, that Sita had forced him to go in search of his brother. And I had grabbed her and hurried back, without a thought for Maricha. The eventful journey back and my happiness in bringing home my daughter to Lanka, had kept the dark thoughts of Maricha's death at bay. But as I watched my aunt's face, the emotions of failure, guilt and my own worthlessness, overcame me. I hugged her and pressed my lips hard together to control my tears. She looked into my eyes, read what was plain to see, and collapsed in my arms.

Sita refused to enter my palace. She made her home in a shady nook under the Ashoka tree where Meghanada used to play as a child. That was after I had failed in my persuasive attempts to get her to move into my palace and had wearily asked Trijata to keep a watch on her. That was after I had shut myself in my room and cried for the loss of my dearest friend and counsel, Maricha; after I had explained to his bereaved widow and my sceptical wife, why I had left Maricha to the mercy of barbarians; and after I left them, unable to suppress the guilt I myself felt for failing my uncle.

The night wore on and I tossed on my bed. It was a moonless and sultry night and I could sense that Mandodari was not asleep either. I moved closer and touched her but she did not move. I waited for her response. I wanted her to hug me and say what I had done was the right thing to do. But she did not move. Slowly, I withdrew my hand and turned away from her.

I woke with a start. I thought I had heard the sound of sobbing. It was not coming from Mandodari. *'Had I imagine it?'* I moved to the window and peered out. It was pitch dark outside. A few dying torches in the garden accentuated the darkness of the night. Then, without any warning, it started to rain. The torches died with protesting hisses and somewhere, a window swung back and forth, creating dull and rhythmic thuds which echoed through the empty corridors.

A deep fear grew within me. I imagined my daughter, all alone, drenched and miserable, out there in that darkness. But I did not move. I was afraid. I was afraid of myself. As the sky screamed and poured and the earth shivered in the drenching tears of heaven, I sat on my bed, alone, terrified of the prophecy and the curse of Vedavathi.

41 The police station

Bhadra

Today I saw a strange sight and wondered whether I should report it to some bigwig in the government. It was getting late. I had loitered around the whole day and the few coins I had earned cleaning the fat merchant's chariot, I had spent on toddy. I was hungry but knew there was nothing to eat at home. In fact, it had been almost six months since I had eaten good food.

I remembered Maricha's grand funeral. Initially, none of us knew how Prince Maricha had died. He had been old, but was not ailing, and the last time I had seen him riding his black horse, he seemed sprightly. His death was a shock to us. The official communication said that Maricha had died of old age, and that his demise had taken place near the northern borders of the Asura kingdom, on the mainland. It was said that Maricha had been cremated there. Why and how he had reached so far before his death, was another mystery. People had seen him just the previous day and it was impossible for any man to travel such a vast distance so quickly. Tongues wagged about the flight of Mayan's magical bird. Some people claimed they had seen the Emperor fly north with Maricha in this iron bird. But it really did not matter. There had been no time to stand and gossip as my wife and I hurried towards the palace where we had heard that the poor would be fed well that day and new clothes would be supplied as well.

All the streets leading to the palace were packed with people. As I neared the palace, I saw there was already a huge crowd. People jostled for space; there was a deafening din; and the choicest abuses were flying about fast and furious. The crowd shoved, pushed and stamped. With bodies slippery with sweat, feet caked in mud, lungs choked with dust, the crowd inched forward, only to be pushed from behind by more people arriving. The sun showed no mercy and the stench of sweat, urine and body odour of thousands of hungry people, was overwhelming. I had gripped my wife's left wrist, but I could feel hands groping her. She wriggled and twisted, but like any other woman in that crowd, she did not have any choice but to bear it. There were freebies to be had, so the pushing and shoving, breast-grabbing and ass-pinching, didn't matter too much. We pushed ahead.

As we got closer, the pushing and shoving got even more intense. I too kicked and punched my way through and grabbed a packet, handed over the heads of other fighting men and woman. I passed it to my wife and then pushed back again to get my share. A soldier shoved me and I lost my balance and got trampled by the crowd. Cursing, I managed to wriggle out. I was disappointed that we had got only one packet between us. We moved against the tide of poor men and woman shoving to get hold of the King's bounty, given in memory of his dead uncle. And I wished then that the King would lose an uncle every day.

Then there was lunch. Holes were dug on either side of the royal highway and plantain leaves were placed inside these holes. Gruel was then poured into these temporary containers and thousands of people like me ate this treat with relish. As we ate, chariots carrying the nobles of Lanka, and a few from the mainland, rushed past us to the palace, throwing mud and dust into our bowls. Flies buzzed around and some stray dogs dared to snatch delicacies from the rows. In the evening, wooden barrels containing fresh palm toddy were rolled down by the palace servants. And another mad rush began. By midnight, all of us, irrespective of sex, were drunk. Four people were killed in brawls that erupted at various places, but we did not know about it till the next day. Not that I cared. My situation got worse by the day. The money I earned was gone in a week. Most of it went to the tavern, but Mala saved some without my knowledge. When I found out, she had hell to pay. I grabbed it from a kicking and screaming Mala and rushed back to the toddy shop. That was the last day I celebrated.

From the next morning, hunger followed us like a determined shadow. Occasionally, I'd get a few odd jobs and we would eat. But, the recurring theme was hunger. We were destitute. The truth slowly sank in. Perhaps there was some truth also in what the Brahmins said about one's previous life and *karma*. We must have been paying for the bad deeds of our previous lives. Most people were poor, so there must have been many sinners in previous lives. But not everyone. The merchant class, the bureaucrats and government servants, the actors and musicians, were all getting fatter by the day. We saw mansions spring up and shops selling glittering clothing and fashionable footwear were frequented by beautiful people in glistening chariots; their houses had real roofs and furniture to sit on; carpets from the distant lands to the west, the cost of one could have fed an entire village for years; smart children going to gurus who taught only the progeny of the rich and so on. There were theatres too but we were chased away by the police if we dared to go near them.

I once knew how to read and write. I was even a trained warrior. Or were these the delusions of an old man vainly imagining past glories and brave deeds? I was not sure. The way I looked now, with my emaciated body and cracked skin, balding hair and sunken cheeks, nobody would have believed I had once been a warrior. I could barely read now. Not that it mattered anymore. I was over fifty years old and there was nothing much left to do. One day I too would be carried away by four people and burnt. Not that I awaited such a journey, though I expressed the wish often. I wanted my wife to comfort me by saying that I was too young to die. Recently though, I found that any comments about my mortality did not get a response from her. Perhaps she wanted me to die. It was not a bad idea. But I was afraid. I did not want to die. I wanted to live forever.

As I walked back home, I gaped at the glittering lights that cast a myriad coloured shadows and reflections on the streets. I smelt the perfume when a beautiful woman passed by. Music softly floated around. A few families were making their beds on the pavement. Poor chaps! Perhaps they were from the countryside or mainland India. They would be chased away soon enough. The pavements were too lovely for such dirty fools to sleep on. I walked past the markets towards my home by the river. Acrid and pungent smells of a thousand spices assaulted my nostrils. Shopkeepers were closing up. Some fat ones sat counting their money. The thugs who were stationed outside such shops, glowered at me as I walked hurriedly past without making eye contact. I turned left at the end of the markets. Rotten vegetables and fish gave the corner its characteristic smell. A few dogs were scavenging in the garbage. One barked hesitantly at me. I stooped to pick up a stone and the dog shot past me with its tail between its legs. It was the only creature afraid of me these days.

In the distance, Ravana's fort looked imposing and impregnable. My son Athikaya might have been with his master, prince Meghanada. Idiot! It had been almost six months since I had last seen him. It was painful to remember that he actually belonged to the palace and I was just his keeper. What if I had remained in my village on the Poorna river and my family, my wife and daughter had lived; what if those blasted Devas had not attacked our poor village? Surely my life would have been better and different. Instead, I had fought for a King's dream, and given the better part of my life so that thugs like Ravana could wallow in riches, glory and power. Alas, I had many regrets in my life and my life seemed to have a mind of its own. At least my son ate well. He lived like a prince. But that thought was no consolation. *'Why only him? Why not me?'* I felt bitter and once again looked at the glowing palace. It was then I saw the strange sight. I stopped and watched. Initially I could not tell what it was. Something was climbing up the citadel. A thief? Which foolish thief would dare break into the palace of the mighty Asura Emperor? He would be skinned alive if caught. I waited for few minutes to see if there were any further movements but all was silent. Perhaps the toddy had been stronger than I had thought. I was about to turn my eyes away and return to my useless life, when I saw him.

He was just a silhouette against the backdrop of the glowing palace and I couldn't see his face. But he was a well-built man and stood atop the fort and surveyed the palace, with a huge club on his shoulder. *'Who was he?'* With a start, I remembered the great Vanara king, Bali. This man resembled him. But why should the Vanara king enter the Asura Emperor's palace in stealth? I remembered the rumours that the great Vanara king was dead, killed by some Deva hunter who had hidden behind a tree and shot him on the sly. When this man turned his head, light reflected from the expensive ear stud he wore. *'No, that is not Bali!'* Then, with an agility which only the Vanaras could aspire to, the man jumped down and I saw the canopy of the trees shake with the impact. Emptiness stared back at me as I stood frozen. Someone had just entered Ravana's palace. I stood there confused. *'Should I inform someone? Or should I just go home and sleep?'* If someone entered the King's palace, it was the King's problem. Why should it bother me? Then the images of just such an entry into my home by the Devas long ago, flashed into my mind and I ran back the way I had come. I had to find someone who could do something about it. Danger lurked around the corner.

By the time I reached the police outpost on the royal avenue, I was panting like a dog. But I hesitated as I approached the station house. There was a torch burning brightly inside and four guards sat huddled together, engrossed in a game of dice. A fat police sergeant slept with both his feet perched on the table. Flies buzzed around the torch that burnt brightly in one corner.

"Sir," I called out. There was no response. "Sir," I called again. One of the guards raised his head and his eyes grew big in surprise. I cowered as my legs trembled. *'I'm not a criminal.'* But I was poor and that was a bigger crime.

"What do you want?" the guard barked at me. He was clearly irritated at my intrusion.

"Sir, I saw a man. . ."

"So have I," and he laughed at his own pathetic sense of humour as the others joined in. The sergeant opened his eyes, blinked a few times, and then slipped back into slumber. I wanted to go back. Let the King save himself. So I began to walk out. "You there! How dare you come here with a stupid story and then walk away," the guard screamed at me.

"I did not abuse you, sir." I tried to gather some dignity.

"Are you talking back to me?" And what came next was quite unexpected.

In a flash, he was upon me and had planted a kick between my legs. I collapsed, tears of anger, shame and pain blinding me.

The other guards had left their game. They had found better entertainment – me. "You beggar, you scoundrel, what are you doing at this time on the royal avenue?"

I tried to parry the next blow but I was too weak. "Sir, Sir, please listen to me. Someone has broken into the palace." A hit across my face sent me sprawled onto the ground. The policemen kicked and punched as I clawed at the ground. Then suddenly it stopped. When I raised my head, the sergeant stood towering over me. He pulled me up by my sparse hair and I blanched. Then he pushed me towards his table and I collapsed on the floor. I looked up and saw his heavy body perched on the table. It creaked under his ample weight but I found the noise soothing. Perhaps the table would break.

"Tell me." He ordered. I remained silent so he kicked me. Then I sang. I told him what I had seen. A frown appeared on his face. He chewed something and kept thinking. Then he told the guard. "You go and tell the chief of palace guards." Then, as an afterthought, he added, "Lock up this man. He's pig drunk."

The other two guards dragged me towards the dingy cell in the corner and threw me into a corner. They did not bother to lock the cell and returned to their game. The other guard who had been forced to go on this errand, cursed me and walked out in search of the palace guards. I cursed myself for having been too conscientious. '*What the King does with his palace is none of my business.*' I was such a fool. Some lowly crook was lying in the other corner of the cell. The fat sergeant had settled back in his chair and was snoring again. I hurt in places I did not know existed. More fool I! I sat there cursing my fate and my foolish, impulsive ways and slowly drifted off to sleep.

When I awoke, Lanka was burning.

42 Messenger of death

Ravana

I was woken by the screams and commotion in my garden. People were running about aimlessly. Guards were shouting and cursing each other. The palace was lit with hundreds of flaming torches. Mandodari was awake, looking puzzled. I opened the door and found the guards outside leaning over the verandah and shouting something. As I walked nearer to them, they sprang to attention.

"What's all this noise?"

Gingerly a senior guard stepped forward with a deep bow. "Your Highness, a monkey-man has sneaked into the royal gardens and was talking to that Deva lady. When some of the guards tried to capture him, he fought them and even killed or seriously injured two or three. Now he has vanished among the trees."

I was shocked. Monkey-men sneaking into my palace gardens was beyond my imagination. I worried about my daughter, Sita. She was vulnerable under the Ashoka tree, though my guards kept a watch. Nevertheless, I felt uneasy. It had been barely four months since I had heard about Bali's assassination. The King of the monkey-men had been killed slyly by that Deva prince, Rama. The Vanaras were now ruled by Bali's corrupt and debauched brother, Sugreeva. It was disgusting the way my son-in-law had usurped Bali's power. That coward had hidden behind a tree and shot Bali through the heart. The fact that Rama had done this while Sugreeva

had been engaged in a hopeless and losing duel with his brother, enraged me further. '*What sort of morality and ethics did my son-in-law follow?*' I had been tempted to overthrow the Vanara King and avenge my friend's death. I had even ordered my army and navy to attack the Vanaras. But after my son's victory over the entire Indian subcontinent, from the seas to the mighty Himalayas, my appetite for war dwindled. Besides, Sugreeva had agreed to pay tribute to Meghanada, and the monsoon had set in. We postponed the plan.

But as the monsoon started, Sugreeva, the rascal that he was, reverted to his life of debauchery. I was sure that with an army of indisciplined monkey-men, Rama would not start any foolish adventure. Obviously I had been too complacent. The monkey-man inside my palace garden was proof enough and I cursed my own lack of foresight.

This was an emergency. The Council was required to meet. I told my wife to shut the doors and windows. She seemed worried by my unusual caution, but I ignored her and went out, slamming the door shut with a bang. I walked towards Meghanada's chamber, but found it open. The *durbar* was well lit and the guards were in their places, standing to attention. My ministers stood chatting excitedly to each other.

"Where's Prince Meghanada?" I asked, searching for my son's handsome face.

"Your Highness, he is leading the search party at the western end," Prahastha replied.

"How on earth did such a security breach happen?" As I spoke, my anger resurfaced. There was complete silence as I banged a fist into my palm. "I want an answer *now*!" I screamed. I felt better as anger rapidly replaced worry.

"He sneaked in through the west side wall while the sentries slept. He murdered them and then reached the Ashoka-*vana*. The bodies of the sentries were found in the drain, their throats slit," Prahastha said slowly.

"Excellent! That is good! Not a single Asura saw this man entering Ravana's fort? My sentries were murdered in their sleep. I have more than 50,000 soldiers and a single monkey-man not only escaped detection but still eludes capture. So much for your vigilance and intelligence network." I saw Prahastha and Jambumali eye each other after my tirade.

"Your Highness, actually, a derelict drunkard had reported to the police outpost at the royal avenue that he saw a man sneaking into the fort. But..."

"But, the officer-in-charge did not want to move from his seat. No action was taken and the matter was ignored. Isn't that what you want to tell me?" Where was Meghanada? I was getting worried. The monkey-man could be hiding anywhere. A sly arrow shot from the top of a tree in the dark could pierce my son's throat. This was a dangerous game. This was not war. No rules applied and worst of all, my enemies were devoid of scruples.

An uneasy silence ruled the *durbar*. We could hear the noises outside, men running and shouting at each other, the clanging of swords. Suddenly I heard a huge cheer. Everyone looked up. The voices were calling "Victory to Ravana. . . Victory to Indrajith." I stood up in my excitement and the entire *durbar* rose with me. I wanted to run out and see the prize my son was bringing me but I stood there, trying hard to conceal my excitement and wringing my hands in pleasure and anticipation. At the head of the procession, my tall, proud son, with his bow firmly held in his hand, entered my *durbar*. The entire assembly rose and cheered. Asura guards danced around. *Chenda* drumbeats reached the highest crescendo. I went down and embraced my son.

Then I saw the tall, muscular, dark Vanara standing behind him. His hands and legs were tied with ropes. Muscles rippled across his body. *'I used to have a body like that in my youth, like a chiselled statue.'* I tucked in my belly. He stood almost as tall as Meghanada. He had curly, black hair all over his body and wavy, black hair flowed on either side of his face. He looked a formidable warrior. With a start I realized that he resembled Bali, my friend, who had been murdered slyly by Rama.

I walked back to my throne with deliberate steps. The ministers returned to their seats. Meghanada stood near the Vanara, his sword drawn. With a wave of my hand I dismissed the *Chenda* drummers and other unimportant persons from my *durbar*. Then, after a few minutes silence, I began the interrogation. The Vanara did not answer the first few questions. He stood there staring at me defiantly. His pose and self-confidence were unsettling. He was in the *durbar* of the mightiest king of the world, caught as a spy, and faced with nothing less than a death sentence. Still he stood there as casually as if he was watching children playing games.

I looked at Prahastha for an answer. He stood up, but before he could speak, the Vanara spoke in a deep voice. "I am Hanuman, son of Maruti, and I have come as an envoy from my King and protector, Sri Ramachandra Prabhu. I demand the respect due to an envoy of one King to another. I am sure the Emperor of Asuras, the learned and scholarly warrior-King Ravana Prabhu, would not hesitate to extend the courtesy due to an envoy as per *Raja Dharma*." He ended the speech with a smile that lit up his face.

"Envoys do not sneak in at midnight, Sri Hanuman. We have strong reasons to believe that you are a spy and as per the ethical codes of the same *Raja Dharma* you evoke, the punishment for a spy is death. And as far as we know, your master is not very scrupulous about *Raja Dharma*. As far as my limited knowledge is concerned, murdering unsuspecting warriors who are engaged in a duel with someone else, by hiding behind a tree and slyly shooting them down, is not a part of *Raja Dharma*." Prahastha spoke with deliberate firmness.

The monkey-man looked uneasy. His attempt at establishing a psychological superiority was effectively thwarted by my Prime Minister. He tried another tactic. "I refuse to talk to you, Ravana Maharaja, when I am bound by ropes. Give me a seat and untie my bonds and I shall answer all your questions."

"Throw him into the dungeons. Let us see whether he talks or not once Rudraka starts his art on this monkey's black body," I said, looking straight into Hanuman's eyes, searching for traces of fear. I could not find any. The man remained composed and calm. My guards approached him and grabbed him by his elbows.

Then my brother Vibhishana rose to speak. I looked at him, trying to hide my rising irritation. "Your Highness! Once a man has declared he is an envoy and not a spy, and no deliberate crime has been committed, our ethical code says that he has to be treated as an envoy."

"Uncle!" Meghanada cried out, forgetting for a moment that he was in the *durbar*, "he murdered two of our guards and vandalized our garden. He is a spy and a criminal. He has to be treated accordingly."

"Is there any witness that Hanuman killed those guards? As long as his guilt is not proven, he is innocent. I am not asking that he be set free. My intention is to ensure that no one accuses the Asura Emperor of not following propriety and *Raja Dharma* while dealing with an uncultured Vanara." Vibhishana looked at me as he completed the last sentence.

"I suggest the spy be dealt with in the way the Emperor finds suitable." Prahastha rose up from his seat.

'Asuras. There's not a single thing in the world that two Asuras will ever agree on. Always arguing and so stubborn about having things done their way.' I decided like a wise fool to satisfy them both. "Untie him. Leave only his hands and feet bound. If he wants to say anything, let him stand and say it. Then I shall decide what is to be done with him."

"But father. . ." I silenced Meghanada with a glare and a guard slowly untied Hanuman's bonds.

As soon as the ropes were undone, Hanuman spoke. "I, Hanuman, son of Maruti, of Kishkindha, minister of the Vanara King Sugreeva, and servant of the Prince of Ayodhya, Sri Ramachandra, wish to give His Most Exalted Highness, the mighty King Lankeswara, some friendly advice from my master. You have wrongfully abducted his wedded wife and Queen of Ayodhya, and have kept her in your custody. My master requests you to return his queen to him with all due respect and to beg his forgiveness. If this advice is ignored, I am authorized to declare war on Lanka and the Asuras, on behalf of my master. We promise that, in such an event, we will crush you

Asuras, grind your sinful cities into the dust, and reclaim our Queen."

There was an uproar. A hundred swords were drawn from their sheaths in a mighty hiss. Meghanada pressed his sword to the throat of the impudent monkey-man. These were multiple insults. How dared this monkey come and challenge me, the Asura Emperor? How dared he do so in the name of a drunkard king of semi-civilized monkey-men? How dared he challenge the mightiest king the world has ever seen, on behalf of a wandering hunter who mistreated his wife? And how dared he challenge me openly in front of everyone in my *durbar*?

"*Death by stoning!*" I roared, and the entire *durbar* roared with me. He stood there unfazed, as I pronounced his sentence.

Vibhishana stood up slowly and the pandemonium died down. Then, in a very soft voice, he said, "Your Highness, this person has earned his death and you in your wisdom have given a fair judgment. He forfeited his right to live when he ceased being a mere envoy. His language was more suited to the battlefield than the court of the most exalted Asura Emperor, who rules all of India and Lanka. But. . ." he paused.

"Come to the point, Vibhishana." I was getting impatient.

"But, brother, would it not be prudent to send him back with our own message? Let his master also know that Lanka would give a befitting reply if he attempted any misguided adventure. If we just kill him, we lose the chance to give them a suitable reply. We may perhaps avoid an unnecessary war as well. We can say that we will keep his wife hostage until he surrenders his brute of a brother, Lakshmana, to us, so that we can try him and punish him for the atrocities he has committed against our sister."

'He has a point.' I thought, looking at Vibhishana. But I was still seething from the insult the monkey had thrown at me.

Prahastha stood up and turned towards me and said, "Your Highness, before we hastily kill him or send him back, let us get some information from this gentleman. I request you to give me the honour of personally interrogating our esteemed envoy from Sri Ramachandra."

I wavered in my decision. What I wanted most at that moment was to get back at Hanuman. He could not come to my *durbar*, insult me, and get away with it. It was Vibhishana again who found a way out.

"Let us brand him." Vibhishana said simply. Branding with a red hot iron or fire, was an age-old Asura practice. It was an agonizing and humiliating punishment. The marks left were permanent and the victim would carry the humiliating symbol and pain to his grave. The symbol would proclaim to the world that he was guilty of a great crime, and that the mark of his failure and guilt has been forcefully etched on his body for the whole world to see and snicker at. The more I thought about it, the more I liked it. This monkey would return to his master with Ravana's brand. . . where should I brand him. . . in his broad chest. . . in his taut abdomen. . . or on his broad back?

"Strip him and brand his tail."

"Your Highness, I suggest that we desist from such a dastardly and barbaric act. We should treat him as a spy and deal with him accordingly. Let us not stoop to such depths." It was that irritating Prahastha again.

"Burn his tail. Let him know pain when he sits, stands, lies down or walks. Let him know the pain of insulting an Asura Emperor." I basked in the cheer that arouse from my *durbar* and ignored Prahastha, who shook his head in despair.

My guards ran to fetch Rudraka. The chief of police came with his assistants and bowed deeply to the court. Hanuman remained unfazed. This was a tough Vanara. I was getting more furious by the minute. Rudraka's men prepared the molten lead for branding and the fire roared. It was then that the unthinkable happened. With an ease that belied the rope's strength, the monkey-man ripped the ropes that bound his legs and kicked the sword out of Meghanada's hands. For a moment everyone was stunned. That was enough for the Vanara warrior. He thrust his hands into the naked flames and burned through the ropes. Then, with his hands free, he lifted the huge container that had molten lead in it and threw it at me. I ducked, but the pot hit the silk curtains behind my throne with full force and they were set ablaze. I jumped from my pedestal in the nick of time as the entire parasol above my throne caught fire and fell. Then my *durbar* began to burn.

There was utter confusion. Hanuman pushed Rudraka into the fire. The burly police chief struggled for his life and by the time his men pulled him out and smothered the fire that threatened to engulf him, Hanuman had pulled out some burning logs and set fire to my palace. Guards ran like panicky hares. Some poured water on what was left of my throne. In the confusion, Hanuman escaped to the city, with burning logs held in both hands. Only Prahastha had the presence of mind to throw his dagger at the escaping arsonist, but it narrowly missed Hanuman's ear and hit the *durbar* door with a twang. Meghanada ran after him in hot pursuit but falling pieces of the burning beams slowed down his chase considerably. And I, being the coward, ran for my life. I called Meghanada back from his chase. We could catch the Vanara any time, but for now, the palace was burning.

It was a nightmare. Total confusion and panic ruled. I ran into the women's quarters with my brother and the others who were following. Rudraka shouted, trying to bring some semblance of order among his men, but the guards fled for their lives, ignoring his orders. A huge burning beam narrowly missed us and fell a few feet away, spluttering and hissing their like a living thing. The heat was beyond imagination. A thick pall of smoke hung everywhere. I kicked open a window and jumped out and landed on the hard ground twelve feet below. Pain shot up from my ankles but I continued running. I could hear screams from my harem. The fire had almost burnt down my *durbar* and was swiftly moving towards the surrounding buildings. And there in front of me, my city burned. Orange flames licked thatched roofs clean. A thousand screams of panic and death echoed through the skies. People ran from their homes. A few brave ones fought the fire but were fast losing the battle. The acrid smell of burning flesh, wood, and clothes, filled the air. Horses bolted from their stables and ran madly through the streets, kicking and trampling people in their way. I ran towards my harem. My wife was there, my sons were there. I had to save them. But the flames beat me in the race. The entire roof of the palace caught fire. My throat was hoarse from shouting instructions and orders. But there was no one to listen. '*Where were my guards? Where was my mighty army? Where were my ministers?'* I stood and watched helplessly as my palace burned down.

It was then that I saw the huge black figure running recklessly towards the burning harem. I called out for the mad man to stop but he dived into the raging fire and disappeared. I stood dazzled by this display of courage *'Perhaps he was raving mad.'* By this time, a few of my ministers, including Prahastha, had joined me, but I dared not to say a word to them. Rudraka had brought some sort of order and his men tried desperately to douse the fire. Part of the palace had been burnt completely, and it looked like the fire was being brought under control on east side at least. But the fire had ravaged the harem and I tried not to think about the plight of my family.

About sixty elephants were brought in to fight the fire. Then the huge black figure which had disappeared inside the burning harem, jumped out of a first floor balcony, cleared the fire and rolled onto the lawn. It was then that I saw he was carrying my queen, Mandodari, on his back. We rushed towards the man. As we approached, I recognized him with a start. It was none other than my illegitimate son, Athikaya. He was fussing over the Queen, trying to revive her. I saw that his hands had been badly burnt. But before I could say anything, Athikaya ran back into the burning palace. This time, an entire group of guards followed him. The intensity of the fire had come down but it was still dangerous.

The fire was slowly controlled inside the palace, but outside, it continued to rage. Somewhere in my mind, I registered that Meghanada and Jambumali had rushed out of the palace towards the city to direct the fire-fighting activities there. Rudraka had renewed his search for the monkey-man who had wrecked such ruin. But I was beyond any thought of revenge or punishment. I was too dazed and overwhelmed by the sudden and horrific turn of events. I was worried sick about my Queen. Guards brought out bodies from the harem. Some were alive but gravely burnt, or unconscious, others charred to death beyond recognition.

Slowly, my Queen opened her eyes. I hugged her. I could not control my tears. But she pushed me away and struggled to stand, not bothering to cover her bosom, "Akshaya, where is my Akshaya?" she muttered. I looked around. Where was my little boy, my eight-year-old Akshaya Kumara? I stood up but feared the worst. I did not have the courage to face my wife. Prahastha bowed and called the guards and whispered something. They ran towards the palace. But I noticed everyone avoided my eyes. I told myself not to lose courage. Shiva would protect my boy. I hoped against hope. I barked out orders, search here, look there. . . a lot of nonsense. I knew it was futile. But I wanted to do something.

A wail came from behind me but I was afraid to turn. Someone put a comforting hand on my shoulder, but it failed to comfort me. I was angry. I knew the meaning of the wail and the man who had caused it. But then my anger passed and I collapsed like an old rag. The warm ash-strewn ground hit me in the face. I lay there, my face bleeding, my tears mingling with my blood. I could hear footsteps and whispers. My men were afraid to come near me. Maybe they respected my grief. Or was it just voyeurism? Who knew and who cared? Ravana's sorrow was his own. Why should I share my grief with this indifferent and cruel world? My boy, my little prince, had been burnt alive like a chicken. No, I did not want to see him now. Let my last memory of him be that beautiful smiling face. The innocence, the curiosity about the world, the charm, the little one wove in this serious and cruel world, and made it bearable for an arrogant brute like me, had been taken away. I staggered up. Through the hazy light, I saw my wife cruelly beating someone. Some people tried to tear her from the huge black crouching figure of Athikaya. "Why did you save me alone. . .how could you leave my little boy who was sleeping with his hands over me. . .you brute. . ."

She pummelled the huge man with all her strength. He just stood there, his head bent in shame and guilt. Or was it anger at this cruel and undeserving treatment from someone whose life he had saved at the risk of his own? I didn't know nor did I care. Athikaya and their anger or guilt was not important to me. I have just lost my little one. I walked towards the row of bodies neatly laid out on my once-green lawn. Grotesque shapes awaited me. I kept walking and then I found the little bundle. Guards bowed respectfully, but I would not have cared if they had spat on my face. I took the charred little body in my arms. The little face leered at me from its burned blackness. My boy mocked everything about me... my vanity, my life, my achievements, my ego. I knew it and was angry at fate and at the Gods who had done this to me. My servants came running to take over my burden, but I refused. This was my burden and I would carry it alone. Was anything worth this? Was my kingdom worth it? To save one child, I had sacrificed another. I had brought disaster on the people I was supposed to protect.

Then, shattering the deadly silence of the night, I heard the cruel laughter of my daughter, Sita. "Ravana, you wicked Asura! You deserve your fate. You and all your kin will die such horrible deaths at the hands of my husband, Rama of Ayodhya."

'I deserved it my daughter? I deserved it? I just sacrificed your little brother for you. I may lose everything but still I will stand up for you. Once I forsook you, but never again. You will understand what sort of a husband you have, only when the protection of your old father ends. Then, alas, my dear daughter, it will be too late.' I wanted to yell all these things at Sita but I had no strength left. I walked away alone, carrying the dead weight of my little prince, into the dark depths of the night. Perhaps, there I would find some solace, someone to dry my tears, and where I could lay myself in the lap of darkness. I kept walking, my dead little one sleeping peacefully in my arms.

43 Let my city burn

Bhadra

The city was burning. The policemen had vanished and the front section of the police station was on fire. My escape route had been blocked and at any moment the fire would reach my cell. Thick curls of smoke billowed in as I sputtered and choked. I was trapped. I tried to run through the raging fire but lost my nerve when faced with the intense heat radiating from the inferno. It had become difficult to breath. I did not know what to do but I am a survivor. But this time I wasn't so sure. The orange tongues of flame hungrily devoured everything in their path. A part of the roof collapsed and the dark sky burst into the room. The smoke escaped and the air cleared a bit.

I tried scrambling up the wall but could not find anything to hold onto and fell back again. I searched for something to stand on. The inspector's table was burning as a huge beam from the roof had fallen across it. I tried pulling it out and finally, after many anxious and tense moments, it yielded. I pushed it hard towards the wall. My hands burned but I was barely aware of the pain. That would come later. I stepped onto the table and then jumped over the wall and I ran for my life.

It was utter chaos outside. Houses, shops and everything on the streets, were burning. I could see the palace burning in the distance. I ran towards my house. The fire had killed people indiscriminately. Brahmins, untouchables, slaves, barbers, merchants, drunkards, pious men, guards, gamblers, prostitutes, old ladies, babies, saints, rowdies –

were all dead. The acrid smell of burning flesh filled the sky. Many were trampled upon. A few were barely alive. Some were fighting the fire. Others wailed the loss of loved ones and possessions. I ran through the streets where death had done its fiery dance. I was afraid and hungry but I kept running. I do not know how or why but as I left the main streets and turned towards the humbler dwellings, I saw the fire had not done much damage there. People had come out and were gawking at the raging inferno licking our city clean. Many tried to stop me and enquire what was going on. I continued running. All I wanted was to reach home and get away from kings, palaces, spies, and their deadly games. Let the city burn and men and woman die, I wanted to be safe in my house. By the time I reached my street, it all seemed like a bad dream. The silence was only broken by a few stray dogs chasing the huge rats that infested our gutters.

As I reached home, I was startled to see the door slightly ajar. I slowly entered, ignoring the creaking noise of the old wooden door as I opened it. In the faint light I saw the silhouette of my snoring wife, blissfully unaware of the raving fire ravishing her city. I cursed her and moved to my bed. It was then that I saw someone lying on my bed. I was startled. The flickering light emanating from the burning city did not illuminate the figure. I searched for my dagger, but could not find it at my waist. I was too afraid to move.

"Father. . ." the voice trembled.

"Who. . .?" I shivered.

"It is Athikaya. . ."

"Why. . . you fool. . . you. . .you. . ." I moved towards the figure now sitting up on the bed, with his head buried in his hands.

"I killed the Prince. . .I killed him. . ."

"What. . .?!" What had this fool done? Had he killed Prince Meghanada? What was going to happen now? I began to panic. '*Would the entire army hunt us down?*' My wife woke and blabbered incoherently. I screamed at

her and she cowed down. I shook Athikaya and slapped him hard across his face. "Idiot! you wake up and stop talking nonsense.. stupid fool."

Then, bit by bit, I extracted what had happened. I was relieved to find that this stupid son of my mine had played no part in the death of the little prince. Rather, he was the hero who had rescued the Queen. Then I felt bitter. *'No one, neither the King nor all those fair-skinned ones who hung around him, will ever acknowledge the heroics deeds of people like us. No bards will ever sing paeans to the selfless acts done by common people like us. Forget the bards. Who needed them?'*

I left my wife to fuss over my incoherent son. Outside, the sky was tinged red in the east by the rising sun and by the burning city in the west. Wearily I stretched my limbs and walked towards the river wondering what the monkey-man had gained by killing innocent babies, men and women, and setting fire to a beautiful palace. The procession of the dead had started towards the funeral ground on the other side of the river. I could not see the faces of the men and women who accompanied the bier, but I could imagine their teary eyed faces. I watched indifferently as the first pyre was lit, and thick smoke curled into the sky. I went home and sat on my mud verandah to watch the smoke over my burning city.

44 Messenger of peace

Ravana

It was Prahastha who insisted that I come out and take a look at the city. I was angry with him at the time, but he insisted. He told me it was the duty of the King to see how his subjects suffered and to take action to mitigate that suffering. I shouted at him and even threatened to dismiss him, to behead him. But he stood his ground without saying anything in return other than to calmly insist that I do my duty. Finally he wore me down and cursing, I agreed.

I saw the horrible sufferings that had been inflicted upon my citizens. I walked with Prahastha, dressed in simple clothes and ceased to be a king. I was a fellow sufferer. Houses were gutted, streets were strewn with odd rags and charred furniture. Heaps of trash lay smouldering in various corners, looking suspiciously like flesh. Many buildings had collapsed and broken walls, black with soot, stood haphazardly. Some had only windows or doorframes with no roof above. Some buildings had only a few pillars standing in the mounds of smoldering ash. They looked like relatives stricken by grief, standing around the funeral pyre of a loved one. Men and women stood in corners, devastated by their loss and stunned by the suddenness of it all. I heard the stifling sobs and occasional wails that broke through the thick walls of the houses that stood precariously on the verge of collapse. Half burnt, animal carcasses lay strewn around. It was sickening. I wanted to go back to the palace and get away from this scene of abject human misery. The loss of my young son seemed small in comparison.

But the sudden thought of my dead son opened the flood-gates of sorrow. I looked pleadingly at Prahastha but he only looked grim. Unable to control my tears, I was also angry at the monkey-man, at Prahastha, at the world at large, for bringing me to this situation. But I was too stunned to move. The road was soggy with soot and water and mud clung to my clothes and sandals. A sickening breeze wafted through these lanes of death. I was overcome and retched, clutching my stomach as I emptied myself on the road. It was then that an old woman recognized me. She came running from her house, letting out a high-pitched shriek. I was taken aback and stopped retching.

"You scoundrel! See what your lust has brought us to!" she screamed. Prahastha tried to stop her but she pushed him away with great force. Then she beat her breasts and wailed, "I brought up two fine sons with so many sacrifices. Their wives, my grandchildren, all gone. All gone in the flames of your lust. . .you have a wife like an angel and you still have to lust over Deva women? And see what she has brought to us Asuras."

A crowd gathered around her. There were angry murmurs and some clenched fists. I stood pinned to the ground. I was afraid they would lynch me to death. What kind of a ruler was I? I felt disgusted. Lanka burnt on all sides. Whatever I had built, whatever my people had built with their dreams, ambition, passion and hard work, lay crumbled in ruins around me. I had failed as a king. I could not protect my citizens from a lowly monkey. I was a failure as a father. I could not protect my small son from being roasted alive. I was a loser. It needed Prahastha to make me come out to see and empathize with my fellow sufferers. My knees gave away and I collapsed on the ground. With trembling hands, I tried to touch the feet of the angry old woman.

"Mother. . .forgive me. . .I. . .I. . ." A gasp went through the crowd.

Prahastha lifted me up but the old woman fell at my feet. "Forgive me your Highness. . .you are our Emperor. . .you should not fall at my feet." She dissolved into sobs. The crowd which had been angry enough to lynch me to death suddenly became indifferent and moved away as I staggered towards my charred palace, leaning on the old but strong arm of my Prime Minister.

"*Jai* to Ravana." Someone cried out and then the entire crowd responded in unison, "*Har Har Mahadev!*"

"We will follow you unto death sir!" someone yelled.

"Death to the Devas. . ." another voice joined in.

"Lead the Asuras to victory. . .we shall avenge the brutal attack sir. We shall build the city back with our hands; brick by brick."

"*Har Har Mahadev!*" shouted a hundred voices. "Death to Rama and death to the monkey-men."

I could feel the energy flood into my veins as I climbed up to my citadel. I was no longer afraid of Prahastha. I could see the streets full of my people. The crowd was electric. Thousands of swords glistened in the sun. I waved my hands and a huge uproar went through the crowd.

"*Let us rebuild Lanka!*" I cried and was greeted by another uproar of *Har Har Mahadeva*! "By Shiva, we shall avenge this brutal attack of the monkey-men and the Devas."

"*Yes we shall!*" answered the crowd.

Prahastha stood smiling beside me. I whispered to him, "Let us start rebuilding the city." He bowed and left my side to make arrangements in his usual efficient manner. The bumbling but brilliant Professor Mayan, the minister of city administration and engineering, was summoned and he came running like a happy child being offered a treat. As the cities had grown and developed, he had been left with the monotonous job of administrating them efficiently. Now he was being again given another chance to rebuild the burnt city and return it to its past glory. I left my two ministers busy in consultation.

The palace was in darkness and I returned to the reality of my dead son and my personal loss. The energy I had built from the cries of thousands of my citizens and their never-say-die spirit, left me at the doorway to my palace. Noises of a city walking from the dead filtered through the dark and gloomy curtains of my palace, but sitting alone, buried in my personal tragedy, I became just a grieving father who had lost his little one. Even the love of my subjects, looked frivolous to me. Everything seemed a pretence, even my grief before the woman in the street. *'Had I really felt empathy towards that grieving woman? Or was it an instinctive reaction to save myself from the angry crowd itching to lynch me to death? Have I led many people to misery and death, just to achieve my personal ambitions?'* the doubts lingered. My mind felt numb. *'I loved my people. Had I not built an empire out of nothing? And had I not given back self-respect and pride to a battered and oppressed people? But, what if it was all guided by selfishness and not by ideals?'* Why I am thinking in this way? Had I not glorified selfishness and greed as the two great pillars of human progress? But then, why was I feeling like scum? Why was I am feeling like a charlatan who had led his people to gloom and hell?

The door creaked and after a moment of pregnant silence, the tall silhouette of my Queen appeared in the slanting sunlight at the door. Slowly, she walked to me and sat down. I did not dare to stir and look at her. I knew my eyes were moist and any movement on my part would expose the tears waiting to flow over the rims of my eyes. She put her hands on my shoulders and tears began to trickle down my cheeks.

"I will be with you always. Do not leave Sita to her husband. We do not know how he will treat her. Whatever may come, we shall face it together. She is our daughter. I understand you, Ravana."

I shook my head. *'If my daughter did not want my protection, why should I sacrifice everything for her?'* Till then, I hadn't thought of returning her to her barbarian husband, but as Mandodari raised the issue, I began to think of returning her to her fate and continuing with my life. *'Who am I to bring destruction to my own people for the selfish reason of saving my daughter?'* I may not have been a perfect human being or a perfect king, but I did not want the curse of mothers who had lost their children and their dignity, to haunt me forever. Enough! I would call Vibhishana and ask him to return Sita to Rama.

As if reading my thoughts, Mandodari said, "No, Ravana, no. We know how Devas treat women. Now that she has lived among us, they would consider her impure. We have already lost one child." She squeezed my shoulders hard. "Let us not lose another."

"Prahastha seeks audience in the *durbar*," announced a guard. I stood up without looking at my wife, went to the basin and washed my face. In the cold water, I allowed my tears to flow freely. When I looked into the mirror, I saw an old man staring back at me. He had grey hair and stubble. The dark circles around his puffy eyes and wrinkles, gave him the appearance of a broken man. Where had youth gone? Where was the Ravana who had challenged the Gods? Where was that King who had wanted to achieve so much in life that he had not cared about the feelings of others? Where was the fiery youth who had led battles after battles and destroyed cities, slaughtered men and woman, and built an empire that stretched from this Pearl Island to the southern banks of the Narmada on the mainland, the man who gave the Asuras self-respect and more glory than the legendry King Mahabali? And where had the love for nature, music, art and life, vanished? Where was Ravana?

The answer stood at the door, with his head held high, his bearing proud and manly. Ravana, with the fire to conquer and the hunger to live, Ravana in his youthful glory and a million dreams, Ravana of the unquenchable zest for all the good things in life. The Ravana missing in the mirror stood at the door, beckoning me back to life. It was Meghanada. "Father, the Council of Ministers are waiting for you."

I turned and adjusting my *angavastra*, put a hand on Meghanada's shoulder. I could not afford to wallow in self-pity, I had a country to rule. Drawing energy from the youthful fire of my son, I walked to my *durbar* leaning on him a little, to take on my life again. I left my sobbing wife behind and listened to the sounds carried in by the breeze – the sound of the Asuras, my beloved people, rebuilding their city and their lives after a brutal terrorist attack. Hope began to sprout again. I left my son behind and entered the *durbar*. As I sat on my throne, I could not help but notice that the repair work was shoddy. Brushing away this little irritation, I began the proceedings. And in my mind, once again, I became the Emperor and the greatest monarch on earth. There were many more battles to be won.

We sat discussing war plans. I personally itched for revenge. Though I wanted Rama to be captured alive for the sake of my daughter, I wanted to slit Lakshmana's throat for what he had done to my sister and kill Hanuman with my bare hands. I was impatient with the endless war planning and strategy. I could see the same impatience in Meghanada too. Nevertheless, Vibhishana pitched for one last peace effort. He said that he would personally go as an emissary and reason with Rama. Prahastha was of the opinion that it would be dangerous for a prince of Lanka to go to the barbarians for peace talks. They could hold him hostage and demand Sita's release in return. Finally, it was decided that Vibhishana would go with a sizable army and Varuna's navy would protect him from the sea. Vibhishana also assured us that if required, he would use force and capture Rama, if he did not see reason.

Prahastha was dead against any such move. "We should move fast and finish off Rama's puny little army. We shouldn't lose the advantage of surprise. Regular rules of war are not applicable this time as they began the offensive by first deforming an Asura princess and indulging in terrorist activities against the Asura empire." Vibhishana didn't agree. I grew tired and told Vibhishana he could go as an emissary. I also instructed Varuna to stand by as a back-up if Rama tried any of his ignoble Deva tricks.

Prahastha was furious, but once I had made my decision, he carried out the arrangements to ensure that Prince Vibhishana got the best trained platoons to accompany him on his mission. Wearily, I disbanded the court and returned to my room. I was tired and needed to sleep after having cremated my little son just hours before.

45 Looming war

Bhadra

The siege began. Essentials disappeared from the market. Prices shot through the roof. Bad times had come. But people like me, with our calloused hands and coarse dress – invisible, irrelevant and silent, we suffered even during good times. In bad times we starved and died. We discussed the impending war in hushed tones. Many of the younger generations had never seen even small skirmishes, let alone wars. True, some had accompanied Meghanada on his northern campaigns, but those were wars fought in other people's countries. The men and women who were killed, raped and looted, were like us, the poor and the hungry of other countries, another race and another skin colour. But the battle was now coming home. Fear hung in the air like a nasty winter mist that never goes away.

We had a fool for a king. Otherwise how could one explain such stupidity? Ask any common man on the road and he would say what a hypocrite and how evil Prince Vibhishana was. Only a gullible and naïve king like Ravana would have trusted such a mission to Vibhishana and Varuna. A few days ago, the public had sent off Prince Vibhishana after a grand public function. Thousands assembled on the beach with Asura flags. Forty-two warships carrying the entire royal navy and almost three fourths of the Asura army, set sail towards the mainland to capture Rama and crush his monkeys. Everyone knew that talk of peace was only a ruse. We waited for the ships to come back in a fortnight with the barbarian Deva prince, Rama, in chains.

But, even after a passage of twenty days, there was still no news about the Asura navy and army. Rumours flew fast and quick. The monkey-men had routed the Asura forces near the Shiva temple on the shore near Mahabalipuram. The sceptics like me, however, were sure that Vibhishana had switched sides. And then the royal announcement came. We were right. From every junction and corner of the island, it was announced that Prince Vibhishana and Admiral Varuna had switched sides. The Emperor's brother had the audacity to send a message requesting Ravana to relinquish the throne in his favour and to hand over Sita to Rama. Varuna also wrote to say that Ravana was no longer the suzerain of the Asuras as Rama had declared Vibhishana, King of Lanka and the Asuras, in a ceremony at Mahabalipuram. There was also a joint letter signed by the two villains that a majority of the Asura army and the whole of the Asura navy, had switched their loyalties to the Devas.

Ravana did not have a chance. To save Lanka from a second destruction and unnecessary bloodshed, Ravana had to hand over the throne peacefully to Vibhishana and retire to the Himalayas with his family, if he valued his life. But Ravana urged every citizen to rise, defend his motherland and culture from the barbarian Devas and the treacherous Asuras who want to impose Brahmanism and caste hierarchy. Not that every citizen of Lanka or on the mainland led a prosperous life and enjoyed a life of equality, without any hierarchy or caste discrimination. Though we had seethed under the slow spread of caste and colour discrimination and had rued Ravana's rule, in our hearts we knew that the king had not been directly responsible for the rot in Asura society. In fact, he and Prahastha had checked the spread of casteism seeping in from the north, though Vibhishana and his Brahmin followers had slyly tried to introduce the discriminatory religion through the back door. Now, the same Vibhishana had allied with the Deva King and had threatened to overthrow Ravana. People shuddered to think how life would be if Vibhishana and the Brahmins were given ultimate authority. We were afraid.

Preparations for the final battle between the Devas and the Asuras had begun – it would be the final clash of two civilizations. In this decisive battle, the Asuras were going to fight with one arm tied behind our backs. For the common man, our only interest in joining Ravana's earlier raiding parties as mercenaries was only for sharing the loot. After a long time, an established Asura empire would face an attack similar to that faced by the ten kings when Indra invaded India. A way of life, a culture of equality and freedom, a tradition that valued material pleasure and celebrated life, braced itself to face the final assault from another culture. It had long ceased to be a personal matter between Ravana and Rama. People had hated Ravana initially for what they saw as his lust for Sita and the misfortune it brought to the Asuras. But when the people heard the rumours that Sita was an Asura princess, our own King's daughter, they recoiled at the thought of leaving the princess in the hands of Rama. But the king could not drag us to a war over his private affairs. It was a family feud at best but we were paying the price. Nor could I forgive him for the way he had treated my adopted son, Athikaya, who was also his blood. But unlike Sita, the womb that had borne Athikaya, was that of a black housecleaner and not the aristocratic daughter of a great scientist. The Asuras braced for the final war between good and evil.

Rudraka paraded the infantry and cavalry through the streets. People moved tensely. Soldiers and police officers were all on edge and screamed at or beat people without reason. Then the people outside the fort, and the fishermen who lived near the bay, arrived with their fowls and beasts. People began to live on footpaths. Then the Asuras who lived near the port, brought the news – the monkey-men were building a bridge across the water. It was strange, fascinating and fearsome. But the bridge inched towards our little island relentlessly. As it grew, so did its terror effect. People climbed onto temple towers and treetops or any elevated place, and talked in excited tones.

Kalaripayattu, the traditional Asura martial arts centres, came up overnight. The streets were filled with Asuras, young and old, men and women, carrying swords, bows and arrows, spears, and assorted weapons. Ravana exhorted his subjects to take up arms and fight the invaders. Temples that had been earlier closed to us ordinary Asuras, were opened and became virtual army camps. The separation and segregation that the Brahmanised elite of the empire had imposed on society, vanished overnight, as most of them left Lanka to join Rama's ranks. The old sense of equality among the Asuras came back. We were fighting for our culture, our race, our way of life, and our traditions. This was the last battle which would determine if the poor and the downtrodden of India, stood a chance to achieve equality; it was a war against heartless Casteism and Untouchability; against degraded Brahmanism. I smiled at the irony. A war against Brahmanism was going to be fought under a king who was secretly proud of his Brahmin lineage. However, what choice did we poor, unlucky, black ones have? Of all the leaders and kings that we, the blacks of this country, had ever had, Ravana was the best. He was humane despite his faults and the alternative – the kingdom of Rama, or worse, that of Vibhishana, was too frightening even to imagine.

Instinctively, every common Asura knew that this war would determine the future of India and its millions of poor and black people. If this war was lost and Rama won, then we would be kicked into the ditch forever. We knew that a life worse than that of a street dog awaited us then. We would fight for Ravana. We would give our blood, our lives, and everything we owned, for if we lost this war, we would lose something more precious than life. A bleak and dark future awaited our children. We were terrified, hungry and thirsty, yet we eagerly awaited to fight Rama and his monkey-men. Our chances were grim. We knew it well. But we were determined to fight to the end. This was the decisive war – the war between good and evil. We were sure that Mahadev Shiva would not allow evil to triumph.

However, in the deepest corner of my mind, I knew we were the lesser children of the Gods, and even a compassionate and all-powerful God like Shiva, would look at the colour of our skin and flinch. Perhaps we had been born with the wrong skin colour.

46 For my people

Ravana

The palace was dark. Odd sounds filtered through the humid air. Not a leaf stirred. I had been sitting on this verandah overlooking the sea. Defeat and death stared me in the face. I berated myself for not having thrown Varuna into the raging waves that night, long, long ago. I felt numb. The life I had built with tears, toil and death, was crumbling. The torches and lamps the palace servants had lit hours before, had flickered to a slow death. Here and there in the palace gardens, an odd lamp still shone, fighting a final battle to survive.

For hours my mind had been a blank page. Then, like a headache that starts with a small flash of pain at the temples, the feelings returned: *I wanted to see my daughter*. I tried to dismiss the thought and it subsided for a while. But before long, it seized me again. I stood up and walked towards the giant Ashoka tree where my daughter lived. It was dark. The lights that escaped through the palace windows threw huge shadows on the bushes, making them appear grotesque. As I approached the tree, a bird flew away with a loud flap of wings and rodents scurried past. A bat flew perilously close to my head, changed course, and then vanished into the darkness.

She slept. The two dozing Asura woman soldiers did not even know of my presence. *'So much for her protection'*, I thought. I hated myself for the trembling in my hands. I wanted to touch her and go back to her childhood, which I had not seen. I wanted to feel my baby daughter's tiny fingers, to cradle her, and see her growing up. The moon broke through the dark clouds and a reluctant beam filtered through the leaves of the Ashoka and illuminated her angelic face. The dull moonlight played hide and seek with the dark shadows of the garden. A gentle breeze rustled the leaves. She stirred. A small drop of tear flowed from the edge of her eyes over the bridge of her lovely nose, balanced on the tip and fell down. My heart went out for my little precious daughter. She was pining for her husband's love. Did I do a mistake in taking her away from the person whom she loved? Suddenly I was angry. Why can't she see her father's love? What was there in Rama that could make her forget all the wealth I had earned? Then my anger oozed away and in its place a sense of helplessness arose. I had wronged her. I had forsaken her when she wanted me most. I was busy building an empire. In my insane race for success, I lost my daughter's childhood. Now, when she was so madly in love with her husband, I had again taken her away from him. I hated myself for doing so. But why can't she understand? Her husband would never take her back. He was standing at my city gates, roaring death and destruction to an old man, not because he loved his wife so dearly. Or did he? I don't want to lose my child again. I do not want him to take her away from me. She is an Asura princess and she is my daughter. I had lost her once, I will not let it happen again.

Instinctively she awoke and saw me standing there with a look of despair and confusion on my face. I wanted to persuade her to stay with us, her parents. But as I moved towards her, she screamed. The spell was broken and I staggered back, disgusted with myself. She spoke words of abuse, sobbing hysterically and calling on Rama to save her. The Asura women guards woke with a start, looking confused. But before they could see me, I withdrew into the shadows and hurried back to my palace. My heart cried in pain as I entered my bedroom and saw Mandodari sitting on the bed. I could not face her.

"Where were you?" Was there an edge to her voice? I shrugged and lay down with my back towards her. I felt bitter and angry about everything. '*Why did she come into my life*' I shifted in my bed but the thoughts refused to go away. Then I felt a warm hand on my shoulder and turned to hug my wife. Slowly, I began to undress her. I could not remember the last time I had loved her and waited for the rush of desire to overwhelm me.

But nothing happened. I fumbled with her clothes, like a teenager minus passion. I felt her go rigid and stiff. Once again I attempted to stoke those forgotten passions and then gave up. I turned away from her and lay on my back. She put her head on my shoulder and tried to stroke passion with her hands. But nothing happened. I was tired and wished she would give up and leave me in peace. I hated her at that moment and I hated myself for being impotent. I do not know for how many hours we lay like that, but slowly sleep claimed her and she slid back to her side of the bed. But the simple mercy of peaceful sleep eluded me. Millions of thoughts, mostly meaningless, popped up. Somewhere between, a sense of weariness and defeat crept in. I wanted to end it all. Life had no meaning. Everything was worthless. I tossed from side to side and the slipped into a stupor.

Then, when the eastern sky had turned pale, I woke with a start, drenched in sweat. I have been learning astrology and astronomy from Mayan. As I grew older, my own vulnerability had gradually made me more receptive to these abstract sciences. Any subject that interested me, I devoted long hours of study to. Life was so short and there was so much to learn. I was in the process of writing a book, a *samhita,* on astrology and omens. Maybe that prompted the nightmare I had of my daughter Sita being dragged away by tall and fair men and being thrown into a raging fire. Rama sat on a high pedestal, visibly distressed. Somewhere nearby, another fire was raging. More than the horrible fate of my daughter, it was the grotesque face that was hungrily being devoured by the flames that woke me, my heart thudding in my chest. It was the face of the Asura Emperor. Was it an omen, the harbinger of things to come? Astrology was such a veiled science and I did not believe in omens. I wished sleep would claim me back into her bosom, but disturbing images kept me awake and tired. Twice, my servants came to wake me, but I ignored them, feeling their dread through the covered sheet under which I nestled under like a frightened child. Finally, Mandodari came and shook me awake. It was a bleak morning. The sky was overcast and darkness loomed over the heaving ocean.

"Your Highness, the Council awaits." Prahastha's voice startled me and I looked at him with bleary eyes. *Council. . .what Council. . . What do they want to discuss now?'* I was weary of everything – petty politics and egos; bickering and tussles; endless meetings and sycophants trying to impress me with their unfailing patriotism; my glittering palace; my empire; the war I would have to inevitably wage against Rama. I was tired of life. I wanted Prahastha and his kind to go away and vanish from my world. *'Why did I choose to be King?'* I should have chosen a simpler life on the beautiful shores of the Poorna river, dreamt small dreams, and lived and died like the insignificant millions of the world. A small hut, a faithful wife, beautiful children, some fields to till and all the time in the world to enjoy life – but I knew such dreams were just that – dreams.

I sat there for a long time after Prahastha had left. I did not feel like doing my *puja* to Shiva. *'Let him do without a puja today.'* I had prayed enough, even without being sure whether God heard me or not. When I finally reached the *durbar*, the Council members were huddled in circles, chatting irreverently like school kids. There was a sudden hush when I entered and they scrambled to their respective seats. I waited with growing annoyance as many fumbled with their dress and their turbans.

Prahastha stood up but I cut him off with a flick of my hand. I could see the embarrassment and hurt on his face but I cared nothing about his fragile feelings. Once more I waited for the murmurs to die down and then said, "The enemy is breathing down our necks. We are facing betrayal after betrayal. Vibhishana, the brother I cradled in my arms and considered a son, left for the enemy camps. Varuna, the snake, whom I trusted with our navy, and whom I considered my best friend, has become a slave of that Deva upstart. Half our army and the entire navy have switched sides. So much for the Asura empire and the glory of our race, for which I have given my blood, my kin, my dreams, my life."

"We should move to the Subela hills. The fort there will hold against any enemy attack. We have enough provisions there to last for several months. We will wait there and wear the enemy out." Prahastha interfered.

I took some time to register what Prahastha was saying and then felt suddenly angry. "No, I will not run away from two Deva men and their rag-tag army of monkey-men. I am the Emperor of the Asuras, and I will not hide in the hills. I will crush them."

There was visible commotion among my ministers. Then Jambumali stood up painfully and said, "Your Highness! If we can hold out in the hills until the next monsoon, then we can trap Rama's army between the raging sea and the city. We can resort to guerilla tactics and weaken the enemy until then."

"You want me to leave the city to the mercy of those barbarians? I think you fools have forgotten the lessons of history. How many magnificent Asura cities were ransacked and burnt to ashes; how many women raped and ravaged by the Devas in the past? You think the sons of Indra will spare our magnificent city?"

"But, Your Highness! We are weak now. We have to strategize, plan and fight the war on our terms. The Subela hills are practically impenetrable. The retreating monsoon will start any time now and the steep walls of Subela Fort will form a formidable barrier for even the monkey-men. Moreover, we will be out of range of the flame throwers of Varuna's ships." Prahastha patiently waited for my reply.

I could sense the tension in the room but did not say anything. My Prime Minister was right. In the Subela hills, we would be able to keep Rama at bay forever. We could then bribe Varuna's men to come over to our side and strike at Rama later in summer. I knew my Governor Khara, who was now at the northern-most border of my kingdom, in the middle of India, was moving rapidly to encircle Rama from the rear. Once Rama was weak, I was sure that Varuna would switch loyalties again. But he would take a few months to cover the distance with his huge army. Could we hold on till then? Even if we did hold on, what would happen to my city and my people? What if Prahastha was plotting to get rid of me? No, Ravana would not run away like a coward. Strategy or not, I would stay here and protect my people.

Suddenly we heard a rising uproar from the streets. It was faint initially, but slowly rose into a crescendo. The Council members apprehensively rose from their seats and I could not contain my curiosity. Was it Rama's army attacking? I rushed to the open verandah where I usually gave my morning *darshan* to my subjects and heard their complaints. A serpentine procession was marching towards the palace. As far as the eye could see, people, men and women, old and young, were marching towards the palace. The guards at the fort gates tried to restrain them, but the crowd pushing past relentlessly.

"Death to the Devas!" "Har Har Mahadeva!" "Ravana Vijaya!" The angry cries tore at the sky as the crowd brandished all sorts of weapons, from 10-foot spears and swords, to garden tools and even kitchen knives. Drummers frantically beat the timeless Asura rhythms on *Chendas*.

'How could I even think of leaving my people and hiding in the hills?' I waved my hands and the crowd roared back in approval. I gestured to the guards to let the crowd in. *'Who was I to restrain them?'* The crowds rushed in. They trampled the manicured gardens, upset the flower pots and some urchins jumped into the fountains. The palace opened its gates to my subjects. It felt good. I raised my hands to the sky and a sudden hush fell on the crowd. In that moment, I felt like God. I felt the charisma I had lost somewhere in the labyrinths of power, return to me. I felt that I had once again reconnected with my people. I regained my youth.

"Long ago, when I was barely seventeen, I made a promise to you. I promised you a world where all men and women would be treated as equals. I promised to give you back the golden age of Mahabali. We hoped to regain our glory. We had nothing except hope. You reposed your confidence in my leadership and I, in your loyalty. Together, we challenged the mighty Deva empire. With a handful of men, we started a campaign against inequality, Brahmanism, oppression, and meaningless rituals. With your sweat and blood, we built what we see around us today. From this pearl island to the foothills of the Vindhyas, we made the Asura flag fly high.

Prosperity came to our people. We built magnificent cities and made leaps of progress in science, art and culture. Our great temples proclaimed the glory of Shiva. The granaries overflowed with the fruits of Asura labour. We built temples of knowledge and ensured each Asura was literate. Our hospitals took care of the sick and we built roads and canals. We can now confidently claim to be the richest empire in the world." I paused for effect. Cries of '*Har Har Mahadev*' and '*Ravana vijaya*' rose on all sides.

"However, on the march towards progress, we made some mistakes. We strayed from the path of righteousness that our great leaders of yore had so painfully walked upon. We lost purity of thought and the simplicity of life. Like the Devas, we began to think that some men were privileged. It would perhaps been justified if privilege was based on abilities and merit. But the Deva civilization, if one could call it that, though defeated by the mighty power of Asura-arms, slowly seeped in and poisoned our minds. Like them, we began to consider some human beings as divine; that some were pure and others not – not because of their deeds or their minds, but because of their birth. As your leader, I should have seen the evil thoughts of caste seeping into our society. Alas, I was busy glorifying myself." The crowd groaned.

"I forgot our values myself, so why should I blame society? The Brahmins, and I mean no evil to them as individuals, cornered all that was worthwhile, and the majority of you were left in the dumps. I, as your leader, failed you, for I allowed my brother, the traitor Vibhishana, to flirt with Brahmanism and Vishnu. I am ashamed to say I prided myself that I was superior to you because I am half-Brahmin myself. I was secretly proud of my fair complexion and considered black skin dirty and evil."

The crowd stood rapt in attention as the words came of their own volition. "Today, our civilization is at crossroads. I stand before you, not as an Emperor, not as the arrogant all-conquering *Rakshasa* that my detractors like to call me, but as a simple man, as a fellow Asura, with my heart bared. I have sinned, for I am not God, but a human being like you. I stand chastised for the wrongs I have committed. I stand humbled by the simple trust you have placed in my leadership. I pray to Shiva that he gives me strength to shoulder this heavy burden.

This war, despite what many people think, is not about Sita, the beautiful wife of the Deva Prince Rama, and the lecherous lust of your old King for another man's wife. Nor is this war about avenging the humiliation suffered by my sister Soorpanakha, at the hands of Lakshmana, the brother of Rama. This. . ." I paused. Suddenly the words had dried up. The crowd waited in anticipation.

"My dear Asura friends. . .Sita. . .Is my daughter." There was a huge roar from the crowd and I waited for it die down. The mid-noon sun beat down mercilessly, sucking my energy and dulling my brain. Rivers of perspiration ran down my face. Thousands of black, wet faces gleamed below. Angry, confused and excited, the crowd swayed. I did not want to look back and face my ministers, though I suspected they knew about Sita. I did not have the courage to face them now. A few minutes ago I had planned to sway the crowd with my speech about the future of the Asura civilization, now, those words had gone into hiding. I supported myself on the balustrade and waited. I knew the crowd could turn dangerous at this time. I felt exhausted and tired.

'*Victory to Sita Mata! Victory to Princess of Asuras*!' a forlorn cry went up from one corner. There was a deadly silence. Heads turned in surprise towards the sound. I squinted into the sun to see who had uttered the cry. Was it Bhadra, the old rascal? I could see a shriveled, old man, leaning on a staff, with a sprightly, black, muscular youth near him, but I was not sure about the face. Once more the old man cried out, '*Victory to mother Sita!*' And as one, the crowd erupted with cries of victory for Sita and Ravana. The *Chenda*s that had become silent, exploded into wild Asura rhythms and the crowd, swayed and pulsated like a monster snake as it crawled out of my palace, raising a hill of dust in its wake.

As the war cry faded, I turned to my ministers and said, "So it is settled. We will stay put and fight." All except Prahastha bowed. As I left for my chambers with a flourish, I could see Prahastha had a glassy look in his eyes. I caught his eye and he imperceptibly shook his head. Later, in the dark, cool chambers, long after the fire lit in my body by my subjects had died down, I found myself praying to Shiva to soothe the rising panic. A premonition of doom hung in the thick, humid air over Lanka. I could smell it; I could feel it in my hair. Perhaps Prahastha was right as usual. However, I would rather have died and lost everything than abandoned my people to the horrendous monkey army of Rama. I knew it was logical to withdraw now, but I was too proud and too sentimental. I would stay here and fight with my half army. I owed my people that much at least.

In those lonely hours, as I wriggled and fumbled with the logic of head and heart, the fate of India, the Asura empire, and millions of black people, was decided forever. Had I listened to my head, perhaps fate would have decreed differently. But then, I was always a creature of passion. I had lived as Ravana and I would die as Ravana. I did not intend to become Rama, the perfect man and God. There was no dearth of gods in my country. It only lacked men.

47 War without ethics

Bhadra

I shouted with all my might for the Asura princess. I was happy that at least one ruler had been honest enough to admit the truth. The crowd's mood changed after that. Who knows? I might have saved the day for Ravana. I followed the crowd back but was too tired to walk back to my hut. So I slept in front of a silk shop, on the footpath. Many more slept on the footpaths. Policing had become lax once the war fever had caught on.

Suddenly, in the dead of night, flame-tipped arrows were shot towards the marketplace. The war had started with a bang. The marketplace was on fire. Varuna's flamethrowers had shot the fiery arrows from the ships anchored a few hundred feet from shore. Arrows hissed and thrummed in the air; they hit things; pierced men; landed on hay roofs and gutted them. The inky black sky was lit with thousands of tongues of red flame that seemed to dance in macabre delight as death rained on Lanka like the monsoon rain. Had I not been running for dear life, I would have stopped to enjoy the spectacle that Varuna was providing for his erstwhile friends.

People ran out. Screams rang through the sky. Flesh burned. Houses were gutted and thick, black smoke, swirled upwards. It was like being in hell. For the first time I faced war as a common man and not a warrior. I found that I needed more courage to survive like this than on the battlefield. There at least we knew who the enemy was. Here, death came in various forms: as falling beams, as marauding troops, as thick black smoke that choked you, as leaping flames, as arrowheads. Here we wait for death to find us.

The Devas had no sense of fair play. They were firing at the civilians first. Their intention was to cause panic, weaken and demoralize us. With daylight, they would cross the bridge and launch the attack with their infantry and cavalry. '*What was our King doing?*' For all his big words, he could have hidden himself in the Subela hill fort. You could not trust these kings. Where had Athikaya gone? A dull panic throbbed in my stomach. I ran against the fleeing crowds, stumbling, getting up, stamping and trampling on a tide of frightened men and women running like mice. '*Where was Athikaya?*' I was on the verge of tears. I pressed myself against a lamp post and stood there panting. The sky was dark with black fumes. The smell of burning flesh made me retch. '*Where has the Asura army gone? Why were they not doing anything to protect us from the monkey-men?*' A sense of helplessness and utter disgust for our rulers prevailed among the panicky crowd. I could sense their fear.

As if to answer my questions, a cavalry unit suddenly appeared through the thick smoke. Some of the fleeing people paused to look back, but the cavalry pressed on through the crowd, trampling some, physically throwing out many, and hacking a way through the crowd with swords and whip lashes. '*Oh God! Rama's cavalry,*' I thought, but then caught a glimpse of Vajradhamstra in the lead. It was the Asura cavalry going to meet the monkey-men.

People lay dead or injured on the road. I walked towards the palace, equally afraid of both Rama's and Ravana's arrows. Charred carcasses of men and animals lay scattered around. After a few hundred yards, the sky cleared a little and I paused to breathe in some fresh air. The palace stood in deathly silence. Varuna's flaming arrows did not have the reach to touch the palace, so for now, the King was safe, unlike his poor subjects. I looked towards the sea. Varuna's ships were rolling gently on the waves. I could see thousands of armed men shooting flame-tipped arrows towards the main market and residential areas. I clambered up a small hillock, a few yards from the main street, which jutted towards the sea and got a better view from there.

Rama's bridge was almost complete. Men, elephants and horses, had unloaded from the ships and a long, serpentine, infantry column snaked its way towards Lanka. I could see the fluttering Deva flags with the emblem of Vishnu's conch, and feel the rising enthusiasm of the barbarian army as they saw the rich Asura capital for the first time.

I saw Vajradhamstra's cavalry clash with the rushing monkey-men, on the beautiful white sands of our beaches. Till a few days ago, lovers had strolled those white sands, hand in hand and mothers had watched with delight the tiny steps their toddlers made. On the same sands, where life had been so beautiful, now death danced in the steps of Kali. A huge boulder that the Asura army catapulted from a nearby hill, found its mark. Another found its mark, then another, until a ship swayed, and went down. A huge cheer rose from the Asura ranks.

The fort gate opened and the rest of the Asura cavalry and infantry, thousands and thousands of armed men, with the battle cry *Har Har Mahadev!* on their lips, charged forth. I looked around. It was a glorious day. The sea lay like a sheet of glass, reflecting the deep, blue sky. Dragonflies buzzed and flowers bloomed all around me. If I could somehow shut out the smell of blood and death, I would have smelt the freshness of the earth and the dew. Then, in a surprising moment of clarity, I saw it all. The world was indifferent to the trivial pursuits of men. It was indifferent to whether Rama or Ravana won. It was as indifferent to the plight of the Asuras as it was to the plight of a deer in the death grip of a panther. The earth was wet with the blood of men, of beasts, of anything that breathed. Every moment, someone, something, was being killed somewhere – perhaps by the enemy on a battlefield or a killer who had broken into a house in search of victims or a hungry tiger; by an accident on the road; or as a sacrifice to quench the bloodlust of the Gods. Violence alone ruled the world. Everything else was a brief interlude, a pause before violence struck with more viciousness. Strangely, it did not matter. All that talk about honour and pride, of race and skin colour, of morals and traditions, of triumphs and failures, it was irrelevant in the greater order of things.

Yet something throbbed in me. Fear? Hope? Thirst for revenge? Weariness and the meaninglessness of these thoughts throbbed in my head. And somewhere, in this muddle of uncontrolled emotions, I desperately grasped for the meaning of this maddening phenomenon called life. Later, much later, I realized that the only meaning of life was that it did not have any meaning. By then, however, it was too late. Wearily I walked towards the palace. I heard the screams and shouts from the beach where a pitched battle was going on. Dust swirled in the sky. I stood on tiptoe to look for Athikaya. *'Where was my son? I want to find him before he gets himself killed.'* I wanted to go home to my wife Mala, and somehow convince Athikaya, if I could find him, to leave this madness and escape from this mad world inhabited by Ramas and Ravanas. *'Where was he? Or was he already lying dead on the beach?'* With leaden feet, I dragged myself towards the palace.

The palace lay hidden behind the rising cloud of dust. The gates were closed and the guards tense and alert. I stopped, gasping for breath and cursed my foolish son and the stupid men who had started this war. I prayed it to be over. One way or the another. I would have liked the intruder, Rama, to be captured and hanged – not that I loved Ravana. But at least, his rule was tolerable. But was he a match for the sly Deva prince? The sun baked my back. With my knotty fingers over my eyes, to shield them from the blazing sun, I scanned the palace balconies to catch a glimpse of Athikaya. The palace seemed deserted. Then slowly, as my eyes adjusted from the blazing sunlight to the relatively dark palace, I saw the tall and fair Asura Emperor, standing alone on a balcony. He stood staring impassively towards the beach. Here was a man who was watching the glorious life he had built for himself and his people, collapsing around him. Yet, his face remained noble and impassive, his posture erect and proud. With his silvery mane flying in the breeze, he looked divine. In spite of myself, I bowed. He turned towards me and our eyes locked. He nodded and my heart leapt with joy. He had remembered this poor servant, the poor wretch, Bhadra, who had been at his side when he was the hurricane that blasted Deva bastions, long ago, in our youth.

I saw a guard coming towards me. The Emperor had vanished from his balcony. The guard ordered me to enter the palace. As I stepped in through the golden gates of Ravana's palace, and stood drinking in the beauty of the place, I was rudely pushed aside. Before I could protest, a chariot rushed past me at great speed. My curses died when I saw a limp figure with its head smashed beyond recognition. As the chariot turned, I saw the face. It was Vajradhamstra. "The monkey-men hit him from behind!" I heard one of the soldiers explaining in great animation to his fascinated listeners. This was a sick war, with no morals. I wanted to get out of this place and ran into the palace in search of Athikaya.

48 Sons are sons

Ravana

The day ended triumphantly. Rudraka, who had been given command of the army after Vajra's death, and Sumali and Prahastha's brilliant moves in the canoes which cut off Rama's army, saved the day. Rama's monkey-men were butchered like pigs. Prahastha also managed to recapture three ships of Varuna's fleet. This could tilt the balance greatly in our favour in the days to come.

Many people paid homage to Vajra's lifeless body, which had been kept at the palace gates. People who had been terrified of him in life, now flocked to see the dead Asura commander. I had hated his high-handedness, his guts, and his devil-may-care attitude. The way in which he had quelled the Brahmin rebellion had been ignoble. The tyranny he had unleashed during those unstable times had marred the Asura claim of *dharma* and compassion, forever. But, I had built my empire on the shoulders of men such as Vajradhamstra. Without men like him, who did not bat an eyelid to take the life of another; who revelled in cruelty; the empire would have remained a twinkle in the eye of a poor half-caste, half- starved Asura boy.

As I moved out with my ministers and relatives in my wake, the crowd that had thronged to see the dead commander, parted. I stood before the lifeless body of my chief soldier with my head bowed. The muffled cries of his wife and daughter could be heard in the uneasy silence. I could not control the shaking of my hands as I touched the cold feet of the corpse. I

prayed to the all-forgiving Shiva. I prayed for the soul of the man who had committed the greatest crimes possible so that his people would regain their lost honour.

A procession of dead bodies came through the streets. Lesser men who had been slain along with their commander were brought in. As the fiery, red sun immersed itself in the sea, thick black smoke rose from the funeral pyres of my men, who had laid down their lives defending the Asura homeland from Rama's army. Across the sea, on the other end of the half-broken ford, I could see the twinkling fires of the enemy's funeral pyres. But the collective sadness of the kin of the slaughtered could scarcely subdue the general gaiety that filled our camp. We had withstood the superior Devas and given them a thrashing they would not forget. I hoped the barbarians would go away, leaving my daughter with me. I was too old to sacrifice good men in a meaningless war. The hatred I had felt for the Devas had long since lost its edge. I had matured beyond the adolescent pursuits of honour, revenge, war, campaigns and racial superiority. The world was large enough for both the Devas and the Asuras. It was broad enough to accommodate Rama and Ravana. Just let him leave my daughter alone. He had never treated her well and never would. It was in his veins. He was trained to treat women like worms. They made a strange pair, this Rama and Lakshmana – while one was willing to fight and kill thousands of men and women for the sake of a wife he had never wanted, the other left his wife to languish in his palace for fourteen, long years.

As the funeral pyres slowly died out and the crowd of commoners thinned, I walked towards my chambers. The moon was three-fourths full and cast a magical, silvery light over Lanka. The sea was calm and a gentle breeze ruffled the coconut palms. The thin, silvery blades of the palm leaves caught the moonlight on their edges and made lovely patterns on the sand. It was a beautiful night, except for the recently widowed women and orphaned children. I did not wish to dwell on the horrors of the war. *Raga*s were forming in my head. As I entered my chambers, my eye caught the moon reflecting on the strings of my *Rudra Veena*. It was a long time since I had played the instrument. I had got this particular instrument from the foothills of the Himalayas. That was a trip when all of us had been buried under an avalanche. The majesty of the great mountains, the abode of my beloved God Shiva, had overawed me. The near death experience and subsequent recuperation in a peasant's hut, taught me humility. It also taught me about the insignificance of human life. I learnt about the beauty of life and discovered the musician in me in that remote Himalayan, pastoral village. The twang of the *Rudra Veena* had initially irritated my ears. But slowly, it captured my imagination. By the time I boarded my *Vimana* to head back to my southern abode, I had become a virtuoso. Then music became my passion and I experimented with the Asura *Chenda, Mrudangam, Milavu, Timila* and *Maddallam,* with the haunting Gandharva tunes of the flute. Artists from all over the country and beyond came to me as I became known as a connoisseur of fine music. I spent many magical nights in the gardens of Lanka, where I forgot all the tensions and stress of running an empire and floated in the rhythms and tunes of my musicians, in the *Raga*s that flowed from my nimble fingers as they caressed the strings of the *Rudra Veena*.

Today was such a magical night. I was filled with the urge to caress the sinuous body of the *Veena*. As a lover takes his beloved, I took the *Veena* and gently placed her in my lap. Then I forgot the war; I forgot Rama and his monkey-men; I forgot the dead and the living and myself. I became a feather floating in the wind, carefree, rootless, purposeless and weightless. I was bound neither to the earth nor the sky. I was just me, barely aware of the touch of my beloved wife, Mandodari, as she came and sat near me, with her lovely face resting on my shoulder. I was barely aware of the party going on in the garden beneath, celebrating the temporary victory of the Asuras. As my fingers caressed the strings, I was only aware that I existed in the celestial sound that flew from them. That was more than enough for me.

"Where is my son, your Highness?" The spell broke and I came back to the ugly world of wars and death. I woke with anger flaring in my eyes. From the shadows of the curtains, the ugly and stooped figure of Bhadra emerged. *'How dare this beggar enter my private chambers? Who allowed him in?'* Before I could react, he had fallen at my feet and grasped my legs with both his hands. I stood still, not knowing what to do. Then I slowly raised him up. The stench of sweat and stale liquor hit my nose. I gasped involuntarily. Immediately, Bhadra moved away and shrank like a frightened mouse.

"It is alright," I said, even though my voice did not carry any conviction.

"I am sorry for touching and polluting you." His voice cracked while his eyes looked down.

Mandodari moved quickly towards the old man and took his hands. He tried to wriggle away. With more compassion than I could ever muster, she asked, "Bhadra, what happened?"

In answer, he broke into sobs. I was assaulted with various emotions – anger that this fellow had broken into one of the most magical moments of my life; ashamed that he had awakened dormant thoughts of impurity, that had lain hidden in the dark alleys of my mind; sorry that I did not treat the beggar in a kinder way; happy that my queen at least remained compassionate enough to understand the distress of this poor man. With my mind in shambles, I vaguely heard that Bhadra had been searching for his adopted son, Athikaya. In some corner of my mind, I knew Athikaya was of my blood, and that I had deliberately forgotten it. I had pushed such irritating memories into the dark attics of my mind. I felt that this old beggar was invading my private and dirty attic, where I had kept my dark secrets hidden from the world.

My son burst into the room. I could smell his inebriated condition. He smelt of wine, women, and arrogance. Like his shadow, a dark figure entered the room. Seeing him, Bhadra rushed to him. Athikaya pushed the old man rudely away. Bhadra staggered and fell. My face burnt with anger and shame. The scoundrel, black and ugly Athikaya leaned on my son Meghanada like an equal. And they were creating a ruckus in the Emperor's private chamber.

"Father, we thrashed those bastards! You should have seen how I set a *dhothi* on fire. Hoooooo. . . and Athikaya's arrow struck Lakshmana's back. . .ha ha. . . I do not know how he will sit. . ." And Athikaya joined in the laughter and slapped the Prince hard on his back.

"Meghanada. . ." I shouted at the top of my voice. "This is no language to use before your parents."

"Athikaya. . . say shorry to papa." I stepped forward and slapped him hard across his face. He was stunned for a moment, then, without saying a word, he went out, his head hung in shame. Athikaya followed.

Bhadra threw himself forward and tried to block their path. "Athikaya, do not go. Please come with me. We'll go away. We'll go to the mainland. Please come with us."

"Get out of my way, you old rascal." Athikaya pushed Bhadra with a force that made the old man stagger and fall. "May you rot in hell!" Cursing, Athikaya followed Meghanada into the darkness.

Mandodari said something to me but I raised a hand and waved her away. I wanted to be alone. I stood looking at the eerily beautiful, moonlit night. Sons were sons, whether they were born in a palace or a hut. But this kind of arrogance was the harbinger of disaster. But who could find fault with the youth? I had behaved worse with my father. Suddenly, a shriek, followed by a huge commotion, broke out in the palace gardens, where the celebration had been going on. Something had gone terribly wrong. With my heart pounding against my ribs, I ran towards the garden, lithely stepping over the heart-broken figure of Bhadra lying on the floor of my chambers.

49 Death visits again

Bhadra

I got up after a while. My heart was heavy. What was the use of anything? There was nothing now to look forward to. My son had been lost forever. I knew I would never see him again or maybe only as a lifeless body. Strangely, I felt empathy for the Asura King, not as our Emperor, not as the great leader who had given his life and valour for the Asura race, but as one distressed father to another. Stripped of his royal robes and shining crown, he was just like me. Or was I fooling myself? Are the powerful and the mighty unhappy in a different way?

A blanket of silence shrouded the palace. In the faint light coming from the *durbar*, I saw shadows among the shrubs and trees of the garden. Something secret was going on. I had decided long ago that the affairs of important men were none of my concern. But curiosity got the better of me. I peeped through the open windows and saw the Emperor sitting on his throne, his face deathly pale and his ministers huddled around a few limp bodies on the floor. I became tense. Had something happened to Athikaya? I waited with bated breath for someone to move so that I could get a better view.

"It is inexcusable." the Emperor said in an icy voice. The ministers shifted restlessly.

"I woke three hours ago. When I got there, the scene was grotesque. Our people were being slaughtered. It was pitch black. It wasn't clear who was butchering whom. Initially, I thought a victory party had gone awry and our people were butchering each other. I moved away from and called the sentries. As we approached, I saw two dark figures. I am not sure, but almost certain that they were none other than Hanuman and Angada. I tried to apprehend them and threw my dagger at Angada and injured him, but in the confusion, they escaped. That was when your Highness reached the scene. Probably, Angada's cry alerted your Highness," Prahastha concluded and a tense silence followed.

"This is an insider job. I think we are going down in the usual Asura way. We almost triumphed today but then we snatch defeat from the jaws of victory. I think we deserve to be slaves. Two of my senior ministers butchered in my own gardens. We are dealing with an enemy who has no scruples, no sense of fair play and *dharma*. They are ruthless barbarians who will stoop to any level to achieve their goals. And we are infested with spies and traitors. My brother became a traitor, my friend became a traitor. I wonder who else will help the Devas? Sumali and Malyavan were good men. They may not have been warriors, nor did they deserve this end. Rudraka, this has now become an all-out war without scruples. Our aim should be to create maximum damage in the enemy ranks. I do not want us to stoop to their level of dastardly terrorist attacks and killing people in their sleep. But I think we are justified in using ruse to capture them. Find my son, if he has returned to sobriety, and bring him here. Prahastha, you will handle what Sumali and Malyavan did, till peace returns. Let us strategize and give them a lesson in their own way." The Emperor sounded resolute and grim.

I took a deep breath. It was the old ministers. They were good men with integrity in public life, but their deaths were of no concern to me. The world was full of men like them who could be replaced without batting an eyelid and nobody would know the difference. But what was happening inside was fascinating and I stood glued to my position. Soon, I saw Meghanada and Athikaya enter the *durbar*. The ministers were seated in their chairs, but the bodies of the two ministers who had been slain, lay on the floor with their heads turned towards the south. Oil lamps made out of coconut shells flickering near their heads. Athikaya and Meghanada were shocked when they saw the dead. Nobody spoke for a while. The two youngsters bowed to the ground to pay obeisance to the dead. Then Meghanada assumed his seat with Athikaya on the floor near him. Ravana raised an eyebrow at the sight of Athikaya, but the youngsters ignored the distaste of their elders.

"Tomorrow, when Rudraka strikes from the eastern side, Prahastha will attack from the sea with the captured ships and will try to either sink or take more pirate ships. I am sure the brothers will be leading the attack. Since their bridge collapsed yesterday, they might use canoes today and try to take our left flank from the northern side of the city. We will use the hills to our advantage and ensure that boulders are employed to maximum effect. Wait till the enemy reaches our city gates and then shower them with stones and boiling oil. Use the catapults and flame-throwers effectively. Prahastha will surround them from the sea and cut off their retreat, or at least engage Varuna, so that they do not get any support from the sea. Put Dhumraksha, the assistant chief-of-army on that task. He'll have to create maximum impact and create panic in the Vanara ranks. When they are attacked from all sides, Surantaka, the chief of the stables, will let loose the royal elephants by opening the fort gate. They will not expect us to open the fort gate. Draw them in and allow them to think they have breached the citadel of the Asuras. When they are trapped in the narrow confines between the hills and the city walls, let the beasts loose. We will show the Vanaras what we are capable of.

And you, Meghanada, I want to talk to you in private. I will assign you a task which will break the back of the Deva army. Make funeral arrangements for our slain heroes. Visit the homes of those slain in today's battle and comfort their kin. We must assure them that the entire Asura community is with them in their bereavement and that the nation does not forsake its martyrs." With this, the Emperor rose from his throne and so did the entire *durbar*.

The eastern skies were painted saffron and the birds were chirping in the trees. I was both thrilled by and afraid of what the Asura Emperor was doing. I was happy that at last he was leading from the front. He had regained his vigour, now tempered with experience. At the same time, he faced a sly and ruthless enemy who did not care even when civilians were killed and burnt enemy cities through arson and treachery. It was a bloody and brutal war and my son was part of some secret scheme. I did not want him to take any part in this war. But sons are sons. I was tired. I went home, leaving scheming kings and invading princes far behind. I wanted to drink and sleep like a log.

50 For whose sake?

Ravana

The loss of two of my ministers was a great blow. This war was different from any other war I had fought. My palace was swarmed with spies. Assassins struck with impunity. I hoped that today we would finish off that upstart of a Deva prince. I had heard that that the Vanaras believed him to be an *avatar* of Vishnu himself. *'That is a good piece of propaganda, I must admit. Claim that God is with you, or better, you are God, then anything you do, any adharma you commit, becomes divine play.'* I was shocked to learn that many common Asuras had also begun to believe in Rama's divinity. Making your wife suffer exile in the forest, killing a friendly king through deceit, sending terrorist to cities and annihilating innocent men, women and children…were these the marks of divinity? The naivety of the people was mind-boggling.

Today, hopefully, if Shiva was willing, I would tear off the mask of divinity. I was restless and wanted to get into action and see the Deva prince face to face. He was much younger than me, but the strength in my arms remained. Prahastha had advised me not to venture into the battlefield as it would be too risky. There were plenty of traitors in our midst and one stray arrow from my own ranks could finish the Asura empire forever. But I longed for action. How could I remain shut in my chamber when my people were in grave danger? I called for a guard and ordered the sentries to line up in the verandah. I choose the right one who had my build and dismissed the others. I asked the suitable one to strip and kept him locked in one of the smaller rooms. Then I left for battle in his uniform. I knew it was foolish and juvenile, but I could not help myself. I wanted to be in the action and see how my people were faring.

I went to the stables, took the first horse I could find and rode off towards the eastern gates. I could see dust rising like a cloud from there. The confusion and violence that met me as I entered the fray was unimaginable. As planned, Surantaka had let the royal elephants loose on the monkey-men. They were caught in the narrow corridor between the fort wall and the cliff that rose more than 300 feet high. The monkey infantry, who had rushed in when the fort gates had opened, found themselves trapped between the charging elephants and Rudraka's mighty cavalry. I rode to a nearby hillock inside the fort to get a better view.

The Vanaras were being butchered. Huge boulders landed on them with sickening thuds from the cliff top. Arrows rained down from Rudraka's men. Huge barrels of boiling oil were dropped onto the hapless Vanaras and some accidently spilt on the rampaging elephants, driving them insane with pain. Sugreeva had led the enemy attack and I could see him desperately trying to rally his men. Arrows zoomed past, perilously close to his head, and few struck him in the shoulder and thighs, but the monkey-king held on. But his escape route had been sealed. He would not escape this trap alive. Rudraka would see to that. This part of our plan had worked well. I rode towards the northern end, where Rama and Lakshmana were leading the attack.

Meghanada had waited until the attackers reached the northern gates and then the Asura chariots rolled in from outside the fort. The horses had been walked in the dead of the night to a nearby jungle and hidden there. Only a token force remained near the northern gate. The chariots were taken apart and carried into the jungle. Then, before dawn, the chariots were reassembled and by mid-morning, Meghanada's charioteers charged in and attacked Rama from the rear.

Meanwhile, Prahastha had managed to drive Varuna's fleet far away, so Rama's armies had no naval support. With alarming swiftness, Meghanada's charioteers surrounded the Vanara army and started their butchering. Asuras who had hidden in the trees and in the citadel and laid low during the morning attack, rose together as planned, to shower arrows on Rama's men. The brothers were trapped. One flank was closed by Meghanada. *'Who was taking care of the other flank?'* I craned my neck to get a better view. Whoever it was, he was doing a better job than Meghanada. Then when the dust cleared a little, I saw him. It was Athikaya, my son. The Vanara army had been surrounded on all sides and the Asuras were decimating the monkeys. Only Hanuman's infantry held on and fought with grit and determination. The majority of Rama's men were now trapped on the other side of the half-broken bridge to the mainland. Prowling canoes and Prahastha's captured fleet, effectively cut off Rama's reckless front men from the cautious ones who had stayed back on the mainland under the command of the wily old rascal, Jambavan, the octogenarian commander of Bali, still serving under Sugreeva.

I rode back to the palace, half amused by my adolescent urge for heroics. My people were fighting to plan. If all went well, we would be holding a victory party tonight. I had got rid of the disguise by the time I reached the palace gates. But Jambavan's reticence nagged me. *'Why was the wily old enemy commander holding his men back? Was it another ruse? And where was Varuna?'* The reports I got indicated that he had sailed his fleet deep into the sea, far from the island, towards the mainland. But that was unusual for the pirate-King. *'What was it that I was missing?'* I missed Prahastha.

I walked towards the garden to see my daughter. Here in the garden, it was a different world. Faint noises of battle could be heard by discerning ears, but otherwise it was just a normal day. I suppressed my thoughts and worries about the war and Rama, and stood under the shade of a sprawling tamarind tree, soaking in the beauty of the world around me. I could hear the soft whisper of the sea and see the wind rustling the leaves. I found rhythm in the orchestra that the crickets had set up in my backyard. My mind raced back to my glorious boyhood spent in the forests of this island and in the Sahya mountains of the mainland It was amazing how easily the mind forgot the painful past, grinding poverty, daily humiliations, and the pangs of hunger, and only remembered the little moments of happiness. There was a pleasurable pain in nostalgia; a yearning for things that were lost forever; a magic woven over things that could have been but did not; a dusting of secret hopes and sweet frustrated longings. And there were small things in the everyday world, if one listened with your heart, like the cooing of the cuckoo, or the chatter of the squirrels, where painful things remain hidden in the shadows and long-forgotten happiness glows once again.

She looked angelic sitting under the Ashoka tree. Beside her, looking smug, was my niece, Trijata. I was not pleased to find her with Sita. I wished to speak to my daughter alone. Trijata, in more ways than one, resembled her loafer father. Kumbha lived his own life of debauchery. His once grand ambitions had been thwarted by a lack of determination and character. He was usually dead drunk in his chambers. He had yearned for immortal fame and an empire of his own, but never had the will to achieve greater things in life. Perhaps I had overshadowed him. I was always the big brother. And no one resents your success more than your siblings. Perhaps it was plain bad luck that I had become what I had. I was at an age when I no longer thought that hard work, determination and ambition determine one's destiny. The atheist in me had died an unceremonious death long ago. I had seen too many things to naively believe that man created his own destiny and nothing else mattered. Hindsight made me ashamed to think of the childish conversation I had had, years ago, in that dark cave, with the real Asura Emperor, Mahabali. I smiled at the memory of my brashness and stupidity and the kitsch philosophy I had used, trying to impress the old man. There was something beyond the mental grasp of man that defied common sense. Determination, hard work, and all the things the gurus talk about, were useful only to determine how to react to random things that happened. But I saw order in things, the way the day and night alter or the way living things take birth, live and die. Yet many things could only be explained by a randomness called fate.

I was shaken from my musings by Sita's laughter. I looked at her. She seemed so divinely beautiful. She had inherited her spirit and passion from me and her perfect face and body from Mandodari. How could I lose her now?

"Oh! the King of Kings, the Emperor of the Asuras... have you come to pay me a visit? Ravana, count your hours. My Rama has come to finish you and your evil empire. You *Rakshasa*s and all that you have built, all that you are proud of, will soon be ashes. My husband has come to deliver me and I can see your evil empire collapsing. If you value the life of your kin, go and fall at his feet. But I know you will not, you are too proud for that kind of wisdom. Mark my words, *Rakshasa*, your time has come." She dissolved into a peal of laughter and looked positively loathsome in her hatred. Trijata looked at me, embarrassed and afraid.

I turned back, dejected and abashed. *'Why can't I bring myself to tell her the truth that I am her father?'* I had been trying to rescue her from her husband. But how could I look at her face and justify my act of abandoning her because of some superstitions? And how I could ignore the burning love she had for her husband, the Deva prince Rama? Why could she not see that her father loved her more than her husband? Why could she not see that I was staking everything I had, for her happiness? But then, why did not she know that she would never be happy with her husband and the moment my protection was gone, her suffering would start? Perhaps I fooled myself. Perhaps they would live on as the most idealized couple, the dark-skinned Deva prince and his lovely wife, and I would become the evil monster who tried to destroy their happiness. All the omens and astrological predictions indicated misery to come for her and a horrifying future for me and my people. Could Ravana change the future? Perhaps I was right in my youth after all and Astrology was just humbug. I decided my own future and not some remote stars sunk in the inky blackness of an indifferent sky. But why did my daughter hate me such vengeance? No father should be tortured like that. Perhaps my time had come. Why would I gamble my whole life for this woman? I was gambling not just my life, but also the future of a whole race, for my animal passion. Thousands were being killed at this moment – fathers, brothers, sons – families who had trusted me and were fighting for me. Maybe, it was only right that my time had come. I was a worthless king who had dragged his people into an unnecessary war, to death and destruction. But how could I hand over my daughter to Rama, knowing how he would treat her? Let fate take care of the future. I would fight to the last and maybe I would win.

The war raged on outside the palace. The shadows grew long and a heavenly crimson hue spread over the city, bathing everything in an unearthly glow. My daughter's words kept ringing in my ears, 'All that you have built and your people will turn to ashes.' I wanted to get drunk and forget everything. As I entered my palace, they brought in the still body of my commander, Rudraka. Maybe, my daughter had known better than me.

51 A HERO RETURNS

BHADRA

I was sitting on the verandah of my thatched hut. The steaming hot porridge and mango pickle my wife had put down near me had grown cold and sticky. The flies had become bolder and lingered longer on the edges of the bowl. I did not have the will to shoo them away. The familiar but indecipherable clatter of vessels and the stirring of pots could be heard from the kitchen where my wife was busy with her chores. I had a mild headache – yesterday's hangover. Business was dull. Who needed clothes washed now when tomorrow you might be dead?

Though I had resigned myself to the fate of my son, I found myself looking out longingly for the appearance of that tall, bulky figure. Sometimes I hoped he would come home hurt, so that we could nurse him back to health. But I knew he would never leave the battlefield or his friend and brother, Meghanada. Death had come marching into our street many times since the war had begun. Many of the neighbours had already lost loved ones. There was a general numbness in the air now. Initially there had been emotional outbursts. The streets saw funeral processions of slain Asura warriors and emotions ran high. But when the body count increased, death lost its novelty and heroism became cheap and commonplace. A general indifference, except for the small pool of sadness in the immediate family, was the only thing the epic heroism of the slain warriors generated. It was as though the entire country had withdrawn into a shell to brace itself for the inevitable. Fathers placed the still and mangled remains of their sons on funeral pyres with sickening numbness. Mothers huddled together and shed silent tears, while widows withdrew into their holes of lonely bitterness. Over these blunted emotions hung the spectre of fear – of a Deva victory and the horrible future that awaited the poor, black Asuras under Rama's rule, or worse, under Vibhishana.

The streets had become deserted long ago. Many of the common Asuras had withdrawn into the forests and some had fled to the mainland in crude, country boats. However, the majority shut themselves in their homes, with their rickety front doors shut and barred. Before the nobles sensed it, the poor Asuras smelt defeat and destruction, although nobody spoke of it openly. The nights were scary. This war was different and every Asura knew in his bones that he was dealing with a ruthless and unscrupulous enemy led by generals who would, under the cover of night, set cities on fire. An enemy who was led by a prince who would hide behind a tree and shoot arrows to kill a noble king engaged in a duel with his brother. An enemy who was also led by a prince who had stooped to cutting off the ears and nose of a woman. The shadows lengthened and we were terrified as never before.

It had been ten days since the war started and the losses were heavy on both sides. News of the enemy was scarce, but our ministers and generals like Rudraka, Vajradhamstra, Sumali and Malyavan, were all dead. The Asura army was running out of leaders. Only the gritty Prahastha, who kept Varuna at bay and had blocked Rama's retreat by sea, and crown prince Meghanada, were the experienced warriors left. Old and bumbling Mayan was offered command, but we heard that he had declined it. The geriatric minister of finance, Jambumali, was too old to even walk. The situation must have been grave indeed if octogenarian scientists were being asked to command Asura armies. Ravana himself should have taken over the command, but perhaps the Emperor was too old for such a task. I had the impulse to walk towards the palace. Perhaps Athikaya was lying there somewhere, injured but alive. I could bring him back. Wiping my hand on my dirty *dhothi*, and without bothering to inform my wife, I walked towards the palace. For some time I was alone on the road. Then I saw men huddled together near small eateries, gossiping. Most of the houses were shut and looked deserted but some had defiantly opened their front doors and were putting up the pretence of normalcy. Muffled cries could be heard behind some of the closed doors. Perhaps a son was dead, or a husband.

The sun was fierce over my head. Perspiration poured from me and I smelt and felt sick. I should have had a bath. As I neared the palace, the absurdity of imagining that Athikaya would be nursed inside the palace hit me. Athikaya was no prince. He was just the son of a poor, illiterate, black Asura. If he was injured, he would have been left for dead on the battlefield. When had the lives of such fools been valuable to the government? But, where did he spend the nights? He had stopped coming home long ago. *'Did he sleep outside Prince Meghanada's chamber, or did he spend his nights in the guard's quarters inside the fort?'* I was determined to see him today and persuade him to leave this stupid war of important men and come back home, though I knew it was futile.

The palace loomed ahead, impregnable and sinister from a distance. Its golden dooms and spires glittered in the sun. '*Gold – the Emperor uses gold to decorate his roof when men like us do not eat one square meal a day*'. Maybe he deserved to go down. But at least he was not cruel and had tried his to uplift his people. I shuddered to think what Lanka would be like under Vibhishana. In Ravana's kingdom, though there were nobles and commoners, in theory anyone could rise through sheer hard work and luck. Examples of men like Rudraka, who was a common butcher before he became a heartless daredevil, and Sumali, who had been just a clerk in Kubera's spice export department but rose to be minister and commander, were quoted by people who glorified Ravana's rule. But I was a non-entity, one among the millions of poor Asuras in a country that was being rapidly Brahminised. At the end of the war, I would end up an untouchable, the scum of the earth. I badly needed a drink but there was nothing nearby. I sat down to wait and catch the attention of some important official who might recognize and take me inside the palace. I had to see if my son was there.

It was late evening when I was woken from my tired slumber by the clamour of the army marching back into the fortress after the day's battle. Gravely injured or dead men, who had been important enough, were carried back. Ordinary soldiers were left for the vultures in the battlefield.

I could hear my heart pounding in my chest as I looked for my son in the army marching past. The soldiers were in high spirits. There he was! *'No, that is not him. Was he dead and left in the field since he was just a black Asura?'* I desperately ran to the tired soldiers, seeking Athikaya among them. I tried to stop the march and called for my son. There were some jeers from the group and angry murmurs, but I didn't give care. I kept running in and out of the marching columns, craning my neck to see the faces of the dead and injured. I got pushed and shoved but ignored it. With growing desperation I looked for my son. There, there he was – in the chariot, with Prince Meghanada. Tall, dark and bulky, Athikaya stood erect. The Prince bled from the wounds on his limbs and shoulders. Athikaya had a horrible gash on his chest which he had dressed crudely with a blood-soaked rag. I ran towards the chariot but was crudely shoved away by the bodyguards of the Prince.

"Athikaya, my son..." My hoarse voice did not carry through the din the soldiers were making. I looked hopelessly short among the tall and bulky Asura warriors. *'How tall the boys grow these days.'* I waved my hands frantically and jumped and shouted, desperately trying to catch his attention. Suddenly I caught his eye. I waved, trying hard to push myself towards the royal chariot. I saw his eyes grow wide with wonder and then the wonder turned to embarrassment. My son was having the time of his life riding along with the Asura Crown Prince and I, the poor washerman, a nobody, was trying to intrude into his high life. With that one look, he killed even the slightest hope I had dared to cherish within me. But then I was just his foster father. He did not belong to the shack of a poor, black Asura. He was of the Emperor's blood, ill begotten yes, but a half prince nevertheless. He belonged to a world where worms like me did not exist. He belonged to a world of mighty men and legendary heroes, who would be talked about for thousands of years after their deaths. Men like Bhadra did not matter.

Suddenly the Prince saw me. He gestured and the row of bodyguards parted. For a moment, I stood there dazed, then I walked towards the chariot apprehensively. *'Had the entire column stopped for me? Would I be rebuffed once I got near?'* The Prince looked at me intently with a tired smile on his lips. I stood respectfully a few feet away. My son looked away from me, as if my old and worn out form caused him shame. I was growing increasingly ashamed of myself. I should have had a bath. I stank of liquor and decay. The prince beckoned but I stood rooted to the spot. A soldier near me barked, "You oaf! Don't you see his Highness is calling you?"

Nervously I moved towards the chariot. As I neared, the Prince held out his hand to me. I shrank from touching the royal fingers, but in a swift move, he pulled me into the chariot. A gasp went through the crowd. A lowly, stinking beggar sharing a ride with the Asura Prince? I felt proud. Not once had his father, whom I had dared to think of as a friend, make any such gesture. Then I turned and saw the hatred in the eyes of my foster son. I shared his shame. The prince was scoring a political point by sharing his moment of glory with a lowly person. It was perhaps a noble gesture from a genuine heart, but I was so weighed down by my experiences in life that I could not bring myself to think benevolently. Everything the rich and the mighty did, even in charity, pity or generosity, smacked of selfishness. That was one of the hard lessons I had learnt in my useless life. I had seen pity in the eyes of the rich; I had seen pride in being nice to people like me; but above all, I had seen fear, even in the eyes of the mighty King Ravana. They were afraid of us, the docile, animalistic, ignorant, black, poor men and women of the world. The pity, patronization, charity, arrogance, pride, and indifference, were all part of the defense mechanism of the rich to escape their fear.

Suddenly I felt I had power over the Asura prince – power of the mundane over the spectacular. It was all very clear. He would wilt away like a half-blossomed flower, in the war, still in his youth, but I would live. He would seep through the gaps in the pages of legend and history, but I would be there forever, scraping life from the streets, fighting my little everyday battles. No poet would ever sing songs about me, but who cared about poets? No one would deify me like a God but Gods were useless and who wanted to be one? This war would end soon and so would the life of heroes and villains. But my battle would continue, and millions like me would continue to wage their little wars in the different corners of the earth, for food, water, air, shelter, and a little dignity.

I was still lost in my thoughts when the Prince said, "Your son saved my life today. You are a hero's father. I bow to you, sir." I felt sick. I did not want any part of this. I was angry at being used by the Prince as a political stunt. Had life made me so cynical that I suspected a truly noble Prince, one who had shared his royal chariot with a stinking tramp like me? I kept quiet, trying to hold down the tears filling my eyes. I tried valiantly to control the trembling of my lips, but I broke down and cried. The Prince hugged me compassionately and kissed my cheeks. My son looked away. I kept sobbing. The chariot started to roll and the soldiers cheered on either side.

As the fortress gate opened, I saw the King and the Queen standing at the top of the steps that led to the palace. The balconies brimmed with courtesans, servants, and all those *durbar* creatures. They all cheered the Prince. The setting sun painted the Emperor red and Ravana looked every bit the mighty Asura Emperor he was. His silver mane blew in the breeze and he stood tall, erect and proud, as he welcomed his son home.

It occurred to me then that this was a victory procession. *'Was the war over?'* Ravana raised his hands and the crowd cheered. *'Har Har Mahadev!'* ripped through the air and electrified every Asura. I caught a jubilant whisper from the crowd that both the Deva princes were dead, slain by Meghanada. *Chenda*s beat furiously and flowers were showered on the victorious soldiers. A great weight fell from my heart. We were safe. My son was safe and alive. The Asuras would not bear the yoke of Brahminism and casteism. Untouchability, racial discrimination, and all the horrors associated with the Deva culture, would remain as the exotic cultures of the semi-civilized north Indians, to be talked about in jeering tones while feeling smug about the cultural superiority of the Asura civilization. Perhaps the Prince was indeed noble if he had saved the Asuras from imminent disaster. This was the beginning of a new era. Rama and all the Vedic atrocities he represented, were buried in the sea.

And my son was a part of the victory. He was the hero of the victory. No wonder Meghanada had felt obliged to take me into his chariot. Actually, as the hero's father, I should have been accorded much more respect. As the chariot came to a stop in front of the steps, the Emperor came running down. Before the proud father could get near his son, his mother ran to and hug him tight. Meghanada's father stood a few feet away, irritated that he could not hug him and feel the strength in the limbs of his young son. Athikaya stood clumsily a few feet behind, a dark shadow of the fair Crown Prince, a stupid and embarrassed grin on his plain face.

Once Mandodari released her son, father and son eyed each other stiffly. After a few moments of tense silence, he hugged Meghanada tightly. The crowd roared in approval and *Chenda*s were beaten furiously. Then they moved into the palace. Like a dog behind its master, my son followed them in. Not a word, not even an acknowledgement that I was here. I stood there stunned. The crowd beneath started their revelries. I did not know what to do. After a while a guard tapped my shoulder. "From the Prince." he said, offering me a suspicious looking bundle. Tentatively I opened the cloth. There were odd things. Some used clothes – silk, but used – a few copper utensils, some sweets. Here was my reward for having fostered a hero – sent with love from the Asura Prince Meghanada, the vanquisher of Indra. This was the price the Prince had put on his own life. The guard watched me with envy and feigned indifference. He waited for his *baksheesh*. '*This country will never change. Grab everything whenever you can – that's the mantra.*' Greed was the basis of this rotten country.

Without speaking, I stood with the reward dumped on me by the government. The courier and faithful government servant, was determined to get something out of me. Disgusted, I dropped the entire reward into his hands and walked away. Without batting an eyelid, the guard took the bundle and walked into the palace. I joined the sea of revelers celebrating Rama's death.

52 A PRIME MINISTER'S MISSION

Ravana

Finally, it was over. My son had vanquished our greatest foes. I was so proud of him. But I was also worried. Something was wrong. He and his friend Athikaya, had managed to cut off Rama and Lakshmana from their generals, and trapped the Deva princes in deadly hand-to-hand combat. Prahastha had landed half his troops on the eastern side of the island the previous day, and had made them trek for the whole night to attack the Deva army from the rear. He had managed to draw Hanuman and Sugreeva from their masters and give them the impression that the Asura army was in retreat. Encouraged, the monkey-men had pursued the Asuras, and when they were sufficiently far away from Rama, the Asuras had turned back in deadly combat. I watched the battle from my citadel and was impressed by Prahastha's generalship.

Rama was left with only a few guards and was soon outnumbered by Meghanada and Athikaya. They hacked their way through Rama's determined and desperate army. They didn't have much time and Meghanada went in for the kill. The Deva princes were quick and accurate with their arrows and wounded my son and his servant many times. It was Athikaya who suggested that they get close to the Princes as quickly as possible so they would lose the advantage of their arrows.

Meghanada and Athikaya abandoned their chariot and rushed forward with drawn swords. They zigzagged through the fighting clump of men, and suddenly descended upon the Deva princes. It was a sign of how quick

Rama was with his arrows; that is, in a split moment, he had half drawn his bow and managed to land an arrow on Meghanada's shoulder. With one sweep of his sword, Meghanada hacked Rama down, while Athikaya struggled in mortal combat with the younger Deva prince. Lakshmana abandoned his bow and arrows and drew his sword. The Deva sword is a deadly weapon. Unlike the curved, heavy, iron sword the Asuras used, the Deva sword was a long, thin blade that was used like a dagger. Meghanada rushed to Athikaya's aid but as he turned, Rama, whom he had thought was dead, caught hold of his leg and tripped him up. In the split moment that Athikaya turned to look at his master, Lakshmana thrust his sword into Athikaya.

Lakshmana turned swiftly and with his sword raised high with both hands, he went for the heart of my son who lay face down on the ground. It was then that Athikaya, who was on his knees, moved and dragged Meghanada away. Lakshmana's sword narrowly missed the Asura prince and plunged deep into the soil. Meghanada thrust his sword deep into Lakshmana's abdomen and he saw the younger Deva prince roll over, writhe in pain and then go still.

By this time, the old general of the Vanaras, had descended upon the small band of the Asura army from the hill he had been hiding in. From a height on the hill, the wily old general had watched the progress of the battle and directed its course when he saw Prahastha's ploy. He rushed in with his band of men, to aid Rama. Sensing danger, Athikaya urged Meghanada to retreat, but Meghanada had lost consciousness by then. Athikaya carried the prince on his shoulders, though he himself was bleeding profusely. He hacked his way back to the chariot and tried to revive the Asura prince. He could see Jambavan's men closing in

Jambavan had sent a message to Sugreeva and Hanuman to return to aid their leader. As one body, the entire Vanara army turned and charged back to close off Meghanada's retreat. Prahastha's army in the rear gave chase. I could see that my son was trapped, though I was unaware that he had lost consciousness. From my citadel I could only see the flag flying on his chariot. I worried when I saw the chariot in the middle of the battleground. *'How could the boy be so reckless as to abandon his chariot and go after the enemy in hand to hand combat?'* That was not the way seasoned warriors fought. It wasn't just dangerous, but foolish too. But boys will be boys and finally, through reckless bravery and luck, he vanquished the evil forces. It was then that Athikaya shouted at top of his voice, "Rama and Lakshmana are dead. Victory to Prince Meghanada." Victorious cries rang through the Asura ranks. I could faintly hear what was happening, but my war hardened eyes noticed the way the Vanara armies charged. Imperceptibly they slowed down and that was enough for the Asuras. Jambavan tried to assemble his forces, shouting over and over again that it was an Asura ploy. But the news spread fast.

For the Vanaras it was unbelievable. Rama was a God to them, an invincible force of nature, and it was inconceivable that he had been slain by an ordinary Asura prince. The column led by Hanuman slowed down considerably and Prahastha's men caught up with them to engage in combat. Athikaya's men dashed out of the confusion towards the fort. By this time Meghanada had regained consciousness. He too cried out that he had killed Rama. The morale in Rama's army sank further. For all practical purposes, the war was over. I saw Prahastha's forces round up the remaining Vanaras. But Jambavan tried to reach the place where the bodies of the Deva princes had fallen.

I was enraged to see my brother Vibhishana rushing towards the slain Deva princes. The scum that he was, he would be on all fours licking my feet, once he was sure the Asuras had won. I saw Jambavan's men lift the limp bodies of the Deva princes. *'Something was wrong. Something was seriously wrong.'* I could see it in the way the Vanaras changed. With the bodies of the princes in the chariot, the wily Vanara general turned his army and dashed towards the sea. Prahastha tried to follow, but was vigorously held back by Sugreeva and Hanuman. I saw a boat approach the beach and the bodies of the Deva princes being laid into it.

By then, Meghanada's victory procession had reached the fort gates and my worried wife rushed out. She nagged me to come and receive her victorious son. But my eyes remained glued to the unfolding drama in the sea. The boat rowed away furiously towards one of the small uninhabited islands that dotted the north-western sea towards the mainland. As soon as the boat was at a safe distance, Hanuman's column fled towards the sea over Rama's bridge. Prahastha was in hot pursuit when suddenly Varuna's army appeared to his rear. This was a ploy to allow the monkey-men to escape. Hanuman's men crossed the bridge and destroyed the connection with the island.

With the news spreading that Meghanada had slain the enemy chief, the Asura army assembled and the celebrations began. There was the small matter of finishing off or conquering what was left of Rama's army, but that could wait until tomorrow. Prahastha tried to rein in his indisciplined Asura soldiers, who had rushed back to the fort to celebrate the victory. But something nagged at me and I anxiously waited for Prahastha to report back. I was happy about our victory, but I was also worried by the way Jambavan had carried the princes. *'Were they really dead?'* They were seriously injured, I knew that for sure. I was irritated that Meghanada had not cut off Rama and Lakshmana's heads. The boy had been under tremendous pressure and had fought valiantly, but it was little details like that which changed the course of battles. Meghanada should never have assumed the enemy was dead from a few sword thrusts or some arrows. But only a miracle could get the vanquished back to life once his head had been severed. That was a lesson I learnt a long time ago in the dense forests, under Mahabali and Brahma.

Had I had such an opportunity in my younger days, I would have severed the heads of Rama and Lakshmana and raised them on poles for his men to see. The moment you get the chief, the war ends. It kills the morale of the warriors. I have seen it in the many campaigns of my youth. I had been in grave danger of being hacked to death, when many a time I had recklessly charged at the enemy chiefs with my Chandrahasa and somehow killed the enemy chief. No matter how many foes surrounded me and how close I was to death, the moment I cut off the head of their chief and make sure all of them saw it, the battle was over. The fool that Meghanada was, he did not ensure that Rama's and Lakshmana's heads were chopped off. That was a tactical error. Meghanada still lacked something that only the big league of great warriors had. Was it ruthlessness? The boy was too soft at heart to be a real warrior. I would have done the deed without batting an eyelid. So would have Bali, Rama,

Hanuman, Prahastha, Rudraka or Mahabali.

That meant that the enemy was not yet dead. There must have been life left in Rama and Lakshmana or why would Jambavan have ferried them to the island? The enemy could still strike. *'Foolish Meghanada.'* The boy had not seen the harshness of life, he took for granted the things I had built with my sweat and blood. He had yet to feel the utter helplessness of not knowing when or if the next meal would come. He has not seen the sorrow in the eyes of a mother who could not feed her children. I blamed Mandodari. She doted on her son like he was the only precious thing in the world. He was so handsome, loving and compassionate, that one could not help adoring the rascal. But, I should have brought him up better. A golden opportunity had been frittered away in battle. Fool!

I went in, wanting to grill him for his stupidity. He smiled at me with glowing pride. I waited for some time as I wished to get him alone. The other fool, Athikaya, was sitting on the floor like a happy mongrel. I wanted to bash the heads of both together, for what they had done. There they sat like heroes after missing the best chance the Asuras could have ever hoped for.

"Ravana, see how his body has been cut, my boy could have been killed." Mandodari sobbed and showed me the various cuts and injuries. Meghanada was actually enjoying all the attention. *'What did she expect? He had gone into battle. This was war. Why was the woman fussing over him?'* Then it struck me. Mandodari was seeing war for the first time. All my other campaigns had been fought in faraway lands. I had worried when I sent him alone to fight, for I knew the horrors that could happen in the fraction of a second on the battlefield. I agonised about the stray arrow that could land in his eye and pop his brains out. If women saw the battlefields where foolish men slaughtered each other, there would have been no wars in this world. I did not have the heart to break into this scene so I went out of the room. Prahastha came to me and bowed. I clasped his hands and led him towards the balcony.

"What do you think? Did Rama die?" I asked, knowing the answer well.

He shook his head.

"The boys botched it up, I think." I said, and he smiled sadly.

"We cannot blame them. Meghanada is too inexperienced and soft, but this could turn out to cost us high." Prahastha avoided my eyes. I could feel the frustration in him. "He should be stopped." Prahastha said, concentrating hard on the distant island where Jambavan had retreated with his injured leader. I looked at him confused.

"Your Highness, the information I got was that both the princes are on the verge of death, but the Vanaras medical knowledge is legendary. They know how to extract life-saving juices from the most unlikely plants. They do not use chemical powders like we do. Instead, they use a system of medicine called Ayurveda, where the thrust is on plants."

"What do you suggest?"

"We are unsure if Rama is alive or not. He was gravely injured and could even be dead by now. But if he is alive, or if the Vanara doctors have somehow miraculously saved him, they will need to brew their medicines. The kind of plants they use are usually found only in three areas of India – in Lanka, on the tropical, south-western coasts of the mainland, and in the Himalayas. The Himalayas are too far. They cannot enter Lanka as it would be too dangerous, but they might try and we have to be alert to such a possibility. The only option left is for them to go to the west coast of the mainland. The Vanaras will explore both options urgently."

"Why don't we attack and take the island tonight?" I was not confident about this option, but I sounded out the idea with Prahastha.

"No. Varuna's fleet is standing guard. It is too risky. What we can do is hope that Rama and Lakshmana die. Then we can cheaply buy off the greedy Vanara King, Sugreeva. Meanwhile, our island security also has to be strengthened. It could be Angada who attempts to get into Lanka. Your Highness, we should alert Lankini, immediately"

Lankini was the Asura governor located at the southern tip of the mainland, where the three oceans met. She had ruled the southern provinces of the mainland with a just and iron hand. Though she was

under my suzerainty, I had stopped my annual visits as she never defaulted in sending huge sums of money for my protection. She should have assisted me in attacking Rama from the rear, but like any good sovereign under my imperial thumb, she sat on the fence to see how things would work out and then align with the winner. I had sent many messages to her for reinforcements, but the letters remained unanswered. I was bitter, but also knew that this was life.

"How will we inform Lankini?" I grew more and more apprehensive about the whole scheme, but somehow, what Prahastha said, made sense. I considered launching an attack on the Vanaras who had withdrawn to the island and weighed the options. But that would be a reckless venture, tempting fate rather too far. No, the best bet was to ensure that Rama died. I felt a pang of pity for my daughter, but brushed it aside hastily.

"We have to move quickly. I'll take one of the snake boats and go myself," Prahastha talked to himself rather than to me. Snake boats had been exclusively used by Mahabali's navy when he had ruled from the west coast of the mainland. They were long and sleek and needed more than 120 oarsmen each. They were ideal in the lagoons that dotted the west coast, but were rarely used in the open sea. But they were the fastest possible way to travel, other than the *Pushpaka*.

"Your Highness, I'll undertake the mission myself. I have to sneak past Varuna's fleet and reach the mainland by dawn. It is dangerous and given a choice, I would have avoided it. But no one knows the waters better than I do. I'm sure the Vanaras will not attempt an attack until their princes recover. I will start now. And it would be a good idea to give the command to Kumbakarna."

Bowing, he left before I could stop him. '*Give my brother command?*' That was easier said than done. My younger brother has been lying drunk for many days. His addiction to drugs and alcohol had become habitual and I could see him wasting away and disintegrating before my eyes. Was it because I sensed a rival in him that I had not made enough of an effort to wean him away from his bad habits? I do not know. I had not even thought about him for many days. I hadn't for a moment thought of Maricha. I had not even spared a though for Akshaya Kumara, my little boy who had been murdered by Hanuman. And now, when I was so short of good men to take command, Prahastha reminded me of my brother. I had to find him in one of the dark holes of the palace and pull him from his dark world of happiness to fight my war. It wasn't going to be easy.

53 Violation

Bhadra

It was in those moments just before the dawn, when the darkness is so thick that you feel it sticking to your skin, that I heard footsteps. My animal instincts had not weakened with age. My ears picked up the sounds of danger even though I was as drunk as a hog. I did not dare raise my head, but somebody was moving silently and that meant trouble. I listened intently for any sound. The last of the oil lamps had died long ago. The sky was overcast and there was no sound other than the intermittent cries of a night fowl. I listened, afraid to even breathe.

This time it was unmistakable. There were many of them. I could sense their presence in the night. They were on the treetops, slowly treading over the hundreds of snoring Asura soldiers. I slowly opened my eyes. I could see the limp figures of the Asura guards at the palace door. I heard a rustle in the trees close to the first floor balcony and some dark figures jumped onto the verandah with graceful ease. It could only be the Vanaras.

A chill went down my spine. *'Why are they here?'* The guards were drunk from yesterday's victory party and had passed out. Slowly I crawled towards the palace on all fours. I feared the worst. As I reached the doors, I could see the guards had been killed, their throats slit open. The enemy was inside. Should I shout and make a noise? But would anyone wake up? I had to warn Ravana. I knew where the royal chambers were. But I was afraid. The enemy could have been anywhere. In the dark shadows of the palace, death was waiting to pounce on me. I had always believed that I was ready to die. If I died, nobody would bother, perhaps not even my wife, certainly not my son. Still I wanted to live. I knew what was at stake if Ravana lost. My people would die a thousand deaths all their lives at the hands of the Brahmins. I pushed my tired body, trembling at the slightest sound, afraid even to breath, to the first floor where I knew Ravana slept. That is, if he was not already dead. I wished I had more strength in my body and that I was young and daring again.

I climbed up the stairs on tiptoe, avoiding the slightest sound. I heard a muffled cry and then a thud and the noise of something being dragged. With my heart pounding, I peeped from the stairs and saw a few Vanaras scamper away. I recognized their evil prince, Angada. He carried a limp form on his shoulder and was running from the room. Some of the guards who were still sober had finally woken up and tried to stop Angada. He did not even break stride, just thrust and hacked his way through the stunned guards with his sword. I rushed to the entrance of the royal chamber and found the guards lying in pools of blood. The guards who had dared to confront the Vanara prince were dead or writhing in pain with their guts spilled out and blood spurting all over the beautiful carpets.

I looked at the swinging doors of the chamber and hesitated for a few seconds. Then bracing myself to see the Emperor with a dagger stuck into his heart, I pushed open the door. The chamber was empty. There were no dead bodies anywhere. Only the bed looked as if it had witnessed some struggle. Then it occurred to me. '*Angada had carried away Mandodari, the Asura Queen. He had come with murder in mind but not finding the Emperor in his chamber, had kidnapped his wife instead. Ravana had to be informed. Where was he?*' I ran through the corridors of the palace, banging on doors and crying loudly, calling for Athikaya. Many people woke up and I shouted at the top of my voice that the Queen had been kidnapped by Angada. Initially there was no reaction. No doubt many thought I was blabbering after having had too much liquor. Then the panic started. The guards woke and ran here and there like headless chickens. Many wailed loudly, some shouting orders, but there was no one to obey them, and others sat blinking and not understanding what the ruckus was all about.

It was almost half an hour before I located Meghanada and Athikaya. I kicked my son awake and he jumped up from his drunken stupor. Anybody could have come in and murdered the Asura Prince and his servant. So much for Asura security. If someone wanted one reason for the downfall of the mighty Asuras, it could be summed up in the word, liquor. It was the bane of my race. The Prince came to his senses quickly and by the time I had explained what had happened, he was alert. He jumped up, drew his sword and ran out. I followed the Prince, shouting what I had seen. Athikaya caught up with us when we crossed the front courtyard and Meghanada ran towards the fort bell. Meghanada took the stairs at the double. I was exhausted and did not follow him up. Athikaya darted past me, trying to catch up with the Prince. Soon the entire fort rang with the continuous peels of the huge fort bell. *'Why hadn't I thought of that myself?'* Within minutes, the entire courtyard was full of alert guards.

"What is going on?" The loud voice of Ravana boomed across the courtyard as the Emperor rushed towards the bell tower. Meghanada explained what had happened and Ravana's face went white. Then the colour rushed back. His anger was back as he slammed his fist on the bell tower wall, sending dust and plaster flying. "Catch that bastard Angada and bring him to me."

"Father, I will lead the search. This could be a trap and you should remain in the palace. If the Vanaras attack when the fort is left without a leader, we will be in deep trouble."

"You remain here Meghanada. It is my wife they have dared to kidnap. I will lead the search party and teach those bastards a lesson. And I think the time has come to wake up Kumbha. I need him desperately. I have been trying to put some sense into that oaf's thick head the whole night."

Ravana mounted his favourite horse and plunged into the darkness. The search party, with hundreds of soldiers carrying flaming torches, struggled to keep pace with the galloping Asura Emperor. Soldiers ran behind the horses with their spears and clubs, making a lot of noise, but generally useless for anything other than making a nuisance of themselves. I joined them.

By the time we reached the edge of the Subela hills, the horses had been abandoned and the search parties were almost a quarter of the way up the steep hills. The thick, dark jungle of Subela with its huge, overhanging boulders, loomed large and formidable. I was not sure my tired, old body could take the rigours of the climb. But curiosity is a great motivator and I dragged my body up, panting and puffing, to catch up with the young guards who had enthusiastically followed the path made by the official search party.

Only the occasional flicker of torches through the thick foliage guided us. Twice I tripped and fell, but ignoring the pain, and suppressing my fear of the poisonous snakes that abounded in these forests, I tried hard to keep up with men twenty-five years younger than me. I found I was stronger than I had believed. The memories of such adventures I had been a part of, with the same man who was now the Emperor; when both of us were younger; the heady feeling of daredevilry and courage; the youthful thrill of facing danger with ease; came flooding back to me and I felt many years younger than at the start of the chase.

We were all perspiring copiously and panting hard by the time we reached the small clearing, hundreds of feet below the peak. We could see the earlier search parties huddled together in the distance. The eastern sky had a streak of grey and the stars had grown dimmer. Many of the torches had died down. I sat down to catch my breath as the younger ones in my group rushed to their friends at the edge of the clearing. Then slowly I dragged myself uphill.

I pushed my way through the crowd. There, lying on the bare earth, was the Queen, naked and unconscious. Ravana stood, stunned, weeping silently. I stepped forward and taking off my tattered shawl, covered the naked body of the Queen of the Asuras. My hands brushed against her breasts and she stirred. Slowly she opened her eyes. Ravana caught her in his arms and hugged her. She looked at the crowd gawking at her for a moment, without comprehension. Then her nudity, her shame, the violation, dawned on her. She let out an animal cry and tried to cover herself in my stinking shawl. She scrambled up and tried to run. With a jerk, Ravana caught her arm and hugged her tightly. She buried her face in his shoulder and wept. The crowd reluctantly moved away. Some ran to fetch water, others collected some clothes for their Queen, and some put together a makeshift stretcher to carry the Queen back. I stood nearby, wondering at the twist of fate. She repeatedly said she did not wish to continue living with this shame. Angada and his boors had violated her when they realized that she was not Sita, as they had at first thought. She did not want to remain Ravana's wife anymore; she wanted to die.

Ravana did not speak at all except to say that she was his lawfully wedded wife and that she would remain so. It was embarrassing to witness his intensely private pain. But I felt a growing admiration for the man who thus stood by his wife in her trial. As a ruler, nothing worse could have happened to him, not even his own death. The Queen was forever tainted and the easiest thing for him would have been to fling her away like a used rag. But he chose the tough way, to live with snickering subordinates who would make lewd comments about his wife the moment his back was turned. Perhaps, in such choices lay his greatness and also his weakness. At the time, I doubt whether I completely appreciated his gesture towards his violated Queen. It was later, much later, when I witnessed the behaviour of another man towards his chosen wife, in circumstance that were much less serious, that I understood why Ravana would never be deified. He was too humane to be a God.

I wanted to slip away silently, but Ravana saw me moving away. "Bhadra," he called and I stopped to turn back. I could see he was both embarrassed and angry that I had witnessed what was essentially a private moment. He did not look at me but asked, "Where is Meghanada?" I did not know, but someone answered that the Prince and Athikaya were pursuing Angada and his men.

"I hope the bastard is caught alive." I felt sorry for my King. He was trying to pick up the pieces of his shattered dignity. Soon, a makeshift palanquin was assembled and the King and Queen were lifted up and carried down the treacherous path towards the palace.

"Fancy that, the King will now taste the leftovers of a dirty monkey." one of the younger soldiers commented. Many around him snickered.

"He should have finished her off then. Now, imagine the shame of having a queen dragged by her hair and stripped naked by a monkey. Who knows what else he would have done to her," another joined in. There were more sniggers and whistles.

"Have a heart, you bastards." one of the older soldier shouted back. "What he did was truly noble and right. How many men would accept a wife who has been shamed like this?" There was a lot of laughter until the captain of the group turned back and shouted, "You boys will not understand. Had you been born when the Devas were raiding and razing city after city, you would not have spoken this way. You owe your dignity to the man you are making fun of for standing by his wife at the time of her need."

A lot of jeering and snickering followed the old soldier's words. Cursing them profusely, he became silent. I thought about what he had said. *'Was it such a great thing that the King had done? I too had done the same thing. That King raped my wife and sired my son, Athikaya. Didn't I bring him up like my own? Did I throw my wife away?'* The more I thought about it, the more I believed that what had happened to the queen was sweet justice. I felt sorry for her, but he was reaping what he had sown. There was nothing noble about accepting one's wife, even if she had been raped, and here there was doubt. If you were a man, you stood by your wife. Or you were a swine. There was nothing great about it. But, perhaps the standards expected from a common Asura and those expected from the nobility, were different. The nobles were expected to be bastards. So what Ravana had done proves he was crude and common like any other Asura. Strangely, the thought that he was like us was comforting. Maybe there was some hope if he won the war with Rama.

As we neared the palace, I saw that the shawl that I had covered the Queen with, was lying discarded on the path. I barely recognize it. It had become even more tattered and torn, more like a dirty rag, after having been stamped upon by so many marching feet. Initially I thought of kicking it into the open sewer, but on second thoughts, I bent and picked it up. Maybe this humble rag had served its purpose for queens and kings, but for a poor man like me, it might still be useful. I could perhaps mend it and reuse it. I did not have a spare one, so I had to make do with what I had. Maybe, if I washed it carefully, it would wash away the smell of the Angadas and Ravanas.

54 The end of an idealist

Ravana

The still body of Prahastha was brought to the palace at sunset. When I came out of my personal hell where I was hiding with my wife, he lay on the cold floor of the *durbar* hall. His body had turned blue and he looked older than he was. He looked worn out with the worries of an empire, with the plotting and planning, thwarted ambitions, straight jacketed self righteousness, by the impossible wish to strictly adhere to *dharma* and a thoroughly colourless life. I suppressed a tear for my best friend and worst enemy. I leaned down towards his lifeless body. A few tears tore themselves away from my hard practiced self-restraint and made a strange pattern on the floor. *'Who was this man?'* Once, long ago, I had been afraid of him. I had been sure that he was after my throne. He had been all that I always wanted to be, but never could be. He was all that I never wished to be, but could have been. He had been the restraint that had kept the wild beast within me leashed. He had been my conscience. He had been what kept me from becoming a *Rakshasa*. I had feared him more than anyone. And in my heart, I was sure that he would have been a better leader for the Asuras than me.

He was the ideal Asura leader, the real successor to Mahabali. Brave, moral, honest, upright, incorruptible. He would not have invited the disaster that was Rama onto us, like I had done. He would not have strayed from the right path. He might not have built such a vast empire but he would not have fallen hopelessly in love with Vedavathi. He would not have thought twice about sacrificing a daughter for the Asura cause or if he had believed the prophecy to be nonsense, he would have had the courage to proclaim it to the world. Once he lost his daughter to Janaka, he would not have lacked the courage to get her back through force or diplomacy. He would have brought his daughter home long ago. Nor would he have let his wife be molested by monkey-men. But. . .perhaps, he would not have taken her back and loved her in quite the same way, because of the shame. He would not have done many of the things I had done, but then, he would not have been Prahastha or I Ravana.

My courtiers remained silent. Jambumali was most distraught. Prahastha had been his friend from childhood. They belonged to the same generation in their thinking. When old friends die, they take something of your life with them. I wanted to hug the old man in his distress, but did not have the courage to face anyone. I had to be practical. Prahastha had to be cremated before sunset. I wanted to hug Prahastha's still body and tell him that, more than anyone else, I had respected and loved him. I also wanted to tell him that he had always got on my nerves with his unwarranted advise and talk about Asura *dharma*. Suddenly I hated him from deep within. '*You were after my throne. And you would have been a much better king, for you were a much better human being than me.*' If he had been King and I the Prime Minister, how would I have behaved? I couldn't even imagine that as I could not have remained in that position for long. I would have got rid of my master and assumed my rightful position. '*This man had so many chances to do that to me. He could have poisoned me, had me stabbed while we shared beds during our campaigns; he could have got rid of me in a hundred ways.*' But even the cynic in me did not think Prahastha would have done that. I had trusted him. He had been too deeply tied to his own principles and *dharma* to stoop so low to assume kingship. He prized his soul more than a blood-stained throne.

I stood up and a junior administrative officer came and bowed. I ordered that the funeral arrangements be made quickly. Then things happened in a blur. The people who were proficient in the matters of last rites took over. My Prime Minister was covered with the red Asura flag and his bier lifted up. I too wished to put my shoulder to it, but thought it would be rather melodramatic. After all, I was still the King. So I walked behind the humble funeral procession. People had lined both sides of the road and filled the balconies and treetops. The procession snaked its way through the war-ravaged road, through the streets that had seen a thousand violent deaths. I was shocked to see what had happened to my beautiful city.

I wanted it to end so I could go home and sleep. I was tired. Yet I had to do my duty. I owed that much to my slain friend and dearest foe. I walked amidst the weeping crowd and was surprised to see how popular he had been. He had never reached out to people and he had taken many unpopular decisions. But he stood his ground when it came to doing what was right rather than what was popular. And he was always fair. That was something new to me. People loved you not for the short-term popular things you did for them as a ruler, but because you were just. The country silently wept for a man who had been like a strict father to them.

And suddenly, I was afraid of the past. All that had stood between Prahastha and my throne was his sense of fairness and doing the right thing. All these people who were thronging to catch a glimpse of Prahastha, could have just cremated their own loved ones just a few hours before. Still they thought it was important to be here. Had he made one call to these people, I would have been swept away like a feather in the wind. But Prahastha had never lived in the palace and would vanish to his country home a few miles away from the city whenever he could. He always said that the country air suited him better. Thinking back, he had never once mentioned his family, had never recommended a relative for a government job, or sought little favours from me like most of the others around me had. I had put it down to his bloated ego and resented it. But now, as the funeral procession wound its way to his country home, I could see that he had chosen to do so because of his convictions. The neighbourhood he had lived in was neither posh nor rich, but had a rural charm and the people were rustic.

The procession halted before what looked like a peasant's dwelling. It was Prahastha's home, a neat and clean hut, with a thatched roof that gave it a cozy feel. The yard was neat. There was a cowshed and a well nearby, a few fruit trees and flowering vines, and a duck pond. I now understood why my Prime Minister wished to escape from my gaudy palace to this rustic haven. It was not poverty he had chosen, but rich simplicity. I had not known this side of the man I had once hated and feared. There were many people, not the rich and social types, but poor villagers and petty officials, who stood in groups. As I moved in, a sudden hush fell and I felt I was intruding into their private grief. A man who resembled Prahastha came out and bowed. Someone whispered that he was the Prime Minister's son. I patted his shoulder and walked in. In the darkness of the hut, I could discern the smooth forms of women, hunched over in grief. A woman slowly stood up and walked towards me. As the light fell on her face, I recognized my slain Prime Minister's wife.

"I am deeply sorry," I said, but my words sounded hollow even to me. She did not move, just stood there. I grew uneasy. I had never been comfortable with ceremonies of death. They reminded me of my own mortality. I could hear the men of the family cutting down a huge mango tree to prepare the pyre. It was our Asura custom to plant a mango tree when a baby was born. The tree grew with the child and gave its fruits to all living things, making the world a better place. The child was expected to do the same when he grew up. And when it was time for the final journey, the tree gave its final sacrifice for its namesake, vanishing into the smoke of the funeral pyre, along with its companion.

Finally it was over. Prahastha and whatever he had stood for, turned into formless smoke and slowly vanished into thin air. The grief throbbing through the people made me jealous. But they slowly dispersed to their own lives, to their own woes. It had grown dark and the crickets were chirping. My attendants waited outside for me to make a move. I emerged from my stupor. I felt heavy hearted and wanted to say some soothing words to the widow and the son or perhaps his daughter. '*What kind of a leader was I? I didn't even know how many children my Prime Minister had. Where had the lofty thoughts of my youth gone? What happened to the ideas I had carried, about being a caring leader, a man of empathy and kindness? In what poor condition my Prime Minister had left his family. They were peasants now, dirt poor.*' When the lord of the house had been Prime Minister of the empire, their simplicity had charm. Maybe it had even been a political plus. But they were nothing but poor wretches now and it was my duty to help them.

I was about to send for Prahastha's son, when he appeared and bowed respectfully. With some hesitation he deposited a bundle of silken cloth at my feet and bowed again. One of guards looked at me. Reading my consent, he opened it in front of me. I was furious. The bundle contained a gold bracelet with the Asura insignia on it, a gold chain with its gold-tipped tiger claws' and a few neatly folded silk dresses. They were the personnel possessions of Prahastha, the only vanity he had allowed himself when he attended my court.

"What is this?" My hands had gone to the hilt of my sword.

The young man stood silently for a moment and it seemed I had frightened him. Then slowly he raised his eyes and said, "Forgive us, your Highness. It was our father's wish. He used to say that these did not belong to us, but to the people of the country. They had just allowed him to wear these ornaments, like the uniform of the palace guards. The moment he resigned or retired or died, the same was to be returned to the King, who would hold them on behalf of the people. I am just obeying my father's wishes."

There was a deathly silence. Then, like water draining out of a leaky jug, my indignation melted away. Tears welled in my eyes. Prahastha had been the one who deserved to be Emperor of the Asuras. But then, had he had my charm? Had he possessed the ruthlessness I did? Maybe he had possessed all these, but he had chosen to live and die by something beyond them. Above all, this country had chosen me over him, that was the nasty truth, and he knew it. I had become the ruler. This country and its stupid people had not deserved Prahastha. They deserved me or even worse, selfish rascals like my brother Vibhishana, who would sell the country and his kin for a fistful of gold to the white-skinned invaders from across the sea.

I walked away from Prahastha's humble hut. I already missed his arguments, his stubbornness, his advice. I longed for our youth and the tense relationship we had shared. If I came out of this war alive, I would build up my empire again, but with more compassion, more probity for government servants, more transparency in governance, and make it less bureaucratic and more people oriented. Prahastha may perhaps have had more influence on me dead than alive. I hoped his sacrifice would not be wasted, but then, which sacrifice had not been a waste?

Lankini. She betrayed us. But then, I had half expected it. Asuras would not be Asuras without betrayals. That had been why I had wanted Prahastha to stop Hanuman with the help from the wily Governor of Kanyakumari. *'How could all this happen in one day? Yesterday, we were on the verge of a stupendous victory. Now the tables were turned.'*

The reports I received were sketchy, but the picture that emerged was typical. Prahastha had been delayed by bad weather and by the time he reached the mainland, Lankini had struck a deal with Hanuman. Lankini, who had a lot to gain in siding with Rama, let Prahastha believe that Hanuman had yet to reach the mainland and insisted that he rest. Prahastha's food had been laced with drugs and then Lankini had stabbed him to death in his drug-induced sleep. By then, Hanuman had returned with the essential medicinal plants he had been sent to fetch for the princes. I did not know whether they had succeeded in reviving Rama and Lakshmana but Lankini had been audacious enough to send the slain body of my Prime Minister to me. I decided that once I had finished off Rama, I would ask Lankini some pertinent questions.

I was so tired of the war. But I didn't have the power to stop it. The juggernaut rolled on. It would stop when the time was right and not when the participants wished. And it would destroy whatever came in its way – pride, power, life, honour, everything.

It had grown dark by the time I reached the palace. The torches sputtered in the cold, salty breeze that came from the sea and the world danced around in the ever-changing play of light and shadow. The sky was an inky blanket with holes where the stars flickered, faded, and glowed bright again. I was tired but hesitated to go to my bedroom and face my wife. I went instead to see my daughter. The night was cold and she was all alone under that Ashoka tree, where she still lived. I thought of my sons, Meghanada, Akshaya, and even Athikaya. I hoped Rama was dead and the monkey-men had returned to their jungle kingdom. There followed a few seconds of bliss, when all thoughts ceased.

From far away, where the sea was a moving grey living thing, faint sounds of cheering rose from that island hidden in the darkness. I had my answer. . .Rama was alive and the next day he would attack me with a vengeance. Somehow I found the thought comforting. War, after all, was a catharsis for my numbed soul. One way or the other it would be decided soon.

A soldier stood before me and bowed, "Your Highness, Prince Kumbakarna is awake and seeks audience." With a nod of my head I gave permission and Kumbha walked in. The moment I saw his face, I knew there was going to be trouble.

55 Kumbhakarna's attack

Bhadra

Rama and Lakshmana were saved by some miraculous Vanara medicine. The brief splutter of hope that had arisen in our hearts, died. I watched mutely, too exhausted to even stand up, as the fort gates opened and hordes of Asuras marched to meet Rama and his monkey-men once again. Riding amidst the column, on a tall elephant, was Prince Kumbakarna. This march was different. The majority of soldiers did not not carry bows and arrows or swords. The front columns carried long, bamboo poles sharpened at the edges. They were followed by Kumbakarna, who led a platoon of war elephants. There were no chariots this time. They were a disadvantage on the soft, white, sandy beaches of Lanka. Kumbakarna, in a single day had found the weakness in the Asura defence. The Asuras had been fighting the war like they would have on the plains of the mainland. It was a good defence strategy and suddenly I felt enthusiastic and trotted along with the marching soldiers, unmindful of the danger. Kumbakarna was taking the battle to the enemy camp.

I found that many commoners had joined the ranks. A few were my acquaintances and they invited me to join them. It was madness, but I joined them anyway. The column stretched for miles behind us. It was then that I saw two shining figures on horseback. The sun was behind them so I could not see their faces.

"There is prince Meghanada and his servant," said the part-time barber who doubled as assistant to the priest of the street temple near my home.

He carried a stone club much too big for him. I then recognized, to my horror, Prince Meghanada on the white horse and Athikaya faithfully following him on a black horse. In the sea of club brandishing and black, glistening bodies of Asuras, the two of them stood out and their ornaments glittered in the sun. *'They were easy targets for Vanara shooters. How foolish can the young be?'* I tried push my way towards my son and the Prince, but was carried away in the tide of marching fighters.

I could see the long column of Vanaras stretching to the sea. There were many more on the bridge which they had rebuilt. Varuna's ships stretched right to the horizon. There were Vanaras everywhere on the beach, screaming and creating a din, as well as on the boats that were being launched from the ships. The first arrow from one of the flame-throwers on Varuna's ship, whooshed overhead. Men screamed. The Asura archers who were perched on the trees on the cliff, showered arrows back on the Vanaras landing on the beach. Many Vanaras fell, but like locusts they kept on coming.

Kumbakarna called a halt before our army reached the clearing on the beach. Swift orders were passed and there was a lot of confusion. Captains screamed commands and there was a lot of pushing and jostling, but finally the army spread out in an arch, in the cover of the tress instead of stepping into the clearing. The Asuras waited. The elephants had giant logs and trees in their trunks and waited at the edge of the clearing. I could see Prince Meghanada getting restless on his horse and pushing his way towards the Commander. He finally succeeded in reaching Prince Kumbakarna, followed faithfully by Athikaya.

Suddenly the murmur in the Asura ranks died down. The two Princes were arguing. Kumbakarna got more and more agitated, but Meghanada kept screaming at his uncle. Athikaya too joined in abusing Kumbakarna. Meghanada wanted to attack immediately, but Kumbakarna had a plan which Meghanada did not think was brilliant. He called Kumbakarna a coward and an old woman and the Commander ordered his men to arrest Meghanada and Athikaya. The situation became ugly. Kumbakarna's men circled Meghanada and Athikaya with their swords drawn. Meghanada's men fought their way towards their leader and soon the fight had spread to the whole army. Asuras do not need Devas to be defeated. I just wanted to get out.

It was at this moment that a few Vanara soldiers chose to rush out of the woods. The Vanara Commander, Jambavan, screamed at them to stay back, but I saw that the foolish raid was led by none other than Prince Angada. *'Why do the young try foolish things to defy the old and more experienced elders?'* Kumbakarna gave the order to attack and the infighting stopped. The elephants advanced, massive hills of flesh with huge logs in their trucks, they moved with unbelievable speed towards the Vanara army. Angada and his men, who were full of enthusiasm and bravado a few minutes before, tottered in their advance and took to their heels towards the safety of their group. But the mighty mountains advanced relentlessly, smashing the Vanara ranks and driving the panic stricken monkey-men into the sea. From the rear, the Asura army advanced and caught the fleeing Vanaras trying to desperately escape, and clubbed them to their death.

The elephants wrecked havoc in the Vanara ranks. The column of men brandishing long poles, pierced the Vanara ranks. Soon the hairy men were in a state of panic and despair. From the cliff, huge boulders rolled down on the fleeing Vanaras. Angada was caught by a war elephant which flung him far away. The arrogant Vanara prince landed with a sickening thud among his fleeing troupes. He would have got trampled by his own people but managed to scramble up and dislodge one of the riders fleeing the battle scene. In disgust I saw the coward fleeing for his life towards his own camp while the man he had unseated, died under the galloping horses.

The flame throwing from the ships had stopped as they retreated to the high seas. Soon the Asuras had gained a clear edge in the battle that was being fought on the land and the sea. I didn't venture into the frontlines and watched the Vanara men being torn limb from limb and trampled by the elephants. By afternoon, the Asuras had advanced onto Rama's bridge and were chasing the fleeing Vanaras. A small group of Vanaras led by the spirited Hanuman, was all that was left between Rama and the complete annihilation of his army. Hanuman, effectively controlled and utilized his men, creating a great din with huge drums that confused the elephants, all the time shooting well aimed arrows at the men riding the animals.

I wondered where Meghanada had gone, when a curious whirring sound ripped through the air. The noise increased and many people stopped hacking each other to death and actually looked up. Flying low over this crowd, was Meghanada in Mayan's flying contraption. The huge fans of the machine whirred furiously, whipping up sand and water. I could also see Athikaya in the machine and they were shooting flame-tipped arrows at the Vanaras. Some of the Asuras cheered on their hero but I saw Kumbakarna's face twist in anger. He shouted something which no one could hear and gestured frantically at the *Pushpaka*, but was only answered by a daring manoeuvre of the flying machine that almost touched the Commander's crown. Kumbakarna tried hard to control his elephants. They were edgy and did not respond to the commands of their *mahout*s.

Many of the flame-tipped arrows found their mark and many Vanaras were killed. But with the Asuras busy watching the spectacle in the sky, the pace of the attack slowed down considerably. It was then that disaster struck. With a curious change in sound, the flying contraption sputtered, its fans slowed, and then it fell like a stone into the water near the bridge. It sank and then bobbed up to the surface. My heart sank. '*My son, Athikaya*!' I rushed forward but was stopped by stronger men hurrying to see the spectacle.

By the time I got a clear view, I saw that Meghanada had managed to climb onto the bridge and was trying to pull up the contraption. Hanuman, seeing his chance, commanded his men to move forward and capture the Prince. Athikaya clambered onto the bridge and tried to aid the prince in pulling up the machine. Kumbakarna rushed forward to save the Prince. In his excitement, Kumbakarna was some distance ahead of his army, trying to reach his nephew before Hanuman could get to him. Kumbakarna's great elephant was hardly ten feet from Meghanada when an iron-tipped arrow pierced the elephant's head and entered almost two feet into its brain. The great body shuddered violently as it crashed down, trumpeting loudly. Kumbakarna was thrown from his mount.

Arrows whizzed past Meghanada and Athikaya, but fortunately none found their mark. They had almost managed to get the machine onto the bridge and were using it as cover. Many of the arrows struck the machine or zinged past it. Kumbakarna ran towards his dead elephant to get his club. I could see Rama and Lakshmana, sitting on the shoulders of mighty Vanara men, shooting arrows at Kumbakarna and Meghanada. The Asura army hesitated, too shocked to believe what was happening in front of them. Hanuman and his men were only a few feet from Meghanada, while Kumbakarna tried to pull his club out from under the mighty carcass of his elephant.

I watched in rising panic, when that wily, old rascal, Jambavan, cleverly used the moment to instruct his flame throwers to aim at the elephants. On the beach, the elephants moved as a mighty wall and were easier to control. On the narrow bridge, where one elephant followed the other with a heaving sea beneath, the animals became unwieldy. When one of the flaming missiles found its mark, the elephant panicked, turned around, and ran back at great speed. It crashed into the elephant following it, which in turn panicked. Soon there was total chaos in the Asura ranks. Elephants ran amok, smashing everything in their path. A few ran towards the Vanara ranks, barely missing Meghanada and Kumbakarna, leaving death and destruction in their trail. But the majority of the panic stricken elephants ran towards the Asura ranks. A few fell into the water.

I ran for my life and clambered up a coconut palm. Below, men on both sides fought the beasts rather than one another. With a mighty crash, the bridge collapsed. Meghanada, Athikaya and Kumbakarna were struck on the other side, with thousands of enemies against them. The Vanara army succeeded in slaying the few elephants that had strayed to their side. Kumbakarna had succeeded in freeing his heavy club and stood brandishing it between Hanuman's men and Meghanada and Athikaya. The Asura army was in disarray. Meghanada and Athikaya, to my surprise, had got into the flying machine and were trying to get it to fly. '*They weren't trying to defend their uncle.*' Kumbakarna continued forward using his heavy club to deflect a few arrows as he advanced swiftly to crush the heads of Hanuman's men.

Kumbakarna was too close. Rama and Lakshmana, and the other archers could not get the range to strike Kumbakarna as he almost merged with them. He smacked the Vanaras with his huge club, smashing their skulls and limbs before they could brandish their swords or aim their arrows. And so one man single handedly held the mighty Vanara army on that narrow bridge. Jambavan shouted at his men on the boats to surround Kumbakarna and attack his rear. But some Asuras had regained their wits and prevented Jambavan's boats from getting within shooting distance of Kumbakarna. The battle started in the sea again. I could see Varuna's ships turn back. Canoes were launched at a distance and fast approached the shore. *'How long could we hold on? How swiftly fortunes had changed and all because of that foolish Meghanada showing off.'*

By this time Sugreeva, the Vanara King, and Hanuman, had broken through the ranks, brandishing huge, iron clubs themselves. I tried to train my eyes on the enemy chief. *'Where had Rama and Lakshmana gone?'* They seemed to have vanished. The fans of the flying machine started rotating slowly, sputtered and stopped, and then, after a few moments, whirred again and stopped. All this time, Kumbakarna had been fighting a duel with Hanuman and Sugreeva. Alone, he held off the two great warriors while his nephew fiddled with the flying contraption. The Asura army was now leaderless, and saw both their Princes struck in the middle of the enemy, fighting for their lives.

With a strong blow, Kumbakarna sent Sugreeva crashing into the water, but Hanuman broke through his defence and rushed towards Meghanada. Kumbakarna turned and almost flew to catch Hanuman by his feet. Both warriors went down fighting. A few arrows struck Kumbakarna and Hanuman too was injured. The western sky had turned red when I saw Kumbakarna lift Hanuman up and smash him on the floor with great violence. Hanuman lay there without any movement and I uttered a jubilant cheer. At that moment, an arrow struck Kumbakarna's neck from behind and the tip that pierced his throat, caught the crimson rays of the setting sun. Slowly, the huge body of the brave Asura prince collapsed lifeless onto the bridge and then crashed into the sea, taking a huge chunk of the bridge along with him. Finally, Jambhavan had managed to gain a strategic position and Rama, an expert at shooting arrows at people from behind, had not missed this time either.

With horror, the Asuras watched their Commander die and the Vanara army rushed in to finish off the trapped Prince and his servant in their contraption. I felt dizzy. Was I going to witness my son being torn to pieces? Then Hanuman stirred and the Vanara army who had thought that their general was dead, were taken by surprise. They halted as Hanuman came to life slowly. He staggered and swayed and steadied himself on the flying machine, when its fans suddenly came to life. He panicked and jumped back, and before the Vanaras could comprehend what had happened, the fan started rotating furiously. Jambavan cried out orders to stop the machine as it lifted. The monkeys rushed forward shooting arrows, throwing clubs, and hurling themselves on the machine that was quickly rising. A few brave ones tried to hold on and got chopped into pieces by the rotating blades.

As the sun set, the Prince and my son escaped in their machine to the safety of Ravana's palace, leaving the poorer folks to the mercy of the Vanaras. And the men who had left their families for the greater glory of their race, fought and killed, and got killed. So also the poor Vanaras who fought for the glory of someone they had never even heard of a few months ago. Later, when Jambavan ordered his men back and the Vanaras retreated to their island, I climbed down from my perch. On my way back, I scared a few jackals and bandicoots who were feasting, and without a second thought, stepped over the dead body of the part-time cook and priest who had shown me the impressive sight of Prince Meghanada that morning. Another Prince, Kumbakarna, was now food for the sharks, who fortunately did not value heroism and enjoyed both heroes and villains with equal delight. I would have given anything for a drink. It was a beautiful night, dark and strange, a night to get drunk and sleep like a log.

56 While they pray

Ravana

I was fuming at Mandodari. I wanted to finish off my son. Fool! I did not know what to make of him. Sometimes he showed great valour; he thought and behaved maturely and showed real leadership; at other times he made an ass of himself. The reports I received were clear. It had been this fool's bravado that had lost us the best general in the war. Kumbha's death hurt me much more than Prahastha's and Maricha's.

Twice in the last two days, my son had fritted away the chance to win. And the fool always rushed to the safety of his mother. And what was that black rascal doing in the King's chamber? He stood discretely, trying to hide his huge frame. I rushed towards Meghanada but once again Mandodari intervened, "Leave the boys alone, Ravana."

"Leave the boys, leave the boys, indeed! When will this idiot grow up? It is the company he keeps that has made him thick-headed." I glared at Athikaya, who seemed strangely hurt.

"Ravana, do not make me say things I will regret later. Do you really want me to remind you why this war began? Do you want me to say that the entire Asura race is being destroyed because of your adamancy and pride? Please do not let my tongue speak."

I felt helpless in my anger. It hurt because it was true. "Mandodari, mind your words. You are speaking to the Emperor of the Asuras." The words sounded ridiculous even to me.

She just glared at me, "Ravana, it would be best if you go and rest."

I stood there for some time not knowing what to do. Then I walked away. I felt lonely and let down, bitter and angry. Why did such terrible things have to happen to me? Why was I so unhappy and unlucky in life? Why did I have to struggle for everything? I would never have committed the stupid mistakes that my pampered son had done. He would one day inherit the largest empire the world had ever seen.

Kumbha, my brother, I forsook you long ago. I never tried to stop your slide. Maybe I even encouraged it as it suited me. I was afraid of you. I could see the ambition fluttering in your mind and feel your envy. You wanted to be King. Little did you know the perils of kingship or how power corrupts and corrodes the soul. You drowned your ambitions in opium and wine, but the opium of power I took, was far more potent than anything you had. Your intoxications fed on constant intake of poison, mine in many acts of tyranny. You were a giant asleep in your ignorance, I was a little man wide awake in my power. Your ambition was raw and your feelings always transparent. You made me afraid for I loved my throne more than you. I loved power even more than myself. I feared that one day you would wake up and plot behind my back for my throne. When wine claimed you, I was relieved. Yet I kept a watch, I ensured that you remain intoxicated and asleep.

You Kumbha, were the one who disturbed my sleep. But when treachery came, it did not come from you. It came from the little brother we were all fond of. How we used to pull his leg, laugh behind his back, and make up amusing stories about the Asura boy who desperately tried to be a Brahmin. Now the joke is on us. The enemy is at our gates and our little brother is leading them in with a torch. He is about to steal our dreams and turn them into nightmares. My mistake brother, my mistake. Forgive me, for I thought you were the dangerous one and forgot to keep an eye on the snake.

Kumbha, you were always right. I remember that you had expressed doubts about Vibhishana's sincerity long ago. But I was naïve and thought you were plotting behind my back, trying to make me fight the younger one so that your path to the power would be smooth. But when I needed you, when this godforsaken Asura race needed direction, I sought your help. You were courageous enough to point out my folly, but desisted from advising me too much. Now I realize who you were, but it is too late. The war is turning against us. Soon, the civilization that we reclaimed, the ideals of equality for all men, the beautiful cities and palaces, the majestic temples and royal highways, the ports where merchant ships waited for the finest spices and cloths, the art and theatre, will all be crushed under the feet of a Deva tyrant. You are lucky. You won't be there when the great Asura dream vanishes without a trace. You will not be there when Brahmins will be the brain; Deva warriors the limbs; and crooked men like Kubera, the torso of our grand society. A society our little brother wishes to build on our corpses. Brother, you have gone beyond the misfortunes of mere mortals. I might soon follow you. My only fear is, when I meet you again, will I be able to look you in the eye?

Mandodari came and stood near me. Her touch broke my thoughts. "Ravana, the boy is heartbroken by what happened to his uncle and thinks it is his fault."

"It is his fault. War is not a place to show off his daredevilry to impress people. Losing Kumbha is the biggest setback for us and I am ashamed that my son was the cause of it. I do not want him in the battlefield anymore. The Asuras cannot afford such mistakes."

"Ravana, the boy is already devastated. . . can't you forgive him?"

My anger was roused again. "It is the company he keeps. What business does he have to tow that black servant along with him. . ." I faltered before the look in Mandodari's eyes.

"Enough Ravana, enough. Why continue this war? Why don't we compromise? Why not give Rama his wife back?" She was almost sobbing.

"You think I don't have any honour or pride? After losing my best men, my brother, my friends, you want me to fall at Rama's feet? You want the Emperor of the Asuras to beg for mercy from a small time adventurer and prince of a tiny barbarian vassal kingdom?"

"The barbarian prince of a tiny vassal kingdom has swallowed more than half of the Asura empire now. How many men do you want to lose before you stop this stupid war? For whose sake are you fighting this. . ."

"This war is for the honour of the Asuras. A war to stop the spread casteism and Brahmin hierarchy. . ."

"Save your political speeches to fool the masses. You are fighting this war for your own selfish reasons."

"Mandodari, you are forgetting that this is the same Prince who insulted my sister and disfigured her. Are you saying I should swallow that?"

"The same sister who you made a widow. . ."

"Enough! What do women understand about. . ."

"I understand well enough, Ravana. Spare me the noble face that you want to project to your foolish subjects. You are a creature of passion. Irreverent, arrogant and lustful. You want to project yourself as a rational man who is not swayed by the superstitions and irrational beliefs that plague the common Asura. But in your heart, you are as superstitious, as afraid as anyone in the street. What prevented you from bringing back our daughter from Janaka when you regained your power? How many hours would Mithila have lasted, had you launched an invasion? But you were afraid. You were afraid that if our little daughter came back, she would bring destruction in her wake, the end of the Asura dream. So you denied her a mother's love. You denied her a father's affection. You were drunk with power and loved your crown more than your family. You were afraid of the prediction. But when Soorpanakha was disfigured, it was a mighty blow to your pride and you chose to steal your daughter from her husband. What shame! You should have fought Rama instead of stealing his wife, even if she is our daughter. Now, when the enemy is at our gates and the predictions are about to come true, you hold onto your stupid pride and ego and forget that you are a king first and a father later."

"I've remained silent and suffered your arrogance and ego. I remained silent when you raped my maid and made her pregnant. I remained silent when I heard that you were fooling around with that Brahmin woman. I suffered silently when you mourned her death. I was silent when I heard you muttering Vedavathi's name in your sleep. I have lived in silence when you left me for years, busy building your empire, fighting violent wars, doing the same cruel things that you people accuse the Devas of, running long campaigns in far-away lands. I, like the other women, have been silent while you foolish men painted the earth red with the blood. And see what you have brought us to. Just this once, listen to me my beloved. . . give Sita back to her husband."

"Shut your mouth, woman!" I exploded, "you are talking too much."

I didn't know what to say. It was as if I stood naked on the road. My innermost thoughts had been laid bare and they were not pretty.

"Do you think I relish the thought of sending Sita to Rama? But Ravana, I love you more than I love our daughter. I do not want to lose you. We will lose this war, Ravana, we will lose this. The moment you brought her to Lanka, I was afraid - for her, for myself and for you. I wanted you to send her back to her husband. But before I could do anything, you started the war. Thousands have been slain. Have you ever thought how we women suffer? I have lost a son. But I am just one of so many poor woman who have lost sons, husbands, fathers, brothers; their homes, their honour and their pride. Only you have pride? You know what your enemies did to me. And what did you do? Did you even go to the battlefield? No! You sent your son, your brother, your friends, your ministers. But you hid here like a coward..."

"Be silent. . ." I grabbed her by her throat.

"Go on. Kill me!"

I threw her down in disgust and stormed out of the room. I fumed with impotent rage. I felt worthless and sick. Involuntarily I turned towards the Ashoka tree where Sita sat. I could see the hunched figure in the darkness. A small lamp threw rays of feeble light. As I moved near, she looked up and turned her back towards me. I wanted to touch her, to hug her and say, *'See, how much I am sacrificing for you."* But something held me back. I stood there for a long time, trying to pick up the courage to talk to my daughter. Then, in a voice that was barely audible, I said, "Daughter. . ."

There was no reaction for some time and I did not have the courage to call her once more. Then I saw that her little body was trembling and I could hear her faint sobs.

"Sita, you are my daughter. . . I loved your mother more than anyone else in my life. But now I love you more than I love myself." Except for her sobs, nothing could be heard. I did not know how to continue but said, "Will you stay here with your father, as Princess of Lanka? If you say so. . . I shall ask for a truce. . . Rama does not deserve to be your husband. Stay with your father always."

There was no answer from her. She did not even turn.

"Please. . .please do not go with your husband. . . He is a barbarian."

With a flash of anger, she turned and said, "I love him. . . I am his wedded wife."

I was taken aback by this sudden display of fury. I did not know what to say but I made a final attempt. "Sita, I am your father and-"

"My father is King Janaka, and my husband is Lord Rama."

I stood there, utterly helpless. Pain gnawed at my soul as I turned back.

"Uncle. . ." It was then that I noticed Trijata. I did not want to face her now. She would have heard about her father. "Uncle, did my father fight like a brave Asura warrior today?"

"I am sorry, Trijata. . ." I had no words left for her.

"I have heard from my mother that my father was always a great warrior, better even than you, before wine claimed him. But, while I was growing up, he had already wasted away. It was not easy for me to grow up with the tag of being a drunkard's daughter. How I wished he would be sober and normal like the fathers of my friends. I hated him. But now, when. . ."

"Trijata, your father was a brave man, a better man than many..." I hugged my niece as she wept against my shoulder. As it was dark and there were no one else to see, I too cried. Honour and pride can cause so much misery. This wretched war, this wretched life, and the eulogizing of heroism and violence – I was sick of everything.

I was woken from my indulgent self-pity by a messenger who came panting up to me. After that, everything that happened was meaningless. Nothing mattered anymore. I had become a cog in the wheel of time. I became a stepping stone for somebody's climb to greatness and godhood. After that I was just a minor player in Rama's heroic epic. In that moment, everything changed.

"Your highness!" The poor man was sweating profusely and one look at his face made me stagger. The blood drained out of me.

"Your Highness, something has happened to Prince Meghanada..." He stood staring at the ground. I pushed Trijata away and ran past the messenger, who followed me.

"Where is he? What happened?!" I did not wait for his answer. I feared the worst, but kept denying it in my mind. I rushed past the sentry post and grabbed a horse. The fort doors opened and I rode towards the hill fort like a mad man. I heard the roar of fire as I passed the city borders. I turned back to see my city in flames but did not stop to watch. *'Let the city burn, let entire humankind perish. Where was my son? Meghanada. Oh Shiva, let nothing happen to the boy.'* I could smell the sticky sweat from the frothing horse, yet I seemed to be riding all too slowly. As I neared the fort, I could see that its gates were wide open. I rode past the slain soldiers, lying lifelessly in their own blood. The fort was sunk in deathly silence. I dismounted and walked with dragging feet towards the palace. I did not want to go there. I knew what lay in store for me. Yet I walked past headless bodies, limbless torsos, and blood stained walls.

"Your Highness!" The voice startled me. My minister of finance and the keeper of the fort, Jambumali, was sitting on the floor, with his back supported by a pillar. He was covered in blood and the old man was trying to stand up.

"Where is Meghanada?" I asked, knowing what the answer would be. He pointed towards the prayer room where my son used to pray before a huge idol of dancing Shiva, Nataraja. A glimmer of hope fluttered in my mind. "Meghanda! Meghanada! Son! " I called out, half expecting him to come out with his sheepish grin. With trembling hands I pushed open the door. There lay my son, dead. I collapsed on the floor, averting my eyes from the horrible sight, yet strangely drawn towards it. Meghanda's head rested on the foot of Shiva, severed from his body which lay a few feet away. Four arrows had pierced his back. It was evident my boy had died before he knew what was happening. He has been shot from the back. After he had collapsed, they had hacked him into pieces.

"It was Lakshmana who broke into the fort. There were almost forty men. No one knew how they came and entered the fort or how they knew that the Prince was here, praying." The old man sobbed uncontrollably. "The prince was in very low spirits when he came here. He told me that he had lost the war and had been responsible for his uncle's death. He wanted to pray. . . but. . .see how. . .he. . ."

"Where is the other boy?" I had grown almost numb.

"Killed, perhaps lying somewhere outside. Everyone was killed. They spared me, maybe because I am an old man."

A small movement behind the huge Nataraja idol caught my attention. But I did not have the courage to go there because I would have had to walk around the hacked body of my Meghanada. A huge black hand clutched the idol and slowly, the black body of Athikaya stood up. He was covered in blood, but he tried to walk towards us. He saw Meghanada and a piteous animal cry rose from his lips. He looked at me blankly and then at Jambumali. Athikaya's face contorted into a ferocious scowl. I looked at my old minister. He had grown pale. Athikaya rushed towards Jambumali with all his strength as Jambumali ran. Before he could move further, I grabbed him by his arms and held him still. But before Athikaya could reach us, he collapsed onto the floor, his face hitting the wet surface. He tried to rise once more but fell back. I pushed Jambumali towards the opposite corner, from where he could not run out without passing me. He sat in the corner with his body trembling with fear. I moved towards Athikaya and turned his face towards me.

"It was he. . .he opened. . .the gates. . .I tried to save the Prince. . .forgive me. . .I could not. . .I tried. . .I really tried. . . Lakshmana had come and. . . Jambumali guided them here. . .I was outside and saw it. . .Prince. . .wanted to be. . .alone. . .so I left him and. . .was outside. . .near the gate. . .when I came back. . .I saw him. . .standing over the body of. . .I fought. . .but they. . .escaped. . .I tried. . .I tried. . ." His life was ebbing fast. I tried to lift him but it was difficult to raise his huge body. Slowly, as I watched, my illegitimate son died in my arms. I put him down gently. I wanted to cry out aloud but I slowly stood up. The old man Jambumali sat quivering in the corner like a rat. I went near and kicked him between his legs. He screamed as he grabbed my foot. "Mercy. . .mercy. . .your Highness." he squeaked. I took out my dagger and hacked him into pieces, slowly, very slowly, taking my own sweet time. Now I had all the time in the world. I was undecided at first, but then I started with his eyes and worked downwards. And I relished the task. His screams were music to my ears.

57 Funeral of martyrs

Bhadra

I rushed to the palace when I heard the news I had feared most. It was very early in the morning. It was finally over. My son, the fool, had got himself killed along with the Prince. I knew it was bound to happen one day. And I could not do a thing about it. The love of a father for his son is always one-sided. When I reached there I cried aloud and beat my breast and rolled in the street. I could not help myself. I told anyone who would listen, that my son had been killed for the sake of the Prince. But no one cared. They were all rushing to mourn the death of the Prince and enjoy a grand funeral. There was a huge crowd on both sides of the street. I wondered why there was no war today. It had become routine now, so it seemed strange that a day could dawn without a battle. They blocked my way into the palace. I pleaded with them and tried to bribe my way through, but the guards were rougher than usual and pushed me away.

"My son has been killed. My son has been killed for the Prince. My son. . ."

"You beggar, move out of the way." A guard pushed me away with such great force that I lost balance and fell on my face. But I stood up angrily. My son had become a martyr for the country, and instead of treating me with the respect due to a martyrs father, they were treating me like a beggar.

"Please let me in. . ."

"You fool, the bier carrying the Prince's body is on the way from Subela." One of the ruffian-guards shoved me to one side. Helplessly, I stood panting. No one listened to me. My son had died and there was not even an iota of pity or sympathy from anyone. I was getting angrier by the minute and abused Ravana and everyone else I could think of. For some minutes people ignored me, but after a while, a guard walked towards me and slapped me hard across my face. My head spun and I fell into the drain. I lay there moaning, without the energy or will to get up. When I heard the distant rumbling of chariot wheels, I crawled up from the gutter. People moved away as I tried to push my way through to the front.

The chariots drew near and a huge crowd jostled, pushed and shouted slogans, thoroughly enjoying their sadness. Wails rose from the crowd as the biers carrying the dead bodies of the slain men slowly crawled towards the palace. People competed with each other to wail the loudest. Flowers were thrown onto the bodies. Everyone cried for Prince Meghanada. *'My son was dead and these people were making this into a spectacle.'*

At the head of the procession, Ravana sat, his head bowed. On his lap, lay Meghanada. Silent tears and sweat dripped from the King's face onto the face of his beloved son. The Prince's face was bloody and grotesque. Death had taken all his youth and beauty. As they neared me, my heart pounded in my chest. *'Where was my son, my Athikaya?'* The crowd grew frantic as the procession neared. I pushed forward but the crowd pushed me back again. I saw there were many bullock carts following the royal chariot and many more dead bodies of lesser men had been heaped on them. Maybe Athikaya was lying in one of those.

Many people ran behind the carts, some with heart rendering wails, and I joined them. I was panting hard by the time I reached the last cart. Limp bodies of slain men were thrown like vegetable sacks into the carts. Blood dripped and made a trail in the street. Crows landed surreptitiously on the carts to get a peck of human flesh. Death was cheap. But my son was dead. *'Where was his body? Had they forgotten to bring him?'* I desperately tried to get a glimpse of the faces, but all the dead men looked alike. My eyes blurred. *'Why did the boy not listen to me?'* He was in bad company. I should have left Lanka long ago. I should have left for my little village on the banks of the Poorna. Why did I stay? What did I have to do with the Ravanas and Ramas of this world? They and their wars. Ravana had raped my wife and given me a son. Then he took him away when I had learnt to love him.

I cried out loud in impotent rage, at the loss of my son and everything I valued in my life. They were going too fast now. How could my old legs keep pace? They were taking my son away from me. By the time I reached the palace gate, they had started arranging the corpses in a straight line on the ground. Guards with huge sticks cordoned off the area from the shoving crowds trying to get a glimpse of the slain heroes. The chariot carrying the dead Prince had gone in, past the gate to the palace gardens. Somehow I pushed my way to the front. The dead were arranged in a line. The wood for cremation was dumped down from a cart and a few got busy arranging the pyre. I pleaded with the guards, saying that my son was there somewhere and I wanted to have a look. Finally a guard took pity on me and led me by the hand to the line of still figures. I scanned each of the faces of the unfortunate men who had been killed in this meaningless war. But he was not there. *'Where was my Athikaya? Was he still alive?'* A flicker of hope ran through me. *'Maybe the boy had lost courage and gone into hiding. Maybe he would come back chastened after a few days.'*

Then I noticed the huge palace gates closing slowly, pushing away the crowd trying to force its way in. Inside, there were two pyres being prepared. On one lay the body of Prince Meghanada. On the other was the unmistakable bulk of my son. I ran towards the closing gates. I kicked, screamed and fought my way through the crowd and somehow managed to reach the gate. The guards were covered with sweat and looked irritated and exhausted after dealing with the unruly crowd. I tried sneaking in through the small gap but was pushed back rudely. I punched the face of the guard who had blocked my path, surprised at my own strength. The mighty guard lay flat in the mud, knocked out by an old man. Before the other guards could gather their wits, I ran past them. Other men behind me, who saw their chance, also tried to push their luck. This ensured that the other guards were kept engaged in fighting off the crowd. This helped me reach the funeral pyre.

I saw my son lying there peacefully on the sandal wood pyre the King had arranged for him. He had hundreds of wounds and his face had lost all that rustic charm. He looked like an ugly monster in death. Yet he was my son, my only purpose in life. No King was going to claim him. In life they had taken him away from me. In death, they were taking him beyond my reach. He had a mother waiting for him in our small hut. No Ravana could stop me taking my son to his mother.

The King stood, his face a mask of grief and misery. The Queen was lying on the ground, her hair undone, quivering with silent sobs. The palace sycophants wailed out loud, competing with each other to show off their grief, making a thorough nuisance of themselves. A few men arranged the sandalwood logs that would consume the Prince and my son. He had never had a place in this palace in the first place. When he had been alive, he had not listened to me. He was just a dog in the palace. In death at least, he could reclaim his manhood. I went to the King and stood there defiantly. I did not even bow to him. *'Let him chop off my head.'*

"I want my son." I told him, but he gazed through me. He did not even seem to hear.

"I want my son back!" I shouted and got the attention of everyone. The King did not seem to register my presence. *'Do I have to grab him by his hair and scream in his ears?'* I was in the mood to do so. Slowly the king looked at my face.

I sobbed uncontrollably. He put his hand on my shoulder but I shrugged it off and screamed. "Give back my son!"

The Queen, shaken from her world of grief, came to us. "Ravana," she said slowly, as if the very act of speaking caused her pain, "Give him his son. Let him take him."

The kings face contorted in rage. "He is my son." he whispered to the queen.

"Not at all. You should have claimed him when he was alive. Your son is Meghanada and no one else. Had you admitted your mistake and taken him into the palace in his infancy, I would have brought him up like

Meghanada. But you forsook him. Now we do not have any claim. In fact, we never had."

Ravána looked at me and at his wife, with anger blazing in his eyes. But the Queen met his eyes unflinchingly. I did not have the courage to face him so I hid myself in piteous sobs and turned away from him.

"Take him. Take him. Had he not been my Meghanada's friend, not even a dog would have cared about his death." the mighty King hissed into my ear.

'Yes I know, my King, not even a dog cares for the death of young men like my son, who died for you. The round medals you give away, the petty jobs you offer to the kin of those who die for you, the paltry compensations which you throw from your brimming coffers, are nothing but bones, to entice more dogs to die for you. Let me take my little dog from you. He has served his purpose. You showed young men how glorious it was to die for such abstract causes such as the motherland and racial pride. You honoured him, and fooled the public, in arranging such a big procession for the dead. Everyone is happy that our country has not forgotten the young who laid down their lives for their motherland. Everyone who has been martyr will be remembered – until the next meal. Great show, my King. Now, more young men will come to die, enticed by your petty bones, two minutes of glory, and a stone memorial by the street corner which real dogs will piss on. My son has served your purpose, now let me take him to his mother.'

I did not say any of this. If I had had the courage, then many like me would have had the courage to echo it, and there would not have been any Ravanas or Ramas left. I went to the limp body of my dear son and hugged him. I tried lifting him up, but he had outgrown me long ago. Two soldiers helped me lift my son. His body had gone rigid and he weighed much more than the shoulders of his poor father could carry. A hand cart was dragged to my side and I delicately put my son on it. With the nerves in my arms straining, I pulled the heavy burden towards my little hut. His mother was waiting to see him.

By the time, I crossed the palace gates, I heard the loud wail of the women as the funeral pyre of Meghanada was lit by his grieving father. As I turned from the royal highway onto the dirty back streets leading to my home, the Prince of the Asuras had vanished into thick, curly smoke. His friend, companion, servant and half-brother was forgotten the moment this poor Asura laid claim on him. I walked alone, dragging the cart with my dead son. The sun pounded relentlessly with a thousand fists and I sweated from every pore. I did not see any of my neighbours or friends. They had all gone to see the spectacle of a Prince being cremated.

As I neared home, I could see the hunched form of my once beautiful wife at the gate. She had waited eagerly for her son to return and came rushing towards us, but stopped at the cart. In a flash her joy was replaced by shock, then denial, then acceptance of the cruel blow of fate. She fell on Athikaya's body and pounded and shook him. She tore at her hair in grief.

I left the wailing mother and the dead son to their world. I had practical things to attend to. I wanted to give my son a decent funeral. The sun was setting and I did not want any rituals. I just wanted it to be over before the sun set. I was sick of being in misery. My son was dead and it would remain a stone in my heart till I died. I desperately searched for some firewood to burn him. Nothing was available. It had been a long time since we had cooked. We survived on the odd rats I trapped or some unlucky squirrels or rabbits that had strayed onto my path. Far away I could hear the cry of the crowd. I could hear some enthusiast crying himself hoarse about the valour of Meghanada and the crowd taking it up and roaring in reply. Anger rose in me in waves as the slogan shouting rose in crescendo. I was sick of everything. I was sick of my race, of being dirt poor, of not even having firewood to cremate my son who had so foolishly died for his Prince.

When I struck my first blow with the axe on the main pillar that supported my poor palace, I had the face of Ravana in my mind. Then with each blow, I imagined I was chopping off the heads of the great men I had seen or heard about. My wife stopped her wailing and came running to me, screaming that I had gone mad. I kept chopping my palace to pieces. It had become a game now and I was thoroughly enjoying it. I gave a blow each for Vibhishana, Kumbakarna, Prahastha, Rama, Lakshmana, Sita, Mandodari, Jambumali, Vidyutjihva, Kubera, and Varuna. But before I could chop off their heads as I would have liked to, my hut came down with a crash.

I rushed towards the cart that carried my darling son and pushed the cart into the rubble. The cart toppled over and Athikaya's huge body fell on the heap of wood fragments. I ran to my neighbour's home. He always had a lamp burning in his *puja* room. I pushed the door open and rushed to the corner where the small lamp was. I took off my *mundu* and dipped it in the oil. The cloth caught fire quickly and with that burning torch, I ran outside.

My wife was trying to recover her petty possessions from the heap that we had called our home till a few minutes ago. I pushed her aside and threw the blazing cloth into the heap. For a moment I held my breath as the flame died down. Then, with a vengeance, the fire leapt up, licking clean everything I had ever owned. The flames voraciously ate away my son. Athikaya had followed his Prince. He had died an equally heroic death as his half-brother, but the poor boy had been born with the wrong skin colour, and had grown up on the wrong side of the city. So there was no one to call out slogans and no idiots to roar back and shake the sky and the earth with their voices. Yet the fire did not make any distinction. It had an equal appetite for my son and the King's son. I watched with satisfaction as the fire licked its plate clean. Hot tears burned my sunken cheeks. As the last of the flames died and the ashes crumbled to the red earth of Lanka, the skies broke and rain fell in torrents. By the time the fury of the rain had ebbed, it had washed away the last remnants of my son and my home. My loss had become a dull pain somewhere in my mind. My wife had not moved from where she lay when I torched our son's pyre. I felt hungry. Maybe they were serving food outside the palace gates, as they usually did for the poor and invalid, at such times. I stood up, shaking away the water that had clung to my body. Maybe if I hurried I could get something to eat and if I was lucky enough, I could carry a packet back for my wife. Maybe, someone would offer me a drink. I started to walk towards the palace.

58 Did I fail as King?

Ravana

The enemy was so near. I could see the end, though I did not want to accept it. Yesterday I lit the funeral pyre of my son. Now, there was nothing, other than to fight Rama to the end – either his or mine. *'But what was I fighting for? My empire had collapsed, my son had died, my Queen's honour had been drugged in the mud. What was left now?'* True, I had this beautiful city I had so meticulously planned and built; a fortune which I had plundered from the Devas long ago; and my daughter, who happened to be the wife of my enemy.

But as things were taken away from me, I clung more and more desperately to what was left. Yet, like a tidal wave hammering away at the solid rock on the seashore, I was getting battered. I was withering from within. The will to live was ebbing away. Things that I had cherished and taken for granted had become meaningless now. Rama was just an immature prince of an irrelevant kingdom of the north. The boy was barely a few years older than my Meghanada had been. I was an Emperor, the mightiest that India had ever seen. Ayodhya was just a vassal state, a backwater village kingdom. Yet, how did my empire crumble like this? Was it the death of Bali that turned the tide? Or was it Vibhishana's betrayal? When did I lose my perspective? Asura empires had all gone down to the Devas, despite our economic, cultural, and technical superiority, because of the consistent in-fighting amongst ourselves. I knew our history and I knew my people. I had ruled my empire with an iron fist and ensured that I had only trustworthy people in powerful positions. I had kept an eye on people I suspected would turn against me – men and women who I thought were unscrupulous and were after my throne. What a fool I was.

I watched men like Prahastha; I ensured that Kumbakarna was always mired in his world of alcohol and *bhang*; I made sure that inherently cruel men like Rudraka did not accumulate too much power. I foolishly believed that I could buy a pirate like Varuna with impressive titles like 'Commander of the Seven Seas' and 'Grand Admiral of the Asura Navies'. I had killed my brother-in-law, Vidyutjihva. But I had been betrayed by men and women like Vibhishana, who looked pious; like Jambumali, who looked like a bureaucrat mired in his own world of accounts; women like Lankini, who never tired of publicly proclaiming her love and affection for King and country. I had powerful friends, but when the need arose, I was all alone. I thought my empire was built on steel, but when the shove came, I found out it had been built on nothing but straw. Whoever I had trusted betrayed me. I was so proud of my intelligence, so how I did I commit such fundamental mistakes in judging people?

I want to begin again, but life is too short for second chances. I had been given one chance and I had grabbed it with both hands. I had built up something great, but now, times had changed and everything was crumbling around me. I had no regrets. I had lived a full life. Enough of this self-pity. The time had come to do my best. I knew I might fail, but I owed my people one last, grand failure. They were the only ones who had not betrayed me. What did I do for them, for the love they have given? I was proud that I had built a great empire for my Asuras, I thought I had given them dignity and freedom, but perhaps I erred. I was a tyrant, maybe a benevolent one, but I was no Mahabali. I had not kept my ears and eyes open. And I had become blind to the sufferings of the people. When I strove for bigger things – for bigger cities, magnificent temples, wider roads, better ports, larger ships, increased trade, improved business, making a name among the nations of the world, making my country the richest in the world – I forgot something simple and basic. I forgot my people. I thought glittering cities marked progress. I forgot about the people who lived in gutters. When I gave lavish banquets, I forgot that most of my people had nothing to eat.

Prahastha had pointed this out to me but it was such a boring subject. I thought the wealth would trickle down. I imagined the freedom I gave my people to protest on the streets and the liberty to express their thoughts, would suffice and they would be content. I was proud that I was not like the other rulers who were mere tyrants and brutes who controlled their people through sheer force and terrorized them with military rule and brazen genocides. I was proud that the Asuras had evolved a system in which the King was powerful but nominal in the sense that the real power lay with the *Panchayat*s, the elected people in the villages, and I had held this up as a model to the world. Yet, the poor and wretched whom I had ignored, stood by me. They knew they had the most to lose – the freedom that gave them the hope that they could do better in life. The rich and the middle class whom I had pampered, either blatantly crossed over to the other side or sat on the fence, waiting for a clear winner to emerge in the battle. Today would be that decisive day.

Was everything predetermined by some unknown power who was conspiring against me? My tragedy could be that I still don't know what I did wrong. I made errors of judgment about men, but they were hardly reasons for such a large empire to collapse. It sounds absurd, but I am now mature enough to know that things happen randomly and we poor humans get caught like straws in the wind. The middle class was saying that I was a great sinner, that I had no right to keep another man's wife in my palace. The rumour was that I had raped many women in the past and I still had many woman in my harem. They called my government corrupt and claimed the officials had amassed riches at the cost of the common people.

I am the greatest fool in the world. I had pampered these people by building great roads so that their gold-plated chariots could rush past the ruins of the demolished hutments where the poor had eked out a living. I had driven away the peasant from their fertile lands so that these gossiping fools could build their bungalows and pleasure gardens. I set my police onto the pavement dwellers because they were such an eyesore for the middle class. I chased away the poor who had flocked to my cities for their livelihood and had cornered patches of land that were smaller than the space occupied by a rich man's chariot, for their entire families. I had diverted water from the fields to my cities, so that these gluttons would have their fountains. I had damned rivers that had irrigated the countryside and diverted the water to the cities so that these people could have their beauty baths. The poor had to go thirsty, die or else flock to the city to be the servants, gardeners, cooks and hewers, to the privileged.

My elephants had pulled down little huts to build huge shopping spaces, where silk, ornaments of gold and precious stones, were sold to this crass class. My coffers were full as I collected taxes on all this trade. And because I taxed them, they demanded that I build more roads. They complained that the ports did not have enough berths for their luxury boats; they were frustrated that they did not have enough entertainment options. They shouted that nothing worked in this country; complained that the entire establishment was corrupt and urged me to do something for them to justify my rule. So I demolished more huts, built more dams, displaced more poor farmers, and clogged my cities in the process. I built bigger temples where god-men fleeced the public, and wider streets; I planted flowers so that the people who did not have a meal could enjoy the beauty of the flowers; I allowed temples of debauchery where wine and women were tacky and spicy, and I became the darling of the middle class. I became intoxicated with their praise. They praised me for development and I, stupid fool that I was, thought I was taking my country forward. I saw the glitter of my cities and closed my eyes to the darkness of the shadows where misery clung, smelly and putrid. I believed the glitter was all that mattered.

Then Rama stood at our gates and everything changed. When the enemy came calling, the middle class vanished without a trace. They buried themselves in their drawing rooms and hid their able bodied sons from the State. The country had paid to have their children educated, in the hope that when the country needed them, they would render their bodies and minds to her cause. But alas, none came to her aid. It was the peasants and pavement dwellers who sacrificed their sons at the altar of patriotism. The foreign-educated, Sanskrit-speaking, betel-chewing wealthy, gave me advise from their hiding holes, but nothing else. The poor repaid the crumbs I had thrown their way with their life-blood. When my capital city burnt, the peasants flocked from the surrounding countryside to rebuild it. Some of them were looters who took whatever they could lay their hands on, but for once I ordered my police to look the other way.

If I got a second chance, I would teach the rich a lesson. I would make military service compulsory, irrespective of whether the person was the son of a rich merchant, ugly priest, or poor beggar. I would make it mandatory for everyone who passed out of the technical and medical schools, to serve for at least five years in the countryside. I would. . .what did it matter?

That I was thinking these thoughts showed I was never to be given a second chance. They were utopian dreams – vestiges of my own lower middle class wishes, long-forgotten titbits of the shattered fantasies of my youth. Power would corrupt me again as it had done before. Ideals would die and be buried like they always had been. True wisdom lay in understanding that idealism was just a tool of power. I could die tomorrow or Rama could, but the world would go on. The wretched would remain wretched, the poor would remain poor. New revolutions could happen; new ideologies flourish; new codes of ethics and morality replace the old; new prophets be born; new kings rule the earth; new religions sprout and fight each other and new discoveries be made, but everything would remain the same. What was the point of feeling guilty? I did what I could. I could have done better, but then, who could not have?

The winner of the battle would take everything – fame, money, power. He would be the truth, for whosoever wins, would be called the truth. Bards would sing paeans about the victor. As time passed, legends would grow. The victor would become the paragon of virtue, the best among men. Like every man, he too would commit good or bad deeds in life. But as is the nature of the world, the good deeds of the victor would be exaggerated and the bad deeds obliterated from memory. And if the doings of the victor could not be justified by the prevailing moral codes of society, he would be elevated to godhood, for who could question a God? In this way, my country produced many Gods. Every person who had won by whatever means, had become a God or *avatar*. For the vanquished, it would always be the other way round.

Yet, strangely enough, I felt that none of this concerned me. I could feel my own insignificance within the higher order of things and that made me curiously self-centered. If I did not matter in the larger order of life and was just an insignificant dot, then the only thing that mattered to me was me. With my death, everything would end for me. What happened to my people after my death was not my problem. I knew that death would be the final halting point and there was nothing beyond. No *atma,* no heaven, no *moksha,* no hell, no God, no afterlife awaited me. I would vanish, earth to earth, water to water, air to air, fire to fire, and everything would stop. Yet, given a choice, I would have loved to come back again. Who would not?

I walked towards my garden where my obstinate daughter Sita was still sulking. I wanted to see my daughter. Then if time permitted, perhaps I could spend a few minutes with Mandodari. Then I would meet Rama in the battlefield, face to face.

59 I WISH YOU DEATH

BHADRA

Last night, by the time I had reached the palace gates, the food distribution was over. Everyone knew that less than half the designated quantity reached the poor. From the purchase of food grains from the farmers to final distribution, there was a chain of swindling and racketeering. The farmer in turn cheated the public purchase official in both quantity and quality. He bribed the petty clerks who wrote the accounts to show larger quantities than the State actually received. Then the official stole some of the grain and sold it in the black market. By the time the grain reached the palace warehouses, there were such glaring gaps between book stock and physical stock, that the supervisors were forced to buy grain from the black market at double the price. The supervisors then fudged the accounts to show some loss due to pestilence and used the state treasury to buy back grain from the black market. Since the supervisors could not be expected to pay for the shortfall, they fudged the number of the poor, bloated the numbers of benefactors and swindled more grain in the process. Bribes flowed thick and fast in all stages. Everyone who touched the grain made a profit.

Idealistic ministers like Prahastha had been fooled by these crooks. He had been happy about the welfare schemes he had initiated. Some others like Jambumali, used the system to their advantage, to grow immensely rich. And wheeler dealers like the Varunas, transported huge stashes of illegal gold and cash from the officials of the empire to northern countries. It was a vicious but meaningless cycle, where the only losers were those who were honest and straight forward. Everybody cheated to their own capacity. And everyone was aware what was happening. But, since everyone from the poor farmer who cheated the government by under-reporting his yield; his farm worker, who cheated the farmer himself whenever possible; to the clerks, merchants, government officers, and ministers were all crooks of varying capacity, there was no anger among the people. They joked about the corruption in the system and raved against the politicians. Baiting politicians became a major amusement for the Asuras.

So, though I was disappointed at not getting anything to eat, I was not really surprised. In fact, I was relieved that the distributing clerk had not been overtly rude to me. He just told me to get lost and closed the shutters. It hurt my pride every time I had to beg for their munificence, but I had learnt long ago that I could not eat my pride. I decided to wait under my favourite Banyan tree. Maybe tomorrow I could be first in the queue and get some food.

The war not far from ending but one way or the other, it had to end. I had lost many my acquaintances and friends in the war. I had cheered for our side. The loss of life was sad but necessary. Were we not fighting for a cause? When others' sons were dying, I was there in the crowd to cheer the martyrs. When death visited my neighbours' homes, I was secretly happy that my family was intact and my son hale and healthy. The fear remained that I too would lose my precious son one day. Yet, I foolishly hoped that God would spare me the horrible death of my child. Had I not suffered enough? Had I not shared whatever little I earned with the Gods and their men? I had helped to fill the coffers of the temples with my humble offerings. In short, I had bribed the gods. But they were our Gods and they were like us. They would accept our bribes and offerings but there was no guarantee they would do us any good. Life was a series of bribes – bribes paid to the Gods; to Godmen; to petty officials; to government servants; to the King; to family; to friends. From birth to death, our culture had trained us to bribe and to take bribes and endorse bribes.

Athikaya's face haunted me. However hard I tried, I could not remember him as a baby. But I remembered little incidents that had made life liveable. I remembered how we sang songs as old as the human race; how I carried him deep into the dark forests; how I told him stories in which Gods, animals and white demons flitted in and out. How he would cling to my tattered *mundu*, scared of the demons; how he would laugh at the pranks of the animals that talked with Gods and men. I recalled the joy and feeling of contentment that had not depended on a fat purse and a mansion, but on little things that wove their magic. Yet I could not recall his little face. The face I saw was the one I had seen on his funeral pyre, mauled by the claws of fate, smashed on the hard rock of racial hatred and crushed under the weight of prejudice. I wanted a drink. The pain was too great to bear.

I lay there under the tree with raindrops still dripping down even though it had stopped raining. Mosquitoes buzzed around and tried to squeeze out whatever blood was left in my veins. I did not even bother to swat them. There were a few lights in the street and the palace itself looked gloomy and ill lit. Somewhere an owl hooted and then after a few moments, another answered. The frogs had woken after the rain and were croaking to their hearts' content. Crickets buzzed in the bushes, adding their own bizarre notes to the strange symphony that was being played around me. I lay there imagining that sky was my blanket and the wet earth my bed. There were a million stars. Were they the gods? They seemed so far away, cold, indifferent and irrelevant – silent witnesses to the drama unfolding on a tiny rock called earth.

There was the frantic cry of a frog in its death throes. Moments before, it had been crying for its mate, hot with sex, trying to fulfill its only *dharma* in life – propagation. And then fate interfered as a slithering snake, dark and silent, struck with its poison. But the strange drama of birth, propagation and death, repeated itself a million times all over the earth. In what way was the death of my son or a king any more significant than the death of that unknown frog? The earth had its claim on every living body. Our life was loaned from the earth. A borrowed life. And at any time, earth could call back its loan.

The grief for my lost son kept coming back into my mind, crushing my speculations on the philosophy of life. I clawed the wet, red earth with my crooked nails. I must have moaned loudly because someone came near me. My rheumatic eyes could barely discern the dark figure. I was terrified.

'Was it Yama, the God of death?' It was inauspicious to even think about death. It might just come your way. I had been speculating about the irrelevance of death, seeing no difference between the life of my son and a frog, just a few seconds ago. So when the dark figure loomed over me, I was terrified to my bones. The figure stooped and put its dark, crooked fingers under my nostrils. I held my breath. A wet palm felt the skin of my brow. Then the figure stood up and called out. Two soldiers ran towards us. *'Was I getting arrested?'* My feverish brain frantically searched for the crime I might have committed.

"He is dying. He is running a very high fever." A craggy face, with a long flowing white beard, loomed near my face. I was relieved. It was that mad scientist, Mayan. The guy was eccentric but totally harmless. "Carry him inside the fort." I heard him say.

"But sir, he is a drunkard. Should we. . ." There was annoyance and a jeer in the soldier's voice.

"He is dying and needs medical help. Take him inside. The poor man could be starving. This bloody war. . .why do people kill each other? Saturn is on the ascendant. Mars is very powerful now. If I could develop a machine eye that would enable me to see the planets more clearly. . . Is there any relationship between the millions of planets and human fate? There are lakhs of planets and stars. . .we are just specks sitting in this vast ocean of planets. . ."

I could hear his voice getting fainter as the mad scientist walked away into his own world. I could not make head or tail of what he had been blabbering about. The soldiers stood there hesitating. They clearly did not want to touch me. I reeked like a pig. But they could not afford to defy the orders of a senior minister. Probably Mayan had forgotten all about me by then, but it was a risk for the poor soldiers to take. I could see them faintly as I swam in and out of consciousness. I found myself half-dragged and half-lifted by the soldiers towards the fort. They dumped me near the gate and there was an angry consultation with the watch captain, who did not want anything to do with me and denied us entry. So I was dumped in a corner near the moat and lay there without the strength to even lift my head. It was much later, after mosquitoes had grown fat with my blood and worms and insects had burrowed their way into my skin, that Mayan returned from his wanderings.

"Ah good, good! You have brought him eh? Take him to the verandah of my quarters. I will try to save him." Maya ordered the hapless captain and went away.

The captain cursed me, his job, the minister, and life, for ten full minutes after the scientist had left. Then he gave orders that I be taken to Mayan's verandah. I was so weak that they had to carry me the whole way. Like a sack of coconuts, they dumped me on the cool, polished and clean verandah. After a while the scientist came out with an assistant and some evil smelling liquid. The assistant closed my nostrils with his fingers and when I gasped for breath, the bitter liquid was emptied into my open mouth. Mayan shut my mouth before I could gag and the fiery liquid burned a fiery path into my stomach. I writhed with pain and convulsed, terrified that I was dying. The two men held my twisting body till I lost all my strength and slipped into unconsciousness.

When I opened my eyes I had a splitting headache and felt drowsy and tired but much better than the previous day. Maybe the old man Mayan, knew a thing or two about medicine. I stood up slowly and found that some food and a tumbler of buttermilk had been placed nearby. I grabbed the food and gobbled it up as fast as I could. Strength returned to my limbs. I wanted to thank the old man and go home as early as possible but he was nowhere to be seen. I did not have the courage knock on the imposing, tall door. These were important men and I was too insignificant to go knocking at the doors of the mighty and powerful. Forget the old man, I just wanted to get out of the place.

As I was about to leave, I saw the King, Ravana, walking towards the Ashoka tree where Sita had camping adamantly. Strange, he was alone and walking fast. I wondered what the King was up to and followed him, careful to move stealthily. By the time I had hidden behind a bush of Jasmine, the King stood mutely before his daughter. I shivered at the thought of the terrifying past that connected me with Ravana, Sita and

Vedavathi. Here, in front of me, was that little bundle I had been entrusted to kill years ago. The memories were vivid. Father and daughter glared at each other with unmitigated animosity and hatred. She had ruined his dream. And he had dragged the future of an entire empire into the mud because of her. I should have killed her when she lay throbbing in my dark hands three decades ago. It would have been so easy to close her nostrils and choke her to death. Instead, I felt pity for the little one. Fool that I was. I should have stayed away from their business or gone the full measure and committed murder like Rudraka or Dhumraksha.

"I love my husband and whatever you say will not sway me from my love for him." She glowered with indignation.

"To hell with your Rama. I do not want to kill the fool. I do not want his blood on my hands. Already people are accusing me of murdering Soorpanakha's husband. I do not want any more blood on my hands. But your husband is stupid and evil. Why do you want to lead a slave's life with him? Deva men treat their women like beasts of burden."

"What do you know about Deva culture? Women are worshipped as Goddesses. Our world is a far cry from yours. Here women have no morals. They move around unveiled. Men and women mix freely and there is no sanctity to marriage in your kingdom. Your women are loud. They drink and dance with men. Your world is uncouth, with women marrying men of their choice, instead of being obedient daughters to their fathers. Your women are pretentious and think they are the most intelligent creatures in the world. You are just creatures of pleasure. Your men are like women. A monkey-man burnt down this hateful city of sin. And what did your mighty army do? Look at the kind of women you people have produced. Look at your sister, how promiscuous she is. Look at this dirty, dark, fat and ugly Trijata, your niece. . .and you want me to live here, leaving my Rama. . ."

I seethed with anger. Trijata, who stood a few feet away, burst into sobs. She had been a friend and companion to Sita since the day she had been brought to Lanka. It was for her that Ravana was losing his empire and his dreams. It was for Sita that so many poor Asuras had died. I could have choked her to death at that moment.

Ravana stamped a foot and drew his sword from its sheath in great anger. "You. . .you. . . I had staked everything for you. I have lost my sons, my honour, my city. . . everything, so that my daughter could be happy. And this is what you say? I sacrificed thousands of men for your sake." He raised his sword and I anticipated the swift swoosh of the sword severing the head of that hateful Deva woman. She looked at her father, unfazed, her eyes taunting and challenging the great Asura Emperor to behead her. Ravana's sword came within an inch of her throat but stopped dead there. Then slowly the strong arm of Ravana that had severed many enemy heads over the past four decades, went limp. "Sita. . .you are my daughter. . ." the King muttered as the famous *Chandrahasa* fell onto the red earth of Lanka.

A jeering laugh was the answer. "Daughter! A daughter who could be thrown away when inconvenient? A daughter your people never wanted? And what a *father!*"

I wanted to leave my hiding place and grab that obnoxious woman by her hair, but to my shock and surprise, I saw Ravana stand with his head bowed. He stood with silent tears flowing from his reddened eyes. Then slowly he turned and walked back to his palace.

"I wish you death! A painful and prolonged one." shouted Sita, as the King of the Asuras walked away with heavy steps.

Ravana aged ten years before my eyes. Death awaited the old King, and as wished and prayed for by his daughter – a long prolonged and painful one. I wanted no part of this bloody, family feud, between father, daughter, and son-in-law. But what choice did people like me have, or had ever had?

60 End of a dream

Ravana

I started out to the battlefield in a depressed mood. Mandodari had been emotional. She had not wanted me to go. She asked me to hand Sita over to Rama and appeal for peace. Peace. . .a word for cowards. *'Women! They will never understand reason.'* I had to literally prise her away from my body as she shouted, cried, tore her hair and beat her breasts. That too, in front of all my soldiers. It was embarrassing. She accused me of sacrificing everyone for my pride. She cursed Sita and I became angry. I shouted back and threw a tantrum that cowed the poor woman. She was still to recover from the shock of losing her son and I should not have behaved so harshly with her. *'But then I have always behaved badly to her. Why just her, to all the women in my life.'*

In my anger, I broke my Veena into two. I had loved music and I did not want any monkey-man playing with my instrument after I had gone. I had tried to codify the ragas and lyrics I had composed. Hopefully, they would survive me and my empire. I had experimented with paediatric medicine and astronomy and meticulously jotted down my notes on palm leaves. Those I had sent to Mayan. Perhaps that mad man would have some use for them. By the time I put on my battle dress, she had shut herself in her chamber. I called to her many times but she would not open the door. Finally, cursing her, I turned and walked towards my chariot. I heard her open the door and come running to me, calling my name piteously. I did not turn back. I was afraid to look at her face again. All my arrogance and false confidence would have melted, and I would have become just the average, middle-aged, pot-bellied, balding husband of a good and kind-hearted woman instead of the King of the Asuras. I knew that if I turned to look at her face, all my resolve would vanish and I would succumb and follow her bidding. I jumped into the chariot and barked to my charioteer to proceed.

As the fort gates opened and my army rushed forward to meet the Devas, I tried hard to suppress the melancholy feeling of a life wasted, of what could have been. I left behind a lonely woman who had suffered me and my antics silently for more than three and half decades; a woman who had sacrificed her children in a useless war started by her foolish husband because of his unbridled passion; a woman who had the courage to question the man the world feared. Tears welled in my eyes. I loved my wife more than anything in the world. I should have said good bye to her. Now it was too late. Rama was waiting.

I looked around and saw the glistening, sweating, bare, black bodies, bobbing around me. How many of them would return alive today? How many wives would be widowed by evening? How many of these poor souls would wet the red soil of Lanka with their blood? How many children would be made orphans? For whose sake were these fools fighting? How easy was it to fool these poor bastards. Far away on the beach, Rama's army lay waiting. What were the monkey-men were fighting for? For the sake of some northern prince and his wife? None of those poor bastards had even seen Rama's wife and they had no enmity with the Asuras. But they came, ready to die. Many among them would also leave their little ones orphaned or their parents without shelter.

Rama's army erupted with loud shouts as we turned the corner and raced towards them. I had placed my elephants at the front. It was a gamble. Elephants were notoriously undependable. They could turn around and create a stampede among my men. But I did not have much choice. My ranks had dwindled and Varuna's navy was pounding my forts with huge stones from the sea. I had positioned my flame-throwers strategically at the top of the low hills overlooking the beach. Because of the height, they were out of reach of Rama's archers or Varuna's catapults and could reach their targets much more accurately. They kept the Vanara army at bay and sunk many catamarans and boats with their flame-throwing. As my elephants thundered towards the Vanaras, I could sense a ripple of fear go through the enemy ranks. They tore through the feeble Vanara ranks, smashing and trampling many underfoot. The Asura army charged and the cavalry surrounded the Vanaras on three sides.

It had been a long time since I had led a battle from the front and I wondered if I had lost my touch. But the sight of Rama's army panicking pumped the blood in my veins. Suddenly I was not an old and tired king nearing six decades of life, I was once again that sixteen-year-old, with passion and ambition burning in my veins. What was Rama after all but a mere hot-headed young man who had somehow arranged a hotchpotch of semi-civilized tribes to challenge the mightiest Emperor on earth. Today, I would ensure that he became an example to all those arrogant hot heads who thought they could ride rough over the Asura Emperor and get away safely to their homes.

I barked commands and runners were dispatched to all sides. With satisfaction, I saw that Rama was in real distress. His captains put up a brave yet futile fight. If I could get him and pierce that throat with a well aimed arrow, this foolish war would end. I asked my charioteer to drive through the left flank. Arrows fell thick and fast. It was dangerous but I was in a giddy mood. Anger and enthusiasm pumped through my veins and nothing could stop me from getting him. This would be the last time a Deva prince would dare to challenge an Asura king.

Suddenly I was swamped by men running in panic from the rear. I cried myself hoarse and asked them regroup. Rama had laid a trap. We had been ambushed from behind, with Vibhishana leading a cavalry charge from the city end, trying to put pressure on my rear. I sent runners to the hilltop to command them to aim the fire at the rear of our formation. The firing could catch some of my own people, but that was inevitable. We were being trapped between the retreating, yet fiercely fighting Vanaras from the sea, and Vibhishana's army from the land. I divided my cavalry and ordered a group to engage Vibhishana. This relieved the pressure from the rear. I rued the fact that I had lost all my experienced commanders. I had underestimated Rama. I should have taken the war to the Vanara country the moment Hanuman came and burnt down my capital. But we had been too complacent. Had I done that earlier, we could have smashed the Vanaras and taken Rama prisoner. Instead, he was leading the war against my empire and I was struggling to contain him. Today, I would finish him.

Both armies fought with desperation and courage. Heroes and martyrs were created every minute. Soon, Lankini's Asura army attacked our position on top of the hills. Wave upon wave of her soldiers attacked my soldiers on the hilltop. I sensed danger. We were outnumbered six to one. It meant that we had to kill six enemy soldiers for each of our soldier being killed, just to keep our position. The other way was to capture or kill the enemy commander. But I could not see where Rama was. Hanuman was commanding and leading from the front. I looked for Rama and Lakshmana, but could not find them at all. The battle raged on with no clear victory for either side.

It was almost three in the afternoon and both sides had lost many men. My ranks had dwindled, though the civilian and untrained population of my city had joined my ranks with whatever they could lay their hands on. They were no match for the highly trained Vanara warriors, but from a distance, I was sure that my civilians looked menacing to the Vanaras. It was also good for our morale and bad news for the enemy, as they could not see any dwindling of the Asura ranks. But I had no doubt that this situation could not go on forever. Already two or three hilltops had been captured by Lankini's soldiers and they were now training their fire on us. Our elephants had managed to smash the enemy lines and tear off portions of the bridge. Many of Varuna's boats had been captured by my enthusiastic troops and we opened another front from the sea. The battle hung in precarious balance.

Time was running out. Dark clouds formed in the western sky and the sea was getting choppy. Varuna's vessels bobbed up and down in the rough sea. The elephants were getting restless and I was afraid that at any moment things would change for the worse. I had to do something daring and dramatic. *'But where was Rama and Lakshmana?'* My best chance would be to lead a surprise attack towards the Deva prince and capture or kill him. Like him, I too was well hidden from enemy eyes. As a part of the deception, more than seven chariots flew the royal Asura flag to confuse the enemy as to which was my chariot. I became desperate. My age was catching up with me. A few arrows had struck me and I was exhausted from the bleeding.

As the first bolts of lightning hit the sea, I saw them. They were near the bridge. They were urging the Vanaras to rebuild it. Hanuman had lit a huge wall of fire that kept the elephants at bay. As the wind shifted and flame wall moved, I saw Varuna's master vessel moving towards the bridge. With horror I saw reinforcements arriving to help Rama. Horses were being lowered and warriors slid down the ropes towards the bridge. Our men directed their arrows towards the slithering Vanara warriors but the enemy numbers were growing quickly. To my rear, Vibhishana was butchering my civilian fighters and advancing. My time was running out. Unless I killed Rama before I got totally swamped, everything would be finished.

I assembled my best fighters and formed a rapid action team. I told them the plan and was annoyed to see the look of fear in their eyes. The plan required extreme daring in its execution. But I explained that the situation was desperate and without waiting for their confirmation, I jumped out of my chariot with my favourite sword in my hand. I unshackled my favourite horse. My charioteer was in tears and I hugged him. He collapsed weeping like an old woman at my feet. Ignoring him, I jumped onto my horse and raised my *Chandrahasa* to the darkening skies and bellowed, "*Har Har Mahadev*".

All around me the war cry echoed from a hundred tongues. Lightning struck here and there as massive waves smashed the boulders on the beach. It was almost dark and rain fell in huge drops. I galloped towards the wall of flame, past the slain soldiers lying on the wet ground, past the writhing men with torn limbs, over the dying men, past pools of blood and trampled flesh, I galloped towards Rama. My men thundered behind me. Blood pounded in my ears. I could feel the reins tremble. My horse frothed from it's nose but I egged it on. Faster and faster I galloped, ignoring the odd arrows that struck my thighs or biceps. I could feel the heat and my horse hesitated, but I kicked her into galloping faster. With one mighty swoop she jumped through the wall of fire towards Rama. My men followed me and we landed in front of the terrified Vanaras. My hair and the mane of my horse had caught fire and I could see the terror my figure had struck.

I could see his eyes. Even at that moment, my feelings were of surprise. *'How dark skinned he was.'* He staggered back with a look of absolute terror. As I raised my sword to thrust it through his heart, Hanuman jumped up and grabbed my legs. I lost my balance and fell from my horse. I kicked at the monkey-man's face. With a grunt he fell into the sea. I scrambled up and hacked my way towards Rama and Lakshmana. They were shooting arrows indiscriminately and had hit some of their own soldiers, though a few arrows managed to hit some of my troops also. We advanced faster towards the Deva princes, when the skies opened in a flood. Rain pounded down on all of us, making movements slippery and cumbersome. Gigantic waves crashed onto the bridge and carried away many men from both sides. A portion of the bridge collapsed, cutting off Rama and a few of his men from their main army. He was trapped. I just had to reach him. He was finished. With renewed vigor, we fought our way towards Rama.

That was the moment I thought the war was finished and I had won. Once again, with pluck and determination, I had managed to turn my luck. Many times in the past I had led my troops to victory from seemingly impossible positions. This was just one of those. In a few minutes Rama and Lakshmana would join my brother Kumbha in the deep sea. I could see fear on their faces. Their heavy bows were slipping from their hands as waves pounded the bridge and sprayed the fighting men with salt water. The wind howled and lightning cracked in the dark skies. Rama's hands trembled and he was not able to aim accurately. Arrows whizzed past me, but in my frenzy I did not even bother about an accidental one striking me. I hacked my way towards my enemy. Countless Vanaras fell dead as the rain lashed us and the bridge shuddered. A few more men to slaughter and I could severe the head of Rama with my *Chandrahasa*. I relished the thought.

It was far too late to realize the fatal mistake I had made. In leaping across the firewall built by Hanuman, I had assumed that there was nothing to fear from my rear. In my rage against Rama, I had made a fundamental error of judgment. The torrential rain had managed to kill the fire and now my rear lay wide open to attack. I had forgotten my brother Vibhishana, who had been fighting his way towards me. With no fire to stop him, he had stealthily reached me. It was only when his sword thrust deep into my back that I realized my folly.

I turned and tried to attack him with my sword, but he ducked and I lost my balance. He kicked me and I almost fell into the raging sea. I recovered my balance but blood poured from the wound he had inflicted. My hands went numb. The heavy armour I wore pulled me down. Rama and Lakshmana, seized the opportunity to shower me with arrows. But the arrows bounced off my armour and could not penetrate it. I did not have any time to lose. I was about to pass out. I had to get to Rama before I became too weak. I kicked Vibhishana and he fell into the sea. As I rushed towards Rama with my sword held high, Vibhishana somehow scrambled back on the bridge. I did not notice it. My mind was totally focused on Rama. As I leapt forward, Vibhishana's sword once again fell on my back. The sword missed my body by an inch but severed the knots that held my armour tight against my body. Instinctively I turned back and kicked Vibhishana. He vanished into the raging, swirling sea water. As I turned again to face Rama, my armour fell and I stood exposed to my enemy's arrows.

Rama seized the opportunity and aimed at my abdomen. I did not want to give up but the blood dripping from my body made my head spin. My steps faltered and my advance became painfully slow. When arrow upon arrow pierced my guts, my only thought was of open defiance. With each painful step, another bout of arrows ripped my bare body. Slowly, I fell and the last thing I remembered was being swallowed by a dark green wave. Then my world went blank.

When I opened my eyes, there was a deathly silence. The earth was dark and cold. Some men were standing around me, but I could not see their faces. Then a tall, dark figure came and stood near my head. '*Rama. . .*' I wanted to grab him by his throat but the earth held me firm. She was about to reclaim my body. Rama mumbled something in Sanskrit, something about finding a place in heaven. I wanted to burst out laughing. In mock obeisance, I brought my palms together. The last thought before I passed out again was that the fool had believed I was doing obeisance to him. My macabre joke had been lost on him. Men and their blasted egos!

61 Victors and their ways

Bhadra

Today is his funeral. It was late afternoon and I stood amidst the crowd, dozing in the humid heat. There was a lingering sadness and terror in the air. The conquering armies had entered the city last night. The Vanaras had pillaged, raped, and looted the way through the city. Most people had fled to the jungles while some had bravely tried to defend their small possessions. Others surrendered to the ravaging Vanara army but they were in no mood to take prisoners. The fools who expected mercy were cut down mercilessly. The granaries were torched and the temples looted. Ravana's impressive palace was almost pulled down, but Vibhishana intervened and ensured that everyone inside the fort was safe. So once again the nobles saved their skins and possessions. The Vanara plunderers were let loose on the hapless common folk of Lanka.

By mid-morning, a semblance of order had come and many poor Asuras were captured from the surrounding jungles by the Vanara soldiers and brought forcefully back to the city. Last night I had sneaked into the beach to foray for any valuables left by the slain soldiers. It was risky, but it was easy money. Besides, it was a safe place to be. It would have been the last place they would have expected an Asura to be. Two or three other men like me scavenged for valuables among the dead or gravely injured, but we kept a discreet distance from each other.

It was then that I stumbled upon the Emperor himself. In the dull glow of a moonless night, I recognized my King and master. He was breathing

heavily and writhing in pain. Jackals were eating him alive. It was the shimmer of gold from his bracelets that had attracted me to him. I was not sure initially, but as I leaned to have a look, he emitted a grunt. *'How the mighty had fallen.'* This man had fought for a race and a people who had lost their dignity, their freedom, their values, and their culture, to foreigners who had invaded and conquered them. Ravana gave the Asuras dignity and self-belief, instilled confidence and pride in our ancient culture and took our civilization to new heights of glory. Yes, he may have been a tyrant. He had destroyed the democratic and egalitarian society of the Asuras and made it into a mean fighting machine. Yes, he wallowed in luxury and did whatever he pleased. The society he had created was not perfect. The majority of us remained poor. Yet we knew that hard work and luck could make us rich and powerful. There were no congenital, privileged castes such as the Brahmins were among the Devas. Despite our crushing poverty and the seething anger we felt for the rich and privileged, we enjoyed one luxury compared to our counterparts in the Deva kingdoms – we were treated like human beings. Most of us were poor, but there was a silent dignity in our poverty. But as I leaned over my fallen King, I did not know any of this. It was later, much later that these things became clear to me. But by then it was too late.

The old King mumbled something but I could understand what he was trying to say. I touched his forehead. It was burning hot. He had fever and wheezed heavily. He was dying and it was unbearable to watch. He mumbled something again. I could only make out that he wanted me to take him somewhere. Poor man! I began to cry despite myself. I took his head in my hands and hugged him close to my bosom. *'I was hugging a real King.'* The exhilaration I felt then! In my excitement I told him I would seek revenge. "I will complete you work, your Highness. Do not worry and go in peace. I will do it for our race." I could not believe what I was saying to the dying man. "My methods may be different, even ignoble, as per your standards."

Ravana wheezed heavily. I moved my mouth towards his half-eaten ear. The stench of putrefying flesh made me gag, but I controlled myself and whispered in his ear, "Once, I too was a warrior, but I have grown old.

Arms frighten me now. I am terrified of war. I cannot beat even an eight-year old. Nevertheless, my methods are deadly. I will have my revenge, for you, for me and for our blighted race. Rama will not go free for what he has done to you and our race. Believe me and go in peace."

As I said this, I felt a purpose had come to my life. At least my thoroughly unremarkable life would be of some use. I kissed my King's forehead and gently laid his head on the wet earth. He wheezed again agonizingly. I stood there for a long time, watching Ravana die. When silver streaks appeared in the eastern sky and the cawing of the crows heralded a new dawn, mighty Ravana laboriously and painfully breathed his last. I waited for half an hour more and then I knelt down and divested him of all the gold ornaments he wore. He would not be needing them wherever he had gone to. It was a good haul and I was happy to have stumbled upon my King.

As I walked back towards the city, the enormity and stupidity of the words I had said to the dying man hit me. *'I was not bound by anything, not even by my words to a dead man.'* By the time I reached the outer edge of the city, I had convinced myself that there was nothing wrong in breaking my word as given to Ravana. I was no hero to take on a revengeful mission against Rama. Soon I was caught by the Vanara soldiers and marched back to the city to watch the victory processions. By late morning I had practically forgotten about revenge.

Many people had been hauled forcefully to the royal street and made to sit in the hot sun on either sides of the road. Vanara soldiers mercilessly beat anyone who even dared to shift their position. The Asuras watched with seething anger and a sense of helplessness, as their women were dragged through the streets. Fear hung like a nasty mist that refused to clear long after sunrise. Surprisingly, the day was clear and windy. Everything looked fresh after yesterday's torrential rain. The trees were stunningly green and the sky a deep blue with soft, fluffy, cotton clouds floating about aimlessly. Small puddles had formed here and there and frogs jumped in and out of them in mirth. The whole world was radiant. In less than a day, it was as if Ravana and his fantastic dreams had never existed. I pushed Ravana's ornaments that I had stolen from his corpse down my loincloth. Stolen was not the word, reclaimed was better, for whatever Ravana owned had been taken from us – from me and people like me, sitting here waiting for the next Ravana. The flag of Vishnu flew high from the tower of the palace. We waited to welcome our next master, Rama. Lest we run away from the wonderful blessings that was being promised by the new Lord, we were held forcibly in place by the brutish Vanaras.

By afternoon, men had started to faint in the heat. The Vanaras, used to the fierce but dry summer heat of central India, were sweating profusely from the milder but sultry tropical heat. This made them more irritable and angry. Even the slightest movement was dealt with severe beatings. I sat next to a teenager who stared intently at the Vanara soldiers a few feet away. I could smell trouble a mile away. I knew what was going through the mind of the teenager. I had to get away from this place as fast as possible. But how could I slip away without attracting anyone's attention. The teenager acted before I could formulate a plan to escape. Leaping from his place, he rushed towards the unsuspecting soldiers. Hearing the noise, they turned but caught the full force of the teenager's blows in their faces. They staggered and fell. The teenager grabbed their spears and thrust them repeatedly into their bodies. As if in cue, many of the young men attacked the Vanara soldiers. But the vast majority of men, including me, watched the drama without any reaction. More and more Vanara soldiers ran from the fort to aid their comrades, and within a few minutes, they had managed to kill the young rebels.

The boy who started this farce was hacked into pieces, his limbs thrown into the crowd in all directions. His arms landed near me and I kicked the dirty thing away towards my terrified neighbor, who promptly gagged and vomited. Some blood of the dead teenager had fallen on my face and shoulders and I wiped it off with my palm and then wiped my hand on my *dhothi*. For their slain comrades, the Vanaras exacted a terrible revenge by randomly choosing some of our men and beheading them. It was pure terror in action and succeeded in quenching any thoughts of heroism in the heart of any Asura hero wannabe.

By late afternoon, the Vanaras had got bored of their game and were lazily walking around. Some Asuras had fainted in the fierce afternoon sun and begged for water. I had dozed off lazily when the sudden roll of *Chenda*s woke me. At the far end, the fort gates opened and a procession entered the royal highway. The entire crowd craned to see what was happening. The procession wound its way slowly through the waves of the gasping crowd. I could only see that they had raised something on a staff and it was bobbing up and down in the crowd. An agonized wail rose from the fort end and followed the procession. As the procession neared me, I was horrified to find that it was Ravana's head that was bobbing up and down on the staff carried by Angada. The once stately and handsome face looked grotesque in death, with its eyes missing, part of its cheeks gnawed away by rats and a bloody stub of a nose, half eaten by jackals. Behind Angada, Sugreeva, the cruel and drunken-looking King of Kishkindha, tottered by, barely able to carry his heavy club. Many ugly and hairy, noble monkey-men, walked with their crude clubs and heavy staffs behind their King. Instead of the deer skin clothing they were used to, they all wore the fine silk clothes that had been looted from the palace, in an attempt to emulate Asura noble men. They looked awkward in those clothes but they carried huge, stone clubs and no man dared to laugh. Then followed the Asura men with their *Chenda*s and horns, trumpeting the victory of their new masters. They were followed by Rama, his brother, and a triumphant-looking Sita, glowing with happiness beside her husband in Ravana's chariot.

Beside the royal chariot, on either side, ran Hanuman and Vibhishana, doing odd errands as commanded by Lakshmana, competing with each other in pleasing their masters. The rivalry between these two servitors of Rama, was evident. Rama sat with Ravana's diamond studded, golden crown on his head. He wore a wooden smile and raised his palms slightly as if he showering his blessing on us. I noticed that he placed his bow and quiver of arrows between him and his wife. I also noticed that he deliberately did not look at his wife and consciously avoided even an accidental touch from her.

It appeared strange then, but later, as I became initiated into the Deva culture, it all made sense. The events that unfolded that evening added greatly to my knowledge. Behind Rama's chariot came palanquins carrying the woman of the palace. In one of them, sat Mandodari, her face partially veiled and her head tonsured. She was wearing a plain white sari. More than the head of Ravana bobbing up and down on a staff, it was the sight of the Asura Queen dressed like a Deva widow that shook the crowd. She sat there with immense dignity and self-control as wave upon waves of Asura men on either side bowed down to the earth and wailed at her plight. Vanara soldiers kicked and screamed, trying to stop the Asuras from crying out in distress and prodded them to shout '*Sri Rama jaya*'. Yet the Asuras refused to be deprived of this small luxury to cry for their shattered dreams. Broken bones were nothing compared to vanished dreams. I could not control my tears and joined my neighbours in pounding my chest and wailing out loud.

The frenzy of the *Chenda*s and horns could not suppress the misery of the Asuras' cries. It was the cry of a race facing the deep abyss of extinction. It was the death cry of a culture. Many years ago, the Asuras had seen a shining promise of renewal, but now it lay shattered. As the setting sun bloodied the turbulent sea, we buried our dreams of a world without borders, a world of equality. For many ages, the Asuras of India held up a beacon of hope to the world for a world without slavery and caste, where anyone with fire in his heart and the ambition to dream, could carve his own destiny. That dream collapsed thousands of years ago when our cities on the bank of Saraswathi and Indus fell to the barbarian attacks of the Devas. Yet it found utterance again in its heroes like Mahabali and Ravana.

And that hero was now bobbing up and down on the tip of a staff held by a beast. The procession stopped near the sea. The crowd ran to the beach to see what was happening. The Asura soldiers, who had fought a few hours before with the Vanaras, now joined their foes to control the crowd. They now served the new regime and wanted their salaries, their promotions, and perks, to remain protected. They were public servants, ready to land heavy blows on the public at short notice from their masters. Their *lathi*s fell with sickening whacks on the backs of the hapless common man. They formed a chain to prevent the public from getting too near the leaders. A dais had been raised for the great men to address us. We were all asked to sit down on the beach. We were pushed down, pressed down and when required, beaten down to the ground. After a delay when the sycophants of Rama, then the sycophants of the sycophants, ran around fetching this and that and grovelling before their immediate bosses and barking at their subordinates, Rama climbed onto the dais. A deep frown lined his brow. But the smile was back on his face again as he waved. A few hands waved back and again the frown returned to his face. The sycophants got their cue and runners were dispatched to various police supervisors. Soon we were all waving to Rama and cheering his every word, though we did not understand a word, as he was speaking in Sanskrit. After a while, Vibhishana stood up and whispered something to Rama. Then he translated Rama's speech, sentence by sentence Obviously we had not been clapping at the right places in Rama's speech.

Rama started from the beginning and said that all of us should be happy as we had freed us from the tyranny of Ravana, an evil demon. It was his belief that good always triumphed over evil. It was logical and we clapped for these great words. Then Rama announced that we would be ruled as per Deva *dharma* henceforth. There would not be any councils, or even village level *panchayat*s. The King would be supreme and he would rule as per the advice of the Brahmins. Though many in the crowd did not understand the full implications of this, there was an uneasy silence from the crowd until we were all prodded to cheer. Rama stated that all subjects would be divided into four castes and a profession would be allocated to each of them. The Brahmins, who had come from the face of the God, would be the supreme caste. They would dispense knowledge, act as representatives of God on earth, and it was imperative that everyone listen and obey them. The Kshatriyas, who had the great fortune of coming from the limbs of God, would rule over society as per the advice of the Brahmins.

The Vaishyas, the merchants who had come from the thighs of God, would be given permission to run business and trade and would be under the other two castes. The artisans, small land owners, the ordinary soldiers, all the Shudras, who had unfortunately come from the foot of God, would serve the other three castes. It was so confusing, but we all clapped. I wondered what would happen to the unskilled or semi-skilled peasants, the blackest of black people, who eked out a living doing odd jobs like me – cleaning the streets, washing clothes, being porters. I was curious to know which bodily part of the Deva God people like me had come from. I soon got the answer. Rama announced that all others, who did not fall into the mentioned categories, would be considered pariahs or untouchables. He felt sorry for our plights but asked us to take it as a blessing from God.

The speech went on and on, boring us with details about Deva glories and their way of life. Finally, he announced that he did not wish to be King of Lanka or the Asuras. He raised the hand of Vibhishana and proclaimed, "Behold! The King of Asuras". A few more blows by policemen ensured a smattering of applause. Vibhishana fell at Rama's feet. We watched what our King did with revulsion. This was a convenient arrangement for Rama. He could enjoy power without the responsibility. This was our fate, to be ruled by a spineless ruler under the advice of a foreigner. Vibhishana began his speech. He apologised to the Devas and ended with the lament that his wayward brothers, Ravana and Kumbakarna, had not recognized the divinity of Rama. As the sun set and darkness and gloom spread over Lanka, Vibhishana said that he would perform the last rites of his slain brother as per the Vedic tradition of the Devas. A wave of protest rose from the crowd and died at the sight of more policemen surrounding them with raised swords. A few Brahmins arrived on stage and Rama, Vibhishana, Lakshmana, and Sita, all scrambled up in respect. Rama, Lakshmana and Vibhishana, fell at the Brahmins' feet and received their blessings.

But when Sita tried to touch their feet, they jumped back in revulsion. A hush descended on the crowd. We sensed something dramatic and sensational was happening. One of the Brahmins whispered something to Rama and we saw his face grow darker. Rama spoke to Lakshmana and the colour drained from his face. For an awkward moment, no one did anything. Then Lakshmana grabbed Sita's hands and pulled her down from the dais. She tried to wriggle away, but her brother-in-law gripped her hard. She was pushed into a corner just below the dais, where she stood burning with shame, indignation and embarrassment. One of the Brahmins came forward and spoke in Sanskrit.

Then Vibhishana stepped forward and translated the Brahmin's words. He sounded ecstatic when he said, "See, my countrymen, how fair the Brahmins are. Rama, my Lord, is King of the world, but even he is not above the law. His wife, Sita, as we all know, was held captive by that demon Ravana. It is our sorrow, that because of him who I once called brother, a virtuous lady like my beloved Lord's wife, has been polluted. Please have no doubts, Sita Devi is like a mother to me. But, we should be proud of the way the learned pundits have applied their laws to all equally. In their wisdom they have ruled that Sita Devi will have to prove her purity and chastity in the time-honoured way of the Devas." Vibhishana paused to gulp some water. It was evident that he relished this opportunity to demonstrate a new order.

Sita had stopped weeping and stood defiant. The veil fell from her face as she stared at her husband. The resemblance was unmistakable. She might have looked like her mother, but in her posture and the fire in her eyes, she looked every inch the daughter of Ravana. She glared at the husband for whom she had waited so patiently. Rama looked away, unable to face her. His hands trembled yet that wooden smile never left his lips. He was trying hard to contain his emotions. He sat there not like a warrior who had vanquished the most powerful king in the world, but like a man stricken by fate. Mandodari, seated a few yards away, looked shocked at this new development. She tried to get up but was pushed back on the orders of the Brahmins. They barked that widows were not allowed to be seen in the sunlight. They had already sinned by allowing her to witness her husband's last journey. This would be Mandodari's last day in the sun. A funeral pyre was set up and the head of Ravana was taken down from the staff. A body which was supposedly Ravana's, was carried in by four dark men, my fellow untouchables.

The sun had set and dark clouds loomed large in the western skies. It was the season of evening showers and the earth got ready for her ritual bath. Vibhishana walked towards his brother's funeral pyre holding a flaming torch. Vibhishana ordered for another pyre to be set up near Ravana's. He ordered that finest of Sandal woods to be brought for this pyre was meant for a divine purpose. We waited with baited breath. Soon another pyre was lit. Specially selected Asura ladies dragged Sita towards this special pyre that would tell the world whether she was pure or not.. We did not understand what was happening. What was this time-honored method of the Devas to test a woman's chastity? As the Brahmins croaked their *mantra*s and sprinkled water on all and sundry, Vibhishana walked three times around the pyre of his slain brother. Some of the drops of water fell onto my skin and by impulse was to smell the water. It stank.

My neighbour whispered in my ear, "It's cow's urine and *gobar*. They use it for purification." We, the untouchables, were purified with bullshit. Small drops of rain fell. Soon the skies would open. Lightning crackled, tearing the dark skies into pieces.

Just before Vibhishana lit the funeral pyre, he dramatically raised the torchand proclaimed, "This is the end of a tyrant, a demon, a *Rakshasa*. Let his life be a lesson to all those who defy the supreme power of *dharma*, whose earthly manifestation is our master, Lord Sri Ramachandra of the heavenly kingdom of Ayodhya. Let today be the end of the evil and decadent ways of the Asuras. Let today be the holiest of all days, when Lord Rama, the *avatar* of Vishnu, showers his immense mercy upon us. He shall, in his infinite compassion, lead us to an exalted way of life. By the time Ravana's sinful body has crumbled into ashes, a new dawn of Deva *dharma* will rise over our dark horizon. A *dharma* in which every man will know his place; and learning will be valued; the prowess of the warriors will be respected; and the skills in business appreciated. No longer will we be burdened by hard struggles to succeed in life, nor will we indulge in mad competition to get further ahead than our neighbours. We will cast away the evil society of the Asuras under Ravana, when men thought that merit and hard work alone could assure him happiness.

We will not, from now on, forget that we are but puny little beings, and that our actions and merit is nothing compared to the supreme power of God. Our material or spiritual success flows from his compassion and love. If you have had the misfortune to be born a pariah, do not grieve. In this life you will face difficulties because in a previous life you have done wrong. For your *karma* you have been born a Shudra or pariah. Do your duty and serve your masters faithfully; do not become overly ambitious or jealous of the respect and riches your superiors enjoy. Only with humility can you ensure that God, in his infinite compassion and wisdom, will show mercy and ensure that your birth in the next level of *varna* hierarchy in your next life.

Vishnu, is the preserver of the social order. The Lord promised that whenever there was a threat to this order, he would take birth among us mere human beings and restore *dharma*. Ravana and the ideology he perpetuated, was dangerous and disrupted that order. He would say that being a mere peasant boy of half-caste origin, he had created the mightiest empire in the world, with only his own bravery, hard work, ingenuity, and a few men to aid him. His temporary victory might have dazzled many. But I put my faith in God. Now, everything Ravana achieved is mine. Did I work for it? Did I use great wit? Did I form an evil company of men like Prahastha, Kumbakarna and Rudraka? The only thing I did was to put my complete faith in God. Ravana was killed and the kingdom and the richness he created is mine now.

Earlier, another usurper of this social order, who foolishly believed that all human beings were equal, ruled the western coast of India. You might know Mahabali, who ruled from Muzuris and challenged Vishnu's social order. At that time the mighty Emperor was defeated by a small Brahmin boy, Vamana, who was none other than another *avatar* of Vishnu. That should have been a lesson to Ravana. I tried to warn him, for I loved him once as my brother. But he was too arrogant and proud to listen to good advice; too engrossed in life to worry about death. He thought his armies would save him. He thought he had given a good life to his subjects, so they would save him. He thought he had created architectural marvels in the great Shiva temples he had built and so Shiva would save him. But when the time, Ravana had no answer. There were no one to save him, except for the destitute and the poor, who did not understand what was right and wrong.

When Rama came, I fell at his feet, for I recognized God. So did all the noble men of intellect and wisdom, whether it was Varuna, or Lankini, or Jambumali. And see how we have been rewarded. Government servants, merchants, the police, and the army of Ravana, most have now recognized their folly and pledged support to my reign in Rama's name. I am sure all of you, who had foolishly believed in Ravana or Mahabali's utopian dreams, will now start leading your life as prescribed by our *smrithi*s. Only by complete submission to *his* supreme will can one achieve *moksha*. The laws of our *dharma*, as defined by the great sage Manu, are eternal and divine. These laws cover every aspect of life. From birth to death, these *dharmic* laws will show you the path.

Knowledge is a dangerous thing in the hands of people who do not know how to use it. The Asuras had so far made the mistake of educating everyone without thinking of the consequences of equipping evil and ignorant people with knowledge. We made the mistake of seeing every human being as equal. But things will be different now. We will not continue with this folly. Only the first three castes will have the right to education and that too, it will be restricted to what is strictly required for their profession. The salvation of others lies in serving their masters with dedication and sincerity, without worrying about the results of their *karma*. This is the law ordained by Lord Vishnu himself. Let any man who thinks he can change or challenge this law, do so at his own peril."

Vibhishana paused and frowned at the crowd. We sat stone-faced. Then, licking his lips, he continued, "This soil is blessed, for the great God Vishnu himself took *avatar* here. Men were defying fate, men were defying the Gods. Ravana tried to teach the world that mere human effort and will power could lead to success. He was worse than Mahabali, for Mahabali wisely surrendered his kingdom when Vishnu came as Vamana. But my brother, I am ashamed to say so, chose to fight God himself. Ravana was a brave man, but he was conceited and vain, and thought that he could be a match for Vishnu. He taught you wrong by teaching you to defy fate and encouraging you to think that you were in control of your own destiny.

God has put an end to the chaos unleashed by the evil genius of Ravana. The peaceful order of *varnashrama dharma* has been restored. No longer shall the men who clean drains and toilets think that they are equal to those who learn Sanskrit and chant the *Vedas*. No longer shall the toddy maker consider himself equal to the merchant selling silk. No longer shall the tiller of the soil think he is equal to an accountant. Everyone has their place and knows his place.

Mandodari, has taken the lead in setting an example of what a virtuous widow's conduct should be. We all know the shame that befell her in the heat of war. Great crimes were committed by both sides and she was an unfortunate victim," Vibhishana paused and suppressing a smile as he looked at Mandodari.

There were a few snide remarks and cat calls among the soldiers, but I could feel the impotent rage and hatred that burned in all our hearts. Bastard! He had no intention of stopping. The air was thick with impending rain and the light played hide and seek among the coconut palms. If I could somehow shut up the man who dared to call himself the leader of the Asuras. . .

"What happened to the Queen was unfortunate, and Lord Rama has punished the men responsible for it. But to our shame, my brother accepted the Queen after what had happened. He, like any other Asura, did not guard the notions of chastity and purity of woman. How could he accept her after what had happened? But, he did not know what was good and what was evil. Why did this war start? Was there any reason for the devastation? He could have remained King, as a vassal of the great God Rama.

I am ashamed to say, Soorpanakha, my own sister, started this war. She cannot be blamed completely. She was a product of our culture that allowed women the freedom to lead a loose life. She tried to seduce the handsome Lakshmana. This impudence of a widow to fall in love cannot be tolerated by any man. He punished Soorpanakha by mutilating her nose and ears.

Ravana, instead of accepting what God had ordained for our immoral sister, decided to wage war against Lord Rama. Such arrogance, such false pride. See what happened to him. I have banished Soorpanakha out of the country. She is my sister but I wanted to set an example and prove my master that the Asuras have decided to shed their old ways. My friend Varuna ensured that she was banished to land of barbarians across the seas. She is now a beggar and a destitute, eking out a living with her begging bowl. I am sad at the fate of my sister, but she deserved nothing less.

Then my brother kidnapped Lord Rama's wife. I have heard rumours that Sita is the daughter of Ravana and by kidnapping her, Ravana was trying to save his own daughter. There cannot be anything more deplorable. How could a low-born Asura have fathered a Deva princess? Rama is not like Ravana. Sita, his beloved wife, for whose sake he waged a bloody war and staked his own and his men's lives, has also sinned. I am sure, Sita, by virtue of being a Deva princess and wife of Lord Rama, has remained pure. Ravana did not dare to violate her. But, Lord Rama knows that the lustful eyes of Ravana and other Asuras have wandered over the pure body of his wife. Which husband would tolerate that? Lord Rama is a man, unlike my dead brother who accepted a violated wife, who wishes to set an example and prove to the whole world the chastity and purity of his wife. He wishes to burn the lustful thoughts of Ravana and other men from the body and soul of his wife forever.

This is a deeply moving personal affair, but it is also a public gesture by the Deva king for the whole world to emulate. Unlike the Asuras, the Devas believe in the purity of fire and life. Fire is the Supreme God, the giver of life and energy. Fire cleanses everything. The impurity of Sita in having lived with the Asuras and bearing the lustful eyes of the Asuras on her; and in living away from her husband for such a long period; for the baseless rumours suggesting that she is the daughter of Ravana; all these will be cleansed by fire. In front of all of you, in front of the Asuras and the Vanaras, in front of the whole world, Sita will undergo the supreme test the Devas have to test a woman's purity – the *Agni Pariksha*. The divine fire that is burning near the funeral pyre of my brother will determine how pure Sita *mata* is. If she is chaste and pure, she will remain unscathed. If she is impure, the divine fire will devour her.

A terrified hush fell over the crowd. Heads turned to look at Rama, who sat in his high-backed chair. He was looking down and I could see he was visibly shaken and distressed. Yet he did not stand up and say, 'Enough! I trust my wife'. Hanuman appeared tense and nervous, whereas Vibhishana gleefully enjoyed his duties. Lakshmana appeared pale and anxious, but tried to hide it with his trademark scowl. Mandodari, who was sitting in one corner with her tonsured head covered with a white veil, sobbed uncontrollably.

There was tension in the air and as if to match it, the first clap of thunder broke in the skies. I could see the black clouds of a thunder storm fast approaching the island. The sun was nothing but the silver edge of the looming dark clouds. A powerful wind swayed the coconut palms and huge waves crashed against the rocky boulders of the beach. People stood up as they dragged Sita towards the divine fire. Initially she resisted and cried out to her husband to save here. But when she comprehended the monstrosity of what her husband wanted her to do in order to prove her purity, she sagged and looked piteously at her him. He averted his eyes and looked straight ahead, beyond her, beyond his soldiers, beyond us, to some distant point on the horizon. Tears welled in his eyes. Beside him and his scowling brother, fat Brahmin priests chanted in Sanskrit, drowning the excited voices of the crowd and the sobs of Mandodari and the other women.

On the beach, Vibhishana, the newly crowned King of the Asuras and vassal of Rama, stood with a flaming torch in his hand and a satisfied smile on his face. In front of him lay the erstwhile King of the Asuras, dead, his face half-eaten by beasts, his head severed from his rotting body, on a funeral pyre. Near him, the fire that knew what chastity is, raged with its hundred arms.

The Asura soldiers left Sita near Vibhishana and marched back. The excitement in the crowd rose to dizzying heights. Never before had they seen anything like this. The sun set into the red sea that rose and fell. Silver-edged, dark clouds loomed in the sky, creating a dark and evil world of sinister-looking reptiles that twisted, turned and reflected a myriad colours from the dying sun.

"With this I end the evil reign of Ravana. With this I end the audacity of a man who dared to challenge the Gods. With this, I end the debauched life of a demon who nearly destroyed the world. Victory to Sri Rama. . ." Vibhishana thundered over the crowd and lit the funeral pyre of his brother as the rain began to fall.

A deep and inexplicable grief gripped me as I watched Ravana turn into ashes. An era had ended. A huge cheer rose from the Vanaras while the Asuras hung their heads in shame. Sita stood near the burning body of her father without any emotion, lost in her own world of grief and betrayal.

"As King of the Asuras, I proclaim that this day shall be celebrated every year, in every village of India, as the day of Victory. On this day, every man, woman and child shall be reminded of the victory of our Lord, *avatar* of Vishnu, Sri Ramachandra of Ayodhya, over the evil called Ravana. Let Ravana die a million deaths every year on this day, in every village, street, and home of India. . ." Vibhishana raised the flaming torch towards the sky and the Vanaras and a few Asuras cheered with enthusiasm. The sky responded with angry thunder and it began to drizzle. The pyre burned hesitantly as thick, black smoke coiled upwards, flickering, shattering, and re-forming in the wind.

"Now comes the test of purity, the *Agni Pariksha* for the respected and beloved wife of our Lord." Vibhishana announced. An Asura servant poured more *ghee* into the burning pyre. The flames rose high and crackled in the wind. We all watched in horror and excitement, as Sita hesitated, looking at the raging fire into which she was supposed to step to prove her chastity to her husband. She looked at Rama, trying to catch his eye, but the God, like other Gods, looked away when he was most needed. Vibhishana became impatient and ordered more *ghee* to be poured into the fire. Sita stood there for a few moments longer. Then she slowly collapsed onto the floor. There was an awkward silence among the crowd. Had she backed out?

Someone near me whispered, "She might not be as pure as she looks, that is why she is not ready to face the fire."

His neighbours snickered, each colouring their own imagination with lewd thoughts.

I angrily turned and said, "Such nonsense! Even if she is not virtuous, how can it be proved by entering a raging fire? A fire cannot discriminate between a virtuous and non-virtuous."

The man who had made comments about Sita clearly did not like what I said. "So you, an ignorant peasant, knows all about fire. This is what the learned Brahmins have said. Who are we to question them?" Though a few appeared sceptical, most nodded their heads in agreement. I had missed a little of what was happening in talking to these idiots.

Sita had stood up. Again the crowd sensed that something was going to happen. Then with sudden strength, she ran towards the raging fire. Did we hear correctly or was it my imagination? I'm still not sure. Did she cry out, "Father. . ." before she jumped into the fire? A gasp went up from the crowd and at that moment the skies opened up and tons of water poured down. The wind had turned into a full-fledged storm and the coconut palms swayed and coiled, the fronds whirling in a frenzy like the arms of a drowning man. It had grown unnaturally dark and the lightning that blazed gave everyone a ghostly appearance. The crowd pushed towards the funeral pyre of their slain King and soon became uncontrollable. Policemen pushed and shoved back the crowd and there was total chaos. The pyre had gone out and we saw Hanuman carrying Sita to Rama. She appeared limp, but to my experienced eyes she seemed to be alive. So, she was pure after all. I remembered when I had held her in my hands in the Vindhya forests, a small bundle of life given to me by the Asura nobles to bury.

The crowd disappeared after the *mela* as the main actors disappeared into the fort for another night of celebration. I stood there drenched in the raging tropical storm till the crowd thinned and then slowly walked towards Ravana's funeral pyre. It was still raining but not as heavily as before. The pyre was a mess. It was a mush of ash and mud, with bits of bone and half-burnt skull protruding haphazardly. I stood there not knowing what to do. Then I kicked the bones and other remnants of the great Asura Emperor into the raging waters of the sea. After some time, I walked back home to sleep.

62 Life sprouts again

Bhadra

The months after the death of Ravana, were a horrible period in the life of the Asuras. There was confusion regarding the new caste hierarchy and plenty of caste conflicts. Each family got itself aligned to whichever caste which they thought would emerge on top. If it had been only a clear division on the basis of four *varnas*, it would not have been so difficult to find one's caste. The hierarchy would have been well defined and everyone would have just obeyed or fought against it. I do not know whether it was an act of genius or a reflection of muddled thinking, that devised the bewildering system of castes and sub-castes. It divided our society into a million parts, with the Brahmins clearly at the top.

It took me almost three months to understand that I belonged to the caste of washermen, which was theoretically lower than goldsmiths, carpenters, etc, but miles higher than travelling minstrels, woodcutters, potters, and the rest. I was not permitted to walk on the road when those belonging to higher castes, decided to use the road. But I, in turn, had the right to kick a potter if he dared to cross my path. My purity was besmirched if I touched a woodcutter, but, in turn, if I ever touched a carpenter, I could cause impurity. None of these castes belonging to the lowest rung, could walk on the streets or wear good clothes or have fine houses or enter the temples – all of which reserved for the people of the other three *varnas*. It was a perverse system and depended on the base emotions of man to inflict humiliation on those under him. I would have to accept any insult from a higher caste person, because I had the right to torture those below me. And then, gripping poverty cast a pall of doom over the dispirited Asura populace.

After about nine months, a terrible famine broke out in the south of India and on the islands. Trade came to a standstill as the Brahmins decried that crossing the black waters of the ocean would result in losing one's caste. The merchant class, in fear of losing their newly-found privileges, refused to go to sea and soon the Chinese and yellow haired barbarians, took over the trade of spices and fine things. Soon there was nothing to eat. But Vibhishana's tax collectors showed no mercy in extracting the last morsel due to the government. There was one person who could have worked a miracle to set right the leaky dams and canals, and restart the farming in the countryside. But the mad scientist Mayan, was now a prisoner in chains, held in a dungeon. The Brahmins laughed at his theories and proclaimed all that he had achieved had been the result of black magic of the Asuras.

It was a dark time indeed. There seemed no hope of escape other than through death. We were lucky if we got one square meal a week. The only good thing was that I had built a small thatched house with the logs and furniture I had stolen during the disturbed times following Ravana's death. I had buried the gold ornaments I had taken from Ravana's corpse, inside my house. I was afraid to take them out. A man of the *dhobi* caste was not supposed to own valuable things. In the first week of his reign, Vibhishana had seized any personal wealth of the lower castes. But, like me, many had buried their wealth.

When all seemed lost, a flicker of hope came in the form of a rumour. Varuna had been transporting people illegally to the countries of the Far East. No scriptures could touch or Brahmins excommunicate men like Varuna. He made money whether Kubera, Ravana, or Rama ruled. He served only one god – money. I was initially sceptical, but when the pangs of hunger grew and the nagging of my woman became unbearable, I decided to give it a try. No sooner had I vaguely expressed my wish to migrate, than an agent came to arrange it for me.

The agent was a middle-aged man of probably my own age. But since he did not face poverty and hunger like me, I must have looked like an aged uncle to him. To my great irritation and the amusement of my wife, he insisted on calling me 'Uncle'. He was a government officer, having started his career with Kubera, and was now a senior official in Vibhishana's administration. He claimed he was a liberal and did not think too highly of the new caste rules. However, for his wife's sake, he did not wish to enter my house as he was a few notches above me in the caste hierarchy. He also refused any refreshments as his wife would not have approved of his touching anything prepared by a *dhobi*. I fumed, but my wife appeared relaxed. We didn't have anything to offer him anyway, so his insistence on caste purity saved us some embarrassment.

We met under an old tamarind tree near the river. He sat on a protruding root of the tree and then the haggling began. Twice he pretended to walk away from the deal and once I did the same. He kept telling me that he was an important government officer and did not care for the small commission the low castes could pay. But it was evident that he was desperate to fix the deal as he stood to gain an agent's commission from both sides. Varuna did not pay his agents well, so they threatened, cajoled and coaxed the maximum money out of the wannabe emigrants. We nearly came to blows, but my wife took me aside and tried to bring some sense to my agitated mind.

Reluctantly, I returned home and after half an hour of digging and much heart burn, I walked back to meet the greedy public servant, with Ravana's ornaments trembling in my hands. There was a gleam in the agent's eyes as the gold glittered in the moonshine. The bureaucrat had been chatting to my wife about the general state of affairs and how difficult it now was for a middle class family to live, with spiralling prices, the rising cost of education and so on. He absentmindedly took the gold in his hands and weighed it. He was all smiles after that. It was all fixed. A canoe would take us to a ship anchored in the high seas, within two days. We just had to get in and would be assured a first class passage to the lands of the Far East. He sang the praises of the eastern lands, where there was plenty of work to be had and gold coins could be casually picked up from the streets that were paved with gold. He left us when the moon had risen directly overhead and the traffic had thinned on the street. Mala and I stood hand in hand under the old tamarind tree by the river like two love struck teenagers, listening to the sweet rippling of the river and smelling the faint fragrance of Jasmine that wafted on the breeze. Perhaps life was offering us another chance. Who knew?

The canoe did not come for two weeks and I was sick with worry. Twice I walked all the way to the office where the fat officer had told us he worked and was unable to meet him both times. Then, when I had almost given up, on a very dark night, there was a discreet tap on the door. I woke and hurriedly pushed aside the terrifying images of one such dark night, decades ago, when Deva marauders had come visiting my humble hut on the banks of the Poorna. I waited for another tap. When it came, I slowly opened the door and saw the ghostly face of the fat officer lit by a flickering lamp. He grinned and gestured to me to come out. I opened the door and he thrust a palm leaf at me. There were two or three dark figures hiding in the shadows.

I went back in and woke my wife. She became excited when she heard that our ticket to paradise had come. Quickly she picked up our meagre belongings, packed in a cloth bundle, and followed me out. We walked to the river where a canoe was waiting. There were three other couples and a holy man, in the canoe. Silently we got into the canoe and waited. After a delay of half an hour, another couple joined us and the fat man waved cheerfully to all of us. The canoe slowly drifted towards the river mouth, carried by the current. Lanka, the land I had adopted and spent the major part of my life in, slowly drifted away from us as I sat choked with conflicting emotions; lonely among so many people, all lost in their own thoughts and dreams.

A dark ship loomed large in the distance. Slowly the canoe approached the ship. A rope ladder dangled on its side. One by one, we were hauled up. We stood on the deck of the large ship, waiting for somebody to take us to our first class cabins. After some time, a clerk came in with a palm leaf. He checked the tickets and ordered the passengers to their respective cabins. I had struck up a conversation with a young couple and learnt that they had been recently married. The girl was coy, with lovely almond eyes, and the boy looked innocent and handsome. They had sold their coconut grove to a Brahmin and had taken passage. The girl's name was Arasi and the boy, Shiva.

When the clerk approached us, we stopped our chatter and handed him our tickets respectfully. He frowned and asked, "Which caste you are?"

"Why does that matter to you?" Shiva was irritated.

"You people look so dark and uncouth, you might be of the untouchable pariah caste. I cannot take you on board. The other high caste passengers may object."

"What do you mean you cannot take us on board. We paid the full amount for the passage." I intervened before Shiva did something rash and foolish.

"I don't know. There appears to be some mix up. The company will refund your money within six months, once you go to our office in the capital and apply for the refund. I am sorry but I cannot take you. You can get down now as the canoe has not left. Or else you may be forced to swim back." The clerk turned to go down to his cabin.

"Give me your necklace," my wife commanded the perplexed Arasi. Reluctantly the girl unclasped the only precious thing she had left and gave it to Mala, who thrust it into my hands and whispered, "Fall at his feet and somehow save the situation. We cannot go back."

I almost dove to catch hold onto one of the clerk's feet.

"Hey you!" He kicked me with his free leg. 'How dare you touch and pollute me? Get out! Get out I say, you old rascal."

But I did not let go. In my most pitiable voice I cried, "Swami, please do not send us off. We cannot go back. We shall scrub the deck and clean the toilets but please take us with you. Do not forsake us. You are our God. Here is a small offering for you. Have pity on us Swami." I held the necklace up so he could have a good look at it. When he saw it, he forgot all about impurity and grasped the treasure with alacrity. I stood up, crossed my hands over my chest, tucked my palms under my armpits, and bowed my back in supplication. My companions took their cue from me and stood with all the humility they could muster.

He once again checked his leaf and after pocketing the necklace, told us with the air of granting us a great favour, "Go down to the lower deck. I don't want to see your dark faces until we reach the city of the Lion. Make yourself useful by scrubbing the kitchen floors, washing the dirty linen, and cleaning the toilets. Hurry!"

With that, he prodded me down the stairway that led to the lower decks, being careful not to come into contact with any of us. The others followed me. It was dark and dirty on the lowermost deck and the odour of stale garlic and rotten onions came from the kitchen.

We almost broke our backs working on Varuna's ship, constantly cleaning utensils, scrubbing floors, washing linen, and emptying the toilet cans into the sea. We hardly saw sunlight and the constant rolling and heaving of the massive wooden ship made us sick. Eventually, after a journey of almost a month, we heard the joyous shout of men from the upper deck, celebrating the sighting of land. We crept to the upper deck and the bright sunshine almost blinded us. There was the mouth of a river and verdant forests running on its either side. Mangroves stretched as far as the eye could see and the tall, black spire of a temple came into view as the ship entered the wide river. We had never seen a river as wide and excitement flooded our veins. Soon the ship decked at a port where strange looking men wearing white turbans, ran around loading and unloading the goods from the ships.

The clerk smiled sheepishly at us and vanished down the ladder to mix with the crowds. After some confusion, we decided to leave for land and slowly got down. Already a queue had formed at the ticketing office of Varuna's shipping service, and I decided to enquire whether this was the city of the Lion in the east. The first few people I asked, stared back at me with blank faces. But I finally found a man as dark skinned as us and picked up enough courage to approach him. He was talking to two tall and fair men and I waited for a chance to speak. Then I asked him in Tamil, whether this was the city of the Lion. He stared at me as if I was mad and then asked, "Have you idiots come in on Varuna's ship?"

We looked at each other and a chill spread in our hearts. "Why, Swami, why are you asking. . .?"

The black man said something in Sanskrit to his fair companions and they all burst out laughing. Then he turned to me and said, "What caste are you?"

"*Dhobi*, Swami," I answered, though I was not sure what caste Arasi and Shiva belonged to.

"No wonder you people are so stupid. This is the city of the Goddess Kali. Varuna has duped you as he has done to many others."

Arasi let out a loud wail and sat on the ground, beating her head. Mala soon joined her. I seethed with impotent rage. Tears sprang from my eyes and I joined the women. An embarrassed Shiva begged the black man for a solution to our problem. He tried to shove us away, but Shiva was persistent. Finally, the black man bid good-bye to his fair friends. Then he turned towards us and shouted at us to shut up so that he could think. Finally he said, "See friends, this is a small town. You may get a job here, but there is another big city up north-west, called Ayodhya, where King Rama rules. That city is booming now and there are plenty of jobs for coolies like you. The wages are good, I have heard. Try your luck there. There is a rice barge sailing up to Ayodhya through the Sarayu river. The owner is a merchant who migrated from the south. I will put in a word and if you are lucky, you could get some space. For tonight, there is a place near the temple of Kali where they serve the poor free meals. Have food there and come at sunrise to the Rice *Ghat*. Now, do not cry for what has happened. Perhaps, it is all for your good." Saying this, he pointed us in the direction of the Kali temple. "And do not take the front road. Outcastes are not allowed through that road, take the small path at the back." he shouted as he jumped into a small boat and floated down the river.

The night we spent in the city of Kali, we did not go hungry. We got some food at the temple, late at night. I could not sleep as I could hear the roar of tigers from the mangrove jungles nearby and mosquitoes buzzed in my ears. I was also curious about Ayodhya. It was perhaps a year since Rama had flown away in the *Pushpaka* with his brother and wife, to Ayodhya. The Vanaras had carried off as much loot as they could physically haul, and left on foot and by ship, within a few months.

As day dawned we boarded the rice barge and sailed towards Ayodhya. After three days, we reached Rama's capital. The city had grown from the small village it had been when I had seen it three decades earlier, with Ravana's conquering army. Though it was no match for the glitter of Trikota or Muzuris in their heyday, there was now an air of prosperity. But certain things had not changed. Cows roamed the streets freely, blocking the traffic and lying down wherever they pleased but the lower caste and dark-skinned people were not allowed where even dogs, swine and cows could roam. There were open drains with swine and rats playing in them. A perpetual stink enveloped the city.

We roamed around, terrified that we could be breaking some caste taboo or the other by walking through streets where we were not allowed. All the signs were in Sanskrit and people spoke in that strange tongue, which we did not understand. We were pushed and shoved angrily and soon attracted the attention of the city police. We were taken to the local police station where they tried questioning us in various ways. Rama's police were no different from Ravana's police. They beat me with their *lathi*s and kicked Shiva, while the woman screamed and cried.

Finally, they brought in a man who ran a shop across the street, who could speak Tamil. We told him how we had landed up in Ayodhya and he translated it to the police. The policemen laughed at our folly and after their merriment was over, asked the shop owner to enquire about our castes. When they heard that we belonged to the *dhobi* caste, they directed him to take us to where our caste brethren lived. The shop keeper protested. Perhaps he was reluctant to leave his shop unmanned. But after the policeman lashed him, he understood what was important.

The *dhobi* colony was by the river and stretched far to the north. The merchant showed us the colony and vanished before we could even thank him. The colony was a city unto itself. There were people belonging to all races – Asuras, Nagas, Kinnaras, Gandharvas, coal black barbarians, yellow skinned Chinese, yellow haired barbarian races from some cold countries, and people of mixed race. But they all belonged to one caste, *dhobi*. Here, in the north, the caste system was ancient and entrenched. One belonged to the lowest caste of one's parents, though one may not have resembled either of them. Races had mixed for thousands of years but one's caste remained the same. The system was established and a caste headman decided what was best for the whole caste and so ruled like a king.

We were taken to the headman, who interviewed us and allotted us a hut near the river. A tenth of our monthly earnings were to go to the caste treasury, which obviously the old head man controlled. We could not complain as we needed a roof over our heads and food. We took possession of our hut and began a new life.

There was no concept of plumbing or closed drains in the Deva countries and we had to relieve ourselves in the open, near the river. The river where everyone defecated and the buffalos bathed, was considered sacred, and drinking water for the city was supplied from the same place where we washed dirty linen. Slowly our life found its own rhythm. We picked up Sanskrit and were able to communicate better with our neighbours. As long as we kept to our place and did not aspire to be anything higher, the straight-laced caste system of the Devas worked well. The government collected tax through the headman, who then negotiated his own percentage. No policeman or any other government official, ever entered the *dhobi* village. It would have been the same with the potters or weavers villages.

Once a fortnight, we went to the market outside the city and bought whatever we needed. Life was simple and straightforward, with none of the complexities of the freewheeling, fiercely competitive, urban world of the Asuras. The caste system was brutal and the indignities heaped on the lower castes were inhuman, but inside one's own caste village, there was a strange kind of equality, with the possible exception of the headman's family. No upper caste members entered the village.

One of the greatest advantages of this Deva system was the lack of competition. Each task was assigned to a caste and all the members of the same caste were assured of a job and two square meals. Unlike Ravana's cities, like Trikota or Muzuris or Gokarna or Mahabalipuram, where different cultures and races mingled; where people dared to dream about making it big; where trade, science, art and architecture flourished; where urbanity, planning, design and aesthetics all had their place; where fiercely competitive men and women fought in different spears of life to create a mark in the world; where men of immeasurable talent and scientists like Mayan flourished; but which also forced a huge population that had fallen back in the rat race to live in inhuman slums, barely able to keep body and soul together; Rama's cities like Ayodhya or Mithila, were different. These cities were an agglomeration of self-contained caste villages that interacted with each other for their minimum needs. Unlike the dynamic and brutally competitive, materialistic, yet magnificent cities of the Asuras, the cities of Rama presented a picture of a closed and static world, with the caste system forming its foundation. It put each one firmly in their place, depending on the accident of birth. In this system, dreams had no chance and aspirations were dangerous. We immigrants would soon discover this.

Life went on smoothly and as the years passed, Arasi gave birth to a son. We named him Shambuka, after Shiva. The boy grew fast and was intelligent beyond his years. Slowly I found happiness in my life. In playing with the boy, teaching him to swim, training him to hunt for small birds, I had rediscovered my youth. I had stopped doing hard work for several years and Shiva, who had become a son to me, took on the additional burden. He was such a hardworking man and enterprising too. He had begged and bribed his way to get the contract for washing the palace linen and it was our ticket to worldly success. That he was able to prosper, was perhaps due to the inherent competitive nature of his Asura heritage that was aroused when the opportunity presented itself. We expanded our home and added two cows to the donkeys we already had. We were slowly moving up in life. My days were spent gazing at the calmly flowing river; the serene, cloud-filled sky; the barges that floated lazily down the river;

and the wild Herons and Kingfishers that dove into the water for fish. Many times Shambuka accompanied me on these excursions, calling me Grandpa and nagging me for something or the other. My heart filled with joy and pride whenever I heard his boyish prattle and once again I started to fall in love with this beautiful life and this wonderful world.

63 Childish dreams

Bhadra

It is always when everything appears dream-like and life seems to possess a never-ending charm, that foolish thoughts and dangerous aspirations take birth in the minds of humans. Shambuka was intelligent and handsome, but that was no reason for Arasi to think that he should grow up to be more than a washerman. Once such thoughts enter a mother's mind, that her child is special, nothing can shake them free. She wished her son to be an important official, or perhaps a famous poet, or a great merchant – anything other than a lowly *dhobi*. I warned her that people like us should not dare to dream. Shiva also tried to reason with her but she remained adamant. Mala joined Arasi in demanding that Shambuka be educated. The women reasoned that we had money and the boy had talent, so why should he be left illiterate? But the boy was eight years old and it was too late. Had he lived in one of the Asura cities, he would have become fairly competent in reading, writing and mathematics by then.

They kept nagging and finally, against my objections and protests, Shiva relented and decided to find a way to send the boy to school. I did not like the decision, but was fairly confident that no one would teach a *dhobi*'s son anything, so I was not overly worried. But I had not taken into account the fact that money can break even the most strict taboos. Shiva found a teacher who was almost a recluse, living across the river.

On the other side of the river Sarayu, lay a thick jungle. With the fowls and beasts, there lived a few ascetics who did nothing other than smear their bodies in ashe, wear skulls and bones as ornaments, and sometimes stand in difficult and acrobatic postures for hours together. Ostensibly they were in search of God, or their inner selves, or *brahman*, but they were a seedy crowd who did not fit in with the rigid caste system of the Devas and found sanctuary in their reclusiveness. As a rule they were addicted to intoxicants and a few punished themselves in exotic ways. The common people were afraid of this motley crowd and whispered in hushed tones about their mystical powers. I had ventured many times to those parts and had struck up conversations with a few of them. They were surprisingly blind to casteism and I went there for the freedom their company offered. They were the only people who never asked me about my caste and some were even happy to share a drink or a smoke with me. That was my secret world.

Shiva had found one of the ascetics who could not have cared less about caste purity. He loved his wine from the city and yearned for some herbs to smoke. I was deputed to supply him with his fees, in exchange for his services in teaching Shambuka. I found myself enjoying his company and his herbs. He was a learned man, equally well versed in Sanskrit, Tamil, Naga, Gandharva, and Kinnara dialects, and a handful of barbarian languages. He was also well versed in the Brahmin Vedas, astrology and other sciences. Shambuka could not have had a better teacher. The ascetic only insisted that he be called Guru.

In one of his drunken spells, he spelt out his earlier life. He was a Brahmin from the land of the five rivers, but had travelled to Ayodhya in his early youth. He had done odd jobs and was on the verge of making it big as a government official, but became disgusted with the caste system, though it gave him privileges as a Brahmin. He was in Ayodhya when Rama relinquished his right of inheritance to respect his father's vows and had witnessed the meeting of the young Deva prince and the saint Jabali. Jabali had argued with Rama, trying to convince him that there was nothing called God or afterlife or soul, and one had to live this life and enjoy it till one died. But the puritan and self-righteous Rama, had refused to accept all the logical reasoning of Jabali and had left for the forest with his young wife and his younger brother. However, Guru had been impressed by Jabali and had impulsively decided to relinquish his high paying government job and become his follower. When Dasratha, Rama's father, had been King, he tolerated all shades of opinion and Jabali was allowed to roam free in the city, declaiming the absurdity of the caste system. But when Bharata, the younger brother of Rama, ascended the throne in the name of Rama, he hunted down any dissenting men and ensured the orthodoxies were kept intact.

Jabali and his followers had been banished to the other bank of the Sarayu, and soon other men with differing opinions and schools of thought, also found asylum on that bank. Jabali was dead but his traditions lingered on, along with the other conflicting schools of thought. After Jabali's death, his followers took it as a mission to educate as many as possible, irrespective of caste. But over the years, the iron grip of the system had tightened and only a few dared to become educated. Those who did, escaped from India to the lands across the mountains, to China, or to the lands beyond the seas, where only the merit of a man mattered and not his accident of birth.

Shambuka listened to all this with eyes wide open and I was disturbed by the strange gleam in them. Later, when I would row him back across the inky black waters of the Sarayu, he would speak of his dream of becoming a great poet who would mesmerize his audience with his dazzling poetry. I kept rowing as the young boy brimmed with life and promise. Then one night, with a million stars as witness, with the cold waters of the Sarayu rippling over the heart of India and the silver moon reflecting in his black curls, Shambuka broke into melodious song. He sang about a world of freedom, a world of hope, of a tomorrow that was never to be. His song dissolved in the breeze that caressed the lowly huts of the poor and curled around the palace towers where the Gods resided in the guise of men. I reached the shore of the Dhobi *Ghat* when the lights had gone out in most homes. The boy had fallen asleep. With a heavy heart, I tied up the boat and carried the sleeping boy home on my tired shoulders.

64 The sword of *Dharma*

Bhadra

As the days passed by, the boy developed wonderfully. His voice grew rich in its tenor and his verses became lyrical. People began to wait at the *Ghat* for our boat to return at night. His songs reached the shore before the prow of our boat disturbed the little pool of golden light near the shore where men and women sat listening rapturously to the sweet voice that wafted over the dark, gently rippling water. Every night, as I walked my little boy through the admiring crowd, with his small fingers clasped firmly around my wrinkled wrist, the audience sometimes sung with him, sometimes clapped to the rhythm, or silently wept with him. He sang in Sanskrit, but the emotions that pulsed were universal and the yearnings that radiated were primeval. It struck a chord with everyone who chanced to hear it even once. It penetrated the thick muck of religion, caste and custom that had pasted itself over men's hearts and instead, appealed to the inner goodness of all human beings.

As his fame grew, my fear increased. I tried to prevent him from going out of our little caste village, to make him understand that outside, a dark and cruel world was waiting to snap him up, a world inhabited by Gods and their chosen men, who would brook no challenge to their supremacy. But the boy had tasted the sweetness of freedom. He could not be tied to a stinking village of outcastes with the chains of tradition. He was at a stage of life when everything appeared sunny and bright and the future spread ahead infinitely with grand promises. That was the danger of education.

It gave birth to dreams that had no legs to stand on firmly in the real world. I tried to reason with him, saying that as per the Vedas, we, the outcastes, were not supposed to learn anything other than our caste duties. Not that I knew much about the Vedas, other than what I had heard about from the Brahmin priests, who quoted obscure phrases for no rhyme or reason. Instead, he surprised me with his clear rendition of the Vedas and translated the meaning for me. He challenged me to show him a single verse that sanctioned caste.

I did not care whether the Vedas sanctioned caste or not. But this was a revelation to me. As an Asura, I had been taught to hate all that was considered holy by the Devas. Shambuka said that his Guru had taught him the real meaning of the Vedas and they were not the monopoly of any single caste or profession. They were a collection of the thoughts of poets who had lived thousands of years ago, who came from varied professions such as fishermen, priests, woodcutters, potters, hunters and many more. It was only later that selfish men appropriated the Vedas for their own means and used them as a convenient tool to beat others with.

Shambuka had become too smart for his own good. I wanted to murder that Brahmin, that disciple of Jabali, who had muddled up my little Shambuka's brain. Even if all the things he said were true, they were dangerous truths and not to be uttered even in private. And that Brahmin had taught my naïve little grandson to sing it in public. I pleaded with the boy but he remained adamant. I pleaded with the father and mother of the boy, and my wife too, but they were all in a dream world, misty-eyed at the success of their little one in the world. He began to go out of the village and sing. He quoted eloquently from the Vedas and then added spice to his speech with logic and the rendering of folktales. Men and women flocked to hear the little boy's sweet voice. They crowded onto the streets and showered him with flowers. He became too famous for his own good.

Then it happened. It was inevitable, so I was not shocked. The boy was confronted on the royal highway by a group of priests who did not wish the lower castes to pollute the highway. The boy refused to move and challenged them on the very authority which they themselves used to condone such an atrocious thing. Enraged, the head priest rumbled forth some obscure Sanskrit verses, which he imagined would intimidate this low caste rascal. The boy, with his head full of the knowledge his Guru had imparted, challenged the priests with accepted interpretations of the verses as well as his own version. By the time the news reached me and our family had rushed to the spot, a huge crowd had gathered to watch the debate. The crowd cheered whenever the boy opened his mouth to render a melodious verse in Sanskrit.

The crowd had forgotten all the taboos assiduously built by the Brahmins about who should use the public road and when, and who could or could not touch whom, along with all the other complicated rules of the caste system. They jostled together, polluting each other and getting polluted by touch and sight, just to hear Shambuka sing. The boy questioned the rituals and the sacrifices, just as his Guru had taught him, and he challenged the idea of caste and the supremacy of one human being over another, based merely on the accident of birth, as the crowd cheered him on.

The high priests of the kingdom were getting more and more agitated as the boy continued to question them, not using the rational atheistic arguments as the master of his Guru, Jabali, would have done, but using the verses from the Vedas and the Upanishads. He recited verses from the Vedas and then translated them into Prakrit for the common people on the street to understand.

The crowd howled and cheered madly as I grew more and more uneasy with every passing moment. Shambuka asked the questions which everyone on street had always wanted to ask, but had never dared to. He asked for the truth and I, from the vantage of my advanced years knew what the fate seekers of truth had always met with. With growing trepidation I watched the army surround the crowd. I could sense a change in the mood of the crowd. The cheering grew less and less in volume and slowly died altogether. There was tension in the air but the boy seemed unaware of what was happening around him. In the thick silence that enveloped thousands of impotent, cowardly men and women, his voice rose in a sweet melody.

A chariot came in fast and stopped at the corner where Shambuka stood in a trance, reciting the Vedas loudly and sweetly. From the chariot, King Rama stepped down. The priests ran to him and whispered something in his ear. He became uneasy and shook his head. He looked as if he was pleading with his priests, but the head priest, a dark, fat man with an immense torso, angrily demanded something of the king. The King's shoulders sank as he heard what his priests were telling him. He moved forward as if to wake Shambuka from his trance. The crowd waited with baited breath. But the fat priest moved in-between and saved the great King from such a polluting touch. Shambuka also sensed something and woke from his trance. He looked bewildered at the sight before him. The boy became afraid and started to cry. The crying broke the spell. He was no longer a great poet and singer who could move men to tears. He was just a small boy of fourteen, a mere untouchable, a black Asura and a non entity. He looked at his King and protector and made a deep bow. Rama again looked helplessly at his priests, who angrily pointed at the boy, shouting.

The King raised his hands to shut up the Brahmins and asked the boy, "Son, who are you?"

"I am Shambuka, son of Shiva," the boy murmured.

"What caste are you?"

"I do not have a caste, nor do you." The boy looked into the eyes of the king.

"Is it true that you are an untouchable?"

"I am not untouchable, nor is anyone else."

"Are you an atheist?"

"I am a firm believer in God, who is within each one of us. I am God and so are you."

"Who granted permission for a Shudhra to learn the Vedas?" Rama was getting angry now.

"Do the birds need permission to fly? Do the fish swim on someone's authority? Learning, for humans, is like swimming for fish or flying for birds."

"You arrogant fool! Do you know the punishment meted out in our kingdom to the lower castes who are arrogant enough to break their caste dharma?" The head priest barked at Shambuka.

Rama looked at the priests, pleading. He had the same look on his face when his wife's purity was tested by fire. He knew what the boy said was true, and his eyes betrayed infinite compassion for the small boy whose soul-stirring song rose above the murmurs of the crowd. He looked at the priests again.

In answer to this question, Shambuka broke into a Sanskrit song from some obscure Upanishad that said death was nothing but a temporary address change for the soul, and just as a man changed his clothes when they were old and tattered and bought new clothes, the soul too, sought a new body. I should really have had a word with that Guru who had taught such nonsense to my little boy. When would people learn the simple things – that death was the end and if you died, your body rotted and dissolved in the soil.

The fat priest, now raised his voice and told the crowd, "This Shudhra, this arrogant untouchable, has dared to break the most important of caste rules. Not only has this Shudhra dared to become literate, he has gone to the extent of learning the holy Vedas. And he is misinterpreting what is written in the Holy Books. There is only one fate that awaits such arrogant hotheads."

He looked at King Rama with the air of a man who has said what he knew to be right and now the responsibility to act on those words had shifted to the others. A tremor passed through the crowd. The soldiers closed into a tight circle, with their swords drawn, spears pointed towards the crowd, waiting for any idiot who was foolish enough to move. A crow cawed, punctuating the thick silence. I trembled at the thought of what was coming. Rama had his sword drawn now. Shambuka's cheeks were wet from his tears and his little, innocent face wore an expression of someone who had tried his best and failed. He looked tired beyond his years. I could hear the thump thump of some women washing dirty linen far away, which gave an eerie rhythm to the hot, sweltering day. It as if someone or something had begun a countdown. When I had counted fourteen thumps, Rama's mighty sword came swishing down and severed the head of my little grandson.

The show was over. The crowd dispersed to their homes, some excitedly talking to each other, others going about their business as if nothing had happened. I pushed towards the place where Shambuka lay without his head. Rama's chariot flew past, cutting the thinning crowd in two. Soldiers pushed men and women out of its way to ensure a smooth passage for the fleeing king, to his palace. I wanted to jump in front of the chariot and pull the man down from the lofty pedestal he clung to; drag him down through the mud and grab his bleeding sword, the sticky, red one that had severed my little boy's neck, and thrust it deep into his heart. Instead, I stood feeble and whimpering, gaping at the disappeared man in his speeding chariot, immersed in my messy grief.

As I stood watching helplessly, the chariot disappearing in a cloud of dust, it suddenly veered to the left and stopped. Soldiers ran to the royal chariot and a commotion developed. I dragged myself there to see what had happened. For a moment, I wished that Rama has been assassinated, but then I ruefully remembered that such things as natural justice exist only in the wistful imaginations of idealists. I was too old a dog to be tempted with that kind of bone.

Rama stood before a distraught Arasi and Mala, embarrassment and anger written clearly on his face. The women had blocked the King's path. Animal screams came from the mother's mouth as she tore her hair in despair. Mala beat her breasts with a violence that surprised me.

"Why did you kill my little one? What were you afraid of? You. . ."

Soldiers rushed to push away the women from the path of the God. But Rama stopped them with a flick of his hand. "Mother, your son broke the sacred rules of the land and as King, I had to protect the *dharma*."

Arasi spat on the ground and viciously barked at the King, "Sacred laws. . .*dharma*. . . If your *dharma* needs to be protected from a little boy, by killing him, if *dharma* is afraid of a few Sanskrit words uttered by a child, think if you can, you ruler of this sacred land, what sort of *dharma* you are protecting and whose hands hold the strings that control you. . ."

Rama stood speechless, his Brahmin aides glowering at the little, dark woman who had asked questions which no one else had even dared to think about. I pushed my way towards the scene, but before I could reach the spot, the soldiers had whisked the women away. When she was being dragged through the street by her hair, Arasi cursed her King with all the rage of a helpless mother whose only child had been killed, "You will pay for this Rama, you will pay for this. You may be a champion of some *smriti*s that treat the helpless, the poor, the weak, and women, like worms, but mark my words. . .never again. . .never again. . .will you know what happiness is. There is a *dharma*, the law of the natural world, that is bigger. . .stronger than all these verses. That *dharma* will come for you..." She kept screaming but the curses grew fainter and fainter and slowly died away as the soldiers dragged her away from the King.

The crowd gawked at this scene, enjoying the drama. They would talk about this for a long time. Before I reached the chariot, I heard the whip fall on the poor horses' backs with vengeance and the chariot shot forward to the safety of the palace walls. I stood there coughing and choking in the swirling dust that had arisen in the wake of the royal chariot. I was drenched in sweat and stooped by the weight of the *dharma* that was crushing us. The crowd melted away. I collapsed on the dusty, red earth and cried for a long time. I cried for my little boy and his parents, for my other son whom I had adopted as my own, but who was claimed by Kings and Gods for their own glory. But more than anything, I cried for my blasted country. I clenched the earth in both fists and screamed, "Cry my mother, for the kind of rulers you beget. . .worse. . .cry my mother, for the kind of men you breed. . ."

Someone kicked me in the ribs. I tried to get up but he kicked me again. He kicked me into the open drain. "Drunken beggar, I would have run over you, you idiot. Why have you chosen my cart to commit suicide? Son of a low caste." It was a merchant hurrying to the market to make more money and I was lying in his way and trying to reform my country. He kicked me into the place that I deserved. . .the stinking drain. I lay in an open drain of Ayodhya and watched the world go by without bothering about anything that had happened. I also watched them carry away the body of my little Shambuka to the *Ghat* to cremate.

It was past midnight when the merriments in the palace and in the homes of the noble and the rich ended and I reached my tiny hut. I imagined for a moment my little one coming out with a song on his lips. But then, had he not gone to the land of nothing, for saving *dharma*? Perhaps, in his next birth, he would be born as a high caste boy so that he could torment others born from darker wombs. There was something soothing about that thought. I did not have the courage to enter the house and walked towards the river and lay down on a fallen tree.

As I drifted in and out of sleep, I could hear a faint tune that the breeze carried across the dark waters of the Sarayu. Some naïve idiot, maybe that rascal Brahmin Guru of Shambuka's, was singing about a world that did not have borders, a tomorrow without wars, a society that did not discriminate, and other such nonsense. I wished someone would choke that idealistic fool to death so that no more innocent ones would be corrupted by such implausible dreams and sacrifice their precious lives for nothing. There was no escaping from the idealists of the world. They breed like rat and infest the world like plague. When they die, they take so many lives with them. To my growing irritation, the song picked up in temper and vigour and when it became too bothersome with its idiotic themes of equality, I walked to my hut and hugged its deep darkness to find oblivion.

65 The beginning

Bhadra

I had been walking for the better part of the year but still there were miles to go before I reached the village of my birth. Decades ago, I had started my journey with a young man who promised us a new world. He gave us hope and filled our dreams with new yearnings. He built an empire and lost it. He had gone to join so many others who dared, achieved and lost. I gave my youth for his achievements. I was gullible enough to be taken for a ride by smooth talking people like Ravana, who promptly made me into a sucker. Later, when I had lost my innocence and the world had taught me a sufficient number of lessons, I buried what was lost in the soil of Lanka, and bundled whatever little I had left and dared to venture again. I reached somewhere I did not intend to be in the first place, but I started my life again. What was life in this land without Gods and their whims? The arms of the Gods caught up with my puny little life and shook it, squeezed it, and trampled on it, until the very last drop of blood oozed out.

After Shambuka's death, life became a living hell in Ayodhya. Shiva tried to drown his sorrows in liquor and the family fell apart as families do when their shared dreams wither away. I would also get drunk and create a scene on most days. The drinking bouts began as an excuse to mourn for a dead child, but later became its own end. Both Shiva and I would get drunk and then vent out our frustrations on the poor women of the house. We would beat our spouses mercilessly and the neighbours would gather to gawk and pass lewd comments. It was during one of those

stupid drunken bouts that something occurred which changed history. My old hag hit me back when I became too drunk and I knew the people in the colony relished this. I wanted to get even for the insults I had suffered. One day, I was not as drunk as I seemed and as the old woman started her tricks, I kicked her down. I screamed her entire past history for the whole world to hear. Her entire life story as a whore in Lanka, her past lovers, her being raped by Ravana, were all laid bare for my neighbors to drool over. I dragged her out of my compound and pushed her into the street saying that, I was neither Rama or Ravana, to accept a soiled wife as I did not belong to the high class who swapped wives. I thumped my chest and said that I belonged to a good middle class family that valued morality and honour above all and ignored the jeering laughter all around me as I kicked my screaming wife again. Then I left for the wine tavern for another round of drinks.

I was arrested two hours later. I was scared when they dragged me to the royal palace. They took me before Rama himself as he sat in his full glory on the throne of India. I did not know what particular laws of the Vedas I had inadvertently broken and what punishment awaited me. I bowed deeply, my nose almost touching the ground. One of the soldiers prodded me to stand up and face the King.

Rama frowned at me and gestured for one of his ministers to question me. That same fat, dark Brahmin minister came forward and stood exactly as far as he was supposed to stand from an untouchable. Then he asked me about my comment on Rama. I denied everything related to the King, but soon the pressure became too great. I did not dare mention Ravana's name in the court of his sworn enemy and so I said that I was not as large hearted as Rama to accept a wife whose chastity was suspect. It was a twisted truth, but that was the best I could manage in those circumstances. The *durbar* went silent and there were many accusing faces and Rama turned red with embarrassment.

To my surprise, I was let off without any punishment. I left Rama's cabinet huddled together in deep discussion, as if the future of the world depended on one *dhobi*'s drunken comment. It was more than an hour later when I reached the shrine where Ravana's old flying machine was kept. I stood at a distance to watch the amusing sight of pious people bowing down with great reverence before the *Pushaka Vimana,* when suddenly a chariot clattered past me at great speed. A distraught Sita sat in the rear seat and a scowling Lakshmana whipped the horses with terrifying violence. I did not think about it then and walked to the tavern for another drink. It was only later, when the neighbours accused us of having shattered the royal family, did I come to know the chain of events my drunken comment had set in motion. The *Pundits* had decided that Sita was impure and that whatever test and penance she had undergone to prove her chastity in Lanka was not valid in Ayodhya. They advised Rama to get rid of this blot from his stainless life and he decided to send his pregnant wife into the forest. The King's wife had to be above suspicion. His logic worked in curious ways. The palace parasites claimed that the King was abiding by the wishes of his subjects as he had always done.

Life became more miserable day by day, with the family situation deteriorating beyond hope. We were almost excommunicated from our caste and the laundry jobs that came our way were few and far between. Whatever we could scrape together, Shiva and I spend on liquor. The women suffered and were sick most of the time, but we did not care. Ten years passed, with life getting bleaker and bleaker.

It was then that our King thought that he ought to proclaim his suzerainty over the whole of India. His advisors told him to conduct an *Aswamedha Yajna,* when they would release a horse to roam free. Wherever the horse went, that place would belong to the King and those who contested this, would have to fight and defeat Rama. There were many wars with the surrounding petty kingdoms and they each surrendered as Rama succeeded in establishing himself as the *avatar* of Vishnu. Indra, the titular king of the Devas, had taken refuge in an obscure hill kingdom in the Himalayas and was soon forgotten by all. It was when the horse entered a nearby jungle that the farce of palace politics came to life.

The horse was stopped by two young boys who happened to be the twins borne by Sita in her exile in the forest. Everyone knew it and proclaimed the twins were invincible. The news went to a pleased King, who condescended to go to the spot. The royal family was reunited as the King found that his banished wife had given birth to twin sons. She had been living in the hermitage of the poet-saint, Valmiki. But what should have been a happy reunion, turned into a tragic tale, due to the handiwork of Rama's advisors. They declared Sita to be impure and her chastity was cast in doubt since she had lived under the same roof as the poet Valmiki. Valmiki was the most saintly person I had ever seen and it was evident that he treated Sita like his own daughter. But there was no questioning the learned men's logic. Another fire was lit on a cliff overlooking the Sarayu river and people flocked to witness Sita proving her chastity again by entering the flames.

I was sitting in my usual tavern when the news reached us that the King had found his exiled wife and asked her to jump into a fire to prove her chastity again. I picked a fight with a bald, old man who irritated me by singing paeans to Rama. I shouted questions at him. "Why did the King go into exile for fourteen years at the whim of his step-mother when the whole city wanted him to stay? Was he not aware of the wishes of his subjects then? Why did he kill Bali through deceit? What was the justification for sending his pregnant wife away when she had committed no wrong? Why was he pushing her again and again into the fire? Why did he kill Shambuka? It soon developed into a heated row with people joining in on both sides and violently beating and pummelling each other with abandon. The tavern toughies kicked all of us out and I cursed myself for my foolish outburst that had ended in my missing a drink. After a while I returned to the tavern for another round, but the bouncers threw me out. Desperate, I walked towards the cliff where the preparations for the trial-by-fire for Sita were going on.

It seemed like the usual circus, with hangers-on, sweetmeat vendors, wooden toy peddlers, and palmists, jostling for space with excited men and women who wanted to witness the miracle. I was directed towards a space allotted to my caste men and I joined them to enjoy the drama. The sun blazed with a vengeance and we were getting baked. People howled and screamed in excitement each time the chariot of some official passed by. The scene in Lanka, where a similar farce had been played out, kept coming vividly back to my mind. The only difference was that instead of tropical humidity and rain, a dry, dusty wind blew from the west, turning us into ghosts.

The sun had moved deep into the western horizon when the chariot carrying the King reached the spot. He waved at the cheering crowd and ascended onto the elevated platform. Sycophants fell over each other to make themselves indispensable to the King, who ignored them. A huge fire was kept burning and it was almost ten feet high now. Servants poured *ghee* and oil and fanned it to make it burn more fiercely. Then they brought Sita. Two ten-year old boys followed, perhaps not comprehending the fact that their mother was to be burnt alive.

The fat Brahmin priest began his usual long-winded speech, but mercifully, sensing the mood of the irritated and impatient public, ended it sooner than he would have otherwise. Some enthusiastic and ambitious wannabe politicians cheered Rama and the crowd took up the cheers with enthusiasm. Sita stood without showing any emotion, silently suffering the humiliation once again. Time froze.

Then everything happened quickly. Sita performed a quick circumambulation of the raging fire and stood still for a moment. Slowly she looked at her husband's face. We all stood with bated breath. Then, with a quickness that took everyone by surprise, she ran towards the river, away from the fire, and vanished beyond the edge of the cliff. After a moment of shocked silence, some people ran towards the cliff where Sita had vanished. Rama collapsed onto his seat in shock.

I ran with all the strength I could pump into my old legs. I ran against the pushing crowd, I ran past the wailing women, I ran through the street where the cloth shops were quickly shutting up and bracing for a riot. I ran past the market where men had overcome the initial shock and were hurrying back to the safety of their homes, fearing the earthquake that follows in India when a large tree falls.

Perhaps I had succeeded in saving the little Asura princess at last from the clutches of a cruel world. As I left the walled city, I wanted to jump in the air and shout in triumph. I wanted to cry out to my old friend and master, Ravana, that I had done my work. I had not planned it, I had not thought about it, but I remembered that it had been one of my drunken bouts that had led to this chain of events. My revenge may have lacked the glamour of violence, yet it had been more effective. No books would be written about me, no poet would compose an epic in my name – I did not wish for such glory. I danced on the street and rolled in the road. I kicked a sleeping dog and it yelped and scurried away in agony. By the time I reached home, I was totally exhausted by my joy. I hugged my old wife and she pushed me away, but I persisted, and after years of deprivation, I had my way that night.

Riots followed and many people died for no reason in the following fortnight. They could not find the body of Sita at all. It was believed that she had been swallowed by the thick mud at the bottom of the Sarayu. I thought that it was appropriate that the last Asura princess lay at rest in the lap of mother earth. There was no King Janaka now to snatch the prize from the river Sarayu, and the river kept her daughter close to her heart. I wondered how differently things would have been had I killed the little girl as I had been asked to do by Prahastha so long ago. Perhaps there was nothing called free will and events happened as fated, as the Devas say they are. Whatever did happen must be one's fate. Who knows?

We were afraid to move out of our shack and watched the red skies at the night in horror. Then it subsided as quickly as it had begun and we were relieved that we had come out of it safe. Rama was a broken man now, without the will to rule. His sycophants started ruling in his name and day by day, the situation became bleaker. The King remained shut up in his chamber, praying and fasting, perhaps begging forgiveness of his beloved Sita. The irony was that he was successful in getting Sita back from the most powerful king in the world, and yet was powerless to save his wife from the clutch of orthodoxy. I grudgingly admit that he genuinely cared about people. As long as his subjects did not stray from the straightlaced path of caste duties, they could lead a peaceful life under his rule. But the moment someone like Shambuka aimed to take their destiny into their own hands, the long sword of dharma would catch up with them. It was difficult to be a just ruler when the entire system was based on discriminations and privileges based on the accident of birth. As long as Rama had some control, there was an uneasy coexistence between the various castes, since he commanded the respect of the people. But after Sita's death, Rama became withdrawn and depressed and the orthodox caucus of priests took over the reins of the kingdom. Oppression and caste rules grew more rigid and when it became unbearable, one by one, families migrated out of the city. We held on for some time as business had slightly improved due to the fact that many families belonging to the *dhobi* caste had vanished and we had less competition. But with the slight increase in finances, Shiva and I revived our drinking habits with vigour and succeeded in making our life miserable again. One day, Shiva stabbed his wife in one of their usual quarrels and two days later, she died. They took Shiva away and threw him into jail. Thus, the only relationship that bound us to Rama's kingdom snapped. After lingering for a few months, with a heavy heart, we decided to leave the city and walk southwards. The euphoria I had felt when I had seen Rama's distress, vanished, and all that was left was a terrible sadness. Everything appeared meaningless. We bundled our humble belongings together and started our long walk.

We travelled through thick jungles and barren wastelands. There were many families migrating south and twice we were attacked by bandits and those who had something to lose, lost that. We reached Heheya, on the banks of the Narmada, near the Sahya mountains – the capital of Karthyaveerarjuna, and the city seemed prosperous enough. The old King was dead, killed by Parasurama's militant Brahmin group. His son ruled the kingdom now. We stayed for one year, as the caste system was not so rigid and we found work. But the local population began to resent the migrants and soon thugs with long sticks and narrow minds began to target all newcomers. What had once been a booming city, soon became stagnant. A gang of thugs once caught me in the street and beat me, calling me a black south Indian. To escape, I tried speaking in the Sanskrit I had picked up in Ayodhya. That proved to be even more dangerous. I was made painfully aware that they hated north Indians even more than south Indians. The city crumbled due to this rampant regionalism and the King seemed helpless.

Once again we journeyed on, and when we reached Gokarna, the city where Mayan had designed and built the grand Shiva temple at the behest of Ravana, we were too tired to move. We decided to stay there for some time, at the edge of a jungle, far away from the city which, as outcastes, we were not allowed to enter. We eked out a living and had slowly got our rhythm back, when Mala caught a fever and died. It was sudden and unexpected, though she had past seventy years. It left a huge void in my heart. I buried her by the river and resumed my walk. I was near Gokarna when I heard the news that the priests had made Rama order the execution of Lakshmana. The younger prince had begun to question many of the rigid and absurd practices decreed by the priests. He had begun to take an interest in governance and found that many of the rules were bizarre and caused sufferings to the common people. The economy was crumbling as skilled labour and artisans began migrating away. The priests waited for their chance to get even with Lakshmana. One day, to their delight, Rama himself gave them the opportunity. A group of holy men had sought a private interview with the King. Lakshmana was instructed by Rama not to allow anyone into his chamber as he had granted an interview to one set of Brahmins. Another *Maharishi* insisted that he be allowed in. He threatened to curse the entire clan of Rama. Terrified, Lakshmana allowed him in and so angered the other group. They quoted at length from various scriptures and the end result was that Rama ordered the execution of his brother for this 'grave crime'. Thus ended Lakshmana, the great warrior and slayer of Meghanada; the man who had left his young wife in order to follow his brother into exile for 14 long years; the man who had served his brother with utmost devotion since childhood. All his sacrifice, devotion and love lay at the feet of a man obsessed with his image as a perfect ruler; a man in the control of his advisors; a man who suffered silently and gravely, yet did not dare to cross the lines drawn by his priests.

As I was crossing the river Payaswini, I heard of Rama's end from a travelling holy man. Rama had sacrificed the two people who he loved most, for the sake of his *dharma*. He became more and more depressed and withdrawn and finally found eternal solace in the dark waters of the Sarayu. It was an inglorious end to a king who had defeated one of the most colourful and glorious men in history. Rama struck to letter of the scriptures. He led an unhappy life and sacrificed everything - his wife, his brother and his conscience, for that *dharma*. I still cannot forget the helpless look in his eyes when he raised the sword against my little Shambuka. His image was in complete contrast to the man whom he had vanquished.

Ravana was a man who lived life on his own terms, doing what he thought was right and caring nothing for what was written by holy men; a man who lived life fully and died a warrior's death. Like their lives, beliefs, values and definitions of dharma, the manner of their deaths were also contradictory. However the final truth remains that both were actors in a grand farce and it is only the small detail of who won, that decided the hero and the villain, in their epic life stories.

As time goes by, Rama may become God and Ravana the demon, for one was putty in the hands of the priests and the other as obstinate as a rock, self-willed and unorthodox. The Ravanas of the world are dangerous to those who wish to use the scriptures for their own purposes and lord over others, exploiting everyone. The Ramas of the world are used by such oppressors, as models to justify their way of life. But as time passes, even the Ramas and Lakshmanas become dangerous, as their inherent humanity starts rebelling. When the hands of Rama shook while beheading a little boy, the ungodly coterie knew he may turn dangerous later. Deifying him was the only solution, since they had already vilified his enemies. They are thoroughly distressed with the Ravanas; they can manage the Ramas for a while; but what they truly delight in are men like the Vibhishanas, Kuberas and Varunas. It is not the righteous and straight-jacketed like Rama or the proud and rebellious like Ravana, who inherit the world, but the men who do the bidding of the fanatics; men who can kill, maim, fight and do any inhuman thing in the name of religion and the scriptures. For people like me, those insignificant, irrelevant and dumb nobodies, remembering this lesson is the basic tool for survival. Once in a while we get swayed by the peddlers of impossible dreams, like Ravana, Rama, Mahabali, the guru of Shambuka. . . And we idiots who fight for abstract dreams and follow such leaders, pay the price, always. But sometimes dreams do not die and survival becomes unimportant. There may be glory in living and dying like Ravana or Meghanada, there may be satisfaction in standing steadfast for some abstract idea like *dharma* and sacrificing everything like Rama. But such glories are unaffordable luxuries for men like me.

After a month of walking, I reached the place of my birth. When I saw the river Poorna as a silver line in the valley, my heart leapt with joy. Memories came rushing back and I felt choked with emotion. I climbed down as fast as I could and reached the river. I jumped into its crystal clear water and swam like a duck. I felt my youth return. I swam for a long time, floating on a thin layer of inexplicable joy. I was rudely shaken from my dreams by a stone that hit my forehead, "Pariah! How dare you pollute this holy water?"

As I scrambled up the steps, I saw a group of high castes, glowering at me. I ran for my life, away from the waters that belonged to the Gods. Later, I came to know that my land has now become God's own country and there is no place left for man. Parasurama has succeeded in overthrowing the last opposition from the Asuras and has established the most rigid and cruel caste system imaginable. Rama's Ayodhya was heaven compared to the hell Parasurama has created. Gods lurk behind every stone; they hang from every tree, hide at every corner and make the lives of humans miserable. Parasurama has brought sixty-four Brahmin families from the North. The elite of the defeated Asuras have joined them as their servants and become their cruel and strong tools, to oppress all others. My place of birth has become a mad house with perplexing caste equations and taboos. I want to run away from this land of God, as many are doing, by sailing away across the seas to the hot deserts to the west. But I am too old for another journey. I was born here and I want to die here. The earth is bountiful in my land and it does not discriminate between skin colours. Coconuts and jackfruits, rabbits and wild berries, and the cool waters of the Poorna, these are more than enough to sustain life in my hunched and tired old body.

Once in a while, I trek to the majestic falls in the upper hills of the Poorna and sit watching the river cascading over the rocks. I do not know why, but it gives me peace of mind. I sometimes wonder how I had dared to jump into these majestic falls as a boy. Sometimes I lie back on the black rock that protrudes over the falls and look at the vast, blue sky with little, puffy clouds sailing across it. The sound of the waterfall fills my ears, along with the screech of parakeets. The universe seems eternal, infinite, and without any barriers. Sometimes I feel it is indifferent to the trivial pursuits of man and his strivings. Sometimes I feel a gigantic eye watching us. I have long given up my quest to find meaning in life. Maybe I am just a fool, since my colour is black.

But on certain days, especially after the rains, when nature blooms in a myriad colours and the grass flowers with a sweet fragrance, I hear snitches of songs that waft across the river. They sing about the golden times when the Emperor Mahabali ruled over the land, when every human was considered equal, when there was perpetual peace and no fraud or disaster. I sometimes smile at the naivety of the singers. But mostly, a mixed feeling of sadness and hope fills my mind. Maybe across the river, there are villages of black-skinned people like me. They may be celebrating Onam, waiting for the return of a golden era, waiting for a king who is long dead and buried somewhere in a cave in the northern Sahyas. Yet there is sweetness in their hope. There is a beauty beyond words in the impossible dreams that hide in men's hearts. No holy books can erase that, no taboos can bind that, and no Gods can steal that away. Men may die, but such hopes remain. I am old and may die any day like the millions who leave without any trace in this world. Maybe, like the Brahmins say, I shall be born again and again. If so, that is the greatest hope. Every death is a temporary pause in the symphony called life. There is immeasurable beauty in the thought of returning to this lovely world again and again. Perhaps, in one of my returns to this wonderful world, who knows, I may find that the words of that lovely song have come true.

Glossary

Agni pariksha	Trial by fire. In ancient India, a woman's chastity was tested in this way; the woman entered a burning pyrand if she emerged unscathed, she was considered chaste.
angavasthra	Shawl worn by nobles
Ashoka	An Indian medicinal tree; in the epic *Ramayana, Sita* spends her captivity in Ravana's Lanka, in a grove of Ashoka trees
astra	Arrow/shaft; epics often describe them as having divine powers
Asura	Hindu mythology portrays *Asuras* as demons of darkness – the antithesis to *Devas,* the Gods
Atharva	The fourth *Veda,* which speaks of magic, spells etc
atma	Soul
Ayurveda	Ancient Indian system of medicine
baksheesh	Bribe, but with the undertone that the receiver considers it his right, rather like a tip or commission
bhang	A mild narcotic made from the female cannabis plant
bindi	Red dot worn by Hindu women on the forehead
Brahma	One of the Hindu Trinity of Gods – Brahma created the universe. In this book, it is the generic name of an ancient tribe of *Asura* origin
Brahman	The one supreme power responsible for the creation and existence of the universe, according to Hindu beliefs
caste	Hindu society was divided into four *Varnas* (see under Varna for details), and further sub-divided into various

	Jatis or castes. Castes varied from region to region (eg. a Brahmin from Kashmir in the north and Brahmin from Andhra in the south, belonged to same Varna, but did not intermarry because they belonged to different castes.
Chaitra	Indian month when Spring begins
Chandagyo Upanishad	One of the most important of the Upanishads
Chandrahasa	Ravana's sword – according to mythology, it was gifted to him by Lord Shiva
chenda	A south Indian drum, beaten with a curved stick; even today it is called *Asura Vadhya* or 'musical instrument of the *Asuras*' and is still used during festivals in Kerala and parts of south Karnataka and Tamil Nadu
Chettis	Merchant caste of south India; corruption of the word Shresti
crore	One hundred lakhs
darshan	Literally 'view'; it was customary for Indian monarchs to appear at a balcony and hear petitions from their subjects
Dasamukha	Ten-faced
dasa	Servant or slave
Dharma	Rough translation : 'duty, righteousness etc'; but Dharma encompasses more – it is the code of life; antonym: adharma
Dharmayudha	Ancient ethical code of battle
dhobi	Washerman caste
Dhoti	Traditional lower garment for men, made from an unstitched length of cloth; the dhoti was also worn in a different style by lower-class women in ancient India
Durbar	Court or assembly
Gandhara	Present-day Kandahar in Afghanistan
Gandharvas	Singers in the courts of the Gods; they were considered to be supernatural beings pining for love and acted as messengers between the Gods and men. In this book, they are just another aborigine tribe, living on the fringes of the clashing *Asura* and *Deva* empires.
ghat	A broad flight of steps leading down to the bank of a river and used by bathers or washermen

gobar	Cow dung
Har Har Mahadev	Hail Shiva, the Greatest God
Indra	King of the Gods; in this book, it is the generic name of the tribe who are the nominal rulers of the *Devas*
Indrajith	'One who had vanquished Indra' – another name of Meghanada
Jambu Dweepa	Ancient name of the Asian continent
Jay, Jai	Hail; victory
Kala	Time; also God of Time and God of Death, who is commonly known as Yama (derived from the unit for measuring time – *yamam*)
Kalaripayattu	The traditional martial art form of south India, especially Kerala
karma	Action or deed
Kingara	Servants; soldier-slaves
Kinnaras	In Hindu mythology these were celestial musicians who were half-horse and half-human. In this book, they are treated as just another tribe.
Kubera	In Hindu mythology, he is the god of wealth, patron god of business men. In this story, he is just a man running a huge business empire
Kurta	Indian shirt
lakhs	One hundred thousand
Lankeswara	Lord of Lanka, another name of Ravana
lathi	Cane stick usually used by police to control crowd
lungi	Traditional lower garment of south Indian men, made from an unstitched length of cloth which is wrapped around the waist
Malayans, Vannans	Tribes from the Western Ghats (Sahyas) of India. These tribes were priests before Brahmins became prominent. Even now, many rituals in the Malabar region are conducted by people of this caste.
Mata	Mother
mehendi	Application of henna as a temporary form of skin decoration, especially for marriage

mela	Gathering
mlecha	Barbarian/ uncivilized people
moksha	Rough translation: 'salvation'; nirvana in Buddhism
Mrudangam, Milavu, Timila & Maddallam	Percussion instruments, which like the *Chenda,* are known as *Asura* instruments
mundu	Traditional south Indian lower class, formal garment, worn by both men and women
Nagas	An ancient tribe, literally meaning 'serpents'
Onam	The only Indian festival celebrated in honour of an Asura King – Mahabali. It is the state festival of Kerala, where people still believe that the reign of this Asura King, who was cheated of his kingdom by Lord Vishnu in his Vamana avatar, was the ideal, when every human being was considered equal.
pallu	the loose end of a draped sari worn by women
Panchayat	Indian village council, usually with 5 members
Parameswara	Literally 'Supreme God' and another name for Shiva, one of the Trinity of Hindu Gods (the other two being Brahma and Vishnu)
pariah	The lowest and most discriminated-against caste
Parvati	Consort of Lord Shiva
Pasupathi	Literally 'Lord of the Beasts', usually applied to Shiva
patala	Nether world; in this book it means the capital of the *Asuras* in exile
Poorna	River in Kerala, also known as Periyar
Prabhu	Sir, an honorific; also used to mean a rich man
Puja	Religious ritual conducted in reverence to a God
Ragas	Indian musical scales
Raja Dharma	Code of ethics of a ruler
Rajasooya	Sacrifice performed by ancient Kings of India who considered themselves powerful enough to be Emperors
Rakshasa	A mythological evil being; Ravana is often called *Rakshasa Raja* or 'King of Demons'
Sarswathi	A mighty river which once flowed between the Indus and Ganges but which has now vanished

Rudra Veena	Ancient string instrument
Sahya	Mountains parallel to the western seaboard of India
samhita	A collection of holy hymns/science/knowledge
sari	Traditional attire of Indian women, made from 6 yards of unstitched material
Sarpanch	Village chief or head of a *Panchayat*
Shiva	One of the Hindu Trinity of Gods – the Destroyer, who after every eon, destroys the Universe, after which Brahma recreates it. In this book, it is the name of an ancient Asura King who became a God by virtue of his great deeds.
Shravan	Fifth month of the Hindu calendar; considered to be a holy month
Shudras	The lowest of four *Varnas,* the other three being, in order of precedence: *Brahmana, Khshatriya,* and Vaishya
Sindhu	Indus
smritis	'That which is remembered'; Hindu laws written by different sages, including Manu Smriti, the code for society in ancient India
Soma	An important ritual drink during Vedic times
swayamvara	Ancient Indian custom wherein a girl chooses her groom from a gathering of suitors, sometimes through competition
tapsya	Penance
Timila	A percussion instrument used in India, also known as an *Asura* instrument
Trimurthi	Trinity of Gods
Upanishads	Collection of holy books; they, along with their commentary called *Brahmanas,* form the basis of Indian philosophical thought
vana	Grove
Vanaras	Literally 'monkeys'. In this book, they are a race of mixed *Asura* and *Deva* origin, dominating south-central India
varna	Literally 'colour' but meaning 'social groups'; Hindu society was divided into 4 basic *varnas,* with the Brahmana or *Brahmins* (priests and teachers), as supreme. The *Khshatriyas* were the warriors who formed the second rung; and *Vysyas* or merchants formed the third. The

Shudras were at the bottom of caste hierarchy – they were farmers, craftsmen, foot soldiers, petty traders, dancers, musicians, etc. Below the 4 basic varnas were the poorest of the poor, the untouchables etc

varnashrama dharma In the ancient Hindu way of life, the ideal lifespan of an individual was divided into 4 stages: student, householder, retiree and renunciate. This formed the basis for the ideal varna-ashrama-dharma system of life in which society was divided into 4 social groups *(varnas)*, according to one's natural talents and propensities – the intelligentsia and priests *(brahmana)*, administrators and warriors (kshatriya), traders *(vaishya)*, and the proletariat *(sudra)*.

Varuna God of the Seas in Hindu mythology. In this book, he is a pirate who lorded over the Indian Ocean

Vedas The four holy books *(Rig, Yajur, Sama and Atharva)*, of the Hindus, considered to possess all the wisdom in the world

Vijaya Victory

vimana Flying machine; the great epic Ramayana, speaks of Ravana's flying machine called *Pushpaka*

Vishnu The second of the Hindu Trinity of Gods, who protects the rhythm of the Universe and is the Preserver. In this book, it is the name of the clan which worked for *Deva* supremacy.

Yajna Ritual of sacrificing herbal preparations in a fire, accompanied by the chanting of Vedic mantras

Yakshas Supernatural beings who also sometimes the patron gods of trees and forests in Hindu mythology. They are believed to guard hidden treasures. The female of this species, called *Yakshi,* has the notoriety of charming unsuspecting travellers into the forest and drinking their blood or eating them. In this book, they are just a tribe that got marginalized by the conquering *Devas*.

Acknowledgements

Asura owes a great debt to many people. First and foremost I owe a lot to my parents, the Late L. Neelakantan and Chellamal Neelakantan, for opening the magical world of Indian epics to me. I also owe lots of thanks to my brothers, Loknathan and Rajendran, who, with my parents and neighbors, created many enchanted evenings when Indian philosophy, epics, and folk stories, were discussed and debated. The role that my sister Chandrika and her husband Parameswaran, played in my development, both as a person and author, cannot go unacknowledged. The irreverent and often mischievous criticism, mostly unsolicited, from my nieces, Divya, Rakhi and nephew Dileep, has kept me from indulging in flights of fancy which I tend to otherwise do. The book would not have taken shape without the heated debates I often had and still enjoy, with my friend of 25 long years, Santosh Prabhu. I also owe thanks to Lakshmi Nair, who took pains to correct my first draft, and my friend and collegue Premjeet in reading and correcting the final draft. I also owe to Rajiv Prakash who took time to read through the entire story and patiently point out typos and errors.

I am grateful to the entire Leadstart team for giving Ravana and Bhadra the opportunity to speak out. The encouragement which Chandralekha Maitra, Editorial Director of Leadstart extended, was phenomenal and I owe a big thanks to her. Without her support and guidance, *Asura* would have been nothing but a few word bytes sleeping in my laptop. Andrea Barton D'souza, who went through the painful process of correcting and

editing the draft of a debut author, deserves an award for patience. I owe Mishta Roy thanks for her wonderful cover design and Subu and Ashok of Amplecreations Studio, for the illustrations.

The book would not have been possible without the support, love and encouragement of my life partner, Aparna. I owe her a hug. And our two little imps, Ananya and Abhinav, who are more interested in the stories I tell than the stories I write, I owe you nothing less than a hundred stories for the next hundred nights. Lastly, I owe gratitude to the unknown storytellers of India, who have kept alive the tradition of storytelling for three millennia. And to my country and its inexhaustible treasure trove of religious mythology, I owe the most.